THE
SECOND SIGHT
OF
ZACHARY
CLOUDESLEY

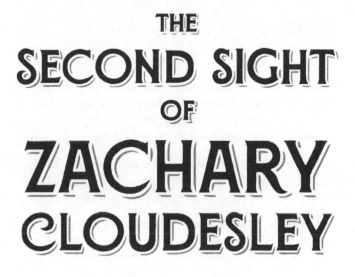

THE
SECOND SIGHT
OF
ZACHARY
CLOUDESLEY

SEAN LUSK

UNION
SQUARE
& CO.

NEW YORK

UNION SQUARE & CO.

NEW YORK

First published in Great Britain in 2022 by Doubleday,
an imprint of Transworld Publishers
This 2023 paperback edition published by Union Square & Co., LLC.

ISBN 978-1-4549-5043-1
ISBN 978-1-4549-5044-8 (e-book)

For information about custom editions, special sales, and premium purchases, please contact specialsales@unionsquareandco.com.

Printed in Canada

2 4 6 8 10 9 7 5 3 1

unionsquareandco.com

Front cover design by Marianne Issa El-Khoury / TW
Cover illustration © 2022 James Weston Lewis
Interior design by Gavin Motnyk
Maps: courtesy of Wikimedia Commons;
pattern background: Sunspire/Shutterstock.com

For Sally, and the miracle of persistence.

CONTENTS

PART ONE

◙

PART TWO

◙

PART THREE

ABOVE: *A New and Accurate Plan of Constantinople from a Late Survey,* 1770.

FOLLOWING PAGES: *The Seraglio & Gardens of the Grand Seignior,* 1752, a map of the Yeni Serai, or New Palace, of the Sultan.

THE SERAGLIO & GARDENS of the GRAND SEIGNIOR

REFERENCES

1 The Entring Gate. Call'd the Only Gate, also the Nest of happiness, and the Unshaken foundation of Power.
2 Horse Armory; Antiently the Vestry of St. Sophia;
3 The Azamoglans's Lodging, and the Yard wherein is put the Wood for the Seraglio's Fools.
4 Gallery Under which the White Eunuchs meet On the Divan's day.
5 Appartment where their Chief Manager of the Mosquies keeps his Office.
6 The Seraglio's Infirmary.
7 Place where the Sultan's Officiers Exercise the throwing of the Javelin.
8 Oven and Bakeries.
9 Seven Kitchens; Over it are the Offices.
10 Reservoir that furnishes Water to the whole Seraglio.
11 Second Door, Call'd the Passage of Justice or Threshold of Obedience and of Martyrdom.
12 Particular Stable, for thirty of the Grand Seignor's Horses.
13 Lodgings for the horselers and Baltagis or Axe-Men.
14 The Office of the Divan's Scriveners Chief Clercks, and Scriveners.
15 The Office of the Director of the Council's Papers.
16 Gibbi-Divan or Privy Council of the Grand Seigner.
17 Building where the Ambassadors are who assist at the Divan.
18 Lodgings for the Black Eunuchs Mutes and Dwarfs.
19 Gallery through which the Sultan goes to the Divan.
20 Lodging of Kislar-Agazi Chief of the Black Eunuchs.
21 Bath for the Sultan and his principal Officers.
22 Lodgings of the White Eunuchs.
23 The Volory for the Hunting Birds of the Sultan.
24 The Lodging of the Dogangis, or Faulconers.
25 Fountain where the Bashaws Condemn'd to Death are beheaded.
26 The third Door Call'd of Felicity and Happiness.
27 Appartment wherein are kept the Records and part of the Treasure.
28 Lodging of the Itchoglans or Pages of the Sultan.
29 Their Baths.
30 Their Mosquey.
31 The Fourth Gate Call'd the Sublime Gate The Bashaws kisses the Threshold of it when they go to their Government; And from it the Ottoman has taken the Name of the Port.
32 Lodging of the white Eunuchs Chief and his privy Garden.
33 Room of the As-Oda, in which the Sultan gives Audience.
34 Appartment where the Jewels of the Empire are kept.
35 Mosquey for the Grand Seignior and of his Sultanesses.
36 Winter Appartment } of the Sultan
37 Summer Appartment }
38 Great Bason.
39 Kiosk or Belvedere of Amurat.
40 The Sultan's Flower Garden.
41 A Long Building that Contains two Halls, One Call'd Bayuk-Oda, the other Chuckuk-Oda, for Women.
42 Bath of the Odaliques.
43 Building where the Odaliques gathers to do to Work.
44 Building where the Lady's are Taught Musick.
45 Appartment of the Mother Sultan and of those Women that Waits on her.
46 Her privy Garden.
47 Separated Appartments for the Haisekis.
48 Infirmary for the Odaliques.
49 Sinan Pacha-Kiosk, Lodging of the head Gardner.
50 Fountains, Basons, and Summer Houses.
51 Terrass of Sultan Achmet.
52 Kiosk of Soliman.
53 Fountain whose Water the Greeks attribute a Miraculous Virtue.
54 Great Gate where the Sultan Embarks.
55 Barge houses wherein are laid up the Seraglio's Gondolas.

PART of the CITY

St. Sophia

Ibrahim Serai

2000 British Feet
300 French Toises

Publish'd according to ...
ly J. Rocque Chorograp...
Highnesses the late and ...
Wales. Near Round Cour...

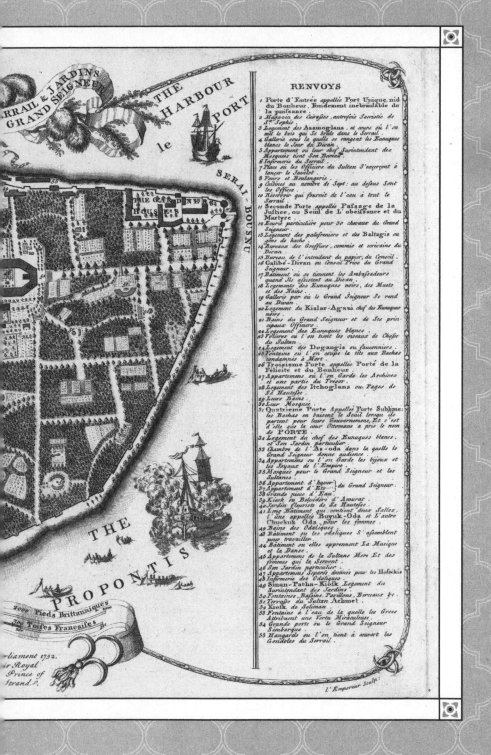

A NOTE ABOUT OTTOMAN HIERARCHY
IN THE MID-EIGHTEENTH CENTURY

The Ottoman, or Turkish, Empire covered an area in the 1760s stretching from the borders of modern-day Romania and Croatia in the north to Greece in the west, Tunisia, Libya, Egypt and Arabia in the south and Iraq and Syria in the east. Named *Ottoman* after the ruling family descended from Osman I, its capital was Constantinople, as it had been capital of the old Eastern Roman or Byzantine Empire until 1453. The city was also known as Istanbul or Stamboul, from the Greek *Στην πόλη*—Stin Poli—"in the city."

The **sultan** was emperor. He had many titles, among them Padishah, or in Western countries the Great Turk or Grand Seigneur. His power was absolute in theory but tempered by the possibility of coup and replacement by a brother or son.

The **grand vizier** was, in effect, prime minister, wielding authority over foreign and domestic policy, but the sultan dismissed grand viziers frequently, and often the position was held only for a few months.

The **kizlar agha**, or Chief Black Eunuch, was in charge of matters within the seraglio, or palace, and many were enormously influential in affairs of state, despite being, in effect, slaves and usually drawn from humble backgrounds.

The **seraglio** was the palace (*serai*) but served as shorthand for the royal court. Within the seraglio sat the harem, the women's quarters. Often given a salacious connotation in Western literature, largely because its life was hidden from outside observation, in practice it had considerable autonomy within the palace, and important decisions about the conduct of the empire were taken there.

The **Sublime Porte** was shorthand for the administrative center of the empire and for diplomatic activity, named originally for the entrance gate to the seraglio, from where policy announcements would be made. By the mid-eighteenth century, the offices of government had moved across the road from the palace to a dedicated building, and these new offices were in effect the new location for the Sublime Porte.

The **divan** was the building within the seraglio where the viziers would meet to discuss policy, sometimes being joined by those making petitions to them or by ambassadors of other nations. It also became the name by which the collection of viziers, or what we would call the cabinet, was known.

Janissaries were the elite troops who formed the sultan's household guard as well as performing a wider role within the Turkish military. Until the late seventeenth century, janissaries were taken as children from Christian families and bound into servitude to the sovereign, though they were trained, well paid and ultimately given a pension. Over time the janissaries became a powerful force within the political as well as the military structures of the empire.

Frank was a generic term for all those Westerners living in the city as diplomats, merchants or visitors. They were required to live in Galata, then called Pera, a neighbourhood of modern-day Beyoğlu, on the opposite side of the Golden Horn from Sultanahmet, where the seraglio and principal mosques were—and are—to be found.

PART ONE

CHAPTER ONE

LIFE AND DEATH

March 1754, London

Leadenhall stinks this morning; of soot and shit and, inexplicably, of nutmeg. Dr. Pike has been in the bedchamber all night with Alice, ejecting Abel from the room four times already, wafting his meaty hand in the air along with words of greasy reassurance. It was Alice's aunt who insisted they engage him, this pompous "midwifeman to ladies of distinction," but he disgusted Abel from the first, there being something of the ox about the fellow, large and slow and clumsy so that he hardly seems the man for a woman's parts.

Terror has crept up on him over the long hours of his wife's confinement. At his last expulsion, not an hour before, she'd been too weak to offer him even her faint smile. "Go, Abel, go," she'd mouthed, and he'd felt her terrible disappointment in him; in everything. He has ceased to think of the unborn creature as a thing of hope and innocence and begun to conceive of it as an incubus, scrabbling its way out of his wife's belly with devilish claws.

He takes a breath, a slower one, and tries to calm himself. A ladybird lands on his sleeve, drowsy, roused early from its hibernation, and he is grateful for the fleeting distraction. Putting a fingernail to its red and black shell he bids it fly, to escape while it can.

Another cry from above, this time Abel matching it with one of his own. A man scuttles past and, pausing, gives him an odd glance. "Good morning!" Abel declares, feeling obliged to offer an explanation. "My wife is at the childbed. Those are her cries you hear." He craves the uncertain sympathy of another being, wants to discuss something inconsequential, as strangers do: the peculiar red dawns they have had that month, perhaps, or the heavy yellow mists that linger long after the breakfast hour. Striving for a jaunty tone, Abel confesses to the cries being his own, too, but the stranger gives him the barest of glances before striding on at even greater pace. "Lobcock!" mutters Abel after his flapping coat, already vanishing into the mist.

The air is clearing, a thin sun breaking through the clouds. A little way along the street a boy leans so far out of an upstairs window that he seems sure to fall from it. Abel is about to shout out to him when he hears a cry from above, a baby's lusty shriek. Every despairing thought flees as he turns and bounds up the stairs, his feet barely touching the wood as he flies, his heart keen and sharp. Ah, Alice! And Pike, good old Pike. He is the man, after all.

Stumbling into the room his first sight is of Pike's back, his face turned toward the window. Next he sees Alice's maid, Kate, whose features are twisted as if in fear, though he has never raised his voice to her or any of his household, nor ever would. In her hands she clasps the source of the cries, small but determined, its little face red and crushed as a rosebud in the hour before it opens. "I am sorry," declares Pike to no one in particular, his sorrow that of a craftsman dismayed with his work; hardly the sorrow of one mortal for another. "A weakness in the wall of the womb. A severe haemorrhage."

It is what lies upon the bed that explains all, a vision of hell thrust into this world from another: Alice's blue-white body twisted upon a rage of crimson blood. Abel rushes to her, presses his lips to her still-warm mouth and will not, cannot let go. After some minutes or years or lifetimes someone pulls him away and he cries out. Coming slowly to his senses he hears himself exclaiming hoarsely to all who might hear that he has murdered his wife with his own seed. Even the baby has fallen silent.

Pike and Kate watch him, Kate rocking the baby from side to side, regarding Abel as if he were a dog that might foam at the mouth and give her a mauling. Turning at last, Pike places a slab hand on Abel's shoulder. "I have sent your servant to fetch out the reverend." Thinking he has not been understood, he repeats: "The priest is coming."

Abel tries to respond, but all he can do is make a sound, a whinny like an injured horse. He knows he should reach out for the child, take it in his arms, yet there is something abhorrent in the prospect of fatherhood now.

Kate holds the swaddled bundle out to him, her face still stricken. Nervously she says, "You have a little boy, sir. A son, it is."

Abel takes him and holds him, looking into his fierce dark blue eyes, their gaze fixed and penetrating, as unnerving as some creature wrenched from another universe entire, and asks him quietly whether he knows what a great calamity has accompanied his arrival, his tears falling on to the child's face. He loosens the swaddling to examine the wonder of him more thoroughly, causing his son to squirm and whimper and grasp Abel's index finger in his own tiny pink hand. He grips with such remarkable strength that it makes Abel wince. Are all newborns so strong, he wonders? Perhaps this resolve is what a motherless infant is given, as a fledgling cuckoo is given the vigour to push the other hatchlings out the nest and into oblivion. But there are no other chicks, thinks Abel. They are quite alone, the two of them, father and son.

Pike, who has been watching Abel cautiously, coughs. "I can attend to . . ." He hesitates. "If you would like to leave the matter in my hands."

Abel, holding the infant close to his chest, knows that Pike speaks of his wife's body and tries to control his anger with a shake of his head. "I thank you, Dr. Pike. Your services here are at an end—definitively so, as you see. I shall take care of matters now." He turns away but a few more bitter words spill in Pike's direction without effort or intention. "No doubt the Reverend Hale will want to mumble his incantations, and then I shall call for the undertaker. I know him well, you understand. We have had regular trade these last few years: first my father, lately my mother, my sisters and now my wife. It's a wonder he does not leave his hearse waiting outside my door."

Pike moves to leave, the now useless bulk of him suddenly dark and looming in the shadowed room. Hesitating, he says, "Your son is strong, sir. Take some comfort in that. He is as strong a newborn as I ever delivered."

Abel looks at him blankly. "He will need to be, will he not?"

With Pike gone there is an abrupt intimacy between Kate and Abel, so that he feels impelled to thrust his son into her waiting arms.

"Shall I ask Grace Morley to be wet nurse, sir?" she asks. "She has newly taken a room on Bishopsgate and not long had a little one of her own. She was born not two miles from my own home in Suffolk."

Abel is silenced by the irony of it: three daughters born dead and poor Alice's abundant milk an agony after each. Now a son born living and his mother has no milk for him because she has no breath, no life at all. A transaction must be made, he understands that; a woman must be found with milk to spare. His hand goes unconsciously to his own breast, as if by some miracle he will find a softness there, a swelling. "But Mrs. Morley is a stranger to me."

"She is clean, sir."

The baby cries and he sees the urgency in it. "Let it be Mrs. Morley," he says without conviction.

"She has a touch of palsy," says Kate over the baby's protests, as if to safeguard herself from future criticism, "but no other impairments. Or none to speak of."

"Then let them not be spoken of," he says with a defeated smile. He does not feel like a man entitled to preferences now. He bids the maid leave him, his son in her arms. Alone, or almost, he becomes aware of the scent of blood and sweat and of something else; the tugging, sweet smell of fruit strewn on the ground and soon to rot, though the taste upon his tongue is of metal; indigestible and perpetual. He sits on the bed, taking Alice's hand in his. Can this astonishing, clever, capable, funny, beautiful, stubborn woman really be gone from him, from everyone who ever knew her, from everyone she knew? Not two nights ago she had played the fortepiano loudly and badly for an hour, intending that all should share in her discomfort. She'd told Abel how different she felt this time, how strong the child was with his kicking and squirming and twisting. "He will leave me in a hurry, Abel, and jump, furious, into your arms." She had called him he. The thought that she was right, the knowledge that she will never see the boy makes him crumple. He slips from the bed to the floor, and weeps.

There is a knock at the door, so soft at first it might be nothing more than a shift of air, then more determined.

"Come!"

The Reverend Hale enters, out of breath, his hat in his hand and his wig half off his head. He regards Abel, still prostrate, with sympathy. "I was prepared"—his chest heaves—"but not for this, Abel. I am truly sorry."

"It is so." Abel stands, brushes himself down. "And I believe . . ." He gestures toward the bed, but he no longer knows what it is he believes and his thoughts trail into silence. The vicar moves to where Alice's body lies and delivers his prayers while Abel goes to the window and looks out on to the street, watching the scuttling movements of those below, as inconsequential to him now as mice arguing over breadcrumbs. Aware that Hale is standing beside him, he turns.

"Have you thought of a name?" asks the priest. "Perhaps Alice—"

"Alice? For a boy?" Abel frowns.

"No, no," says Hale, gently, "I was not proposing the name Alice for the boy, merely wondering if dear Alice had expressed some preference, some . . ."

Abel turns to look once again at his wife's body before leading Hale from the bedchamber and out on to the landing, having no wish to be overheard by the dead. "We dared not think of a name," he whispers, as much to himself as to the priest.

"No, I understand. But a name is needed, nonetheless."

Abel knows that Hale has a preference for speedy baptisms. The clergyman is a believer in efficiency, thinking that it is inefficiency that threatens faith, as if belief were the product of constant manufacture, and prayer a sort of flywheel keeping heaven aloft and God in His proper place. "What do you propose, Reverend?" asks Abel, weary.

"John is an ever-popular name."

Needing to contradict Hale, needing to inflict some provocation simply to remind himself that he still lives, he says, "Perhaps an Old Testament name?"

"Old Testament? Old Testament. Yes, well, there is Isaac, of course. Or Daniel."

"Hmmm."

Warming to his theme, Hale offers other possibilities. "There is Absalom, who is the father of peace, and I would wish that this child brings you peace, Abel."

"I think I shall have little of that now."

"Or Zephaniah. Zephaniah was hidden by God, and this child, too, his, his . . . goodness has been hidden from you, from us all, on this strange, dark day of fearful loss. And so—"

Abel places a hand on the minister's shoulder. "Enough, Reverend. Zephaniah will do well enough. I like the idea of a name that begins with the end. It fits with Cloudesley, does it not? Or Zachary, perhaps."

"Zachary, yes," says Hale, relieved, "Zachary is serviceable." He turns and lurches down the stairs in pursuit of the infant, eager to begin his ministrations and no less eager to remove himself from Abel's grief.

It is already late in the afternoon when Abel goes next door to the workshop, from where comes the low murmur of voices. He must face his men, all twenty of them. They will have heard the news and must offer him their sympathies as he must receive them; a ceremony equally hideous for them all. If he were five years old he would be permitted to howl and sob and spoil his breeches and no one would think it unreasonable, but he is an adult and must deliver his lines with what authority and grace he can muster. All the men stand as he enters the low workshop, their solemn faces lit with the warm glow of beeswax candles, the brass and glass of the finished clocks winking from their shelves. Richie Harris, the oldest man, his eyes hidden beneath white eyebrows so heavy that he peeks out from beneath them like a badger in its sett, steps forward. He has been deputed, then, though he is hardly the most fluent. "We are awful sorry, Master Abel. We are so awful sorry for you. There is joy in a son, to be sure, but to lose Miss Alice. . . . Well, it is a tragedy, that be certain, and we are all so awful sorry for you."

They call him Master Abel, not *sir* or *Mister Cloudesley* or any other yet more apple-polishing epithet, because the older amongst them remember him as a boy, working in the workshop, making his little clockwork animals in the hope of impressing his unimpressible father. He knows he will always be a child to them, and that they think his venture to be a father himself was ever likely to end in some misadventure, just as it has. He takes a breath. "Thank you, Richie. Thank you all. I know how well loved Alice was by every man here, as she was loved by me more than life itself. Yet she is gone and life is still here." He smiles as best he can, stretches his arms wide to show the breadth of life, carrying them all along on its current. "So I go on, as must we all. And yes, there is a little one who lives, God willing, and who is to be called Zachary. And so the label we place on our clocks and instruments is true once more: *Cloudesley and Son, of Leadenhall Street.*" This prompts an approving murmuring amongst the men, as he knew it would. "Now, I would bid you all go to your homes and not return here until Monday." This, too, prompts a low noise, less approving this time. It is only Tuesday. "You will be paid, all of you, for these days of idleness, but we cannot be making clocks now . . ." He stumbles, cannot think what to say. "You understand."

It is Seth, the foreman, who comes to his aid. "Now then, men, you heard what Master Abel said. We are to pack up for the week, as a mark of respect."

There is a shuffling, a gathering and, at last, a departing. Some of the men shake his hand as they pass, others rest a hand on his shoulder. A couple of the shyer ones do not even look at him. Richie, to his surprise, plants a kiss on his forehead, stretching up to him as if he had forgotten that Abel is no longer that nervous eight-year-old he once knew. Only two remain, Seth Cartwright and Tom Spurrell; Tom neat and shy and exceptionally dexterous, who assists Abel with his more demanding projects and never fails to create mechanisms of exquisite precision, but who only reddens with embarrassment when complimented. "I pray for him, Master Abel," says Tom in his reedy voice.

"For the baby, Tom?"

"For Zachary, yes."

Tom, uttering his son's name, makes the child real in a way that Abel had not anticipated. It makes him gasp. "I thank you, Tom," he stutters. They hear the baby's cry from up the stairs, the three of them. "Now away to your home, gentlemen, and not back here till Monday." Tom lodges with Seth, and Abel thinks it a good arrangement, the coarse but worldly foreman and, under his protection, this gifted waif of a man.

"I don't like to think of you here alone, Master Abel," says Tom.

"But I won't be alone, Mr. Spurrell, will I? I have all these clocks for company." He smiles, pained by the effort of it, and the two men finally and with surprising reluctance begin to gather their things.

Alone, or as good as, he looks around the workshop. The sound of it is a torment—the ticking, the slow swing of a hundred pendulums, the movement of mechanical hands over brass faces. The weary distribution of time itself feels joyless and without meaning; the hours, he has come to understand, cannot be captured and regulated. It is he who is ensnared in the brass wheels, the fly springs, in the ticking and the turning. At this hour yesterday Alice was chiding him for something or other, and Kate was preparing their supper, Biddy assisting her. How can a day, an hour, a minute change a life so completely? Why can these clocks not be made to run backward and take him to the day before, to the life he had supposed he would have? That, he thinks, would be a worthwhile pursuit for a clockmaker, not simply to mark off time as it passes, but to tame the beast, to make it run this way and that; to make time man's servant, not man its ever more obedient slave.

On one side of the long workshop is a shelf with dozens of the Ottoman clocks they make for the Levant market. They are old-fashioned lantern clocks such as are never sold in England anymore, with a few adaptations for the Turkish taste: the numbers, the hint of minarets on their corners. He takes little interest in their manufacture, even though they are what keeps the business in profit, and his men in work. Alice kept the books, knew the cost of all bought in and the profit of all sold out; she busied herself with the small amounts, the sum spent on mercury for fire-gilding, which amounted to three pounds and six shillings in the last year, yet she never worried what was spent on gold. It was Alice who'd insisted on increasing the price of the lantern clocks from thirty-six shillings to forty-one, declaring that amounts of forty shillings and above were more respectable. The accounts are another thing he has no interest in. He will have to find a man who has.

Alice occupies every dark space around him, her voice filling his head, never saying quite what was expected, talking in one moment of the damned accounts and in the next of the possibility of acquiring a tortoise, or of the height of a mountain in Peru. She encouraged him in his more fanciful endeavours—his clockwork owls and silver mice, his dancing milkmaids and singing cherubs, calling them his "magical proclivities." His father had thought them nothing more than gewgaws, a waste of workmanship. To think of the two of them equally dead seems impossible. Surely Alice cannot be—can never be—as dead as his father? If some people are unquestionably more alive than others, then why not others less dead? Yet he knows there is a terrible equality in death. He closes his eyes and lets the sound of whirring and ticking fill him.

Startled by a hand on his arm, he looks up to see Samuels, their new manservant (another incarnation of Aunt Frances's wishes), and understands that he is saying something to him, though it takes a moment for the clamour in his head to quiet. "There is a woman to see you."

"A woman?" he says, his mouth dry.

"Miss Kate was most insistent, sir."

"Is it the wet nurse, Samuels?"

"I have fetched a woman for you to see." This is how Samuels always is—terse, maddeningly cryptic. Yet Alice thought him indispensable and took a perverse delight in his curt, odd manner. Abel knows he will feel the same about him now, in memory of her.

He steps through the door that connects the workshop to the house and there Abel finds Grace Morley standing next to Kate. She is cooing at his son. Her countenance is, indeed, strange. It is as if her face were made of wax, and that one side of it had been placed too close to the fire. Her other cheek is smooth as marble, and the woman is a surprise in other ways—tall and haughty, like one of those marble goddesses so beloved of the Greeks, a tumble of red hair halfway down her back, a flash of fury kept half hidden in her eye.

"You are Mrs. Morley?"

"Sir."

"You have milk enough for this little one?"

"Aye sir, plenty. I am feeding just my own, Leonora. Your son will stay with me at my chamber on Bishopsgate."

He had not expected this. "Really?"

Detecting his reluctance, Mrs. Morley takes a step toward him. "I prefer to stay there, sir."

Abel hesitates.

"It is my home," she says, defiant.

That the woman has spirit is not a bad thing, he thinks. Better that than a woman easily cowed. "It is irregular . . . is there a Mr. Morley?"

"No and never was. Captain Morley he was, and he is dead."

Abel thinks it best to ask no more about the late captain, or at least not on this occasion. "I may come from time to time to visit my son?"

"Readily. Day or night, Mr. Cloudesley, I shall be there, and so shall you find your Zachary." She gives him a smile, which in its lopsidedness seems more a threat. He would like to turn her away, to turn them all away, to take his son to his own breast, to feed him and love him, but the world is ordered in another way, its rules unarguable.

With a little more negotiation Zachary is gone, together with the wet nurse and Alice's corpse, collected by Coopers the undertakers with sombre and respectful noises and much black crêpe. The hours take care of things, the hands creeping round the dial, and Abel finds himself alone, yet not as he has ever been before, for there is a desolation in loss so much greater than never having possessed at all. He feels like a man who has been basking in the warmth of summer sun and is cast without warning into the bleakest of Arctic nights. Looking down at his trembling hands, he imagines his son nestling there—a heart or some other bloody pulse ripped from its home and placed tenderly in his improbable custody.

Abel is drawn back to the workshop. The candles have burned down and he sits for a while in the darkness before lighting a lamp. There is a shelf that holds his automata and, placing his lamp on a bench, he takes down from it a silver milkmaid, the device ready to spin around on the top of a clock each hour and lift and drop her bucket and curtsey to whichever idle soul may care to watch her performance. She has taken six weeks in the making, her tiny springs and flywheels, her fusee drives no less exquisite than her little silver ankles, her feet turned so prettily. The work is Tom Spurrell's, finer than any other of his men can produce. Abel prides himself on knowing the faint and secret faculties of each man and Tom's work surpasses all.

Raising the mechanism high above his head he throws it to the ground, shattering the milkmaid's silver casing and scattering her works in five hundred pieces across the floor, where they glint celestial and unearthly in the half-light. Next, he goes to the clock shelf and hurls first one and then another to the ground, their sound almost enough to drown out that other sound in his head, that sound he knows he will hear forever.

Samuels is there beside him, stepping from the shadows. With a touch, a shake of the head, he stops Abel from taking another clock from the shelf, before retreating again without a word. He must have been there watching all along.

Fury spent or interrupted, Abel walks over to where the cot he built stands in a corner. It is clockwork, naturally enough, with a rocking mechanism and, in its base, a pinned drum and stack of bells ready to play four different tunes. It was this he had come to destroy; he was going to present it to Alice this very day, the day of the birth of that miracle—a living child. He had been anticipating her delight at its lullaby almost as much as he had been relishing the prospect of fatherhood itself. She would have made fun of it, of course, and of what she called the shallowness of his intentions. Broken glass and bits of brass crunch as Abel goes to it, but as he lifts the cot above his head, he hears a disembodied voice from the corner. "Was that not for your son to sleep on?"

Abel lowers the cot and carries it over to where Samuels stands. "It was."

"And would your wife have not wanted the child to lie in it?"

Abel hesitates. Samuels never dresses his sentiments in unnecessary words but speaks always without artifice, let alone courtesy. His is a consciousness unburdened by feeling, ever practical and, Abel understands, on this occasion, necessary. Knowing what he must do, he asks Samuels the way.

"Follow," says his manservant, leading him out on to Leadenhall and onward to Mrs. Morley's through the evening fog.

◙

CHAPTER TWO

AN UNRELIABLE CUSTODY

June 1754, London (three months later)

◘

Mrs. Morley's rooms are in a sorry sort of building, up a steep stairway above a candlemaker's on Bishopsgate, the smell of tallow filling the hallway. He makes his way up the rank stairs and gives his familiar rap on her door, four sharp knocks, intended to sound light and cheerful, but always seeming too insistent, even bad-tempered. Sometimes she keeps him waiting, regarding him with surprise when she eventually appears, as if he were a stranger, but today the door opens promptly, and her greeting is warm enough. "Oh, Mr. Cloudesley! Your boy has been close to sitting up today. He holds himself quite stiff, you know." Her accent is of the countryside, but she speaks with a brittle confidence, and not without learning.

"Good. That is good?" He frowns. Abel is never quite certain how he should remark on his son's development. She tells him daily of his son's stillness, his quietness, the steadiness of his gaze, his lack of provision of a smile, and it is discouraging, though he wonders whether the explanation is that his son feels no need to add to Mrs. Morley's woes, since her daughter, Leonora, wriggles and writhes and screams and gurgles and farts and pukes in a cavalcade of emanations remarkable for a creature so small. "He is ahead of where he should be, Mr. Cloudesley. Well ahead."

He goes to where Zachary, the seeming prodigy, is lying on a rug before the fire (there is always a fire made up, and the room itself is bright and clean; were it not he would have acted sooner, or so he tells himself) and lifts him as Mrs. Morley has shown an infant should be lifted. "Hello, my little man, my Zachary. Have you been good for Mrs. Morley today? Have you had your breakfast and your luncheon? Shall we have a look out into the street?" Zachary fixes his father with that gaze he has always found so piercing as to be unnerving, yet lately he finds himself able to take an uncertain pride in his son's intensity, for surely it is a sign of a fierce if incipient intelligence. Abel takes him to the window and points out what is happening below, the carts going along Bishopsgate, and what is on them. "See those?" he says, pointing down, making sure that Zachary's eye is following the line of his finger. "Those are barrels of rum, I think. They will have come from far-off Jamaica and are being taken north to be guzzled down in York and Derby. And there . . . there is a cart coming the other way loaded with strawberries to be sold to all the fine houses of the city. Soon you will eat a strawberry and you will think it very fine, too. A sweet, juicy treat. Won't he, Mrs. Morley?" He spins around but she is in the other room, tending to her daughter.

The room seems to fill with the lush, faintly decadent smell of strawberries, causing Abel to wonder if Mrs. Morley has acquired a pottle already. "Mrs. Morley!" he shouts. "Did you buy a pottle of strawberries?"

"Certainly not," she replies, gruff, from beyond the door. "Where would I have got a strawberry from?"

Abel ponders again the smell in the room, which has evaporated as readily as it arrived. He senses things more keenly when Zachary is in his arms, as if his son binds him more firmly to all the world's marvels.

Although he felt awkward in those first weeks at Mrs. Morley's, he has become used to the place and its routines. Putting Zachary back on the rug, he sets the kettle on the fire ready to make tea. It is his habit now, this making of tea, though he usurps both Mrs. Morley's proper role and his own in doing so, and he often brings some treats, crumpets or Shrewsbury cakes, cockles or meat pies. Tomorrow he will bring a pottle of strawberries. He makes sure there is always plenty of tea for the pot and when Mrs. Morley protests that she is "perfectly capable of . . ." he tells her that it is he who is feeling incapable, and that she does him a great honour by allowing him such small provision. He feels almost as he did as a boy when Mr. Catchpenny took George and him off into the countryside near Ely, where they lodged with their tutor, and left them for a night to fend for themselves, telling them that every young man should learn to sleep under a hedge and feel the better for it the next day. They made a fire, picked berries, begged bread from a farm. He lets his concentration drift as he thinks fondly of George, his companion throughout his schooldays and a few years after that, though Alice could not abide him for reasons Abel never fully understood, and he has not seen him for three years or more.

"Are you brewing that tea or fermenting it, Mr. Cloudesley?"

Startled out of his reverie, Abel pours, offering an apologetic smile. He knows he is imminently to upset her, for he has come today feeling obliged to act on the advice he has been receiving from every quarter for weeks on end, namely that his son must come and live with him in his own home—to be brought up in the shabby (though, as he has observed, perfectly warm and clean) rooms of his wet nurse is, it seems, an aberration, a monstrous insult to all the conventions of society. Abel has never been much interested in matters of social order, though he supposes there must be rules, to be observed when their breaching can no longer be tolerated.

When he has poured tea into their cups, and the babies are fed and settled, he says what he must. "Mrs. Morley, it is very kind that you have taken Zachary into your home—"

Irritated, she interrupts. "He is not weaned."

"No, Mrs. Morley."

"If you have found another wet nurse, so be it. But it is not good for an infant to go from one breast to another. They can sicken—I am only saying. You must do as you wish. I'm thinking of Zachary, not of myself." She puts him in mind of a swan disturbed in its swim, raising its head indignantly and beating its wings in an agitation.

"I know, Mrs. Morley. You have taken good care of my son, and I would that you continue to."

She looks at him doubtfully, lifting her cup to her lips but placing it back on the saucer without taking a sip.

"But my son must come to Leadenhall. He must come home."

"Not with me he won't."

"But Mrs. Morley . . ."

"Don't you *Mrs. Morley* me, Mr. Cloudesley," she says, bristling. "If you will have me feed and tend your boy, it must be here."

"But why, Mrs. Mor—madam. Why?"

"I should rather starve than abandon my own little one. You do see that, don't you? I'm not farming out my girl to be fed sugar water by some gin-soaked slut."

"Nor should you. I would . . . I would never ask you to leave your own little one behind. No, you and Leonora shall both come to live at Leadenhall."

Mrs. Morley purses her lips. "I have other reasons for keeping my own rooms."

"Yes?"

"I do not ask you to understand my motivations."

"I can strive to do so." Mrs. Morley and he are about the same age, he supposes, almost thirty and no longer young. Her red hair is already flecked with grey and, were it not for the palsy having dragged down one side of her face, she would be a woman of striking handsomeness. Not beauty, for that is different—he thinks again that she has more the look of a Greek goddess with her pained dignity, and there is something majestic about her, if troubled. The goddesses had their troubles too, after all.

"I have not always had a happy life, Mr. Cloudesley," she declares. "Not as happy as I have now. I have not burdened you with my history. You have not asked, and I would not expect you to." Her tone is matter-of-fact, as if she were talking of someone else, a person of little interest to either of them. "You know that I am widowed."

"Yes, madam. We have that bond, have we not?"

She gives him a look so withering that Abel feels himself shrivel. "I married badly, Mr. Cloudesley. I married in order to escape an unhappy home. My father was a violent man. Violent," she repeats, raising a hand to make clear her meaning, her green eyes blazing in recollection of what he did to her, of what she suffered.

"Really, Mrs. Morley, there is no need . . ." he says, hoping to stop her confession before it goes too far.

"But there is need, you see. You need understand me if you are to be persuaded, and you have to . . . I would be obliged if you gave me that opportunity."

"Very well, madam."

"Oh call me Grace, for heaven's sake. It is my name."

"And my name is—"

"No, I shall call you Mr. Cloudesley. I am in your service, after all."

He is conscious that he has loosened a stopper and her bitterness is flowing unchecked into the room. He looks over to where the infants are asleep, willing one of them to stir, to cry and interrupt her testimony.

"He thought I would always be there to cook his meals and scrub his back and bear his blows, being the eldest of his daughters, and having this disfigurement being unmarriageable, or so he thought." To Abel's alarm she reaches over for his hand and places it upon her collapsed cheek. "People think it a palsy, but it is in fact a burn, a scalding he did to me with a pan snatched from the fire and swung at me. I was nine."

"Dear God, Grace," he says, leaving his hand upon her face a moment, knowing he should not draw it away too quickly in case she thinks him disgusted, though the intimacy is disquieting.

"Him above . . . God, I mean, well, He wasn't much help to me, though I prayed and beseeched and all that. Nothing. So instead I did all I could to protect my sisters from his wrath and succeeded, by and large. They are pretty girls, you see. Mother died with the youngest." She hesitates. "I am sorry to mention that," she says glancing at him, almost sly, watching for Abel's reaction, the renewal of his heartbreak. "I bid the girls marry men who lived far off, so they would be out of reach of the old man's spite. And then comes along a certain Captain Morley to Felixstowe—that is where I am from, or a village not far from it—yes, *Captain Morley*"—she pronounces her late husband's name with bitter irony—"who came sniffing around on account of how he knew my father from years before. He was old and drunk and in general terms disgusting, but he was not my father and it was clear enough what he wanted. Not only that, but he had gold, having recently retired as captain of a slaver, and he paid my father handsomely for my hand. Hand!" She laughs. There are tears in her eyes, but tears of anger, not self-pity, still less of shame.

Abel, emboldened by her earlier gesture and sensing that Mrs. Morley is in need of consolation, leans toward her and rests his hand on hers. She accepts the gesture without remark.

"I was a virgin. Twenty-eight and a virgin! Do I speak too frankly for you? Well, I am frank now, since there is a liberation in it. I do not know why we exalt virginity so. It is a burden on any woman. Or man. I suppose there are men who are virgins. Though that is different, of course."

Abel thinks it best to withdraw his hand and sit back in his chair, allowing her confession to reach its conclusion.

"He went at it well and good, and I was with child before you'd know it. I cannot say I was sorry when he went and died. Peaceful it was, or would have been, is my guess, though he was half burned and the cottage he'd bought us gutted from fire. I was out at the market, with Leonora, thank God, not three weeks old, and had left him with his pipe in his chair. Captain Morley. Pfff! His heart gave way, I suppose. The damnable old bastard." She glances at him to see if he is shocked by her cursing, but Abel has heard a good deal worse. "Most of his money had gone on the cottage, but there was enough left for me to pay a good rent and I came to London for fear of falling again into my father's grasp. I would not allow that for my daughter. London is a place where a woman may disappear—a woman most especially, since we are barely visible beyond twenty to any man. So you see, Mr. Morley, I have fought hard for my independence, and I will fight hard for my daughter's, too. That is why I keep my own rooms." She settles back in her chair and looks about in disbelief, as if seeing the place for the first time.

How odd, thinks Abel, that she has given me her own surname, but he does not remark on it. "But you shall keep your rooms, Grace. I will pay the rent on them, so you will be in no way inconvenienced and, when the time comes, you and Leonora may return to them freely. I . . ." He hesitates, not wanting to sound boastful. "I have means, Grace. My late father's business makes a handsome profit, and as yet I have not so grievously mismanaged it as to change that situation."

She laughs, and at first he thinks she has appreciated the little joke he made at his own expense, but he sees quickly enough that is not what Grace Morley has found amusing. "But I could not possibly! I cannot move in with you, a widower, and me a widow. What will people say?"

Abel is taken aback. Only a few moments ago she was telling him of her loss of virginity, having him feel her face where it was burned, reassuring him that she was in his service. Suddenly she is suggesting that he is trying to scandalize her. He suppresses the thought of whether he might be tempted in any way, in other circumstances. He clears his throat. "I think they would say that you are my infant son's wet nurse and have been given rooms in my home as is only right and proper."

"But there is no woman living there, Mr. Cloudesley. There should be a sister or mother or aunt or someone. Some living soul."

"There is Kate, who is your friend, I think. And Biddy, too, the scullery maid."

"Kate has told me that your men come and go freely into the house from the workshop. Twenty or more of them in their dirty boots, seeking your advice or instruction or showing you their work. She says it is like . . ." She stops herself.

"What does she say?" he encourages.

She shakes her head. "I should not have spoken so. But if you are to make the household a suitable place you need must find some relation to move in there with you. Some female relation."

"But you know, surely, that I have none. I am utterly alone in the world, but for this one." He gestures toward where Zachary lies in the cot he made for him.

"There is one, I am told."

"You have the benefit of much intelligence, it seems."

"You know of whom I speak."

"I do."

"Then why not have her come stay?"

Why not indeed? thinks Abel as he walks back to Leadenhall, his mind jostling with a hundred and ten convincing reasons why not. The evening is long and slow, heavy with the pepper-sweet scent of summer wafting into the city from the fields beyond, though that perfume barely conceals the odour of shit, equine and otherwise, that lies in wait on every corner on warm, dry days such as these. The cry of children playing is oddly distant, though they are all around him like swarming bees. In other circumstances he thinks he might be happy.

Aunt Frances is a high wind that batters at him constantly, and though her grief at Alice's death was absolute, her letters since—three or four each week, demanding that he bring Zachary to Briar House for inspection—have been unreasonably insistent. He has explained the difficulties—the distance (Tring is a day's journey along the appalling Sparrows Herne Turnpike); the wet nurse; the workshop, which requires his attention if not his constant supervision; the household. No doubt she senses his real objection, which is shame: he is ashamed that he took Alice away from her, that he loved her with such selfish, greedy passion, and that his eagerness for a child resulted not in Alice's happiness but the desolation of three stillbirths and an agonizing death. "Oh, how cruel life is," he mutters.

A child looks at him quizzically and he knows he has had his thoughts overheard. "Aunt Frances is not vindictive, but she has her claims on me," he declares to the girl, who is crouched over her spinning top. She has a cloud of beautiful blonde hair. When she turns to him he sees that her face is half consumed with the terrible imprint of smallpox.

He first met Alice at a supper party organized by his mother, who was resolved to see him married in the hope it would make him sensible. She was also possessed of the conviction, fervently held, that she needed to find a woman sufficiently alluring that her son would forget, or at least surmount, the unsuitable affair he had been reported to have had with an older woman in Constantinople. The reports were true and Abel had far from forgotten that woman, though he'd accepted the impossibility of their relationship long before his mother's efforts on his behalf. And Alice had been dazzling, able to make everything light about her, not only illuminating dreary subjects like weather or food or horses but lifting the weight of tedious conversation until everyone's words glittered and floated in her presence. There was no subject on which she was not knowledgeable, nor was her lightness of manner for a moment trivializing of any person. Her disconcerting ability to tell Abel his thoughts and to always be right, and to discern the thoughts of others, only added to her fascination. She was unafraid of being surprising, and delighted in mystifying and baffling. She once told him, as she sliced into an orange, that she had grown oranges and other fruits on a small farm in the hills of southern Spain. "When was this?" he had asked her. "Oh, about two hundred years ago," she'd replied. "You are looking well for a woman of your age," he'd joked, but Alice had quite matter-of-factly assured him that she was speaking not of this life but of one of her previous ones.

He has reached his house on Leadenhall but cannot bring himself to step through the door to greet his solitary supper. Leaning his back against the wood of the front door, which has caught the warmth of the evening sun, he decides to indulge his memories a little longer. The fact that Alice stood to inherit a fortune, though pressed on Abel as a point in her favour, seemed to him a disadvantage since it carried the impediment of allying opportunity with love and the risk of confusing the one with the other. He and Alice had been able to talk of it openly, frankly; equally. She had warned him that her aunt, as her guardian, would need to be won over by intelligence and candour—that she loathed convention, sycophancy and hypocrisy above all, and thought almost all Englishmen guilty of those three sins, though she exempted Frenchmen in their entirety. Frances had been Alice's guardian since she was twelve years old, when her mother and then her father (a distant cousin of Abel's mother, hence their introduction), had died of smallpox. Since Frances had no children of her own and had been left a young widow by Sir John Peake-Barnes, she had taken Alice gladly as her ward. But the inheritance is there, and while it might have slumbered in the background like an old dog before a fire, now the embers are cold it sits there growling, demanding bones to gnaw.

The door opens. It is Samuels. "Sir. Miss Kate asks if you are taking supper out tonight?"

"No, Samuels, I'll be right in." The evening has grown cool while he has been adrift in his thoughts, and the children who were playing in the street have vanished into their beds. He goes inside and, after eating a supper of cauliflower pudding and ham, writes as he must to Aunt Frances, trying to strike a note of cheer (however false), since he knows she cannot abide despondency anymore than she tolerates a bore.

Leadenhall St.

London

Briar House

Tring

Hertfordshire

15 June 1754

Dearest Aunt,

I was indeed heartened to learn that Egbert has settled so well into the aviary and that Dorcas has proved surprisingly adept at capturing additional mice. I share your conviction that your scullery is not infested with the creatures and suspect that Dorcas, despite her quiet manner, goes out at night and prowls the grounds like a panther. Soon all of Tring will be entirely wanting in rodents and shall have no further use for the Pied Piper of St. Peter and St. Paul, the Reverend Ratcliffe performing his miracle of making his parishioners vanish the more they hear the flute of his sermons.

I know that you are eager to meet Zachary as I am certain he is eager to meet you, though he has as yet no ability to give voice to his wishes apart from whimpers and cries, and he is—or so I am told by Mrs. Morley and by certain of the household who have met him—an unusually placid child. I think they mean to unsettle me by implying that he is not quite as he should be, but I see a fierce intelligence in his gaze. You will reach your own judgment, and your advice on the matter will be accepted as eagerly as gold by His Majesty's Treasury, though it shall be spent a good deal more wisely.

You have been most understanding of my predicament here, and my resulting difficulty in making the journey to Tring, and I am grateful beyond words for your forbearance. It was, indeed, most unfortunate that you should have suffered a fall at such an inconvenient moment, so soon after the tragedy. In your last you suggested that you might soon be sufficiently recovered to make the journey to London, and I trust that you will spend some weeks or months with us here. I shall have rooms prepared for you and as many of your household as you care to bring, though as you are aware Samuels is capable, and Kate and Biddy are eager to be of service to you. You will meet Mrs. Morley, who is not only diligent in her duties in respect of Zachary but is a woman of intelligence, despite being low-born.

Dearest Aunt, I look forward to your visit with keen anticipation.
Your ever-loving nephew,
Abel

It isn't a very charming or entertaining letter, but he feels neither charming nor entertaining. It will have to do.

A reply arrives two mornings later.

Briar House
Tring

Leadenhall St.
London
17 June

Dear Nephew,
I went only yesterday for my first ride on Sleipnir since that terrible day in March. He settled quickly and today we have been out jumping hedges and stirring dozy farmhands. He is not quite his old self, but none of us are. I will not remind you again that he threw me not "soon after" but at the precise moment of Alice's demise. Nature knows what mankind does not, and we are fools if we fail to listen to what it has to tell us.

To the matter of my visit: since I am fit and eager, I see no reason why I should not come to you on the morrow. I am not a believer in hesitation, since in delay lies misgiving and in misgiving lies our incapacity to forgive ourselves our sins, and if we are not to forgive them it is unreasonable to expect forgiveness from anyone else. It has not rained for three weeks and the ruts on the turnpike will be as knives. I shall come on Sleipnir and leave the bumping and grinding to Reeve, who can come after in a carriage with Peter and Catherine and Harold in a day or two. They shall also bring Mrs. Jenkins, a wet nurse who comes much recommended and who will return with me to Tring once Zachary has become accustomed to her. Mrs. Jenkins speaks only Welsh, but since a wet nurse requires no instruction in regard to her duties, I should not think that a great disadvantage.

You will not have time to reply and I can only say, as Monsieur Molière said, Ce n'est pas seulement ce que nous faisons, mais aussi ce que nous ne faisons pas, pour lequel nous sommes responsables.

Your faithful aunt,
Frances

He throws the letter to the floor. She has been hinting for weeks that she might take some role in Zachary's upbringing, but does she really imagine he will cheerfully relinquish care of his son to her and this Welsh wet nurse? And her quote from Monsieur Molière about being responsible not merely for what we choose to do, but for what we choose not to do, what on earth does she mean by it?

Samuels picks the letter from where it lies and returns it to him, glancing at its words without seeming to. "Sir?"

"Lady Peake-Barnes is to be with us . . . well, quite possibly at any moment, Samuels."

"Sir." He is sanguine, as always—generally immune to excitement and only ever hinting at emotion, as a dried brown leaf hints at spring.

"She is riding down. Alone!"

"Sir?"

"She will tell you that Harold and Catherine and Peter will follow in a day or two."

"I shall have rooms prepared."

"They will not need their own rooms, Samuels," says Abel in exasperation. "Harold is a crow and Peter and Catherine are parrots."

"Ah yes, sir." He gives Abel a hint of an oddly conspiratorial smile, causing him to wonder with whom his manservant is conspiring, for it most certainly is not him.

CHAPTER THREE

STALEMATE

June 1754, London

◪

By the time she reaches King's Langley it has begun to drizzle, and she finds herself damp, uncomfortable and in a low mood. Even Sleipnir has lost heart. She'd imagined sweeping into London, marching into Abel's house, dandling the baby on her knee, winning immediate affection from the child and taking him back to Briar House within the week. But to arrive bedraggled and in poor humour would set her at a disadvantage, and though Abel is malleable, it is his very malleability that is his strength; he is like an army permanently in retreat but never quite defeated, so that one always has to be on one's guard.

She takes a room at the Saracen's Head and sends a message to Reeve to have her carriage sent on with her things, writing a short note to Abel to tell him she has been delayed a day by the illness of her friend and neighbour Mrs. Margesson—she can hardly admit that she is detained merely by dank weather and an unaccountable loss of spirit.

Alone in her small room at the inn, its wooden floor so uneven that it resembles a series of low hills, its bed having roughly the consistency (and odour) of a sack of potatoes, she finds her confidence has deserted her completely. Frances knows herself well enough to understand that if she is not busy, she is in jeopardy. At Briar House there is always much to do, but away from it she feels like a puffin set down in a forest, confounded by the rustle of leaves and the absence of sea air. Without the household accounts to disentangle (Reeve always ties them into knots that must be unraveled), or Italian conversation with Miss Pellew, or correspondence regarding her coal mines, she loses purpose and thus hope and her very soul sinks down to her feet and out the leather of her boots, down through the floorboards to heaven knows where.

Alice had kept her hopeful, Alice above all; her full moon, her bright new day, her dear girl. Frances hadn't wanted to stand in the way of the marriage, or only insofar as she'd have liked to stand in the way of any marriage; would have liked Alice always at her side. But she is no monster and had resolved long before Abel Cloudesley's appearance that she would not deny her niece that other sort of love, should it present itself. Frances wanted Alice to have those things she had been denied—not that she had been denied love, or not exactly. Sir John Peake-Barnes had been endowed with affection, a prodigious appetite for the pleasures of the bedchamber and much experience in that direction. In addition, he had a cheerful disposition, a fine country house, the largest collection of owls in England, and four coal mines in Leicestershire. But he had been twenty-eight years older than Frances and his heart, though big, was not big enough for all that he strived to be (not least, twenty-eight years younger) and, once stilled, Frances was left with said house, coal mines, and two hundred and fifteen owls. Also, a week after his death, a miscarriage.

There is a mirror in her room, spotted and cloudy, so that the image she sees in it might be of a creature that has crawled from a swamp. Frances is not a martyr to reflection, having no illusions about her appearance. She was always told she was an ungainly girl, and it is true that she was heavy-footed, awkward and not in the least demure, quite unlike her sister, Alice's mother, who was so delicate that she seemed to float from place to place like a sprite. But she has no regrets: her robust disposition has meant she has suffered few ailments. Why Sleipnir reared and threw her on the very hour and moment of Alice's death she cannot say, but she knew when she hit the ground that something far more terrible than a broken ankle had befallen her. When she heard the news, she took opium pills in sufficient quantity to make an elephant pass out for a week. Dorcas found her empty pill box and made her drink saltwater and sour milk until she retched, and then would not allow her sleep but slapped her and threw iced water into her face and walked her a thousand times about her chamber. When Frances had come more to herself and thanked her maid for all that she had done, Dorcas only frowned and said, "Can't be doing with finding myself another position. Not at my time of life, whatever time of life that might be," before promptly leaving the room. She had barely spoken to her mistress since.

Frances might have insisted on a man from a better family for Alice, a man with land, at least, or something more than a trade, but Abel had withstood her early interrogations so thoroughly it seemed churlish not to allow the two of them their experiment in love. Remembering that first visit of his to Briar House, she recalled how she'd been out shooting weasels when he'd been due to call, leaving him to the mercy of Dorcas and Reeve and a dozen birds, having given express instruction that they be encouraged to fly freely about the prospective suitor's head. When she eventually presented herself to him in the library, ensuring copious quantities of blood were smeared across her blue silk dress, he'd stood, bowed and quietly apologized for his impertinence in taking one of her books to read. He appeared to have hardly noticed the crow sitting on the arm of his chair or the parrots sitting on top of the bookcase, still less the droppings on the table where his tea had been placed. The book he had chosen was Voltaire's *Lettres philosophiques*.

"A poor choice, Mr. Cloudesley," she'd declared.

"Oh?"

"You are familiar with the work?"

"Indeed, madam," he'd said, and that had marked him out for a start.

"But Monsieur Voltaire is so obviously wrong," she declared.

"Wrong, madam? In what respect?" he asked in a tone that suggested interest in her opinion—and not merely so he could give voice to his own.

She explained patiently that Voltaire's admiration for the English was misplaced, given that there was so much more to admire about the French. "We all pay too little attention to the muck at our feet, Mr. Cloudesley," and he'd had the good grace to observe his boots and aver that watching one's own feet was very much the best way to begin any journey.

That he was a handsome fellow was undeniable, though more Hermes than Achilles, with something transitory about him—a touch of mischief, a dash of mercury. He was unattached to anything, it seemed, yet was so obviously striving for something more than this ordinary world could provide. He'd been in Constantinople and the experience had left him infected with a wistful sensitivity and an understanding of matters which even the best-educated Englishmen and women were usually content to consign to the realms of ignorance. That evening they had argued for three hours after supper about Mahometanism, or Islam, as he'd insisted it be called, he contending that it was a faith superior to Christianity because it was less corrupted by vanity and saints. Frances, no defender of any church, invited him to agree that God was in any case a mirage and they compromised by agreeing that mankind was ruled by the illusory and heedless of the actual. What had impressed her was not his opinions, since opinions are a currency quickly devalued; it was rather that not once did Abel show the failings that might have been expected of a man in his position: he gave no impression that conversation with a woman was an activity equivalent to talking to a child in need of encouragement, nor did he seem to bear that resentful pride in his own intelligence that was so often the mark of the low-born given a good education. That, and his response to dear Alice when she had returned from the errand she had sent her on, had decided her in his favour. "Has she been odious, Abel?" she'd asked, entering the library, her cheeks flushed, pulling off her gloves and handing them to him in an act of unmistakable intimacy. "I would say that your aunt has weighed me and found me wanting in exactly the right proportions," he replied, casting a modest smile at Frances.

In short, he was suitable, endowed as he was with an excellent physique, his own hair and teeth, sweet breath, and both intelligence and character. To frighten him away from Alice, as she had frightened away so many others, would be like declining to take the one good oyster from a plate of stinking ones for the sake of conformity. Besides which, she doubted he would be so easily deterred. On their wedding day he presented her with a gift: a clockwork silver owl which flapped its wings and descended smoothly from its gilt perch onto a tiny scuttling enameled mouse, consuming it on the hour and defecating it on the half-hour. Though ingenious and amusing, it was hardly fair exchange for Alice, but it would have to do.

Frances looks at herself again in the milky mirror, turning to the side, observing her profile neutrally, holding her belly in and her chin up, pulling her unruly hair back into something like the loose braid and bun that Dorcas usually did for her, and does not think so ill of herself as all that. She is not yet fifty and hopes she might yet find a companion who will look at her with desire, for there is no feeling in the world so fulfilling, as there is none so discouraging as the absence of it. Love is another matter; more important, more durable, but so terrible in its loss that on the whole she thinks it best avoided altogether.

When her carriage joins her at the Saracen's Head the following morning, making a great commotion just as she is about to take breakfast, it is *sans* Mrs. Jenkins. Reeve informs her that the Welshwoman has declined to come to London because the infant she has lately been feeding has developed a fever and to bring it on such a grueling journey would be fatal to it. Frances returns Reeve to Tring on Sleipnir and proceeds in her carriage with only her coachman, postilion and Catherine, Peter and Harold as traveling companions, bumping along the turnpike and endeavouring to read Monsieur Rousseau's new work, though the French words joggle before her eyes so that she can only take half a page at a time before having to look out the window at the startling green of an English summer. By late afternoon a familiar but disturbing smell fills her nostrils. They have reached Kilburn Green and are within sniffing distance of London and its stinking miasma of alcohol fumes, sewage and rotting meat. She is surprised that so many of her acquaintances tolerate it and can only suppose that the prospect of regular intelligent conversation and visits to the theatre dull the nose. Tring is parochial, but at least it does not stink. Living in the country may be but a half-life, but life in London is not whole—it is simply the other half.

Her carriage pulls up outside the Leadenhall house and workshop, from which a sign swings in the light breeze—CLOUDESLEY AND SON, CLOCKMAKERS. It is a tall building of four stories at least three hundred years old, the street having largely been spared the ravages of the Great Fire. With its windows at odd angles and its undulating roof it looks like a house built by a distracted child. The workshop joins onto the house and from it comes the sound of hammering and grinding and low murmur of male voices at work. The wooden front door of the main house opens, and Samuels presents himself in his oblique way, more shadow than light. He comes to help Frances from her carriage, but she bats him away, instructing him to bring in the parrots' cages for fear of theft by curious onlookers, who are already gathering as if she were an itinerant performer come to town.

Abel stands in the doorway ready to greet her, or she supposes it must be Abel. Never has she seen a man so changed. His looks, once so full of vigour, have deserted him, replaced by the ravages of grief and worry. He is pale, thin, stooped like a man twice his age. He offers a smile, so distant it might have been conceived in Siberia.

"Abel . . ." she says, wondering what else she can add to the declaration of his name, her tongue flapping aimlessly in pursuit of the right expression. She had intended a short speech on his dilatoriness in failing to come to her, wanting to make a jest of Bacon's words on Mahomet and the mountain, but finds herself so shocked by his countenance that she cannot bring herself to utter a word.

"Aunt. It is so good of you to come. I . . . well, you must forgive me for not bringing him to you at Briar House." He stands to the side to allow Samuels to bustle past, in each hand a tall silver cage containing a parrot. "Will you not come in? Tea is freshly brewed, and we have a good supply of sugared almonds." He peers at her, she supposes wondering at her silence.

"Abel," she repeats. To her shame she realizes that she had been relishing the battle to come, preparing ploy and ruse over the child, ready to outwit her nephew-in-law, but instead she feels like a general who has marched her troops into a town ready to ransack it, only to find its inhabitants pitiable and starving. She realizes that she should have brought him a gift. She has a silver egg cup for Zachary, but nothing for Abel. Reaching into her purse she hands him her copy of Jean-Jacques Rousseau's *Discours sur les sciences et les arts*, only a little dog-eared. She has not finished the book and is deeply reluctant to part with it but feels she must give him something. "Here, Abel. An excellent edition, I think." She looks at the book fondly, hardly able to hand it over. "It is in French, of course. You will enjoy it. You have read Monsieur Diderot's *Pensées philosophiques*? Very good, very good."

Abel looks at the book uncomprehendingly. "Yes," he says eventually, "yes. You have mentioned him before."

"There are so many fine young thinkers in France. And he is the son of a watchmaker, this Rousseau, just like you." She taps his cheek, trying to lift his spirits and her own. "I have mentioned that to you before, I'm sure. Why don't we have any of our own, do you suppose? Thinkers, that is, not sons of watchmakers." She walks past him and on through the house, noticing the small but telling differences from when Alice had been its mistress. There are no flowers in the vases as there would have been; towering blue spikes of delphiniums and day lilies at this time of year. The smell of cooking emanating from the kitchen below is of watery stock and overboiled mutton. Why is it, she wonders, that the smell of inattentive cooking is almost as depressing as grief itself?

Abel is at her side. "Here, Aunt. Come through to the parlour. We have it set out for tea, and Kate—you remember Kate?—she will be through shortly with milk and, and . . ." He looks at her, his face blank as if he has forgotten why he's talking to her at all.

Frances feels a strange compulsion to take him in her arms. It is not at all how she had imagined comporting herself and yet, yielding to her sudden inclination, he is there sobbing upon her bosom, sobbing like a man who has been waiting for the moment to sob and it being too long delayed is incapable of stopping. When at last his lament subsides and the milk jug has appeared and disappeared in the doorway not once but twice, she says, "It is I who had expected to weep before you, and I had hoped that it would have been you that might have comforted me on the loss of dear Alice." Abel begins an apology for his lapse, but she holds up a hand to silence him. "Your misery, Abel, in its force, in its sheer, unarguable grief, is surely enough to speak for us both." She stretches out her hands and presses them to his cheeks, obliging him to purse his lips. "Now, give your aunt a smile, for we must both face the world bravely, must we not, for little Zachary if not for ourselves."

Abel gives her the smile she bid of him and to her surprise what Frances sees in his expression is not sorrow or self-pity but relief. She wonders whether it is from the release of that pent-up torrent of grief, or because she is being considerate to him when she had given him every expectation that she would be unreasonable. "Now, Abel," she says, "where is the child?"

"Sleeping."

"Sleeping, yes." She glances at the clock to see that it is four o'clock. An odd time for sleep. "And this Mrs. Morley you have told me of. Where is she?"

"Also sleeping."

"It is like the enchanted castle, this household, with everyone cursed to one hundred years of slumber."

Abel laughs. "Well, I am awake."

"I must be frank, Abel, but you look very much in need of rest. A hundred years would be a perfectly sensible prescription."

He grimaces. "I barely sleep these days."

"Opium. I have a copious supply of tablets in my trunk. Take two tonight. I guarantee deep repose and most peculiar"— she pauses, amused by a private recollection—"*most* peculiar dreams."

There is the sound of an infant scream from somewhere in the house, followed quickly by stirring. "That will be Leonora," says Abel, rubbing a hand across his face as if to wipe away the evidence of his exhaustion. "She acts as the prince's kiss to any sleeping beauties we have in the house."

"Leonora? And who, pray, is Leonora?"

"The wet nurse's daughter."

"What's she doing here?"

Abel gives her a baffled smile. "She must live some-where, and it is as well she lives here. I would wish for her to be a more placid child, but I think she screams for Zachary, too, and therefore saves him the effort of it." A moment later a woman enters, tall, red-haired, blotchy in complexion, harassed and resentful, in each arm a wriggling pink thing which Frances mistakes at first for piglets, one screaming and wearing a bonnet, the other still and dressed in a tiny smock like a minuscule farm-hand. "Aunt Frances," announces Abel, "meet your great-nephew, and his good friends Mrs. Morley and Leonora."

Mrs. Morley gives a brief nod in Frances's direction and arrays herself on the settee, an infant each side of her. Her chin is tilted upward, as if in expectation of insult or assault.

"Fearful small, aren't they?" says Frances, more accusingly than she had intended.

"They are, madam, being as they are only three and five months of age," says Mrs. Morley, defiantly.

She ponders the wet nurse's rebuke a moment before turning to Abel. "I mentioned to you Mrs. Jenkins. Should this lady"—she waves a hand in the direction of Mrs. Morley—"cease to be in your employ, then I have Mrs. Jenkins at the ready. She has had the smallpox and so can pass her immunity along to Zachary with her milk."

"That is not a protection," says Mrs. Morley emphatically, "but that it were." Frances glances at Abel, wondering whether he will allow the woman's impertinence to stand. Frances isn't sure how to respond. The woman seems to speak with full liberty. The two babies have fallen quiet and are regarding her with what appears to be appalled fascination. She assumes the smaller child is Zachary, his little face quite stern. Mrs. Morley stands and passes him to her. "Your great-nephew, Lady Peake-Barnes. He is an impassive child, yet he seems sturdy and is not beyond the appreciation of a cuddle."

This is the moment she has been anticipating so eagerly, yet now her hands are upon the infant, she is uncertain what it is she should say or do.

"Here," says Mrs. Morley, taking Frances's hand and placing it more firmly behind the baby's head, moving her other to support his rump. "More comfortable for you and he both."

What a strange authority the wet nurse possesses. "Thank you," says Frances, and takes some time to regard the little one. "Well, hello, Zachary Cloudesley. And where in the world will you find yourself in years to come, I wonder? What will those dark blue eyes behold, and those little ears hear?" She brushes one, as tender as a fresh lamb's lettuce leaf. "All manner of nonsense, I daresay. Well, don't expect your Aunt Franny to bibble-babble at you. I shall attempt to instill reason in you, for we are in great need of it." She glances over at Abel, who is regarding her, to her surprise, with approval. But Zachary's features form themselves into a frown and shortly after comes the sound of a great gurgling from within his diminutive form and the distinctive smell of excrement.

"I'll deal with that," says Mrs. Morley, taking Zachary from her. "Will you keep an eye on Leonora for me? She has a propensity to roll about."

Abel stands as Mrs. Morley leaves the room. It is hardly a necessary show of respect. "Your wet nurse enjoys a position of considerable authority in this household, I see."

"Do you object, Aunt? Should we not show respect to all?"

"Yes, certainly"—she hesitates—"up to a point." She looks at the baby girl who sits gurgling on the sofa. The child has an oddly adult look about her, ruddy-cheeked and, in her forming features, some of the roughness of her mother. "Ugly little thing, isn't she?"

"There is no need to strive to set me against Mrs. Morley, Aunt. Or her child. I am not in thrall to her, if that is your suspicion. She takes good care of Zachary and is a woman of strong character, something which I should have thought would meet with your approval."

Frances cannot think that she does approve, or not exactly, but decides to suspend further campaigning on the matter, and in particular on the question of when she might remove Zachary to Tring, until she has laid the groundwork. She is about to go to her rooms when she realizes that Harold is not at her side. "Where is Harold?" she declares in alarm.

"Samuels will have fetched him in for you, I am sure."

Frances hurries out in search of Samuels, finding him in his small room beside the kitchen, Harold there at his elbow. Upon the desk is an open ledger of accounts, Samuels entering some figures into it. "Ah, Samuels, I see you have Harold in your care."

Samuels stands. "The crow likes to watch me write, I think, madam."

"He likes writing, it's true. The scratching of quill on paper, the smell of ink, they please him. As they do me. And you too, I think, Samuels?" But Samuels responds only with that almost secret smile of his. He grew up in her household, Dorcas's boy, and Frances had hoped for great things for him. He'd had a good education at her expense and might have been an admiral or an engineer yet here he is in service, as if it were in his veins, though in him deference tussles with contempt and his churn of feelings can only ever be part-concealed by that tight little smile. Dorcas claims to have no recollection of who or what the father might have been, as if through such denial she can lay claim to a virgin birth. Her son could be almost any age, like his mother. He looks forty but is not yet twenty-five. "Will you show me to my chamber?" she asks him.

She and Abel spend the next few days in an awkward dance, the one advancing a step and the other retreating. They are polite, without ever seeming to quite see one another as they did on that first day.

She catches herself observed by Mrs. Morley from a window and knows that she is not entirely trusted. Frances can barely resist the temptation to throw Zachary up in the air and catch him, simply to cause the overbearing wet nurse alarm.

Abel is away in the workshop much of the day, and Frances begins to think it might not be so difficult to persuade him that it will be best for Zachary to come home with her to Tring. If needs be Mrs. Morley and her noisy daughter with her spotty face and bilious inclination can come too.

◙

CHAPTER FOUR

A REMARKABLE WRITING GIRL

June 1754, London

※

"Abel, we must speak," she says on the Wednesday, a week after her arrival. He is moving away from her at speed along the narrow wood-paneled corridor that connects the house to the workshop. She catches him by the elbow.

"Yes, yes," he says, pausing a moment before continuing, compelling her to pursue him. "In fact," he says, "there is something I wish to show you."

She has never entered the workshop before (notwithstanding her inclination to give him advice on his methods of manufacture), and it is startling. The ceiling is low, yet despite the dull day the light is bright. There are candles in chandeliers which hang on chains so long they must be walked around, and which produce a warm, bright, yellowish glow. They also make the long room hot, and the smell of wood and metal is blended with the odour of twenty working men, or most particularly their armpits, imparting that oddly earthy and unsettling oniony smell. "Good afternoon, gentlemen," she says, since only a few of them have looked up. Some nod as she passes, though others are so absorbed in their fine work at their benches they do not notice her arrival. Abel makes no attempt at introduction, that not being his intention. He walks through to the far end of the workshop, Frances following to where there is a wooden partition and, beyond it, a separate smaller room where only one man is at work on a half-formed creature the size and shape of a young woman at a desk. In place of hands are steel bones, and where there should be a face is a void filled with cogs and springs and levers. The device is dressed in a fine silk gown of pistachio green, making Frances think of an ancient noblewoman disinterred from her tomb, her clothes the only sign of her former rank, for bones are bones for paupers and queens alike.

"Aunt, it is this I wanted to show you. She is a young woman— an automaton, as you see, but as near a living thing as we have ever built here. She can write!" His pride is obvious, and Frances has no wish to puncture it, though she finds his claim improbable. The young man who is working on the creature glances up, reddens and lowers his eyes, and it is perfectly plain to Frances that she is in fact a young woman dressed in men's clothing. "Here, let us show you her faculties," says Abel. "Tom, engage the mechanism."

The young woman called Tom pulls a lever and, astonishingly, the machine leans further forward and, with a creak and a whirr, its steel fingers take up a quill on the desk, dip it into a pot of ink and begin to write a letter. Frances goes to see what is being written.

Good afternoon, Aunt Frances. I am pleased to have made your acquaintance; I wish I knew my name in order to tell it to you.

Frances brings a hand to her heart to arrest its wild beat. She is no less amazed than she knows she is meant to be. "Goodness, Abel, goodness," she says, breathless, "how . . . how . . ."

"I am able to determine the letters the creature shall write, through this mechanism. See?" He pulls her round to the back of the desk, where Frances sees a board with letters and buttons and levers which mean as little to her as the workings of a church organ. "Tom is a marvel at giving our girl her words, aren't you, Tom?" The young woman lowers her eyes yet again and blushes.

"It is most impressive, Abel, or should I say *she* is most impressive." Frances casts an obvious glance in the direction of Tom, but Abel fails to grasp her inference.

"That is just it, Aunt. I would give her a name, but I have not . . . that is, Tom and I have not . . . decided upon one." His excitement is palpable, almost physical, so that it fills the room like a cloud of bees. It is, she surmises, why he has been so inattentive to her and Zachary this past week. "It is a commission, you see, and for a sum so great it is, well, extraordinary, from the Duke of Devonshire. I believe it was for his wife, Charlotte, but she has died, you know, and now I think he intends that it should remind him of her. But this . . . this is what I wanted to ask of you, to have your counsel upon." He draws a breath.

"Yes?"

"Should I call her Charlotte, do you think, or is that insensitive?"

Very likely to cause offence, she thinks. "I shall consider the matter, Abel. You have not given her a face yet, and so it is difficult to give her a name without one, as it is any creature, don't you think?"

"You are right! Quite right. And on this, too, I wish for your guidance." He is animated by unease, rippling with awkwardness and embarrassment, as if about to make a confession. "Tom and

I have been constructing a face, but I am conscious . . . I am conscious of how much it looks like . . . like . . ."

"I know perfectly well what you are to say, Abel."

"You do?"

"You are to say that she looks like Alice, because it is her face that you see before you at all times."

"It is that, Aunt. Just that," he confesses.

"And you wonder whether I think it in poor taste to give dear Alice's face to an automaton?"

"I do."

"Show me."

"It is not quite ready. We have no hair, have we, Tom?" He laughs uncomfortably and turns to his apprentice for confirmation, as he would a younger brother, though a brother it is clear he holds in high esteem. Can it really be that Abel has not noticed that Tom is, in fact, a sister? She is dressed in male costume, wearing a white shirt of good size and looseness and a jerkin tight enough that it presses down upon her bosom, making it almost but not quite imperceptible. She has not spoken, and Frances determines to oblige her to say something.

"Tom, you have worked with my nephew long?"

"I have, my lady. These past four years." Her voice is that of a woman trying to sound like a man, low and gruff.

"And how old were you when you first came to work here?"

Abel regards Frances with surprise.

"I was but fourteen, madam."

"And you are now eighteen?"

Abel interrupts her questioning. "Even in a clock shop we are not able to make time run either faster or slower than elsewhere.

Tom is not wordy but he has astonishing dexterity and is very skilled with the mathematics of giving a mechanism movement. What do you call it, Tom?"

"Sequencing, master."

"Sequencing, yes. We give the automaton a progression of hundreds of different movements with these cams"—he points to a column of metal discs in the back of the automaton—"which in combination are almost infinite, and enable the machine to blink and nod and raise its arm and, in this, our most remarkable yet, to move its fingers across a page in a series of prescribed movements to write a letter. And Tom calls this a sequence. Wondrous, is it not?"

Frances thinks it best to calm him by appearing to consider the machine they have built in some way ordinary. "And this creature you are making will sit in Chatsworth House and be seen by no one but the duke, I suppose?"

"Most likely."

"It is perhaps as well."

If Abel is hurt he does not show it. "I have no opinion on its future admiration. The pleasure is all in the making. I am not interested in creating a sensation, Aunt."

Frances suspects, nevertheless, that a sensation will be stirred. "Now, the face?"

"It is best that we fit it to the automaton, and you can see it as it is meant to be seen. Perhaps tomorrow?" He takes Frances's arm and leads her back through the workshop, its rows of finished clocks on their shelves glittering, its men bent over their benches, so absorbed that there seems something almost holy in their labour.

Once in the very different atmosphere of the house, with its cooking smells and the sound of Leonora grizzling and Mrs. Morley attempting to soothe her, Frances says to Abel, "I am gratified to see that your principal apprentice is a young woman."

He stares at her in incredulity. "It's true there is something girlish about him, and I have often thought so, but I assure you Tom is a boy."

Frances laughs at the absurdity of his self-delusion.

"He has yet to show a whisker, it's true," continues Abel, "and . . ." Doubt snakes into his voice. "His words are spoken high . . . ever on the edge of breaking . . ."

"You think he must be a boy because he has always told you he is. Is that it? And why do you suppose that is the case? Or is it, rather, that you cannot believe a young woman would be so fine at their craft as she is?"

"It is . . . it is . . ." Abel sits, dropping his head between his hands. When he looks up all the rejuvenating energy that had been there in the workshop has deserted him. "Tom came to me on the recommendation of Josiah Laskins of Colchester," he says, shaken. "He was a shy boy, but dexterous and quick and he learned so fast. He lodges with my foreman, Seth, and I am certain Seth would have told me if he thought Tom . . . if he thought there was anything irregular in Tom's . . ."

"Does this Seth like Tom?"

"They are fast friends."

"Then why would he tell you anything at all, since you would cease to employ Tom if you thought he—or she, rather—had been concealing her sex from you, would you not?"

"I shall speak to Tom now."

"No," says Frances, a restraining finger on his shoulder to keep him in his chair. "No, do not confront the poor woman and force her either to confess or oblige her to tell a lie. Find a way of making it easy for her to tell you the truth in her own way and in her own time."

"I couldn't do without Tom," he says, trepidation creeping up on him. "My other men are very capable, but Tom . . ."

"Find a way, Abel, both of keeping her and letting her be who she is. Perhaps it is not she who has been deceiving you, but you. Perhaps your wits haven't wanted to let your eyes admit the truth."

When they are in the workshop the following day to examine the face of the automaton, Frances sees that it is not quite beautiful. The cheeks are rosy and the nose rather too sharp and long, so that she looks like an invalid made up to look well. She is not really so much like Alice, and that is both a disappointment and a relief. Yet she has eyes that blink and turn from side to side while she writes, and her mouth opens and closes as if she is silently composing her words. On the paper this time she writes:

It was my delight and honour to meet you, Aunt. But what name shall I say is mine?

"Well, Abel," she asks, "what name shall this writing girl be given?"

He looks at Tom, puzzling at her. "Tom, you have an opinion, do you not?" His tone is accusing.

"Why, sir, not really, I mean not properly . . ."

"Just tell my aunt," he says with impatience.

Frances understands that Abel must feel that he has been made a fool of by this young woman. No doubt he is wondering whether some or all of his men have observed what he has failed to observe and have long known what he has neglected to know. "Tom, my nephew tells me how much he values your work and your opinions," she says, "which I have observed you express with great modesty. Do not be shy. Tell us what you think."

Tom coughs, a fist to her mouth, and looks to Abel for approval, which is given with a gesture of resignation. Speaking with an unease prompted by her master's sudden and unexpected disapproval, she says, "I think, madam, that a creature such as this should be given no name, since she is after all but an automaton, and quite without spirit. I would call her simply *Mr. Cloudesley's Remarkable Writing Girl*."

Abel starts to say something about the creature being *Mr. Tom Spurrell's Writing Girl*, but his tone is ungenerous, and for fear of what else he is about to say, Frances interrupts. "I think *Mr. Cloudesley's Remarkable Writing Girl* will do very well, and for just the reason Tom says, Abel. Now come, it is my turn to show you something." And she leads him away.

With the door to the workshop closed behind them she hisses, "You have worked with this young woman amicably and with increasing admiration for her talents these past four years?"

He says nothing.

"Well?"

"Yes."

"And she is of good character?"

"Unimpeachable."

"Then why turn on her so, Abel, thinking her now a female and not a male? It is not fitting. It is not your character, or what I thought you were."

"It is . . . well, it is . . ."

"You are embarrassed. You wonder perhaps that others have been laughing at you?"

"It's not that," he says sullenly.

"Did Alice not notice? This Seth, he must know, if she lodges with him."

"It is the deceit, Aunt, that hurts so, more than my own idiocy. I am familiar enough with that."

"It may be, Abel, that all assumed you knew and were content with the charade."

It is apparent he has not thought of this and brightens for a moment before darkening again. "But if my men assumed I knew, then what must they think when I so obviously favour Tom?"

"But you favour Tom for her talents, not for her sex."

"If they think I knew all along they might assume . . . oh, I don't know," he says, exasperated. "I don't know how I can talk to him now, what to say."

"Would you like me to speak to her?"

He looks at her with unconcealed gratitude. "Would you?"

"When she has finished her work for the day. What time is that?"

"Tom generally leaves with Seth, and that is toward seven."

"Very well."

The day has softened into evening, the light pink as if refracted through stained glass and making everything glow with unreliable beauty when Frances returns to the workshop. Seth is readying to leave, and she asks him if he will wait outside and permit her to talk to Tom alone. Unease sweeps across his face and Frances knows that Seth shares the secret. In the room at the far end Tom is there, writing her sequences. A stack of pages sits at her elbow, upon them notations something like music. She stands at Frances's entrance, brushing down her breeches. She is small and unlikely to grow much bigger by the look of her, her form elfin. Frances allows a portentous silence to fall between them. "I cannot be the first who has noticed," she says at last.

Tom stares at the floor. "No, madam."

"Do you not think it was cruel to my nephew to deceive him so?"

To Frances's astonishment a sort of growl emanates from the young woman, almost bear-like. "What?" she demands, looking up. "What am I supposed to be? Can a woman work at a craft such as this?" Words then begin to tumble from her lips at such pace they blur into one single angry declaration. "I am not as you, ma'am. I come from a poor home. My father was a watchmaker. I would have had two brothers but they were dead before I was born and when I came along my father had no one to teach his trade to, so he teached me and treated me as if I was a boy and dressed me as a boy, so it has always been so, and I called myself Tom and repaired the town's clocks and earned us our money, my mother and I, for my father was dead too by then, but then my mother started to scream and shout at me to wear a petticoat and I couldn't bear it, I couldn't, and so I forged a letter to Mr. Laskins and went to work for him until he noticed that I was turning into a young woman and started doing what most men will do when they have a young woman to do with as they will and, and . . ." As her story reaches its climax her indignation tapers into sorrow and tears begin to spill. Frances encourages her to continue. "And then I forged a letter from Mr. Laskins to Mr. Cloudesley commending my work, thinking that if Mr. Cloudesley were to seek corroboration from Laskins he could hardly deny it given what he done to me and I came here."

"What age were you then?"

"Near twenty, ma'am."

"And why this place?"

"It is renowned, this shop. Large and busy. And London, well, if a man cannot make of himself what he would wish to be here, then where?"

Frances hesitates, but feels she must say it: "But you are not a man."

Tom puffs herself up, as a cat does before a dog. "I am my own invention, m'am. And I would keep it so."

"But now you may be a woman, openly, as your sex dictates, and yet keep your position, and what is more be an example to other women of talent and craft, who may be encouraged. I will make sure of it. I give you my word. My nephew is—"

"I will not be dictated to by my sex or anyone else's!" she insists, angrily. "I have no wish to be other than I am. I am Tom."

Frances ponders this. "There must be difficulties?" She wishes to be delicate.

"Difficulties? *Difficulties?* I will not be ruled by this, which is not my likeness, but the likeness of another being altogether." She passes a hand down her diminutive form, and Frances does not doubt her determination.

"You like your work?"

"It is my passion, and Master Abel is good to me, and he has such ideas, and for me to work at them and make them real, why it is like making life from nothing but bits of brass and silver. It is, if you will, a sort of alchemy, but not flimflammery and lies, but clockwork and movement and a different order of magic."

"And your name, child?"

"I am no child, ma'am. And my name is Tom. If you mean, by what name was I baptized, it was long ago. A different life. I am Tom, and Tom I will stay."

"Very well, Tom." She puts her hands on her hips, signaling the matter is concluded. "You have convinced me, but how will you and I now proceed to convince my nephew to keep you in his employ as you are?"

Tom reddens, his shyness returning as if it had never left him. "Tell him who I am for me, madam, if you will, for I think he will not listen to me until he knows again that I am Tom, and though I am not equipped with all the parts he might have expected, I have all those he needs, and that which he might be troubled by has been given to no man nor ever shall be."

Frances smiles at his delicacy. Tom has precision of thought as well as dexterity in manufacture. "I will do my best, Tom Spurrell," she says, leaving without a second glance at the automaton who looks barely like Alice, and only then if glanced at from the corner of one eye.

She tells Abel what she has heard from his apprentice and suggests that he continue as if nothing has changed, since that is what Tom wishes and what he surely desires, too.

"Yet everything has changed," Abel says.

"Has it? What has changed? Your perception, as if a view you have always admired was seen through a thicket of brush, and one day you wake and walk down to admire that same landscape to find that your gardener has cleared it away, and the view seems to you altered. But it is the same, now only seen more clearly. It is you who must adjust, and whose pleasure should be heightened not diminished by the greater clarity you have gained."

"You are very astute, when you choose to be," says Abel with a skeptical smile. "I will not dismiss him, if that is your fear. I shall talk to Seth, gently, and listen to what he has to say about Tom."

The following day she resolves to take Zachary out for a walk. Abel has devised a carriage that can be pulled along or pushed and that is mercifully free of clockwork. She goes upstairs to where Mrs. Morley looks after the babies, seeking the wet nurse and finding her cleaning Zachary's rump, which is red with sores from where he has been left too long in a shitty tailclout. But his form is as perfect as any cupid's, his thighs plump, his tummy rounded and his little pizzle waving about in perfect innocence, so that he makes her think of a cherub from one of Signor Botticelli's paintings. His face, though, is much more like that of an angel as drawn by Signor Caravaggio—knowing, weighted with suspicion, and holding an anger against the world, as if he has been busy absorbing fury and mistrust along with Mrs. Morley's milk.

Mrs. Morley looks around to see Frances standing in the doorway and returns to her swaddling without comment.

"You do not like me very much, I think, Mrs. Morley."

"It is not my place to like or dislike," she says, without turning.

"For what it is worth, madam, I admire you. I can see that you are a woman of great competence and self-sufficiency."

The wet nurse pauses and turns, putting a hand on a hip. "That you should have an opinion on my character surprises me, madam, since you do not know it at all."

"Abel has told me that you made it a condition of moving to this house that I should take up residence."

"Has he told you that?" says Mrs. Morley without emotion, turning and continuing to dress the child.

"But I cannot stay. I have a household to run."

Mrs. Morley lifts Zachary to her shoulder and bends to where she has left Leonora fussing on the floor, lifting her, too. Armed with both infants she looks at Frances with something resembling condescension. "You have a household to run? Very well, then, run it. I have heard you have a fine estate, and that you have many birds there, madam. I do not like birds in the least. The feathery air is not good for the little ones' lungs. Your parrots fly freely around your chamber here, or so I am led to believe, and that crow of yours is ever hopping about the furniture. It is disturbing. And so, madam, and please do not take this unkindly, I must say I will not be sorry to see you gone."

Frances laughs. "I am quite used to people being pleased to see me gone. I have very few friends, and even they can only tolerate me for a short time. But I had hoped to persuade you to come to Briar House, since it is my intention to raise Zachary as my own."

Mrs. Morley staggers back in such violent amazement that she hits her head against the door frame, loosening her grip on both children, who start to slip from her grasp. Frances rushes forward, taking both Zachary and Leonora (who is screeching) and holding them to her bosom. "Oh, Mrs. Morley! Let me get you a glass of water. Sit, breathe. Goodness." She joggles the two babies until Leonora calms. Zachary watches her attentively, as always. Frances calls down to Biddy to bring a glass of water for Mrs. Morley, who has bumped her head.

Biddy comes bounding up the stairs (she is an athletic girl, always brimming with unspent energy, her sleeves rolled up as if ready for any task she may be given) and presents the half-spilled glass to the wet nurse. "Why, Mrs. Morley, you look as if you had seen a ghost, which wouldn't surprise me," says Biddy. Remembering that Frances is standing beside her she adds, "Excusing me, ma'am," and gives an ungainly curtsey before hurtling away back down the stairs.

Seeing that Mrs. Morley has somewhat recovered herself, Frances says, "You knew that was my intention, surely, to raise Zachary?"

"I did not."

"But why so surprised, Mrs. Morley? You do not seem the type to be made aghast at such a predictable development."

Mrs. Morley's eyes are on Zachary and, most particularly, on Leonora, who is nuzzling against Frances's breast. "She wants to feed," she says.

"And I long to suckle, but alas I am unable." Tucking her chin into her neck she looks down to where Zachary is, as always, observing her with a certain wary attentiveness. "But I can be a mother to this child, with your help, or with another's. It is immaterial to me, but I would see you most amply rewarded."

Mrs. Morley darkens, conjuring stormy clouds as she sits on the overstuffed sofa. "It is that Zachary is Mr. Cloudesley's son, Lady Peake-Barnes, and he loves him most dearly, most, most dearly. I have witnessed your nephew's disposition these past three months and his affection for his boy is unarguable. He loves him." She places such emphasis on the word *love* that it is for once imbued with that meaning which so often eludes it.

"He loves his work, I think," says Frances, deciding to parry. "He loves that automaton he is making next door more than anything else." She sits on a chair opposite Mrs. Morley, finding the weight of the two babies literally unbearable. Zachary, suddenly rigid in her arms, seems just for a moment to become weightless. Leonora giggles. It is as if the child is performing tricks for the amusement of his sucklemate.

Mrs. Morley, failing to observe the infants' antics, stands and lurches at Frances, making her wonder if she is about to be struck by the woman. "Do you not see? Do you not observe? Do you not understand?" exclaims Mrs. Morley, each question louder than the one before. "For one who prides herself on intelligence you are, my lady, inattentive."

"Am I so?"

"You are. Your nephew has attended to his work so diligently since your arrival to permit you the opportunity to make some bond with the child. And on the whole it seems to have been a successful policy."

Frances hands Leonora up to Mrs. Morley and holds Zachary close to her, breathing in the remarkable scent of an innocent scalp. Feigning distraction she says, "I do not believe that you think this child quite as he should be, what with your frequent comments on his stillness, his placidity. It is as if you think him stupid."

Mrs. Morley bristles. "I have said no such thing. I have experience of children, raising my own sisters much as a mother, and now Leonora, and never knew one quite like him. But that is not to say he is not something very special. Probably he is."

"This child could have the snout of a pig and the ears of a mule and I would still wish to care for him, because he is my Alice's child."

"But he is also his father's son. Don't you see?"

"Then why did his father have me come and stay at all? He knew my intentions well enough, even if he did not convey them to his son's wet nurse."

"It is not about you, madam, still less is it about me. It is about Master Abel, as all here call him. He is a good man—"

"I do not doubt it."

"And he has a great desire to be a good father to his son. He was not well loved by his own."

"He has told you so?"

"He always speaks free and honest. It is a fine quality, I think."

"On occasion."

"He wishes to be everything to his son that his father was not to him. And I think you should allow it. Not that it is my place to think anything at all."

"I have no idea what your place is in this household," says Frances, standing and preparing to end their argument, "but I am not willing to allow my nephew to be ruled over by a . . . by a . . ."

"By a what, madam? By a common wet nurse? By a poor bloody widow?"

"By a woman of such schemes," says Frances, lowering her voice to her preferred register for threat.

"I have no designs on Mr. Cloudesley or any man, if that is what you imply. I have had quite enough of them and should be perfectly glad if I never had to encounter another. I only give thanks each day that I was left with a little girl to raise." Her cheeks are blotchy, and in her indignation she has stirred Leonora into squalls of protest, so that she has to raise her voice further to be heard over her daughter's cries. "I pity that poor child," she shouts, nodding in the direction of Zachary, who is still held firm by Frances, "that he will one day grow to be a man."

Frances knows that she should desist from goading the poor woman, since it is such easy sport, but she cannot help herself. "Perhaps, madam, you are not to be entrusted with care of him for fear you will turn him into a eunuch."

"Oh, but you are provocative!"

In the same moment they both notice Abel, who has come up the stairs to discover the cause of the commotion.

Frances turns to him and announces, "Mrs. Morley has been describing her hatred of the male sex in general and of Zachary in particular."

"Oh, but you twist my words, madam! I love that child as much as it were my own. I pity him for his manhood, not hate him for it. Pity and hatred are not the same thing at all. You do see that, I suppose?" In her rage she is close to tears.

"*Stop!*" a voice commands, high and clear. "*Stop*," it says again, more quietly. But it is not Abel's voice that Frances hears, nor is it Mrs. Morley's.

Mrs. Morley, jolted into alarm, says, "Oh no, it cannot be," her tone conveying the preternatural character of what they have just heard.

Slowly, one by one, they turn to gaze in baffled awe at the infant still held in Frances's arms.

She cannot suppress a certain feeling of excitement. She had fully expected her great-nephew to be endowed with extraordinary faculties, and not only because he is her relation. Alice had certain qualities, a gift for sensing what was to come—the routine, certainly, such as might be sensed by any man or woman: a change in the weather, or who was about to come marching up the drive to call for tea. Less humdrum was when she foresaw that Mr. Lucas the costermonger would be drowned a week before the poor man fell into the river and was washed away, or when she announced that the London stagecoach had lost a wheel and the lives of three of its passengers on the Tuesday, when the accident only came to pass the following Friday. Alice dismissed her foreshadowings as nothing more than mildly perplexing embarrassments, as if she were repeatedly missing a B flat in an otherwise perfect melody. That Zachary should be possessed of the power of speech at only three months might, thinks Frances, be only the first of many gifts.

Abel looks sick. "You heard it?" he says.

"I heard him speak, most clearly," says Frances.

"It is not possible," declares Mrs. Morley. "We must have imagined that he spoke. He made a noise, that is all."

They peer at Zachary in turn, seeking some affirmation from him, but the child has resumed his placid, grave demeanour.

"Perhaps," says Abel, "well, I cannot say I am certain I heard a word, as such. A sound. I am not . . ."

"He demanded that we cease our arguing," says Frances. "We all heard it. And we have done as he bid, have we not, and so now he is quiet." She has decided that she will be Zachary's interpreter.

"It seemed to be a word, distinctly a word, and in a child's voice, and yet . . ." Mrs. Morley shudders.

Abel reaches for his son and holds him close, rocking him gently. The silence that has descended on the scene is broken by gleeful laughter, loud and slightly diabolical. It is Leonora's turn to disturb them. Zachary's eyes are locked on the little girl's, though whatever it is he is saying is this time wordless and for her amusement only.

◙

CHAPTER FIVE

AN ACCIDENT

July 1760, London (six years later)

◙

Zachary is ever keen to see bears, which are rare in London, though one can be visited at the Tower of London menagerie and another, clawless, toothless and tormented, at the Spring Gardens at Vauxhall. Abel made him a clockwork bear and Tom made a mohair pelt for the creature so that he could carry it to bed in comfort, but lately he seems to have tired of Arktos, as he calls his pet. His Greek is already excellent, as is his Latin. He is an intense child, generally serious and studious, though given to wild enthusiasms and sudden bursts of vigour, and is fascinated by all that is natural, from the birds that land on the twisted, crabbed branches of the little apple tree that sits in their pocket handkerchief of a garden, to the worms that turn the soil beneath it and the bees that come and feed on its blossoms in the spring. He has his own way of classifying these and other creatures and, contrary to Aristotle's order, avows that it is the smallest creature that is most important, for it is upon the tiniest that all others depend. Zachary is happy to be left alone for hours in the garden or with a book, for he reads as well as a child twice his age, and Abel finds himself having to annex one room after another for his library. Indeed, he has come to wish that Mr. Linnaeus desist from writing yet another edition of his *Systema*

Naturae, since Zachary has come to expect the latest imprint from Stockholm or Leiden as soon as word arrives of its publication.

That his son has an extraordinary intelligence for one his age Abel does not doubt, and, even if he were to question it for a moment, Aunt Frances would soon correct him, for she has concluded that her great-nephew is a nascent genius. Zachary spends two months each summer and a month at Christmastime with his great-aunt in that uneasy compromise that Abel and Frances call, only half in jest, the Treaty of Tring. Frances has made clear that Zachary, as her only heir, will inherit her estate and she is therefore entitled to have a hand in his upbringing. She is vague on the particulars of her fortune and Abel has not thought to press her on the matter, since he would much prefer that there was no fortune at all to get in the way of the free circulation of their affections.

There are times when Abel fears his son will very soon demand a better tutor than his father, for his questions are relentless and exacting, but no tutor lasts long and Abel settles to his task each day with the uneasy apprehension that he is grappling not only with a fierce intelligence that requires tempering and taming but, given Zachary's strange faculties, something altogether more preternatural. The evidence for this is considerable, although Abel tries always to find some everyday rational explanation for his son's oddness. When he was three years old he developed a strong affinity for their good-hearted if clumsy maid, Biddy, which Abel was encouraged by, since Zachary was regarded as an unusually detached and even proud child by Kate and Mrs. Scrants the cook, and he fostered their friendship until the day when Zachary confessed to him that he was being especially kind to Biddy because she was very soon to be knocked down by a horse.

"You mustn't say such a thing," he said to the boy.

"But why not, Papa, if it's true?"

"We cannot see what will happen, Zachary," he tried to explain patiently, "or wish bad things upon people. For that matter I'm sure Biddy is more likely to knock down a horse than a horse is to knock her down."

Zachary had scrunched up his small features, pushed his wispy blond hair from his eyes and sighed in despair at his father's obstinance. "I wish I did not see what was to happen to everyone around me, Papa, but I cannot help it. Tom understands me."

Abel tried to dismiss Zachary's troubling prophecy until, some two weeks after that strange conversation, poor Biddy had indeed run into the path of the Leighton Buzzard stage as it swept out of St. Martin's Le Grand and was, by all accounts, killed in an instant.

Remembering what Zachary had said to him about Tom, he spoke to his apprentice the next day about Zachary's seeming prediction of the terrible accident.

"Did he foresee it?" observed Tom, as if seeing into the future were no more unusual than standing on one's head. "It's a right sad business about Biddy, to be sure, but he sees all sorts of things, does Zachary, master, that others cannot or do not see."

"Such as?"

"Well . . ." he said, pondering which examples of his employer's son's gifts he might offer him with delicacy. "He sees into the past as well as the future."

"We can all see the past, Tom."

"Can we? I'm not so sure. He told me once that he remembers the very day he was born. What child remembers that? Do you? Do I? He remembers you holding him, he says, and that your tears fell on his face. And he remembers things that happened to me, too, things I've tried to forget. He told me that I need not worry about Mr. Laskins anymore, and that I was not to lie awake afearing him. Now how could he have known about Joe Laskins and how that man tormented me, still less how I'd wake at night in a terror thinking he was on top of me?"

"Perhaps he overheard you say something of it to Seth?"

Tom reddened. "Say something? I would not speak of it to any man. I cannot believe I am telling you of it now, but to convince you that Zachary is remarkable, gifted in ways even the child himself cannot perceive."

"Perhaps," said Abel, though still reluctant to believe that Zachary suffered from such an outlandish affliction.

"He is, I think, Master Abel," said Tom with a smile intended in the direction of reassurance, "like the best clock we could ever hope to make."

Puzzled, Abel asked him to say more.

"He is like a clock that tells of time to come and of time past and missed, yet is driven by blood and a beating heart, not by mainsprings and ratchets and bobs of steel and brass."

Today's lesson is in the garden. Abel has set out a bench and has some specimens for Zachary to examine.

"But Papa," Zachary demands, "how many seeds is lots?"

Today is natural science, always a subject at which Abel is likely to be bested by his six-year-old son, and they are in the garden examining the head of an early-flowering sunflower. "Above a thousand."

"But how many?"

"It is hard to tell at a glance, Zachary."

"I shall count."

Abel feels impatience rising in his throat and tries not to let it sound on his tongue. "Very well. It will take you a while."

But it does not take his son a while. He scatters the seeds from the flower before him, inspects them briefly and pronounces his calculation. "Twelve hundred and forty-two, Papa."

"Indeed," says Abel, skeptically. "I shall check your estimate later."

"It is not an estimate," he insists, "I have counted them."

"Have you now?" Not wishing to reprimand his son for exaggeration he changes the subject. "Now, let us look at this beetle. See how its shell seems to change colour as we turn it in the light. We call this iridescence."

Zachary observes in silence.

"It is a rose chafer. And it has this armour across its shoulder blades, which we call a scutellum."

No response.

"As perhaps you already are well aware?"

Still silence.

"And here I have a pupa, which is how the beetle changes from its larva into its adult form. See?"

"Why did you kill the beetle?"

"I, I . . ." Abel does not think the death of a beetle a great tragedy.

"When did you kill it?"

"Well . . . this morning."

"And how? How did you kill it?"

"I . . ."

"It should be alive and flying, not sitting here dead so that we can poke at it," says Zachary, crossly.

"We can go and find more living ones, Zachary."

"Kill no living thing, Papa."

"I will try to avoid killing anything for your sake, then."

Ludo, Zachary's white cockatoo, repeats his master's tautological words: *Kill no living thing, kill no living thing.* A gift from Aunt Frances for his fourth birthday, the bird and his son are inseparable. It is, of course, her way to make her presence felt at all times. Abel wouldn't be surprised if Ludo had the ability to report back to her on his many failings: his distractedness; his inability to organize a nanny or tutor for his son; his tendency to speak his thoughts out loud; his inattention both to his own diet and Zachary's; and his habit of falling asleep when reading a bedtime story. Zachary always returns from his twice-yearly stays with his great-aunt with his impressionable mind filled with odd notions about the wisdom of animals over men and of the good sense of trees to add to those even odder notions he already possesses and, still more gallingly, of the need to disbelieve everything his father tells him.

Ludo bobs down and takes one of the sunflower seeds. "Twelve hundred and forty-one," says Zachary, earnestly.

Abel sweeps the seeds into his pocket. He will count them later, if only to satisfy himself that his son is not endowed with yet another strange faculty. He wants to be both nanny and tutor to him, but perhaps being father is more than enough. He has had three nannies in succession, but the first two lasted little more than a fortnight. The first fled, unnerved, when Zachary told her that he had ingested a teaspoon. He then made the spoon appear from his ear—a trick he had been taught by Samuels, whom he has made his ally in mischief—though whether or not he has troubled Samuels with his strange prognostications Abel has not determined, given his manservant's enigmatic, even secretive nature. The second nanny, engaged for her competence in classics, was infuriated to find that a five-year-old was able to quote from *The Iliad* and correct her. "But I cannot help it, Papa," he'd protested. "I know all of Homer."

Finally, through connections Aunt Frances had with the Blue Stockings Society, he found a woman who was herself sufficiently odd to hold his son's interest. They wrote poetry together and mapped the stars on clear nights. But Abel was obliged to dismiss her when she returned from Vauxhall Gardens one afternoon without him. "He ran away from me, and I simply had not the speed to catch him," she declared. She did not seem unduly concerned. "Your son might only be six years old, Mr. Cloudesley, but he has the ingenuity of James Lind, and will certainly be able to procure assistance when he has tired of the gardens."

"James Lind?"

"Surely you've heard of Lind? Who has cures for scurvy and those other rots that afflict those at sea?"

Abel confessed he had not and dispatched himself for Vauxhall, pausing only to tell the woman that she was relieved of her duties. He found Zachary learning the art of tarot from a gypsy woman in a tent. "He can come and work here as soon as he pleases, this boy," said the woman as he dragged his protesting son away. "He reads the cards well and saw in them that fortune-telling would be his future."

Zachary is a fast runner, it's true. His athleticism is a mercy— it is something he can do with other children, sprinting. Zachary's interests and his manner make him, on the whole, distasteful to those his own age. But running is in some measure equalizing, and even Zachary cannot race and talk (and so cause upset) at the same time. Abel organizes a race out on Leadenhall on Sunday afternoons when the traffic is not too great, a race which Zachary does not always win, since there are eight- and nine-year-olds even faster than he. Abel intends by these competitions to make his son understand that he will lose in life as well as win, and he also hopes to make him less inclined to chase at great velocity around the house and through the workshop. He is a boy who is either still and deep in concentration or running at speed. There is no in between with Zachary.

Mrs. Morley comes for tea once a week, bringing Leonora with her. Zachary, who is usually poor company for any child who is not willing to discuss calculus, is indulgent with Leonora, taking her by the hand into the small garden, picking flowers, finding voles, observing spiders, and telling her stories from *The Odyssey*.

Abel loaned Grace Morley forty-five guineas when she had finished her wet nursing, which she pays him back at two shillings a week. She took the lease on a store near her rooms with the money and has opened a hat shop, which thrives. She has more entrepreneurial spirit than he will ever possess.

The clocks for export to the Levant earn well enough, and he seems to win more and more commissions for his automata from the great houses of the country. Were it not for the war his work would be selling in Paris and Vienna and Stockholm, too, or so he is told. His present commission is for a peacock that struts and pecks, moving its shimmering neck and fanning its tail on the hour. It is for a granddaughter of the king, and engages five of his men, though Tom is in charge of matters.

Zachary is happiest in the workshop, sitting beside the men while they work. Tom is his favourite, as Zachary is Tom's, and he takes pleasure in having him as his assistant, giving him small jobs to do. The peacock's feathers are of gold, enamel and lapis lazuli and the work is intricate, but Zachary is so absorbed by it that it settles him, ceasing his endless flow of questions. Sometimes Abel comes into the workshop to find him sitting in Tom's lap, the two of them working away at polishing a fine piece of lapis, the stone cut very thin so as not to make the peacock's tail too heavy for the mechanism to lift and fan. It gives him ease, to know that his troubled and troubling son finds comfort in the company of his remarkable apprentice, who is called Tom by all and treated as the shy young man he has found himself to be.

Abel has been working amiably with Tom all morning, Zachary running about the workshop, talking to the men, sitting with one or other and asking questions. He sometimes dashes up to Abel, seeking to know some fact that has only just occurred to him.

"When is the princess to have her birthday, Papa?"

"It is on the last day of the month, Zachary."

"And how old will she be?"

"She will be, um, twenty-two, I believe."

"Twenty-three," corrects Richie, who is not only the most patriotic man in the workshop but who has in addition a particular adoration for the late Prince of Wales's eldest child.

"And will she like the peacock, do you think?" asks Zachary.

"It is in that direction that our expectations lie," says Abel.

"And when shall I see a comet, Papa?"

Abel is familiar with the nonsequitous manner of his son's exclamations. "A comet? Why do you ask about a comet?"

"Franny and I looked at Halley's comet through her telescope last year, and I should like to see another now."

"You will have to wait a while to see that one again, I think. It appears but once in a lifetime."

"I shall see it again, Papa. But not until I am eighty-one. I shall see it and then I shall die."

"Well, then." He tries to be patient with the boy, knows that he needs more attention than he is able to give, but goodness how he tries his patience.

"But I'd like to see another, this year or next. Will you make me a telescope, like Franny's?"

Abel wants to press on with the final touches to the princess's peacock. "We'll see."

"Tom, will you make me a telescope?" asks Zachary, turning to his friend.

Tom casts a glance in Abel's direction, seeking permission to agree to Zachary's request, and Abel gives him a nod of resigned approval.

The last tail rod of the peacock for Princess Augusta is ready for fixing at last when Samuels appears in his usual manner, conjuring himself out of vapour. "There is a Mr. Cathcart to see you, sir."

Damn, thinks Abel, ignoring the wild dashing about of his son, who seems to be in much the same state of nervous excitement at the completion of the royal peacock as the rest of them, and is now in addition chattering away to all who will listen about the dimensions of the telescope he is to have made for him. Abel had quite forgotten about Cathcart, the Levant Company's man, come to check on the progress of the orders for shipment in August. He has a thought. "Will you ask Mr. Cathcart whether he would do me the honour, Samuels, of being the very first, outside of this workshop, to see the marvelous peacock that is being made for the Princess Augusta. If he would be kind enough to take tea, I shall invite him to witness the automaton in its first animation in, let us say, a quarter of an hour."

Samuels bows and walks away, and it is at this moment that Abel's world turns abruptly and irrevocably into hell. He has rested the final steel rod, some three feet in length and sharp as a rapier at its tip, on his lap, and as Samuels leaves he feels a judder, a small cry, more of surprise than of agony, and then the distinct sensation of blood, warm and slightly viscous, spattering on to his face. Zachary is, inexplicably, there on the end of the rod, blood pooling around where it lodges in his eye, as if he were a murdered prince on a battlefield, slain not by an enemy but by his own father. He is insensate, his other eye fixed in a look of surprise at Abel's own. "Jesus!" Abel cries out. "Jesus!" he is about to stand when he realizes that to do so would wrench the rod within his son's skull. He turns to Tom, who has fainted. His leather jerkin is spotted with droplets of Zachary's blood. "Help!" he cries. "Someone, help!" He reaches over and, careful not to move the rod any further, holds his hands either side of his dear son's face, keeping him still, the child's blood seeping through his fingers. It is not gushing or spurting, he tells himself, and there is some hope in that, perhaps. Might he live? Might his boy live? Oh God, make it so. Make it so this is not happening. Why was he running so carelessly? No doubt he was rushing to tell him yet another small thing, something observed or more likely imagined, or perhaps just to see the peacock complete at last. "Send for Dr. Clare," Abel says faintly. Nothing more. Then he shouts, "Quick. Quick as you can!"

He tries to stop himself from shaking, conceiving that holding Zachary's slumped body absolutely still is the key to his very being—to his own and his son's alike. He feels the pain of the rod in his own eye, sheer and sickening blue, dazzling, freezing, burning. Bile fills his mouth, and he spits it to the side. "My God!" he says. He begs again, aloud, begs God to let Zachary live, offers his own life in his place, offers Him any price he must pay. He has been a pitiable father, he knows. What sensible parent would allow their six-year-old to run about a workshop filled with such perils? What loving father would have a rapier resting on their lap ready for their beloved boy to impale himself upon? He makes then and there a vow to find some safer place for Zachary to grow up, imploring the God in whom he barely believes to let his son live so that he can make good on his promise.

Mercifully soon, Dr. Clare appears, his brow furrowed, wondering what mischief Zachary has been about on this occasion. He is used to these mishaps, for the boy pushes catkins up his nose, consorts with adders, drinks pond water. But he startles at the sight before him. Kneeling and feeling Zachary's brow, taking his pulse and listening to his heartbeat, his ear to his chest, he falls still and speechless, prompting Abel to think it already too late. "Is there anything that can be done?" he asks, hopeless with fear.

Clare stands. "We cannot move the child," he says, slowly, "it will be fatal to him. I will have to extract the rod here and now. I believe I can stanch the blood and there is a chance of preserving his life, depending on what damage there has been to his brain. He will lose the eye, naturally."

"Naturally," echoes Abel, faintly.

"What effect this will have on his reasoning I cannot say." Clare is controversial amongst the doctors of the city in holding to certain unconventional beliefs, including in the efficacy of hot water and clean towels. He issues his orders for what he requires rapidly and assuredly. Within the hour Zachary is in his bed, his head heavily bandaged, Abel beside him, holding his clammy hand in his. Clare has informed him that his son's chances of survival are no better than one in five at best. The house and workshop tumble into whispers and waiting, almost the only sound that of Tom's weeping, for he blames himself, believing he must have distracted his master at the very moment of Zachary's rushing-in. Abel wishes he could blame Tom, for it would absolve him of the unbearable guilt he feels. As he sits by Zachary, he vows again that he will give his son into the care of someone fit to raise him, since he knows, without doubt, that he is not.

For two weeks Zachary lies pale and feverish on the cusp of life, murmuring words in languages Abel cannot comprehend. Frances comes to stay and pronounces that he is, unquestionably, speaking in ancient Egyptian, though since that is a language lost to mankind Abel cannot fathom how either Zachary would know it, still less how Frances might recognize it. Ludo sits on a perch beside his young master but says only *Oh misery!* from time to time. Zachary is never left alone. Samuels, who rarely sleeps in any case, sits with him at night, allowing Abel, who is otherwise always with his son, sometimes reading to him from *Robinson*

Crusoe, sometimes inventing stories of unicorns and talking bears, of flying turtles and singing slugs, a few hours' rest. Mrs. Morley comes with Leonora and they take turns in singing songs to him. And Tom, once he has calmed his guilt, lies beside him and talks quietly of the magic eye he is making for him. Dr. Clare says that Zachary is in a lethargy, a good sign, for it is the brain's means of repairing itself.

On the fifteenth day after the accident, Zachary sits up and announces that he would like to eat a pickled cucumber. He seems just as he did before, and the house billows with relief. Dr. Clare insists that Zachary stay another month in his bed, else the wound will open and fester. Abel determines to spend this time of healing to repair whatever injuries he has done to his bond with his son, and leaves supervision of the workshop to Seth and Tom. He sits with Zachary and begins to talk to him of a journey he has decided they will make together when he is well enough, a venture to Southend and the sea, and he carefully describes the smell of salt and the sound of waves on pebbles.

"I still have one eye, Papa," says Zachary, "and will be able to see it for myself. You need not pity me."

Chastened, Abel asks him if he would like to be read to.

"I can read to myself," says Zachary.

"But Dr. Clare says you are to rest your good eye a while longer."

Zachary purses his lips and says, sorrowfully, "You do not read well, Papa."

"Do I not?" says Abel, laughing to cover his hurt.

Zachary hesitates, perhaps wanting to spare his father's feelings. "You pronounce your Greek in a very old-fashioned manner."

"But Greek is an ancient language."

"Not in my head it isn't."

"It sounds better in your head, Zachary?"

"Everything sounds better in my head. No, Papa, I should like to play chess with you."

"Chess?" Abel used to play the game constantly when he was Mr. Catchpenny's pupil. He learned the game quickly and was soon beating both his tutor and George with ease. He seemed always able to see the endgame and the path to it and wondered why others could not. Catchpenny encouraged him greatly, finding opponents from all manner of place and rank, even writing to the French master Philidor and inviting him to Oxford, though by the time he arrived in England, Abel had already been sent away by his father to Constantinople. He'd only played a little in Constantinople, and on his return his father's swift and uncharitable death and his new obligations to the business meant he'd not found time for the game.

Zachary's request makes him wonder why he hasn't thought of it before, this gift of his that he might pass to his son; he is certain after all that he has no wish to teach him to become a clockmaker—not after the terrible injury his peacock automaton has done to the boy. "Chess?" he says again. "What made you think of it?"

"Samuels taught me."

Samuels again.

"I am not certain where my old set is," says Abel.

"Samuels has it."

Of course. "Well, I shall go and ask him for it." But Samuels is already there at the door, unbidden, in his hand the old set that was given Abel by Mr. Catchpenny, and also a board and a short-legged table suitable for placing on Zachary's bed. Samuels steps forward with the box, board and tray and leaves without a word. Abel lifts the lid, releasing a smell so familiar it is like far-off music, once greatly loved and almost forgotten. The pieces sit in their red plush cushion and are of bone and a German design, being representations of king, queen and courtiers—the royal court of Brunswick, he fancies. He sets them out, leaving Zachary to play the white.

"No, Papa. You play white."

"Why?"

"Because you must win."

"Perhaps at first, but you will soon learn."

"You are the best player in all the world. I can never beat you."

"Who told you so?" Abel exclaims, laughing, as he opens with his usual Italian game. Zachary replies to each move instantly and without apparent difficulty. They are absorbed in the game for a few minutes before Abel gains the upper hand. "Samuels has taught you well."

"But you will teach me better?"

"Certainly. As much as you like."

"I should like that, Papa," says Zachary. "But first you must make me a promise."

"Oh?"

"Will you promise?"

"I must make my promise without knowing what it is?" Abel smiles, contemplating his poor boy, a bandage covering half his head, his small features solemn and determined as ever. "Anything, yes. I promise," he says with an indulgent smile.

"You promise on your life?"

"On my life."

"You must never, ever again play chess with anyone but me."

What an odd request, thinks Abel, but since he hasn't played in so long, he does not think it a difficult thing to agree to. He reaches out a hand and shakes in agreement, noticing how slight Zachary's hand feels in his own, like a bird fallen down a chimney that he must return quickly to the air for fear its fragile bones will crack, however gentle his grasp.

"You promise then, Papa?"

"I do."

"Good."

They play each day after that, Zachary improving steadily, though his stern insistence that Abel must do his best against him means that no game lasts longer than half an hour. After a fortnight Zachary's impatience grows too great, and he throws back his sheets and declares, "Enough. I am well!" But something is changed, something Abel notices that no one else would. When Zachary is out in the garden, communing with his beloved frogs and believing himself unobserved, there is a tremble to his hand, a slight uncertainty in his step. Abel consults Dr. Clare and is told only that greater injuries were to be expected, and is warned to prepare himself for crueler or stranger impairments to manifest themselves in other ways at other times.

Tom shows Abel the eye he has been making for Zachary from gold and enamel and lapis lazuli. It is as the eye of Ramses, ancient and mesmerizing. "He can wear it?" asks Abel, doubtfully.

"Readily, if you are content, master. I have measured carefully, and taken advice from Dr. Clare on the necessary shape, like a tiny shallow bowl, see, so that it may fit there quite comfortably."

"He desires it?"

"He does."

"He has said so?"

Tom looks uncomfortable, making to leave without answering Abel's question.

"Wait, Tom. You say he desires it. You have spoken to him about the golden eye already? Come now, I will not be unhappy if you have."

Still Tom is uneasy. "It is just . . ." he says.

"Just what?"

"It is that I know what he wants without him quite telling me. He has this way, this way of letting you know his thoughts."

Abel knows enough of his son's peculiar faculties to know that what Tom says has the force of truth. If he thought himself a more competent parent, he would persuade himself that he had a father's instincts for his child's desires, but he knows it is something altogether more other-worldly, and that Zachary chooses how he will speak without words, and to whom and when. "I see," says Abel, uneasily. "I understand, Tom. Let him try the eye for its fit and see how he likes the look of it."

How strange it is that the eye suits Zachary so well, and how odd that it seems almost to match his real, seeing eye even though it looks so different. Dr. Clare gives the eye his seal of approval, finding its shape gives the healing socket protection without impairing the necessary scarring. He shows Zachary how to keep the golden eye clean so that it gives him no corruption of the wound. In the weeks that follow his accident Zachary seems, if anything, an even more confident child than before and Abel is barely surprised when he says to him one day, "You are to send me away, Papa."

"Am I so?"

"You are."

"And what makes you think so?"

"I see it. I see it with my magic eye. You are afraid of me, or afraid of you more, I think. Afraid that you cannot be a good papa to me."

It is true, of course, that Abel lives in constant trepidation of some further accident befalling his son and is only a little less fearful of the increasingly strange hold he has over the household, who believe themselves spoken to by him, even when they have not heard his voice. "If you know all this, then tell me what to do."

"You have already decided. It is not for me to tell you, Papa."

That night Abel writes to Aunt Frances, every word a blow he inflicts on himself. But somehow, too, he knows that if Zachary stays with him some further misfortune will befall him, one from which there can be no recovery.

Leadenhall St.

5 September 1760

My dearest aunt,

How strange it is that we who are both so doubtful about the purpose and efficacy of prayer should have prayed so ardently and sincerely, and how much stranger still that our prayers should have been heard with such indulgence. Zachary is perfectly recovered both in spirit and in almost all respects, though I believe his unusually determined character conceals some injury which in any other child would be more fully revealed.

You are, I understand, au courant with the eye that Tom has made for him, and that was, it seems, expressly ordered by Zachary while he lay prone and unspeaking in his long fever. It looks well on him. He believes he sees further with it than with the eye he was born with, temporally if not physically. He tells me what I am to do and, lo, I find myself doing it.

You will not be surprised, perhaps, when I tell you that I believe I should long ago have heeded your oft expressed wish to give Z a home at Briar House. That he is always happy with you I know, and on the question of his great-aunt's love for him I need no reassurance. He is the beat of my heart and the breath in my lungs, and to lose him would be to lose life itself. But lose him we all nearly did so recently, and I hold myself alone responsible for his jeopardy.

I am lending him to you, then, as winter is custodian for spring, and summer for autumn. Be his guardian and protector, dear Aunt, and may you, and he, forgive me.

I am, as ever, your loving nephew.

A

CHAPTER SIX

COERCION

October 1760, London

◙

It is not long after Zachary is away to Tring that Abel receives a letter he hardly had cause to expect.

Office of the Lord President of His Majesty's Privy Council
Northumberland House

3 October 1760

Dear Cloudesley,
I fear I have been a neglectful correspondent and poor friend, but I trust that I might beg your indulgence and hope for your forgiveness. I received intelligence recently that your dear son suffered a most unfortunate accident not three months ago and am obliged to offer not only my own pity for the thing but also that of a royal princess, who has been told of the manner of the incident and wishes you to be reassured that she would not have wished for such an occurrence by any means what-soever, least of all from a peacock.

It is nigh on nine years since we last met, when you gave me the honour of meeting your dear late wife and we were able to speak fondly together of our days under the tuition of that old rogue Catchpenny, as well as of your employ in Constantinople and my own feeble political ambitions. If the paths of our lives have since gone one north and the other south, or more likely east and west, I trust that they might now converge as soon as they may. Come dine with me this very day if you are able. I have a table most nights at the Fountain Tavern on the Strand. You may join entertaining company, or I shall banish all but ourselves, as you best desire.

I am eager to hear the latest news of your ingenious instruments which astonish all and are, I assure you, much discussed at court. As for me, you might have received intelligence that I have recently been given a position by Lord Carteret, the Earl Granville, as his private secretary. It is a station in which I hear much and see more but am obliged to feign deafness and blindness to all but my master. Catchpenny would have been amused to think me in such a predicament, since he always thought me a garrulous fool, did he not? No doubt he would have found a Greek myth to fit my part—not Sisyphus, more Tantalus I hazard.

Let us, dear Abel, renew that friendship of our schooldays. Come dine with me at the Fountain. My invitation awaits you, as does my messenger who will not leave until he has your reply in his hands.

I hope to have long the pleasure of being most affectionately yours,

Claxton

Abel asks Samuels to give the man who waits in the hall sixpence to send him away, but not even a shilling is equal to the task, and he reluctantly consents to have him return in an hour for his reply. Is it really nine years since he last saw George Claxton? It is in no way untypical of his old friend to make himself known in such manner, adorned in courtesies but demanding his way without delay. George had been abroad at the time of their wedding, but had come to dinner not long after, when Alice had made no attempt to conceal her loathing of him, finding him conceited and insincere; a creature lacking Abel's intelligence but willing to make himself outshine it by reflecting its light with clever words placed like deceiving mirrors. He'd tried to act as George's advocate that night, explaining to Alice after he'd gone that they had grown up almost as brothers, telling her how they'd been schooled together by the extraordinary Mr. Catchpenny; how they'd been rivals, certainly, but also the best of friends. His wife hadn't understood the nature of male friendship; hadn't grasped how men will always try to outdo each other—and that George had outdone him was undeniable, encouraged by his father to go to Cambridge, while Abel's had sent him off to Constantinople, insisting he learn for himself about the Levant trade, though more likely he wanted to save himself the trouble and expense of a university education, which he regarded as a certain road to profligacy and dissipation. By the time Abel had been summoned back from Constantinople his father was mortally ill. There was no deathbed reconciliation, only mumbled counsel against the ruination of the business.

Those years with Catchpenny had been amongst Abel's happiest, apart from his too-brief time with Alice. No education could have been quite so liberal as that provided by their tutor, who had opinions that, had Abel and George's fathers known of them, would have led to Catchpenny's immediate dismissal. Some days he would wander into their classroom and absent-mindedly speak to them all day long in French or Italian, Greek or Latin and in this way and without great effort the boys came to speak those languages, with all their fine stems and curling petals that stood in contrast to the thick trunks and muddy roots of English. He instilled in his charges a sound knowledge of classics, of the natural sciences, of how to pleasure a woman in a variety of ways, and of the works of Mr. Shakespeare; indeed, of all things but religion, of which Catchpenny said he knew nothing that God could not tell them Himself.

For all his surprise at hearing from Claxton after such a long silence, and the faintly uneasy feeling that he is being disloyal to Alice in accepting the invitation, Abel decides it would be churlish to decline. After all, taking his supper alone night after night, working on his latest designs for automata and missing Zachary so terribly that he feels his absence as if a sharp, black stone were lodged in his heart, is hardly a comfort, and this distraction, even from an unexpected quarter, is welcome.

Abel is relieved to see George alone at a table in a quiet corner. A bottle of claret is before him and two glasses, one half full, the light of the nearby fire casting rubies into it. He stands and greets him heartily. "By God, Abel, you are a man in his prime, I must say."

"You mean I have aged, I think," says Abel, without rancour.

"I should hope a man is wiser in his thirties than at twenty-one."

Abel considers his old friend. He has a look of girdling dissipation about him, his open face turned florid, his eyes haunted. But his manner belies whatever it is that ails him, and he is full of jollity. "Tell me about your boy. He resides now with Alice's aunt?"

"Who told you so?" asks Abel in surprise.

"Ah, well, I need must be a man of intelligence these days."

It is no secret that Zachary is in Frances's care, but Abel is sorry it has been mentioned at the first, not least because he has already written to her suggesting that they bring the arrangement to an end sooner rather than later. "It is a temporary arrangement, to help him in his convalescence."

George raises an eyebrow, no more than that, but Abel can see that he is doubted. "I'm sure he is a fine fellow. A marvel and a sensation," says George.

"He is a sweet child, and with a fierce intelligence for one so young."

"I hope to have the honour of making his acquaintance before long." He fills Abel's glass, and they salute each other. "It is so very good to see you, Abel."

"And you, George." He is conscious of the awkwardness between them, though now wonders how he could have possibly thought it would be otherwise.

"You received my condolences, I trust, for your terrible loss? I did not hear the news for many months, being in Pennsylvania and then Virginia."

Abel cannot remember ever receiving such a letter, but America is far away and plagued by endless conflict, and it would hardly be a surprise if correspondence went astray. "Yes. Thank you, George, for your tender words. You were in the colonies long?"

"Not long returned, that's the rub of it." He becomes animated, his hands chopping the table as he begins to tell of his time there. "I was sent to help organize the colonists for Governor Dinwiddie. You know about Dinwiddie?"

"No," confesses Abel.

"He was governor of Virginia, and a shrewd fellow. And the colonists are young and mostly farmers and my task was to encourage the Iroquois—who are the Indians in those parts, you know—to our side and make sure the colonists didn't sign any treaties they didn't understand with the Canadians, who are a cunning lot to be sure, and they have this prodigy, the colonists, called Washington, who is a bright young man, really little more than a boy, but already a colonel, yet he reads French hardly at all and signed a treaty not fully understanding it, which has caused all manner of difficulty, and I have been his mentor in a manner of speaking and . . . well . . ." He becomes conscious that he is talking too much. "Well, enough of America. I have carried myself away." He bids Abel to tell him about his automata. "What are you working on now?"

Abel smiles and waves the question away. "And now you work for the king's favourite minister? And must deal with parliament?"

"Oh, parliament," says George, pulling a face as if to dismiss the whole sorry matter. "It's a tedious affair, really. So many factions."

"Amongst the Whigs, you mean?"

"The Tories are nothing, Abel," he says, suddenly serious, "to be a Tory is to be something antediluvian, you know. Never let me hear you thinking well of Tories. But yes, we Whigs are both government and opposition and a dozen other things besides."

"And your master?"

"Carteret is close to the king, but floats some way above his fellow ministers, and therein lies my work."

"Yes?"

"I spend my days smoothing feathers which my lord has ruffled. He is quite the feather-ruffler, you know."

"I suppose he can afford to be."

"Not in the least. Everything in government is exhausting, Abel, I tell you. It's like trying to stop apples falling from a tree in a storm. One has gravity to battle, and high winds and nature itself, or in this case the Pelhams and the Commons, not to mention sundry dukes and earls in the other place."

"It doesn't sound like a very great pleasure."

"Oh, but it is!" he says, his face flushed with excitement. "I tell you it's better than a gallop across winter fields, or a swim in a cold pond on an August day or, or . . ." He leans forward and whispers, "A servant girl in an attic room."

George always had appetites. Abel says, as generously as he can, "Truly I'm pleased, George, that you are the coming man."

George takes his time to respond, a skill recently learned, thinks Abel. "You have something far more important to care about, my friend, than privy counsellors and motions of the House."

Thinking of Zachary, Abel silently renews his vow to be a better father to him, and to never send him away from him again. "It is a fine thing to be a father, George," he says. "Will you marry, now that you are back in England?"

"My father expects me to be in a good position to find a woman with a fortune. A fat, ugly one, I think." He laughs, and Abel joins in. "It matters not to me. *J'aurai des maîtresses*! If His Majesty can keep his word, then so can I!"

They eat mutton pie, which is the Fountain Tavern's standard fare, and drink a bottle of port. As they are about to leave, Claxton says, "Let's meet next week, Cloudesley. Do you still play chess?"

"With my son I do."

"Then let us play. I never beat you. I believe no man can better you."

Abel offers him an apologetic smile. He has made his promise to Zachary, on his life.

As he walks out the door Claxton shouts after him, "Ever have cause to speak Turkish?"

What an odd question. "Never, I'm sorry to say."

"I remember you telling me that you spoke the tongue well, when I came for dinner that time."

"Farewell, Claxton."

"*Au revoir.*"

George calls on him the following day, the Saturday, insisting that he accompany him on a visit to a new coffee house. On the Tuesday he calls again, taking him out drinking and leaving him groggy the next day. Again and again he calls, dragging him south of the river on carouses with his friends and making introductions to ladies who only pretend to be amused by their company. Abel accepts all this much as a dog accepts any walk over none, even in a direction he does not much care for, and it slowly dawns on him that his old schoolfriend, however exciting his life might be in parliament and at court and however wide his circle of aristocratic friends, is lonely. It strikes Abel as a sort of tragedy, that a man so full of boundless energy and imbued with such a great desire to be loved is, in truth, unloved. Whatever happens to Abel, he will always have his memories of Alice to cherish, and he has Zachary as his perplexing and irresistible devotion, his unalterable love.

When George first mentions the possibility of a return to Constantinople, Abel dismisses the idea: he would be too far from Zachary for one thing; for another he has enough commissions to keep the workshop busy for the next five years and his men depend on him. Yet his objections are not, he knows, quite convincing, not even to himself. Zachary is fully occupied in Tring; Frances has engaged a tutor for him, a Jewish teacher called Mendel who, possessing a knowledge apparently universal, is undeterred by Zachary's restless mind. And he knows that his commissions do not all need to be accepted. What George Claxton proposes is, in any case, intriguing: the continuation of his work, in that city he knows so well and that sits deep within him, and Abel is not immune to George's assertion that it is his patriotic duty to serve His Majesty in the midst of the great world war, for a most particular commission is intimated, one involving all of Abel's skills and experience.

"Think of it, Abel. England is embattled on all fronts in this damnable war. It is intelligence, and intelligence alone, that keeps us a neck and a nose ahead of the French and Austrians and Russians. My master was bemoaning only last week our inability to learn even a hint of Ottoman plans and I thought to myself, well, I thought—well, it seemed so obvious to me . . ." He raises the palms of both hands, as if he had seen no other option but to provide his employer with the name of Abel Cloudesley, speaker of Turkish, master of chess and maker of automata.

"I have no great experience of government work."

"This would not be government work, or not obviously so. No, Abel, you would go to Constantinople, perhaps resume old acquaintances, eh?" George leers. "And using your quiet talents solve our conundrum."

Abel thinks of his time in Constantinople as any grown man remembers his first, clumsy attempts at lovemaking, both delectable and mortifying: how he fell for the place, for its smells and fashions, for the minarets and the call of the muez-zin, for the lapping of the fish-stinking waters of the Golden Horn, for the ancient rules and rituals of the city. He says, more wistfully than he intended, "I cannot imagine what talents you have in mind."

"You need not imagine, for Lord Carteret has ideas. He is a man of such ideas, Abel, of schemes, of plots and intrigues." George, far from finding such characteristics repugnant, seems to believe his master wondrous.

A week later he finds himself at Lord Carteret's house at Hawnes Park. Abel has never thought of himself as in any way important or deserving of special treatment, yet to see the contempt in the footman's eye, even in the maid who brings him a bowl of water to wash his hands, is unexpected. He has visited the houses of earls, of dukes and duchesses. Clocks require introductions to the high-born, and he has acted the chaperone on numberless occasions and received the essential courtesies. At Blenheim, when caught in a blizzard, he was given not only a chamber for the night but invited to join a game of whist with the Lady Elizabeth and her party. But here, at Hawnes Park, he has been kept waiting two hours and given not so much as a glass of water. "My horse will have had more consideration," he declares, not meaning to speak his thoughts aloud.

The footman fails to suppress a small smile of satisfaction.

The clocks are striking nine when he is at last ushered into Carteret's presence. It is growing dark and the Lord President is sitting alone at the far end of a long table in a dimly lit dining room. Before him are the demolished remains of a large meal, an empty decanter and another half full. Becoming aware of Abel standing at the far end of the room he beckons him as he would a dog due a beating.

"Cloudesley, is it?" he says without looking up, his attention upon a long document, which Abel sees is spattered with grease and spots of claret.

"At your service, your lordship." Abel is annoyed with himself for feeling so nervous in this pompous man's presence. He would like to turn and walk away—would do just that, he thinks, especially after being kept waiting so long, but is mindful that Carteret is Claxton's master, and that he owes his friend patience, at least.

"You are soon to go to Constantinople, Cloudesley." Still he has not looked at him.

"I am not certain of that, sir."

Carteret looks up abruptly, startled by such impertinence. "Oh, but you are," he says, smoothly, his voice a low murmur of threat.

Abel, tired and suppressing a strong feeling of being ill-used, puts his hand on the back of the chair before him. Carteret, observing his exhaustion from the corner of an eye, gestures for him to sit, pouring more wine into his own glass. For a moment

Abel thinks he is to be offered one of his own, but Carteret takes down most of what he has just poured in a single gulp.

"I am advised that you are a man of intelligence and with a rare combination of talents, talents that we can put to good use for we have a most particular need of them." He takes a candle and holds it to Abel's face, as if to determine the truth of the claims for himself. "Your Turkish is good?"

"I have not used it in more than ten years."

"That is not what I asked."

"I believe I have not forgotten it."

"You have great facility in foreign tongues, I am told."

"If a man can master French and Latin and Greek as he must, then I believe he can command others, too."

"But what man cares to trouble himself with Danish?" Carteret gives a twitch, almost of embarrassment.

"I have found the Scandinavian tongues have a texture of their own."

Carteret ponders the statement. "It's not many an Englishman that cares to run his hand over them."

"Not many, I think, no." Claxton has told Abel of Carteret's fluency in every European tongue, of how he converses with the King of Sweden in Swedish and the cabinet of the Emperor Frederick in German and, in such manner and with much guile, wins their confidence. Abel wonders if this matter of languages might be a subject he and Carteret can discuss freely. "You, sir, speak all the languages of Europe, and win much respect for it."

Carteret pokes a fingernail between his teeth, dislodges a small lump of meat, examining it for a moment before flicking it across the table. "I am obliged to converse with the King of

Sweden; with our own king for that matter, who is happier speaking French or German than English, as is well known." He yawns extravagantly. "With whom are you obliged to converse?"

"I correspond with European clockmakers. None write in English and some do not write French."

"They are craftsmen, I suppose. Not men of learning."

"But kings and queens have learning, surely?"

"Perhaps not always so much as we imagine, Cloudesley. A horse may be led to water, et cetera, et cetera . . ." He waves a hand in the air. "In my experience if you want to understand a man, speak to him in his own tongue, do not ask him to speak yours. And above all be capable of understanding some small digression they might make, for it is in digression, in nuance, that we give away our true feelings and beliefs. Listen not for words, Cloudesley, but for the timing of silence." He pauses, pleased with his own phrase. "Anyway, what is it that clockmakers have to write about?"

Abel, provoked by Carteret's disdain and seeing an opportunity to make a point that Monsieur Rousseau himself might make, says, "There is all manner of learning in this world, my lord, and strange talents in even the humblest soul."

Carteret offers the briefest smile of disapproval. "Is that what you believe?" he says, doubtfully. He rings a small bell and Abel, relieved that his audience has been brief and, not in the least dismayed that he has fallen well short of Carteret's expectations, is only mildly concerned that his failure will reflect poorly on Claxton. He begins to stand, but before he can lift himself out of his chair he feels Carteret's hand pressing down firmly on his own. A footman appears from the gloom and clears the greasy plates. Soon after he returns with a glass which is set down before Abel. Carteret fills it himself. "You understand the urgency of the matter?"

"Of what matter, sir?"

"Of our position. Of Great Britain's."

"I read we triumph everywhere."

Carteret gusts with hollow contempt. "I sometimes wonder whether a stupid journalist is to be preferred over a mendacious one. England is close to bankrupt. Prussia, our only ally, is finished. And we have no idea of Turkish intentions. If the Ottoman court were to decide to resume their never-ending war with Russia it would . . ." He pauses, a flash of mischief in his eyes, before flicking his own glass toward Abel's, so that both topple, Abel's shattering, the red liquid spilling across the walnut surface of the dining table like a wound. "It would do this to Russia, and save Prussia, and Prussia saved . . . well." He smiles widely. "Why the Turks do not seize their opportunity is a mystery. We have no intelligence. King Louis has his spies everywhere. It is French doing, this Ottoman inertia, or that is my suspicion. Were the Turks to ally with France and attack our interests in the Mediterranean, well . . ." He smiles sourly, running his hand across the broken glass without flinching, slowly observing the cuts he has inflicted on himself with detached curiosity. "You grasp how perilous our situation is." He closes his fist, a drop of blood landing on the table, then another and another, his eyes fixed firmly on Abel's own.

"I do not see how a clockmaker can help," he says, uneasily, trying to resist the lure of the drama he is being subjected to.

"Then think, clockmaker, think," says Carteret in a hypnotic whisper.

"You would have me make exploding clocks?" offers Abel.

"No," he murmurs, "I wish you to be quiet, to listen."

"To spy?"

Carteret leans back, waving a hand in the air, as if clearing a bad smell. He has had enough of the small melodrama. "Call it spying if you will. I call it listening, nothing more. Though it is listening to conversations that are not meant to be overheard. Eavesdropping, let us say. You are to be His Majesty's Eavesdropper in old Byzantium."

Abel's unease mounts, though he knows he can hardly be surprised at the nature of the conversation, the low and grubby character of it. He wonders why he is here at all—to please Claxton, he supposes, though also to satisfy a curiosity which he can hardly confess to. "I do not think I am your man, sir."

Carteret, warmer in his manner now, rings his bell once more, and the footman, who must have been standing in the room all along concealed by shadows, returns, sweeping away the broken glass and spilled wine and, a moment later, setting down two fresh glasses, a full decanter and a clean white handkerchief, bending to wrap it around his master's hand. Carteret pours and raises his glass, bidding Abel do likewise. They drink; the wine is warm and comforting. "Think, then," he says, "of the war against the Trojans. Of how Troy was won. Aren't your automata of which I have been told much like the horse?"

"My automata contain springs, wheels, cams, steel. Not men."

Carteret looks at him almost as a lover might, allowing the silence between them to build until it is charged. "But they could, could they not?" he says at last. "One could contain you."

"Me?" The room is cavernous, and the few candles Lord Carteret has set out around him cannot bring light into its corners.

Here and there the contour of a wooden carving is visible high on the walls, ornate: an angel's face, a trumpet. There is a smell of wax, of wood and, faintly, of the game Carteret has just eaten.

"The sultan's mother was French," says Carteret, now in the tone of one giving a briefing, though Abel has no intention of accepting the role of eavesdropper that is proposed for him. "He is bound to have some sympathies for the French cause, being half French himself. Though we know he admires Frederick of Prussia, and that gives us hope. He likes to play chess, is a collector of clocks, and has a fascination for orreries and other astronomical whatnots. He is a cultured man. He writes poetry, though one must always be wary of poems written by kings, since they more often than not provoke a fit of the colic."

"Forgive me, Lord Carteret, but I still do not understand what it is you wish of me."

"To go to Constantinople, build a chess-playing automaton, one you may conceal yourself within, and build its reputation with the nobles of the city until you are summoned by the Sultan Mustafa. Or rather your machine is."

"Would it not be simpler for me to play chess with the sultan and engage him in conversation?"

Carteret, midway through a gulp of wine, sputters it out. "Good grief, man, are you so naive? Do you think it an easy matter to win an audience with the Ottoman emperor? Even our ambassador cannot see him face to face. Mustafa is the shadow of Allah upon the earth. He talks only to his chief eunuch and his concubines. No, no, I shall find whomsoever plays the game of chess most masterfully in our kingdom and they will challenge you. You must vanquish all comers, first here and then there, so that the sultan is keen to test himself against you. But it will not be you, but one of your automata, and that will make it more alluring still. And you will sit within it and hear everything that is spoken in the seraglio. Yes, yes, this idea of mine is the only way. He will ask to play it, I'm sure of it—you can overcome any opponent, I am told?"

"I seem to have some gift for the game, but it has not been greatly tested."

Carteret, warming to his idea, stands and fills both glasses, again drinking his down immediately. He begins a perambulation around the long table, so that his form recedes into the gloom. "It is really quite ingenious. You will be paid, of course. I know that you receive great sums for your flapping silver birds and writing girls and whatnot. And you will have a chance to reacquaint yourself with a city which captured your heart."

Abel takes another sip of the wine. It is the best he has ever tasted.

Noticing his appreciation, Carteret says, "It is Margoose, 1706. Perhaps the finest wine ever produced. I have all of it. One never knows when there will be another war, an interruption of supply."

"There is always war, it seems."

Carteret steps out of the gloom and brings his face close to Abel's. His appearance is unpleasant, his small eyes set in a head unnaturally large, so that he seems like a myopic and startled hog. "That," he says, his voice containing a dribble of excitement, "is my goal, and now it is yours, too. To bring wars to an end. To achieve a perfect balance in Europe and thus bring peace to our vexed nations. A permanent peace. It is what I have worked for all my life, Cloudesley. But peace does not come without labour, and it never comes with honour. I am not asking you to wield a sword or fire a rifle. I am not asking you to lay down your life. All I am asking is that you make an automatic man that can play chess and to sit within it and listen. And you are the only being alive who may do such a thing."

"And if I decline this employment?" asks Abel, innocently enough, he thinks. As he speaks there is a sudden cooling in the room, palpable, as if an icy wind had blown through it. He half expects to see the candles sputter and extinguish, but they burn on in the gloom.

"Decline?" says Carteret, his tone now unmistakably menacing. "You think it is your right to decline? It is no more your right to decline than it is mine to put your one-eyed son in irons."

Mention of Zachary dazes Abel, and for a moment he thinks he must have misheard. "My son?" he asks, apprehensively.

"Come, come, Cloudesley," says Carteret more gently, once again placing his meaty hand, now bandaged, over Abel's and patting it, "I shall ensure no harm comes to your Zachary. Rest assured." He pauses, eloquently. "Not while you are in the king's service."

It is bare reassurance to him that Zachary is, at least, in the care of Aunt Frances and a little further from the grasp of Carteret than might otherwise be the case. For all his unease about Frances and her indulgence of the boy's eccentricities, he does not doubt her love for him, or that she'd hesitate for a moment to wield her long rifle in his defence. Yet the threat is obvious, unanswerable, Abel's curiosity to meet Carteret and have the tantalizing possibility of Constantinople dangled before him replaced by the terrible certainty that he is a man in a trap, a trap set for him by his closest friend, and that he has stepped into it blithely. He considers arguing, protesting that to threaten the welfare of his innocent child is an outrage, yet he knows he would be no more sensible than a fish wriggling on a hook, tearing out its gills to make its own demise a certainty. Better to fall willingly into the hands of the angler, to be clubbed over the head with a priest and worry about the currents no more. Perhaps he will be doing his patriotic duty, perhaps he will in some way do Zachary some good in accepting this terrible commission. Unable to speak he stands, bows his head and takes up his hat from where he had laid it on the table. Looking at a clock, he sees it is almost midnight. As he retreats, he realizes he is being spoken to. He turns. "Sir?"

"You are a relative to the late admiral?"

His surname. He is often asked. Sir Cloudesley Shovell is still an English hero, despite his ignominious end on the rocks of the Scillies. "Distant, sir. My great-great-grandfather and the admiral's grandmother were brother and sister, or so I have been told."

"Distant, then?"

"Yes."

This appears to satisfy his tormentor. "Remember, Cloudesley, there is not a thing in all the universe that is worthwhile that is not also complicated."

The footman opens the door and Abel slips out of the room, free to leave but now most assuredly a prisoner.

◻

CHAPTER SEVEN

MRS. MORLEY'S GREAT MISFORTUNE

January 1761, Tring

▣

Fire seems to trail me like a pack of beagles on the scent of an ill-starred hare. My shop on Bishopsgate was turning a good profit what with the current fashion for feathered and flowered ladies' hats, there being none to be got from France as we are at war with the Frenchies and heaven knows who besides and they blockade us and we them, which is all to the good for the price of hats. We were busy. Leonora in the main is peaceable and at her hop-scotch, and Sally, my capable if overly meek shop girl, deals with customers while I place orders for summer stock.

It is the beginning of December when a letter arrives from John, my sister's foolish husband in Faversham, saying that I am needed there urgently and on a matter of life and death, no less. I leave the shop in the hands of Sally with the promise I will return within two days. At Faversham I find my sister Amelia suffering from a fit of the convulsive vapours brought on, so John tells me, by a visit to the fair where she'd gone into a tent and seen the dog-faced boy. What I am supposed to do with her I don't know. Her husband wants me to slap her, since he has vowed never to take his hand to her again, but I choose instead to make her an infusion of red wine vinegar, prunella and nightshade water, which is in general a serviceable cure for apoplexies, tending to hasten on recovery a treat, the remedy being so much worse than the ailment.

What I find on my return to Bishopsgate is the sorriest sight I beheld in my life, and I have known hard times so I do not say such a thing lightly. My beautiful shop is as charred and black as an empty coal scuttle. I kick the burnt timbers aside and go in search of a hat or two. There were some that were in steel hatboxes, and I think they might have been preserved, but the fire must have burned with such ferocity that I find them buckled and misshapen by the great incineration. That the buildings either side of my shop are barely scorched is mysterious to me, since we all had fire marks on our properties, mine being with the Phoenix Fire Insurance company as is the one beside it, and on the other side one with Sun Fire, and I had sent Sally out with the insurance money not a month before, me being afeard of fire having lost my home and husband in one such but seven years past, not that losing the husband was so great a loss. But no, I am told, two fire engines had come and put out the fires about, but not my shop, since the fire mark had been taken down the day after I left for Faversham. What outrage is this? I go marching into the office of the Phoenix Fire Insurance company, placing a fire-blackened hatbox on the counter, and declare, "This is your doing, this fire. You sent out a fire engine and let my shop burn." "Madam," they say, "the insurance was due last month and you did not pay." "You scoundrels!" I declare. "I sent my girl to you on the fourth of November with nine shillings for the payment." "I am sorry to say she did not pay it," says the clerk.

Oh, Sally, Sally, Sally. Where are you now? Was it worth nine shillings to make such misery? I have looked for her since, with a mind to break her arms and knock out her teeth, but she will be far off, I suppose, continuing to enjoy the use of her deceitful arms and teeth alike.

I did not despair, for I had Leonora safe at my side and despair is anyway not in my nature. I thought of what friends I had and knew there to be none of great value excepting my benefactor, Mr. Cloudesley, and he was gone to far-off Constantinople, and much against his will I should say. The last time I saw him he seemed to me near deranged, and I was obliged to insist he take some of my Dover's Powder to calm his nerves though these had the effect of over-calming so that he never did tell me the cause of his distress. Counting Mr. Cloudesley out of my reckoning, I resolved to make a little money in the pie trade, since I make a good hard pastry and can think of all manner of meats to slip inside a pleasing crust, and I think of Lady Pee-Bee as she might be amenable to an application for a small loan, since despite her many lunacies she always knew me to be a woman both practical and honest. So I write to her setting out my changed circumstances without any hint of sentiment or pleading and she replies to my letter no less promptly than I had cause to expect, hinting at agreement but with the stipulation that I come to see her at her house in Tring and sending me a guinea to cover the expense of the journey. I should have liked to decline, but poverty is not just poverty but the shame of having to accept charity when it is neither sought nor desired.

Bought, I was, for a guinea.

Thinking that if she could apply terms and conditions then so could I, my reply was accompanied with a firm demand that all birds should be removed from the house, since feathers bring

Leonora out in hives, which is something I lay at the door of Lady Peake-Barnes in any case, from when Leonora was but a baby and Lady Pee-Bee came to stay with her parrots and that discouraging crow of hers. Anyway, and to my great surprise, she consents most readily.

Well, we take the Aylesbury coach, Leonora and I, on a bright winter's day that is all white with frost on the meadows and the branches of the bare trees and the air is crisp, and I am in a humour a little too gentle for what I know must come. Leonora has been a good girl by her lights, only biting the man who sat opposite in the carriage and he was to blame for that for he would insist on smiling at her though I tried to tell him not to, that she was not a good-hearted child. He seemed taken aback when I said so, as if a mother could not possibly say such a thing about her own, but he quickly got the gist of it after the bite. She is not wild, but she has the ill temper of her father, and perhaps of my own father, I am sorry to say. Still, she is my little girl, and she is strong, too. Six years old and she can lift a small pig.

Anyway, we get to Tring and are soon at Briar House, a pretty place, grand but not so grand as to be disheartening, with white walls and an abundance of smoke from the chimneys. We are met by an elderly footman who begins to take our things but seems to forget what he's about and puts them down on the steps and wanders away without a word. Then Lady Pee-Bee is upon us, all arms and shrieks as if she has herself turned into one of her birds, though one too stout to fly. "Well," she says, and, "Well," again, and, "This is quite a thing, is it not, to have you here; it is quite the thing," and suchlike. A maid appears, a gaunt-looking woman with a back so bent that her nose is almost to the ground, yet all she does is peer up at us and then shuffles away. And it makes me comprehend that the household is most likely to be in disarray within and so I find it, with cages and bird droppings upon the furniture and a kitchen that is like a skating rink with beef dripping, and its cook in a chair in the corner in a stupor and smelling of rum.

"What is the cause of this disorder, madam?" says I to Lady Pee-Bee who is flapping about behind me.

"My dear Mrs. Morley, you are not to concern yourself with such trivialities, anymore than I do myself, for you are our guest, you and Leonora, and you must make yourself at ease," she says with a wave of her hand as if to dispel a malodorous air.

"I do not think I could put myself at ease in such a household as this, my lady. No, not in the least."

This prompts nothing more than laughter, as if she imagines I am indulging in some manner of jest. It is quite apparent to me that when Lady Pee-Bee had come to stay at Leadenhall when Zachary and Leonora were but suckling babes she must have exerted her-self to contain her many eccentricities, but that in her own domain she is perfectly without constraint. It also makes me suspect that she is a woman without companions or purpose, and that is the reason why she had been so keen to have Zachary at her side, for her own entertainment, entertainment being one thing that boy is more than able to provide, since his mind whirrs like a waterwheel after a storm and his little mouth knows no more how to cease its torrent of words than a river knows how to stop its flow.

She makes to take Leonora by the hand, and I try to tell her that the child is likely to act up, but I need not have worried, because my girl is fascinated by Lady Pee-Bee, by her flapping arms, her crimson dress and her singing voice and her sweets, which she immediately offers the child contrary to my objections, and then she takes Leonora out to the aviary, despite my protestations that she has the problem with the hives; it is as if Lady Pee-Bee disbelieves me as she disbelieves anything she does not care to believe. So we have hives to contend with and poultices and salves and all of that for the first few days, though at least it keeps Leonora whimpering in her bed rather than breaking things or screaming and shouting.

Zachary is much changed, but not in the least direction I had cause to expect under his great-aunt's influence. I'd imagined her encouraging all the boy's peculiarities—his fascination for creatures, taking frogs and spiders into his bed, his damnable cockatoo, and his counting, enumerating the clouds in the sky and the tiles on a roof and the pocks on a face, and all out loud and all at the same time. She has built him a small menagerie, right enough, in which are those giant and tragic birds called ostriches, also three ill-tempered striped mules which are known as zebras and kept warm by great fires in their enclosures, a dozen haughty-looking creatures about the size of a small horse but with the ears of a hare and that are called llamas. But despite all this indulgence there is a sensibleness about him, almost gentlemanly, or so I think as he reaches out and gives my hand a shake, but then he looks at me oddly, as if he has received a jolt, and says, "You have come to stay, Mrs. Morley. To stay for many years."

"I most certainly have not!" I exclaim. "This is a visit, young Zachary, so that we might see how you fare with your aunt and so you might again acquaint yourself with your friend Leonora."

"No, you will stay," he says, pointing to his eye that he says can see into the future. "At first you will be sorry about it, but soon you will come to see it is for the best."

Well, he always did say strange things and in a strange manner—and in any case, I wonder if he has been cooking something up with Lady Pee-Bee—but then he next says something that catches my attention right and proper and I know it to be more than that. "You must not keep on worrying about that extra shilling she asked for."

"What extra shilling?" says I. "And who asked for it?"

"Sally," he says, soft as anything, his little face all innocence but for his golden eye, that always seems to see right into you and out through the other side.

I try to tell myself that he has heard mention of Sally when I used to bring Leonora on visits to Mr. Cloudesley, but I know I told not one soul about that damnable shilling, though I have thought of it often, whether I might have had that girl's loyalty with it, for she asked for it not long before I went away, saying she had need of it to pay the surgeon who came to do her mother's bleeding and cupping, for she had a canker in her. I declined, thinking that maybe I'd give her two shilling on my return and that patience was a virtue. Damn patience. Damn virtue. I grunt and turn away so the boy will not see my discomposure, and walk right into a man, tall and very thin, with a complexion more grey than alive and an expression so sad it seems made purposely for the provocation of tears. He bows and introduces himself as Mendel, Zachary's tutor. "Oh," I say, "you have your hands full there."

He regards me as if I have spoken in a language he does not fully comprehend, and I am about to repeat myself when he declares,

"I have the best pupil in all the world, madam, for he has a great hunger for learning and everything he is told he remembers."

"Well, he is a curious boy, I grant you."

"Curiosity is a blessing, and the incurious as happy as the sheep in the fields, which is to say not happy in the least."

"Well, Mr. Mendel, I cannot say I have ever speculated on the ecstasies and miseries of a sheep," says I, thinking to laugh, but he is so much in earnest that I restore myself to a stern disposition, as seems fitting with such a gloomy gentleman. Seeing that Zachary has gone off to find Leonora I ask him whether Zachary tells him that his golden eye sees into the future, or whether he has noticed any other strange faculties the child possesses.

Mendel is uneasy with the question, I can tell, and courtesy (even to one such as I) tussles in him with a disinclination to answer me at all. He bends his head as if in mourning and mumbles, not to me but at the dusty floorboards, "Zachary is troubled by visions and apparitions, and he has been told by those who should know better that these are gifts or strange magic when they are simply the result of his *traumateia*—his ordeals, if you will." He looks at me directly, his watery grey eyes a little less far away than before and says, "My task, as given me by the lady of the house, is to instill reason in the boy, for through reason we find understanding, and as Baruch Spinoza taught us, *to understand is to be free.*" And with that he bows to me very deeply and walks away. An odd fellow, that one.

Eager though I was to discuss the terms of Lady Pee-Bee's loan and be away back to London, I knew it would be ill-mannered to ask straight away, and anyway I had to wait for Leonora to overcome her fit of the boils. As I say, the household was not well run, nor wholly clean, and I find myself having to resist a great urge to dust and scrub. Lady Pee-Bee has only nine engaged, excluding Mr. Mendel, who lives in the pigeon loft—none of them very capable apart from the head gardener, who has everything outside in good order, producing oranges from the orangery and pineapples from the pineapplery as well as an abundance of early potatoes and spring greens. Reeve, the footman whose absent-mindedness presented itself on that first day, and Dorcas, the bent housekeeper, were not lazy so much as spent, like old dogs fit only to lie before the fire. They sit in Reeve's small parlour by the kitchen, in turn smoking their pipes and sleeping. The cook, Mrs. Jopling, is a woman so committed to beef dripping and rum that the whole kitchen is a slithering rink and doesn't bear a visit. But I say nothing of any of this and think it instead my duty to busy myself with reading Lady Pee-Bee's correspondence, which is left like all other items scattered about. Since Zachary is in lessons most of the day with Mr. Mendel, Leonora bedbound with her boils and Lady Pee-Bee out firing her rifle or riding about the countryside on her cantankerous horse, I have a good deal of time to myself.

I confess I had hoped to discover some intelligence regarding Lady Pee-Bee's finances so that I might ensure I request an amount in keeping with her means, for it is certainly not unknown for those living richly to do so by means of impoverishing their creditors, and I had no wish to add to the misery of others in seeking to ease my own. Much of what I find is dull and tedious correspondence with a Mrs. Elizabeth Montagu about the import of books from Holland, and letters back and forth with one Elizabeth Carter concerning some poetry to be published in the *Gentleman's Magazine*. There are also letters from Mr. Gore, the member of parliament for Tring and a long-suffering one by the look of things, and several from the Reverend Bradley, the Astronomer Royal, on the best means of measuring the speed of light, of all things. Only such a woman as Lady Pee-Bee could imagine that light is something with a certain velocity, and yet I am amazed to see the Reverend Bradley has condescended to offer a reply and even to agree with her in some small part. There is also an odd letter from a Mr. Claxton, of whom I have heard some mention from Mr. Cloudesley as being a friend, but the letter does not seem friendly in its tone, what with mention of Mr. Cloudesley's guilelessness and his being well out of the way in Constantinople.

I turn next to some letters concerning Lady Pee-Bee's mining interests and these are of very great concern, it being immediately apparent that Lady Pee-Bee is paying far too little attention to her investments. A series of letters from her solicitor, a Mr. Dray, implores her to allow him to authorize moneys for a new water pump but has been torn into pieces, and it takes a good deal of putting the fragments back together for me to read what they say, though I suspect this is also Lady Pee-Bee's intention—to set me a challenge. Then, when I read at what price she is selling her coal, I wonder that she doesn't just let it go for free! Is it up to Lady Pee-Bee how she manages her affairs? Should she not think of those who depend upon her prudence (prudence! Hah!)? Her household? Her great-nephew who stands to inherit nothing but birds if her affairs continue to be run as they have been these past years? As a woman who has always been obliged to be painstaking with what little money I've had, it galls me to see one with plenty letting it be carried off like chaff in the wind.

I am musing on how best to raise the matter with her—whether to confront her with her willful idiocy directly or to ask her instead whether she has taken leave of her senses, when Reeve comes in bearing a letter. "Add it to the pile," says I, waving a hand in the direction of her correspondence, which I have sorted into stacks in date order. He seems unsurprised to see me going through the lady's letters, but I feel obliged to offer him some explanation, nonetheless. "The lady asked me to put her correspondence in order," I say, which provokes a guffaw of disbelief.

"It matters not what the lady said or did not say," he mutters, "the child says it is you who are now to rule over us."

"What child?" I ask.

"The one with the eye. I forget his name. It may be Zebedee."

"When did he say such a thing?" I do not attempt to hide my annoyance from him.

But Reeve only grimaces. "It is for you," he says, holding out the letter, "and you owe me a shilling."

"A shilling!" declares I, for I know the cost of a sheet sent from London to be not more than eightpence. "How many pages?"

"Just the one, and not much written upon."

The villain! I open it and it is a demand for payment for making good the property on Bishopsgate for the sum of forty pound. I confess that I immediately lost control of myself, so that when I come to, I find myself in the arms of Dorcas and my face bloody. She says I passed out and my nose bled, and that she will draw me a bath and I will be the better for it.

"A bath?" I protest, despite my wretched state. "What good is a bath when I am in want of forty pounds?"

"Then at least put on a clean dress," says she.

When she is returned from her riding Lady Pee-Bee comes striding into the library where I sit distraught and covered in blood. She is herself spattered with mud and holding some dead creature which bleeds over her dress and the rug alike, so it is as if the two of us are recently at battle and have retreated to nurse our injuries. Tossing aside the dead thing, which I now see to be a stoat, she tells me she has been told of my new misfortune. Taking me by the arm she says that, though she would most certainly not have wished such a calamity on me, she has decided what is to become of me, and it is to stay at Briar House and take charge of the household and all her affairs, for she finds them tedious and wishes to spend her time on her astronomical investigations and in ensuring that Zachary does not grow dull.

I am at a loss for words, which is not a familiar condition. Eventually I say, "Well, madam, I have observed that your affairs are in disarray, but I hardly think I could be happy in your household, not with matters as they are currently ordered."

"You may reorder them as you please," says she, "my only stipulations are that you allow me to pay off your debts, that Leonora receive a proper education, which I propose alongside Zachary with Mr. Mendel, and that you should leave Reeve and Dorcas to their dozing, for they have earned it."

And that, in short, is how Leonora and I have come to reside at Briar House, though whether I am to succeed in making the house respectable or the lady any less exasperating remains to be seen.

CHAPTER EIGHT

AN UNFAMILIAR CITY

May 1761, Constantinople

When the ship has Constantinople in its sights, the wind drops as it so often does in that treacherous strait and Abel is left, along with the others on deck, to contemplate the hazy city and all it has in store for him. Its unsteady outline of minarets and domes, the distant noise of afternoon prayer being called, the faint hint of cinnamon and smoke on the dying breeze, serve to provoke a nostalgia almost violent in its force. It is fifteen years since he last sailed into the mouth of the Bosphorus, and his memories of his year learning the Levant trade return to him with the potency of a dream that, half shaken off on waking, is found to be no dream at all. He is engulfed in longing, almost a grieving for the youth he was. How fine a thing to be so innocent, so impressionable, so hopeful and yet how pathetic, too—to imagine that love is something in the air that need only be breathed for immortality to be granted. What is youth but the mainspring of a timepiece freshly wound, measuring the hours perfectly, ignorant that time must, sooner or later, outpace the tick and tock of his heart, leaving a man to rot until even his bones are turned to dust.

He catches sight of Tom, who has come up on deck, fooled by the ship's stall to think they are in harbour. He has glued some whiskers on his chin for the journey (Abel has a notion of their source but has tried to think no more about it) and kept his distance from the other passengers, for fear of provoking curiosity or worse. Abel had paid for a private cabin for Tom, which had not come cheap. Even then, Tom had suffered the attentions of the first mate, though whether or not he saw some shadow of Tom's former self in him, Abel had no idea. Tom kept a pistol for such an occasion, and Abel knew he would use it if given cause.

Samuels, on the other hand, Abel has let make the passage with the other common passengers, since he knows his servant will have no trouble from any man, he being that sort who forbids idle enquiry and who may ignore any question or invitation to join drinking or singing or cards without provoking resentment or argument. There is a low, unspoken threat in Samuels at all times, something like the slow beat of a buzzard's wing, serene and almost still so long as it has no prey in its sights.

The automaton, half built and in the hold, held in its great wooden box by wedges and fixings and deep leather cushions stuffed with horsehair, is as cosseted as a brittle and venerated saint in its reliquary. But the finishing touches are to be made here in Constantinople; the mechanism is of extraordinary sophistication, able to make its moves, if need be, automatically, though the sequencing required to win a game of chess against any human opponent with a reasonable grasp of the game has proven beyond even Tom's ability. Abel has tussled with his promise to his son that he never play chess against anyone other than him, but has reasoned that it will be the machine that plays, even if he must direct it, and so is not breaking his vow, though he is hardly persuaded by his own argument. The machine is a wooden horse and

Abel its Odysseus, ready to sit within, determine its moves and listen to the sultan's musings.

It is late in the afternoon when they finally dock, the ropes pulled taut, Abel standing on cobbles seemingly animated by the tides and apparently liquid, so long has he been at sea. He watches his precious cargo brought roughly from the hold by dockers exotic in their costumes—billowing white shirts, red breeches, round hats, long moustaches; Circassians, he thinks, though he cannot now remember all the subtle distinctions of the uniforms and standing of each man in the city. Bakers are Armenian, he recalls, and boatmen Egyptian, traders Greek, porters Bulgarian, and to transgress these ordained roles is no easier than for a worm to fly or an owl to swim. The Turks rule over all from the south bank of the Golden Horn, the quarter known as Sultanahmet, much as the gods on Mount Olympus, making their presence always felt but rarely seen.

His freight is finally heaved up the steep, narrow lanes of Galata to Pera and the English Palace, as the embassy is known, with its fine view over the Golden Horn. Abel is eager to meet again his old friend James Porter, the ambassador, who had been almost a father to him when he'd been here before. But arriving at the palace, he sees packing cases and the unmistakable evidence of departure and is told that Porter and his family are to leave Constantinople the following week.

At dinner that evening, Porter and his wife, Clarissa, are solicitous, seeking a full account of Abel's life since he was last in the city, asking about Alice with a keen sympathy devoid of the mawkishness some think necessary in consideration of the bereaved. They express the keen hope that he will one day bring Zachary to meet them. "You and your son must come and visit us in Brussels," Clarissa urges him, that being the city to which she and James and their daughters are bound. But after dinner, alone with Porter, the landscape shifts into bleaker territory.

"I am not sorry to be leaving," says Porter, his accent holding still the music of his native Ireland, "not in the least."

Abel is surprised, knowing the ambassador's deep affection for the city and how respected he is by all, even those diplomats and merchants from nations with which England is now at war, that being more or less all of them.

"I have received precious little in the manner of funds from London, you know, Abel," he continues, "still less from the Levant Company, which is failing."

"Failing, sir?"

"Now don't you go calling me *sir*, Abel," he says, a hand on his shoulder. "You have surely heard that the company is asking for loans from parliament? It is the East India Company that glitters and outshines all these days, and catches the eye of those who were once investors in the Levant trade."

"The East India Company has opened its offices not far from my own workshop, and they are grander than a royal palace. Yet there are markets here for our wool still, surely, and clocks for that matter, and there must still be demand for Turkish silks and cottons in England?"

Porter grimaces, rubs a hand across his weary features. "The world is changing, Abel, faster than you or I can comprehend. They are spinning cotton now in Birmingham. *Birmingham*," he repeats, as if it were a place more exotic by far than

Constantinople. "I am sorry to say that our country is not the noble land we might once have hoped it was, and the affairs of the world grow grubby. As for you being sent here as Carteret's man, all I can say is I am sorry for it, since I have been Carteret's man myself half my life and I have come to know the cost of it." He looks at Abel frankly. "There, I have said my piece." He leans back as if the better to reappraise his visitor.

"I am grateful for your candour, James."

Porter shuffles his chair closer still to Abel's, lowering his voice as if fearing they are overheard, though none but a footman is within earshot and even he is sent out the room. "I have asked to leave, Abel, and let all know it is because of my intolerable financial position, which no one will doubt since they know it to be true—but it is more than that."

Abel attends his words carefully, since it is clear that Porter wishes—needs, perhaps—him to know his true reasons.

"Carteret is displeased with me, and to displease Carteret is unhealthy for one such as I. And no less is it for one such as you, now, if I have correctly understood your duties here."

"I am not sure I understand my duties myself. I am sincerely hoping for your guidance."

Porter grunts wearily. "I am not sure my guidance counts for much. The French are ready to sue for peace, particularly after the success of Quiberon, and I have told Carteret as much, but the war grinds on, crunching the bones of tens of thousands—no, hundreds of thousands—of young men: French, English, Austrian, Russian, Prussian."

"Carteret told me he wanted peace. He told me he is . . ." Realizing that if he tells Porter all that Carteret said it might be taken as a rebuke, he says, ". . . uneasy about Ottoman intentions, and seeks to know them for sure."

Porter grabs Abel's wrist. "Even the Turks do not know the Turkish intention for sure. Oh, I have tried to explain this to him so many times, Abel. Carteret might have a certain genius when it comes to European diplomacy, but here we are far from that, and it is subtler, more the brush of a feather than the slap of a glove, or should I say more a reflection seen in glass by candlelight, deceiving, flattering and untrue. The sultan is exalted, mysterious—rather more so than is our new King George in his domain, and yes, one sees the grand vizier conducting himself much as our own prime minister, with his plans and policies which are quite at odds with the sultan's wishes, their distrust of each other tumbling into loathing, just as His Majesty detests the Duke of Newcastle and Mr. Pitt. But the damnable difficulty here is finding where true power lies, since all is whispers and rumour, and there are potent figures who never emerge from the seraglio, not even from the ladies' harem—where, it is said, the most weighty decisions are made. In London, one can take a minister to a tavern, get him drunk and learn a good deal. Here one cannot even look a vizier in the eye, let alone the sultan. The Chief Black Eunuch runs the seraglio and with it the empire, or so some believe. Be warned of him. He has his agents everywhere and I wish to God that you should never encounter that corrupt figure, though if he is seen at all it is in disguise. I have been here many years and have little more understanding of how Ottoman affairs are run than when I arrived." He offers Abel a sad smile. "So I wish His Majesty's next ambassador to the Sublime Porte good fortune and a sorcerer's intuition." He brightens with a thought: "And there's another thing, Abel, ambassadors are appointed not to the court of the sultan, nor to the seraglio, but to the Sublime Porte—a damned gate!"

Abel laughs.

"Well, I tell Carteret all this, give him the light and shade of it, but he has lost that faith he once had in me, I fear."

"I am no expert, James, as you know, but in my own meeting with him, and from everything I have heard of the man, I should have thought him quite the man for light and shade."

"I have known him fast on thirty years and liked him well enough in that time. But he is more the man for shade, Abel . . . more the man for shade and always was. That is my counsel." He shakes his head sorrowfully.

"You have done your best, James, I am sure, and I have no doubt you and Clarissa will make a great success of things in Brussels."

Porter considers him for a moment or two, making Abel feel like a portrait doubted as a true likeness. "I am not telling you this, Abel, seeking your comfort. I am trying to caution you. I don't know what it is exactly that you are sent here to do . . ."

Abel starts to explain his understanding of his mission, but is halted by Porter, the palm of his hand held up as if to stop a carriage on the street. "No! I have no wish to know. I have used all fair means to gain intelligence in my time here and have had a good deal of success in it if it comes to that. I know the intrigues of the Russian court, and what is likely to happen if, as seems likely, the Empress Elizabeth should soon die; I know Austrian and Swedish plans and hopes well, for I dine twice a week with the ambassadors of each nation, and though we dissemble when we must, on the whole we share intelligence in a friendly way, for in such manner we may shorten this abominable conflict. But I do not spy."

"I . . ." Abel tries to protest that he is no spy either.

"You are to build an automaton that will somehow find its way into the seraglio, to the very inner sanctum of the sultan. I have been told as much, no more. I cannot imagine how this will bring intelligence from the sultan to the ears of the Lord President. It is not my business to know, but I fear for you, Abel. You are not the innocent young man who arrived here all those years ago, of course you're not. But nor, I am certain, are you so conversant with the dark arts Carteret would have you perform as to be capable of avoiding great peril."

Abel is chilled by his warning, which he knows will not have been given lightly, and feels he must explain. "I was given no choice in the matter, James."

Porter's expression is that of a man reading the label on a bottle of poison he has long warned against. "I am sure of it. Our friend the Lord President has his ways to hold us true to his purposes. I will tell you the threat he holds over me, since you will hear it from others after I am gone, no doubt. It is that he is in possession of certain information about the Baron de Hochepied, my father-in-law, that would ruin him. He has told me the nature of it in cyphers and made clear to me the consequence of my failing to bend to his will. But I have not, or not yet, and that is truly why I am leaving this place. You might imagine Brussels will suit us well, being so close to my wife's home, but it will bankrupt us, of that I am certain. What, may I ask, is his hold over you?"

"It is Zachary."

Porter does not show surprise. "And he has spelled out the nature of his designs on your son?"

"He has no need to. I know how easy it would be for him to arrange for his abduction. I fear it. And doesn't one hear of such things? Of children stolen, brought up in some other household, told they are orphans taken in?" He is engulfed by a great need to confess his true feelings to Porter, believing him in that moment one of the few men both kind and wise he has ever known. "All my life I hoped to find love, to be loved, and now I have a son I love more dearly than life itself, and yet I have proved myself a pitifully inadequate father, as I fear I spoke at undue length over dinner, and now am a poorer father still, a thousand leagues from him for fear of some further injury befalling him." He pauses, the weight of his thoughts making his tongue heavy, so that he almost slurs his next words. "And what will that boy think of me?"

Porter, having no answer, coughs lightly and changes the subject. "I have made you a workshop in the stables, dry, warm, with the equipment I believe you require. You asked for help in finding able assistants who would be reliably discreet." He rubs his hand again across his face. It is after midnight, and the frank nature of their discussion has drained both men equally. "Discretion is not a commodity easily found in this city, Abel—it is a place full of secrets, not one of them long kept, so truth is quickly debased, and rumour exalted, as I have tried to explain." A shutter creaks in a breeze and a waft of warm, jasmine-scented air creeps into the room, as if it, too, were a spy. "But I have found a man I believe you might be able to trust," continues Porter, "a Nubian, come from southern Egypt to the Mevlevi school here."

"A dervish?"

"A dervish, indeed, but sadly unable to perform the rituals, for he has been stricken with a paralysis, a myelitis of the anterior horns, as those who swim in unclean water can fall prey to."

Abel wonders what use a paralyzed man can be to him, but he knows something of the dervishes. He went, sometimes, to the Galata Mevlevihanesi, where he watched the disciples practice their whirling for hour after hour, the bare toes of their left foot gripping a nail driven into the floor, spinning upon it. In addition to their devotions and songs and poems, they manufactured the most remarkable astronomical clocks he had ever seen, clocks with four faces, foretelling events to come—comets, droughts, floods, plagues, based upon the positioning of the stars, all that is to come being known to Allah, ready to be revealed to those with sufficient faith to understand, and orreries, too—remarkably beautiful and accurate moving models of the solar system that were inspiration for his own clockwork devices, altogether more frivolous and vain.

"His name is Naguib Ghalib. I will send him to you and you may see what you make of him."

"Thank you, James." Their long evening at an end, he stands, bows.

Porter walks over to the open window and stares out of it into the starless night. "How everything once fresh and sweet and bright spoils, Abel, how it turns rotten." He turns and gives Abel his sad smile. "We must be glad for those better times, my dear fellow; that we had them at all, eh?"

"We must."

"Good night. You know the way to your chamber?"

"I do. Thank you."

The house is grand and improbably large, another cause of Porter's straitened circumstances, supposes Abel. As he walks along one long corridor and then another, he feels a deep sorrow for his friend, and is unable to shake off a strong sense of ill omen in his departure. His slippers clack-clack on the black-and-white tessellated tiles that, in the dim light of his lamp, seem to shift and buckle before his eyes, and he slowly comes to realize that he is lost. The house is silent. He tries to retrace his steps, but again takes a wrong turn. He thinks if he can descend again to the hall he will surely find Samuels, since he has taken up station there, having formed the notion that the janissary placed at the outer door is not to be trusted, but Abel cannot even find the stairs, the corridors being a maze designed for the single purpose of disorientation. Seeing a door which looks familiar he opens it only to be met by the fluttering of countless wings. The room stinks of ammonia and, in the brief moment before his lamp snuffs out, he sees open windows and a mass of pigeons, rising as one at the impertinence of his entrance. He retreats into the silent corridor, closing the door behind him with relief only to be enveloped by absolute blackness. It is then he feels or hears it: a brush of something cold on his cheek, followed by his son's voice, distinct and audible as if he were standing just before him. Abel gasps, squats, his arms stretching into the darkness as if he might touch him, embrace him. *It is the third door on the right, Papa*, says the voice, *after the portrait of William and Mary. Keep walking until you see the old king and queen. Keep walking . . .* His lamp sputters back into life, and before him he sees . . . nothing. Nothing but black-and-white tessellated floor. The absence of Zachary, usually no more than a dull ache deep within him, is made so painfully acute by hearing his voice that he clutches at his chest as he stands, struggling to regain breath. Was it a ghost? Has something happened to Zachary? He must write, straight away. Though even if his letter reaches England without mishap, he will not receive a reply for many months.

Abel holds up the lamp and sees, not far along the corridor, a portrait of King William and Queen Mary. He counts three doors from it and, opening that on the right, finds within a comfortable, well-lit bedchamber, his trunk at the end of the bed, his clothes hanging neatly before the wardrobe, a chamber pot and basin, water and a vase of roses, their petals white tinged with red, as if dipped in blood. It is incongruous after his frantic wandering, and Abel sits on the soft bed laughing at his foolishness. Taking out his watch he sees it is not so late, a little after one. What felt like an hour of stumbling around the corridors of the palace was probably no more than a quarter. He sits at the desk, takes the quill that sits so temptingly there, dips it in the ink and writes to his son of his arrival in the city, describing its sights and sounds and smells. He ponders on whether to mention in his letter that he thought he had heard Zachary speak to him, guiding him so clearly to his bedchamber when he was tired and lost, but thinks it best not to encourage his son's already overly active imagination. He tells himself he must have known where his chamber was all along, noticed before dinner the portrait on the wall but forgotten it, and his lamp must have had a low flame after all, enough to flare once again in the still air. He tells himself all of this, though without great conviction, for he knows the truth of it; Zachary is imbued with those same gifts Alice possessed, and in him they are even more pronounced. Abel has always turned away from them, not from lack of love for Zachary but because of love, certain that Zachary would be a happier child if he were more like other boys, a little less singular. Besides, a father's role is not to indulge a child's every fancy. And yet . . . he looks down at the half-written page and resolves to tell Zachary how much he loves him and, yes, perhaps to mention that he imagined his voice telling him the way when he was lost in the dark and frightened, and to reassure his son that he will in his turn be there for him whenever he might find himself lost or frightened, though as Abel grows drowsy the quill in his hand becomes a feather and then a castle and soon a white horse that carries him away to a palace filled with viziers and eunuchs and dark shadows and chess pieces the height of lighthouses.

◙

CHAPTER NINE

CORRESPONDENCE

May 1761, Constantinople

Abel wakes, his head on the paper, the candle burned down to its stub and a bright morning poking through the shutters, and feels surprisingly refreshed. At breakfast, Porter, who has already been at work in his office for an hour or more, comes to sit with him, giving him information about the present situation in the city. As Abel drinks the last of his coffee, Porter announces that he has a bundle of letters for him. "Forgive me, Abel. I should have given them to you as soon as you arrived. You must be eager to have news from home."

There are two dozen, tied in a ribbon of light blue silk. He takes them to his room, greedy with anticipation. Several are business letters from the Levant Company, another half-dozen from Seth Cartwright, his foreman, who has been left in charge of workshop production at Leadenhall, written in his halting hand. There are letters from Claxton, two from Lord Carteret, one in cypher. Five are from Frances and, there at the bottom, two from Zachary. He pushes all the rest to one side and reads.

Briar House
Tring
15 January 1761

Dear Papa,
There was snow yesterday, and Franny took us out on sleds.
How strange it is that it feels warmer when the snow is falling.
Franny explained to us how the snow takes the moisture out of
the air to make its flakes, and ~~consequncially consequnetally~~
consequently the air is drier and so feels warmer. We also
took Franny's microscope outside and looked at snowflakes,
which have many different shapes, and when we went inside
we drew snowflakes. Leonora draws very prettily. I do not
have the hand for it, or the patience. You might not ever have
thought Leonora patient, but she is so, now that her head is
made so full with Mr. Mendel's lessons, though Mr. Mendel
is ill this week, and we are only allowed to see him in his
room in the pigeon loft for five minutes for fear of exhausting
him. I had never been to his room before. It must have been a
very grand pigeon loft, for now it is a library, with a bed and
a stove and, being hexagonal in shape, is a very comforting
place to be. Mr. Mendel lies under a dozen blankets and his
face is quite green.

Mrs. Morley rules the house, leaving Aunt Franny to the
aviary and to her astronomical calculations, which I am told
to tell you are much advanced. She hopes to present her find-
ings to the Royal Society in London and promises to take me
with her! Though I will not go if Leonora is not allowed to go
as well, though Mrs. Morley says she will never go to London

ever again nor let Leonora go neither because it is a filthy disgusting place and altogether too ~~combastable~~ combustible.

Papa, I would have you write to Mrs. Morley, please, to tell her that I may read past eight o'clock, for that is the hour she insists I blow out my candle for fear of wearing out my one good eye, so she says. Aunt Franny let me read till midnight. I have asked Franny to come light my candle after Mrs. Morley's curfew, but she says she has ~~relinkished reluinkished~~ relinquished command, as Lear to his daughters, and she only hopes she will not be found howling on the moors or gouging out the eyes of cousins. I am reading Mr. Shakespeare's plays one by one and I like them a good deal for their blood and magic.

Franny says you will be at sea as I write this, somewhere near the Balearics. Mr. Mendel has put a map on the wall of the schoolroom, and we follow your passage day by day without quite being certain of it. I now know all the coast of the Mediterranean and the position of every isle within it. Some I knew already from Homer. If you make port at Mahon or Valletta or suchlike please may you send me a letter from there.

There has been only one matter of great dispute in the house since Mrs. Morley's coming, and its name was Christmas, Aunt Franny declaring it a pagan affair, and that we were to call it the yule. Mrs. Morley, though, favours Christmas and all its traditions, which included holly brought into the house and the making of frumentary, lum pottage and Twelfth cake. Franny said that she would have no part in it, but that Mrs. Morley was to do as she pleased. Leonora and I were each given a horse for Christmas, Franny relenting in her objections, and we are to be taught to ride. Reeve says we should also each be made to muck them out, since he cannot be taking on extra shoveling at his age. I told him all about Hercules and the Augean stables and he wished me well on my search for a river to divert.

> *I am, sir, your loving son,*
> *Zachary Cloudesley*

Zachary is only just seven, but he is prodigious in so many ways that his talent as a letter writer is barely a surprise. Abel reads the other letter from him, of an earlier date, which tells of Mrs. Morley's arrival and of a fire which has destroyed her shop. His son is then as he ever was, in no way ordinary. He thinks of their final meeting when he'd come to see him that last time at Tring, Zachary's little face solemn, his eye looking down at the ground, no hint of upset. Frances had the grace to retreat and leave them to their farewells. Zachary extended his small hand and Abel had shaken it sensibly until he found himself sweeping his boy into his arms and covering him in kisses and soaking him in tears before placing him gently back on the ground like a piece of porcelain he had knocked from a shelf and barely caught before it shattered. Zachary looked up at him and said, "You should not go, Papa. You know that, don't you?" "Yes, Zachary, I know." He could not tell him of Carteret's threat, and that he had been left with no choice. He was leaving to protect him, not abandon him, but he had no idea how to begin to explain such a thing.

Looking through the pile again he sees there is also a letter from Mrs. Morley. Conscious that he should see how preparations are progressing in his new workshop, he decides to read them all later.

The old stables have been converted well, and the smell is of newly sawn wood and fresh paint rather than forgotten horses. Tom is there and a surprise, for he has donned local dress, clad in a red hat with a tassel, billowing white shirt, gold embroidered waistcoat and baggy white cotton trousers. On his feet are a pair of well-turned red leather slippers. "Goodness, Tom. Quite the transformation."

"And tomorrow I shall have a splendid black moustache. I am having it made for me."

"You have settled in quickly, I must say."

"The landlord's daughter at my lodgings is most obliging." He twinkles, such as Abel has never seen him do before.

"It must be something in the air, Tom."

Tom stretches, a hand to his back, yawning like a satisfied cat, and it is obvious to Abel that he has the night before enjoyed that very happiest of consummations. "It must, yes, it must," Tom says.

It is Abel's turn to blush. He cannot ask Tom anymore about the matter. "What think you of our new workshop?"

"It will serve us well, I think, master. We have a month's more work to do, or that is my estimate."

"Indeed."

"And we are to have assistance?"

"On that subject . . ." He is about to say he is uncertain when they hear a tap, tap, tapping across the cobbles outside. In the doorway appears a striking figure, his face quite black, his smile radiant and generous, his body hunched, legs withered, and beneath his arms two crutches. He strikes Abel as a creature from Ovid, a centaur, yet instead of half man, half horse he is something like half spider. But Abel is disarmed in an instant by the candour of his expression; he can see some quality in the man which is neither pride nor shame, neither triumph nor defeat, nor even hope nor hopelessness but something like faith—faith that he will be given a hearing, at least.

"Good morning," Abel says to him in Turkish.

"Peace be upon you, my friends," says the man, who is not so old, under thirty at a guess. "My name is Naguib Ghalib."

"I have been told of you. This is my assistant." Abel gestures to Tom, who bows. "Tom Spurrell."

"Peace be upon you."

They stand awkwardly, wondering how to proceed. "I am told," says Abel, "that you have made clocks at the Mevlevihanesi?"

Ghalib smiles. "My fingers work," he says, raising them and making a little dance with them, "my eyes work," he says, opening them wide, "and this," he says, pointing to his temple, "my brain, it is sharper than any sword."

"Well, that is good to know," says Abel, wondering at the man before him, an intriguing blend of bravado and misfortune. He stands aside to encourage him to proceed into the workshop, where Tom pushes aside some boxes and finds a place for Ghalib to sit. "It would be good to learn something of your work, and of how you come to offer your services," says Abel.

Ghalib smiles patiently, points to his legs. "I am a poor dervish, for reasons that must be clear to you. The sheikh is kind, but they treat me now as if I were made of glass. I want to work, and to be worked hard. You may see the clock I have made at the

Mevlevihanesi, for it is in daily use. And I know of your work, Cloudesley, sir. I have read about your mechanical creatures and believe I can make them move and speak and write and"—he hesitates—"even reason."

Abel tells Tom what Ghalib has just said to him, translating from the Turkish.

"What is this Mevlevihanesi?" he asks Abel.

"It is the lodge, the school and place of worship of the dervishes. They are a most interesting sect, Tom. They believe profoundly in appreciating the beauty of the world and in poetry, meditation and dance."

"Not much like our Church of England, then?"

"Not exactly, no," he laughs.

"I should like to see his clocks," he says, gesturing to Ghalib.

"I show you," says Ghalib in English. "Come. Come now."

"You speak English?" asks Abel in surprise.

"A little," he says. "I learn more. Another reason, yes?" Ghalib gives him a look, almost a wink, leaving no doubt that he wishes to be a part of whatever endeavour it is they are about.

Abel is about to propose they visit the Mevlevihanesi the next day when Tom says, "I'll go with you, Mr. Ghalib. Let's go right away. Why not?"

Why not indeed, thinks Abel. He has other things he needs to do. Let this new, light, bright, confident Tom make this intriguing man's acquaintance. There will be no surer way of discovering whether he is to be trusted. A horse and trap are soon trundling off to Galata with the two of them, Ghalib pulling himself up on to the seat with arms of phenomenal strength.

Returning to his chamber, Abel works through the rest of his correspondence, reaching last the letter from Grace Morley.

Briar House
Tring
17 January 1761

Mr. Cloudesley sir,
I write with bitter regret to tell you that your investment in my hat shop is lost, since the shop burned to the ground, all because my shop girl Sally turned out to be a greedy and deceitful b——. It just goes to shew you never can tell what is going around in circles in the head of a young girl, or for that matter any other creature. Your two shillings a week I shall continue to pay, this amounting to four guineas and nineteen shillings a year, as agreed. Since I think it unwise to entrust gold coins to a postman, I am keeping the money in the kitchen here at Briar House. In the event of any mishap befalling me, I wish you to know that it is in a jar marked "goose fat" and if you open the lid thereof you will see nothing but goose fat, for it has a false bottom, and the coins sit beneath it. Your aunt pays me generously, and I will be able to settle your loan in full when next we meet, since I have no other expenses of late. Lady Pee-Bee can well afford her generosity, since I earn her a hundred times the sum I cost her, given her great incompetence in running her own affairs—oh you have no idea! I will not tell you how grievously she mismanaged the mines in Leicestershire, failing to invest in new water pumps and shewing a perfect indifference to the idleness of her managers

there. They are all now dismissed and replaced by honest hardworking men interviewed by Mr. Mendel, Reeve and myself, since between us we find good judgment through our many disagreements. Your aunt says she is weary of mines and money and, as she trusts us, she is happy to leave matters in our hands. What think you of that, sir? What if we were scoundrels! More than likely we would be, but that we happen not to be.

You will not need to be told that it was never my intention to live under the same roof as your late wife's aunt, since we never did see eye to eye, but she averts her gaze, as it were, and I cannot complain about my treatment from her, not for a moment. She has, in respect of my good self, been kind in her neglect and attentive in her distraction. It is a different matter when it comes to Leonora, in whom she invests much attention, as she does with your Zachary. She fills their heads with foolish notions, such as she is brimful with, but they are mostly harmless I think, being of the nature of women being in parliament and children not being made to work until they are above twelve and such nonsense and I am able to push her fancies back out their heads with sweet reason and exasperation. They have lessons each day with Mr. Mendel to put them on new paths, too. That Jewish gentleman is full of facts and knowledge but is very shy with me, I think for fear that I might find him in some way tempting, but he is too ailing a fellow for my tastes and, as I have made perfectly clear to all, there is not a man in the world I should wish to do more with than pass the time of day.

Your Zachary does well I should say, on the whole, all things considered. He will ever be an odd boy, I fear, but that is only to be expected with his aunt's influence and growing up surrounded by clocks and, I shouldn't wonder, having one eye is no help in that respect either. But he is a marvel with the reading and the writing and the reasoning, and if that should ever come in useful for him he will do all right I daresay. And now I have put an end to his aunt losing five hundred a year he will have an inheritance, too. Leonora has lost much of that savagery that once proved so unmanageable. She is quite worn out with all her learning, thanks be to God and Mr. Mendel.

Well, I have gone on a bit, I see. I trust you are happy in that plague-ridden oriental city. London is bad enough. I cannot conceive of what sort of a hell Constantinople must be.

I am, sir, your obedient servant and friend,

Mrs. Grace Morley

How strange, thinks Abel, that a letter should tell him almost nothing and yet at the same time almost everything.

Back at the workshop Tom is fired with excitement. "Oh, master!" he declares, "You never did see such a clock as Naguib has made. Here, here." He beckons him over to his working table, already ordered with tools and papers. "I have been making a drawing of what I saw." What Tom has drawn with his skilled hand is, indeed, remarkable—a clock face with four hands, pointing toward star positions, the place of the planets on given dates, a foretelling of floods and plagues, droughts and earthquakes.

"It is a rare thing, such a clock, and produced only by these ingenious dervish men," says Abel.

"It is a marvel."

"As is Mr. Ghalib," says Abel, wishing to encourage Tom's enthusiasm for his new friend.

"Oh, he is, isn't he?" says Tom.

"Well, tomorrow we should begin work on our task. Do you think Ghalib will be useful?"

"He has a computing mind. Every calculation he can complete in a moment, as I learned when presenting him with some problems we have faced with our sequencing, and he understood them with ease."

"There is a secrecy to what we are about, Tom—or, at least, I supposed there to be. Though it seems every man and woman in Constantinople has heard of it. Let us hope they have heard only of the horse and not of what the horse contains."

"Horse, sir?"

"I'm sorry, Tom. I am thinking of the Trojan horse."

"Oh, that one," he says dismissively. "I believe Naguib may be trusted, so long as we are to bring an end to war, not be the cause of it, which is what you have told me our task is truly about. He is a soldier for peace. That is what he said to me. I believe he may have lost family in some recent conflict, and he hates all violence."

"Well, yes," says Abel, feeling uncertain. "Yes, it is peace that we are working toward." He hopes it is true. As he is about to leave, Tom looks as though he wants to ask something. "What is it, Tom?"

"Do you think we might take a day or two to make this?" He holds out a piece of paper on which there is another of his drawings.

Abel inspects it but is baffled. It appears to be a chair, but instead of legs it bears wheels. "What is this, Tom?"

"It is a design for a wheeled chair. I believe we have all that we need here for me to make such a thing in just two or three days."

"A wheeled chair? I never did hear of such a thing."

"I have heard of one before, built for the King of Portugal or some such prince. But this is my invention, and I believe it would allow Naguib to propel himself about the workshop more readily. And perhaps beyond, too." His eyes are lit with some vision, presumably of Naguib Ghalib wheeling himself freely about the city at great speed.

Abel is conscious of the need to press on with work on the chess-playing automaton, yet he knows he must busy himself with replies to the correspondence he has received. "Oh, very well, Tom," he sighs. "Let's see how you get on with it, but we must attend to the chess player sooner rather than later if we are not to find ourselves winning the displeasure of our king's ministers."

Tom laughs, though whether in glee at the prospect of making his wheeled chair for Ghalib or at the preposterousness of upsetting the king's ministers Abel cannot say.

CHAPTER TEN

HIGH SUMMER

August 1761, Tring

She rises later and later, always feeling happier even than the day before. It is not a condition in which she ever expected to find herself. But the house is run as if by clockwork by Mrs. Morley, tickety-tock, and very little winding is required. The children will already be in their lessons with Mr. Mendel. After she has taken breakfast and ridden for an hour she will bring first Zachary from the schoolroom into the library for some political discussion or astronomical investigations, while Mr. Mendel teaches Leonora basic French and Latin, since she is well behind Zachary in all of that, and much else besides. Later Frances will return Zachary to Mendel for calculus or geology, and she will spend a happy hour with Leonora teaching her about gravity and how the circumference of the earth is measured. How the girl has bloomed. In less than a year she has grown serene and poised, her pale, blotchy skin and red hair, which once made her seem like nothing so much as a furious toadstool, having tempered into something altogether more promising—a hint of an Erato or Euterpe to come, or whichever of the muses it was who had red hair; Frances must reread her *Aeneid*. She has begun to think that Leonora might grow to take that same place in her affections that Alice once occupied—that of a beloved daughter.

Zachary is a very different proposition. It is not love that binds them together, but absolute possession: his thoughts are hers, hers his. She hardly needs to make a suggestion to him that he has not anticipated, and he makes his own wishes known without a word, yet she is ever ready to comply. He has a power, that boy, a force of will that is unarguable, yet is quiet and true. He is Alice's boy, most certainly, but he is more than that.

The Reverend Ratcliffe is due to call this afternoon, a tedium Frances generally avoids by absenting herself in her aviary or by going riding, but she has been preoccupied all morning in correspondence with Dr. Sam. Johnson, to whom she had sent five guineas on hearing from her friends at the Blue Stockings Society of his latest hardships and from whom she had today received a letter with which she disagreed in every particular, and now she finds herself too late to remove herself from the ordeal of Ratcliffe. Poor Ratcliffe. He tries his best, determined to make Zachary into a good Christian. She has no objection to Christ's teachings, none whatsoever. It is, as she explains to him, the Church she finds discouraging, since it seems devoid of both belief and purpose, and committed only to the propagation of damp hassocks and the overuse of chrysanthemums. "Well, if it's belief you want, Lady Peake-Barnes, go to the Catholic church. Or the Nonconformist chapel," averred Ratcliffe. "The whole point of the Church of England is to do what is expected of us without thinking too much about it. That is the English way, after all." She could not argue. He was not a foolish or unobservant man. It was why she thought the English, on the whole, a dull people and why she concerned herself more with French literature, the Greek classics and the stars.

After months of petitioning by Ratcliffe she has consented to Bible lessons once a week for the children. Mendel is made uneasy by theology, which is one of the reasons she thought him a suitable tutor, since any fool can teach belief. Facts, on the other hand, being so much more mutable in their nature, require intelligence and the subtlety of a mind open to novelty and doubt.

Ratcliffe is one of those men who feels the obligation to fill all peace with noise, for fear that his deeper thoughts might be audible in silence, not least to himself. He signals his arrival through the loud singing of hymns, intending to uplift but having the effect of making the very walls of Briar House groan with dismay. This morning it is "Awake, My Soul, and with the Sun." Frances would prefer it if he went straight to the schoolroom and commenced his Bible teaching, but he seems to think himself under some obligation to pay his respects to her first if she is caught, as today, at home. He is always accompanied by his two dogs, a pair of lawless spaniels called Rags and Pippy, who spend a happy hour chewing her rugs while Ratcliffe teaches the children about Paul's Epistle to the Colossians.

"My dear Lady Peake-Barnes."

She ceased to argue with him long ago. "Reverend, how are you today. Well, I trust?"

A simple yes would suffice, but never comes. "Ah yes, yes, wonderfully well, thank you, dear lady. The sunflowers are pointing their heads to heaven, the wheat in the fields turns its ears to the breeze and there is the powder blue of love-in-a-mist all along the road. What a world of perfection God has made for us."

"Yes . . ."

"My thoughts are turning to the harvest festival, madam. It is a wonderful time for the little ones. We shall have a fine display of pumpkins this year, if your neighbour Mr. Jepherson's efforts are to be rewarded as they deserve to be. I trust I can expect to see young Zachary and his dear little friend Leonora in your pew?"

"Manure, Reverend."

He reddens, scratches the top of his head and, absent-mindedly, removes his wig to scratch more effectively.

"The secret to Jepherson's gourds."

"Yes, yes. All God's creatures."

"Is it not a little early in the season to be thinking of the harvest festival?"

"I am a planner, Lady Peake-Barnes. There is a great solace to be found in planning."

"I daresay." She has no interest in the subject and still less in assisting him in small talk.

"Mrs. Margesson is possessed once again," he says cheerfully.

"Is it the devil this time, or her late husband?"

"Only the devil on this occasion, I'm pleased to say."

"She has asked for your services once more?"

"Yes," he says with a chuckle. "It is nonsense, of course, but I am obliged to do what is expected of me." His affability deserts him and a stricken look crosses his face before he lights up again with contrived jollity. "And so a casting-out of the devil it will be."

A heady smell of sulphur and rotten cabbage enters the room. Frances is unable to endure it.

"It is Rags," confesses Ratcliffe. "He has a tendency to go at the manure in Jepherson's vegetable patch. My apologies on his behalf."

"Ah yes," says Frances. "Well, I am sure the children are eager for their lesson, Reverend."

He gives her an expression of unconditional defeat and his head one more scratch. "That, madam, will never be the case, I know. But to each of us *our daily stage of duty run / Shake off dull sloth and joyful rise / To pay our morning sacrifice*, eh?"

She cannot bring herself to dislike the man.

Mendel has asked to be excused from his evening lessons. He has succumbed to a melancholy, such as often comes upon him on a Thursday. Frances takes the children for a walk since it is a fine afternoon and the fields are, as Ratcliffe maintained, full and uplifting. Leonora gambols along a little way ahead, plucking flowers and throwing them back over her shoulder with a care-lessness fitting for a seven-year-old liberated from learning. Her mother will scold her if her petticoats have grass stains on them or show signs of undue exposure to the outdoors and for this reason Frances keeps a set of clean clothes for her and makes sure she changes into them each evening before she is subjected to her daily maternal inspection at six o'clock. Mrs. Morley is punctual in this as in all else, interrogating her daughter closely on what she has learned that day, ever alert to signs of aberration in her education, most particularly for those unorthodoxies emanating from Frances herself.

Zachary has become somewhat preoccupied of late with his father. "Will Papa be sailing home soon, Franny?" he asks.

"Well now. That depends on whether he has completed his work there, Zachary."

"I see him sailing home."

"Good . . . good." She has spotted a white-tailed eagle, rare in these parts and more than capable of carrying off one of her owls.

"But weeping, broken and old."

She only half hears what he says. "Good, good." But then his words sort themselves into meaning and she turns to him with concern. "Really, Zachary, these are daydreams and signify nothing."

"They are not daydreams," he says, placidly. He is chewing on an ear of corn. "He will not tell me what his work is, or not properly. In his letters he says he is making a chess-playing clockwork man, but why would he go all the way there to make such a thing? He could have made that at home more easily, and had other men take it there in a ship."

"Yes, yes. Quite so. But it needs your father to operate it."

"An orangutan could be taught to operate such a machine." And with that he is off, clambering up a beech tree in parody of an orangutan, making Leonora whoop and clap with delight.

"Higher, Zack, higher!" shouts the girl.

Frances is not concerned, or not unduly. He has a good sense of how high he should climb and is never reckless. His accident taught him the price to be paid for incaution and he knows his limits, though his boundaries are wide, and she makes an effort to keep them so. He is a child who would fade rapidly if constrained; she has always known it.

"I have heard them say he has a woman there," shouts Zachary from his branch, "but it is not that, not that at all." Frances contemplates the boy in his blue coat and white stockings, knees green with moss, and no less does she regard the branch, its bark smooth and grey, stretching its fingers to its tips where a thousand green leaves rustle, darkening and glossy now as summer unwinds. She prefers the fresh beech leaves of May, light green and furry and full of promise. It will have been the cook, Mrs. Jopling, forever gossiping and speculating since that is her wont when she is not insensible with liquor, and more probably to Leonora than to Zachary himself, for Mrs. Jopling finds the boy unnerving. Nor would she ever repeat such tittle-tattle in the hearing of Mrs. Morley, who, for all her bluntness, is so much a devotee of Abel that she will not hear a bad word said of him. She turns to regard Leonora and sees that she is indeed the source, for her cheeks have reddened with shame.

Looking up at the tree, where he sits, swinging his legs twenty feet above, Frances says, "Your father is there to listen, Zachary. Or that is my supposition. He is there to report on what he sees and hears because Constantinople is the capital of a great and powerful empire and England, I am sorry to say, is at war with the whole wide world, or most of it." She sees no reason to deceive the child beyond what is necessary. And though Abel did not tell her precisely the nature of his mission, she knows more of it than Abel knows himself, Claxton having taken her into his confidence. Both were agreed that Zachary would be best left in her charge, without interference from a loving but essentially incapable father. She had urged Claxton to be firm in his resolve to get Abel to serve his master's purposes, and swiftly too, and had undertaken to perform her part in their bargain with no less rigour, for should Abel have once again resumed charge of his son he could hardly have been persuaded to accept the commission in Constantinople, however noble or ignoble it might be.

"And why is England at war, Franny?" demands Zachary from his perch.

Leonora comes to where Frances is standing looking up at the tree and lies flat on the grass by her feet, staring at the sky and giggling at what she regards as a ridiculous conversation.

"I have told you before why we are at war," says Frances to a branch, since the sun has sunk a little lower and now makes Zachary nothing but a shadowy outline.

"But Franny, though you have told me, you have not answered me."

"And so it will always be with this war, as with any war. We can tell each other the reasons for war, but we cannot answer the question of why go to war. Why does any land go to war against another, since war is always a certain calamity?"

He clambers down the tree with confidence. "You said last week it was all to do with Silesia."

"Did I so?"

"And the week before with Nova Scotia."

"It is that, too."

"And then again, all because of the Empress Maria Theresa, whom you like one week and loathe the next."

"She is a complicated figure."

"She is like you."

"I am not Austrian, I am not fat, or not very, and I most certainly do not hate the Jews."

"Why does the Empress of Austria hate the Jews?"

"Yes, why?" asks Leonora from her prone position, thinking she ought to join in the debate.

"Why does anyone hate someone they have never met? Let that be my lesson for you for today," says Frances, lifting Leonora to her feet and, having brushed her down, turning to Zachary and picking the moss and twigs from his coat. "Hate by all means, but never, ever hate anyone you have never met. And most certainly not an entire race of men. That is irrational. Can you imagine a fox hating every rabbit?"

"But they *do eat* rabbits, Auntie." Leonora has taken to calling Frances "Auntie." She cannot think when that began. It was not at her suggestion. She is not unhappy with the appellation but trusts it will not stand in the way of an even closer one in time.

"One rabbit at a time, Leonora. Foxes do not hate all rabbits. If they did they would be in a permanent and furious frenzy, much like English men and women who hate all the Scots, or empresses who hate Jews, or Protestant kings who hate Catholics."

"When the fox got into the chicken coop it was in a frenzy. It tore the heads off every one of them," says Leonora.

Zachary gives her a nod of approval. Sensing the argument is lost, Frances says, "Well, let us hope we are better than foxes. Or chickens, come to that."

As they walk back in the direction of Briar House, its red chimneys and the tops of the pillars of the aviary just visible above the full canopies of the trees, Zachary says, "Your error was to take such a poor example as a fox. However sound your premise, only one conclusion could follow."

"Sometimes, Zachary, you are insufferable."

He smiles at so complete a victory, before adding, thoughtfully, "It is not a daydream I had about Papa, Franny. I wish that it were."

Yes, she thinks, she has begun to wish his visions were nothing more than daydreams, too.

◙

CHAPTER ELEVEN

ENSNARED

May 1762, Constantinople (nine months later)

◙

It has gained quickly that notoriety that was intended for it, not only in Constantinople but far beyond, being reported even in the *Gentleman's Magazine*. They have developed a routine, Tom and Samuels and Naguib, placing the Duke of Derbyshire on a palanquin carried by two strong Circassians and making a parade to the house of the distinguished person who has demanded a demonstration of its prowess. Naguib rides the palanquin up front, his task to introduce the machine to the nobleman or merchant who has invited it into their home. Samuels ensures the Duke is not in any way molested while Tom makes a show of its abilities, making it nod its bewigged head, move its grey eyes, raise its arms and set up the pieces on the board with its neatly manicured fingers. They have given it a voice box, after much experimentation, enabling the Duke to make certain utterances, including *Good move* and *Now I have you* as well as *Check and Checkmate*. To ensure that no one can accuse the automaton of being a fraud, Tom opens up its works before each game so that its cogs and levers may be inspected, as they always are with great interest, for this is a machine of astonishing and unrivaled intricacy. There is sometimes an enquiry made as to the whereabouts

of Mr. Abel Cloudesley, which is answered thus: he is constructing a still more remarkable automaton in his workshop. He does
not enjoy seeing his creations at work, it is said, for fear they will
show those imperfections he knows them to possess. Mr. Cloudesley wishes to make in time a perfect clockwork replica of a
human being, possessed of speech and thought.

Mr. Cloudesley is, in fact, concealed in a compartment within
the Duke, a cushioned chamber hidden by mirrors, lit by a lamp
which expels its smoke through the Duke's hat. Within he has
a perfect replica of the board that sits before the Duke's unsee-
ing eyes and thus knows the position of each piece and, through
a pantograph and levers, full control of the Duke's hand movements. It is a matter of great shame to Tom and Naguib and Abel
that matters are ordered thus (Samuels is, of course, indifferent),
for the Duke is well able to play and win a simple game of chess
without its concealed puppeteer. But the point of the Duke is
to overhear all that is said in its presence and thus, even if the
machine were a more capable player, it would still need Abel
in its bowels to do the listening. To this end, Naguib and Tom
withdraw while the game is under way; Samuels, too, remaining
at some distance. There is a signal that can be given if Abel finds
himself in distress within his compartment, a grinding noise sug-
gestive of clockwork unraveling, which will prompt Samuels to
intervene in such an emergency, though none has yet arisen.

The Duke has played near to two hundred games so far, and
only once has it been bested, when Abel fell asleep within the
compartment during the second game of the night, and the poor
Duke was left to play its own simple moves. He must sit patient
within, even after his many hours of confinement, waiting until

they are safely returned to the workshop within the walls of the English Palace, when he is helped out by Tom and unfolds himself like a moth emerging from its cocoon, slow and deliberate and in some way miraculous. It is his habit to then drink a brandy or two with Tom, though Tom is already in a state of intoxication from the sights of whatever grand house they have just visited, and also from the triumph of the Duke, since he has long ago ceased to think of Abel as playing much part in its victory, or no more than, say, the liver plays in the operation of a man—that is, as an organ both essential and also wholly uninteresting so long as it performs its function. In his excitement he feels compelled to tell Abel all that he could not observe from his tight little velvet-lined box.

"We walked first through gardens that were full of pink roses of the heaviest scent. Did you catch a waft, master?"

"I could smell only my own stockings."

Tom laughs, as Abel intended him to. Abel has asked him many times to call him by his given name, since he regards Tom as his absolute equal, but he insists still on calling him master, saying it has become a habit as comfortable to him as pulling on his breeches and affixing his moustache each morning. "And then once we were within, the pasha was most gracious, as you must surely have heard, and offered us sherbet and sweetmeats and perfumed handkerchiefs. There was a huge portrait on the wall of the poor man when he was both handsome and young, with a dark beard and a hawk on his arm, and he wished to show it to us before the game commenced, as if he needed us to believe in his younger self as well as he who was before us."

"And was he not so young, then, this man I played tonight?"

"He was a bent old soul, toothless and cloudy of eye. Had you known how frail he was you might have allowed the Duke to lose for once."

"His voice was not that of an old man."

"He had a good strong voice, I agree. Naguib said, too, that he was gracious to him, as many are not, he being a Nubian and what with his infirmity and all, and the pasha asked about you and what new creature you were working on."

"What did Naguib tell him?"

"I don't know, master. But I believe he sometimes says you are working on a Medusa, with writhing clockwork snakes on her head and eyes that can turn a man to stone."

"Why on earth would I work on such a thing as that?" He takes a sip of his brandy and leans back in his seat. Unable to assuage his curiosity, he asks, "Does he really say so?"

Tom is flustered. "Well, I don't know. He told me he says such a thing, but now I wonder if he was teasing me. If a Nubian teases?"

"I see no reason for a Nubian either to do or not do any of the things any other person would do."

"Then perhaps he was teasing me about the Medusa"—he frowns—"or perhaps he does say it and teases others. Oh," he says, remembering something important, "the pasha this evening told us that he would like his senior wife to play the Duke, since she is a better player of the game than he."

Abel considers this. "That is an excellent invitation. To be within the women's quarters would permit the gathering of a good deal of useful intelligence. I've heard that the women of the city speak to each other more freely than the men and are often better informed of political developments than their husbands."

"But it would be indecent!" declares Tom, to Abel's surprise.

"Indecent? Really, Tom, you cannot mean it."

"You would be spying on women."

"I would only *hear* what they have to say, since I have no periscope."

"And besides, Naguib would not be permitted into the women's quarters, and nor would Samuels or I be."

"You could be, Tom, if you were to . . ."

"No!" he objects. "No, I am what I am, and cannot be two things."

Emboldened by the brandy, Abel says, "Are you not two things already?" He immediately regrets his words.

"If I am two things then you are many," bristles Tom.

"Am I so?" Their talk is good-natured in tone, more or less, but Abel knows there is hazard in it.

"You are good, but also bad, I think," says Tom, drinking down all his brandy in a gulp.

"Bad?" He maintains his smile.

"You tell us the work we do is for the good of bringing war to an end, but it is spying, and a spy is a low and cunning creature, whichever way you look at it. A weasel or a stoat or a snake or worse."

"What can I say but that you are right, Tom? Shall we desist, then? Shall we return to London?"

"No . . . no, I didn't mean that."

Abel can play this trump card against Tom whenever he chooses, for Tom has set up home with a young woman, Katerina, a sweet-natured and innocent tailoress, and Abel knows he will not sacrifice this happiness lightly. "Well, we should get some rest," he says, standing and stretching. "Tomorrow we are at last through the Sublime Porte, that high and mighty gate to the grand vizier's offices, and the Duke's opponent is the governor of the city, is he not?"

"Aye, he is."

"It is our foot in the door," says Abel, "or our *pied dans la porte*." His quip is unremarked upon. They have worked hard for this invitation, the four of them, building the Duke's reputation night after night, and he is exhausted. But to be so close to the seraglio, where he may overhear small talk not of trade or a new vessel in the harbour but of high politics and military planning, is the very purpose of all his efforts. It is not that he has forgotten the automaton is Carteret's scheme and forced upon him against his will, but like a condemned man obliged to sharpen the axe that will be used on his own neck, he is determined to make the blade quick and glinting. Besides, he cannot help himself from taking pride in the Duke and is reluctant to allow it to lose, as it would if he were not its lungs and heart; its brain. He is ashamed of it as well, of course; ashamed that it is a fraud, and no less ashamed that he is a spy, that low and cunning creature Tom described.

He returns to his quarters. He was given a whole wing of the sprawling English Palace at the time of the Porter family's departure, since it was to be several months before the new ambassador, Henry Grenville, arrived. The abundance of rooms, at first an embarrassment since it was only he and Samuels who needed lodgings, has proved convenient. The new ambassador, the Hon. Mr. Grenville, regards Abel and his automaton much as a man might regard the unfettered opinions of recently acquired in-laws—that is, with courteous disinterest, since he must accept them as a temporary inconvenience until such time as he can move them some hundreds of miles distant. Grenville, being another of Carteret's men, is not ignorant of Abel's mission, at least in its general terms, but he has made clear that he has no wish to be cognizant of the particulars.

The governor of Constantinople lives and works in the new buildings of the Sublime Porte, alongside the grand vizier and other high officials of the sultan. The acres of the Yeni Serai, or New Palace, which is called by most simply the seraglio, sit opposite, behind high walls and gates. The palanquin carrying the Duke makes its way into the building flanked by janissaries, or so Abel is told afterward, for all he can perceive is the dizzying journey and, once set down, the comments of those who encounter the Duke. Naguib's introduction is well polished, Tom's demonstration an assured routine. Once his own men have withdrawn, Abel hears conversations going on in the margins of the game, as he hoped. But these are arguments about how many bakers should be executed for short-weighting their customers. The governor seems a man inclined to the mercy of liberal beatings, but his advisers insist that the correct and traditional punishment is for the bakers to be hanged upon a meat hook in front of their shops. This debate rumbles on while the governor plays, every so often commanding his men to silence while he concentrates. He attempts to move his bishop in the manner of a knight, two squares forward and one to the side, causing Abel to direct the Duke to return the piece to its original square, and emit a blast of disapproval. This must have amused the governor, for on the next move he tries to remove

the Duke's queen without cause. This prompts Abel to make the
Duke sweep all of the pieces from the table.

A new game commences; this time the governor concentrat-
ing and playing a close game, requiring Abel's fixed attention for
the best part of two hours. It is a relief when, not long after midnight, he pulls the lever for the Duke to utter *Checkmate* and
feels himself lifted onto the palanquin and on his way back to
Pera. In the safety of the English Palace, Abel is told that the
grand vizier himself came to watch part of the second game, and
that Naguib heard him say on his way out of the room, where he
passed close to where he was waiting, that he would mention the
Duke's prowess to His Majesty the Sultan, who is known to enjoy
a game of chess and to be frustrated that he has yet to find an
opponent equal to his talents.

"At last," says Abel, too tired for his usual brandy.

The invitation arrives two days later, and the next afternoon the
party is on its way into the seraglio itself. There are many formalities as their small party, on this occasion accompanied by
Mr. Grenville, the ambassador, makes its way first through the
outer gate and into the courtyard beyond, then from the outer
to the middle and finally to the inner. Abel can hear courtesies
being offered, accepted, returned, and the washing of hands at
each gate. Also the sound of fountains and of soldiers parading,
of prayers being called, of Samuels—presumably finding himself
alone with the Duke—asking Abel whether he is comfortable.
Abel responds by making the Duke say *Good move*!

Nevertheless, by the time they are in the sultan's private
quarters he is in some degree discomposed. He has learned to

delay for many hours the moment when he might need to relieve himself but has a small pot for use in an emergency. A sound may be made by the Duke to cover the noise of micturition if needed. He very much hopes he will not have cause to use it when finally in the presence of the sultan.

There is a palpable sense of potency as the sultan enters, a hush, a ripple of power. Grenville makes his humble introduction to the sultan, which is accepted tersely. Naguib says a few words and they are accepted courteously. Then he and Tom and the ambassador are, as Abel expected, instructed to withdraw. Abel knows that Samuels will have been required to wait in the middle courtyard and will be far out of earshot. The game begins and the Duke loses two pawns and a bishop in the first six moves. The sultan expresses some exasperation at the Duke's poor play, and Abel knows he is going to have to concentrate hard. The grand vizier is present and begins to discuss the latest Austrian setbacks in the war, and whether the time is propitious for Turkey to declare against both Russia and Austria. The sultan sets out the disadvantages of action as he sees them, and Abel, taking the opportunity of the sultan's distraction, mounts an attack which puts the game on even terms. His eagerness to ensure the Duke is not dismissed for its poor game has the result of squandering his priceless opportunity to gather the intelligence for which the Duke was constructed in the first place, for now the sultan demands silence so that he can concentrate. In another forty minutes the game is over, the Duke declaring *Checkmate*. The sultan is dismayed, pacing the room and telling his grand vizier that he was certain he would be able to defeat the machine. To his horror he hears the sultan say, "It shall stay here."

The grand vizier tells him he thinks that will not be possible.

"Send the crippled Nubian and the queer-looking Frank on their way with the ambassador and the rest of the English party. Tell them they may have their Duke returned to them tomorrow night. In the meantime, I shall find a way to beat it. Now go, all of you!"

In desperation Abel pulls the chord that makes the clockwork grind and clank, his signal to Samuels, but he knows his action is desperate, futile; it will never be heard. The heavy doors of the sultan's chamber clatter shut for the night.

"Now then, Duke of Derbyshire," says the sultan, "I shall find your secrets, if need be, piece by piece, cog by cog and screw by screw."

PART TWO

CHAPTER TWELVE

ZACHARY FINDS A LETTER

July 1769, Tring (seven years later)

He works alongside Dawkins, the gardener, as he does on these long days of summer, taking comfort in the old man's labours, his grunts and grumbles, his tender encouragements to the fruit and vegetables and his mumbled imprecations to the weeds. It is hot, and Zachary has stripped off his shirt, his torso sheened with sweat.

"Now then, cucumbers, why do you curl so this year? There is a great pleasure to be had in the sight of a bold straight cucumber, and people are inclined to regard one such as you with contempt." Dawkins snaps the curly cucumber from its stem and throws it off into the hedge.

Zachary has been digging a new bed for winter planting. He has not noticed the dozens of butterflies that have landed on his back, drawn to it by the salt of his perspiration. They are mostly Mazarine blues, but one has caught the eye of Dawkins.

"Well I'll be, Zack, if you don't have the Duke of Burgundy sitting pretty there on your shoulder," says the old gardener, whose sight is not what it was.

Zachary twists his head to study the creature slowly beating its mottled brown wings by his ear. "No, Dawkins. It's a gatekeeper, *Pyronia tithonus*. See its dark eyes on its wings. A male."

The old man comes closer and squeezes his brow to gain finer focus. "Ah yes. So it is. I call it a hedge brown, that one."

"A hedge brown, yes. No Duke, but much the handsomer for that."

Dawkins laughs appreciatively and rests a hand on the youth's neck. "You're a great help to me, Zack, with the digging and the heavy labouring."

Zachary doesn't much like the feel of the old man's callouses on his skin, but his affection for him is too great to shrug him off. "It's good for me to work outside," he says, turning back to his trenches and taking up his spade.

Dawkins addresses a black currant bush with dismay. "Now, what are you doing with all those aphids on you?" Addressing the aphids, he says, "You buggering little bastards. Don't say you haven't been warned," and he wheezes away in the direction of a supply of white vinegar.

Zachary finds the physical labour of digging, planting and lifting soothing; it makes him forget himself for an hour or two and forget, too, his worries for the whereabouts of his papa. Franny has forgotten about him or, at least, consigned him to some deep, dark place in her memory where he is interred. Indeed, all seem to have done their utmost to neglect the memory of him, to perpetuate the tale that eventually found its way to them that Papa was seized and executed all those years ago. But Zachary hears his father whispering into his ear in his sleep, feels the faint beat of his heart and knows with absolute certainty that he is alive, half buried and smothered. He cannot explain how he feels to Franny, who disapproves of him talking of it, as she disapproves of so much. She tells him that he must accept the truth of it; that it is a tragedy, but tragedies are a part of life and now that Zach-ary is a man he must face up to them. Yet the tragedy is not his father's death but that he has been entombed undead and that no one will believe him when he tells them so. He and Franny have begun to quarrel endlessly, and when he is not working in the garden he goes for long walks, lost in his thoughts and some-times, finding it has grown dark in his wanderings, sleeping under a hedge for the night, returning to accept Franny's distressed fury with a shrug. During those hours and days of his rambling he sees and tastes nature as he never can in the grounds of Briar House or in the neat fields around Tring; he is absorbed by it, literally he thinks, becoming a thing natural once his boots are soaked with dew and his hair gauzy with seed. There is wilderness and wild-ness to be found in England—the vixen carrying her cubs in her mouth, the song thrush building her nest, the trees snapping in the wind, and there is no place better to sleep a dreamless sleep than in the dry, warm cavern made by the canopy of an old yew in a graveyard.

If he alarms or infuriates Franny with his disappearances, it is because he feels a compulsion to make himself hurt her, despite his love for her. Perhaps it is because he loves her that he must inflict pain, simply to make sure he is felt. There are reasons to loathe her, too: her affectations of learning, which is not so great as she thinks it to be; her strident opinions; her captive, unhappy owls; her obstinacy—her obstinacy most of all that she will not join him in his belief that his papa lives. That she caused Leonora and her mother to flee is something he cannot forgive, no less her inability to understand that Mr. Mendel was irreplaceable. Zachary had tried to impress upon her the matchless nature of the man, but she could not see it, breezily asserting after his swift burial that she would find a better, more suitable tutor. Was he rude to those pocket revolutionaries and doggerel poets she dragged to Tring? He supposes he was, but no more than any of them deserved for their brazenness in imagining they had something to teach him.

She was once willing to believe his convictions, since Franny always had a better understanding of his visions and foreshadowings than any other. They wrote, in those first years, to the ambassador in Constantinople, saying that they believed his assertion that Abel Cloudesley had been executed to be mistaken. Zachary received news from Tom Spurrell, conveying rumours of new automata being seen in the seraglio, machines capable of firing an arrow, shooting a rifle, spitting acid, creations both monstrous and fearful. Even if there had been no word of Master Abel himself, said Tom, he was surely the hidden hand behind such inventions. Along with the letters, Tom sent to Zachary, once a year, a new eye of gold and lapis lazuli, a little larger than the last, so that he always had one to fit.

Samuels had returned from Constantinople to Tring to run the household and take care of Dorcas, his mother now sadly demented and living in two rooms in the attic, and who persisted in brushing the floors every few minutes, resulting in carpets that were spotless but threadbare. Samuels, though he was Zachary's old friend, would tell him nothing of that fateful night when his father was seized, only that Mr. Cloudesley was surely too useful a man to the sultan to be let go, and encouraging Zachary to allow that to be his comfort and reassurance.

Zachary wrote to successive prime ministers on the matter: the Earl of Bute did not reply; George Grenville replied, but only to say that he was bound, with the greatest regret, to concur with his brother the ambassador's reports; Mr. Pitt, the Earl of Chatham, promised to have the matter of his father's incarceration investigated with vigour; the Duke of Grafton said that he had instructed the new ambassador, Mr. Murray (Henry Grenville having been recalled), to pursue enquiries with that delicacy and subtlety that was most likely to prove fruitful. Zachary asked Franny whether he might next write to the king, to which she had replied that, if writing to him, he had better include some proposal for the better propagation of turnips. Taking her at her word, Zachary suggested to His Majesty that fossilized dinosaur feces would prove an excellent source of fertilizer, but his proposal was not, perhaps, taken with the seriousness it deserved. Such is the burden geniuses have carried throughout the ages.

He does not speak anymore of his visions, since they provoke dismay or, worse, contempt. He cannot help but suffer them, since they are so often prompted by the simple act of skin touching skin. It is for this reason he tries to avoid all intimacies, though certain of them are unavoidable. Dawkins is a toucher, and Zachary is obliged to turn away from the old man's bestial visions and pretend they are unseen—flayed bodies hanging from hooks, their intestines spilling from gashed bellies; disembodied screams for mercy. Zachary does not know if these are things the old man has witnessed in his long life, or if they are simply his own dark imaginings.

Franny insists on taking a hold of his hand when she comes to sit beside him, interrogating him about his day or what books he has been reading or how his menagerie of llamas, zebras and ostriches fares. He devotes himself to his animals, which give him no troubling visions but, on the contrary, great comfort. He tries not to see into Franny's thoughts and does his utmost to end their conversation abruptly if they begin to spill out in his direction, for they comprise tiny, bloodied bodies lying on winding sheets, and a longing so deep it feels like a thousand drownings. She conceals her suffering, he knows, with all her excitements and exclamations, with her reckless riding and the shooting of innocent creatures, but he sees into her, much as he wishes he did not.

As for the Reverend Ratcliffe, who will insist on shaking Zachary's hand though he tries to sit far away from him or, when at church, to leave swiftly with a wave—his conscience is so tormented by visions of hell that it is hardly surprising he sings his hymns so loudly and constantly, presumably in the hope of drowning out his torments.

The only person he could ever tell about his visions and get a hearing, apart from Franny, the only person whose hand he could hold and feel as calmed as if stroking one of his llamas, was Leonora. But she is gone along with her mother nine months now, and there is no clue as to where. As to the why, he has no doubt that Franny's slow but certain appropriation of Leonora as her own became intolerable to Mrs. Morley, Franny always seeking to foster disharmony between Mrs. Morley and her daughter, insisting that Leonora call her *mama* not simply *aunt*, and promising her an inheritance if only her mother might consent to her unreasonable suggestions as to her status. He has hoped, ever since that day last October when Leonora disappeared, for a letter, some word. Anything.

Mr. Mendel always helped him to regard his visions as commonplace anxieties, seen more colourfully by him than by most, but not so different, and he told him that instead of letting them frighten him he should make them into whatever he wanted them to be. But Mr. Mendel is no more. That day not long after Mrs. Morley and Leonora's flight, when he'd said he had a terrible pain behind his eyes and could not see anything but black stars, Zachary had thought it was nothing more than his usual Thursday headache coming on, helping him to his bed in the pigeon loft and bringing him a bowl of warm chamomile tea, as he usually took when he had one of his attacks. When Zachary went back to him the next morning and found his tutor cold and unmoving in his bed he didn't know what to do, sitting beside him until Franny eventually came looking for the two of them. He'd said to her, "I do believe Mr. Mendel is in heaven, Franny," knowing he must say something, and that he should not cry, but this prompted his great-aunt to declare, "Mendel would not wish you to believe that, since he did not believe in it himself. Mr. Mendel is dead and we shall have to have him buried in the garden, since he was not a Christian, and in any case has no one to come to his funeral."

The house has fallen into a great disorder since Leonora and her mother left. Half the rooms are closed, the kitchen is able to produce little beyond soup and the occasional stew, the library is losing its books folio by folio to a legion of bibliophilic mice, the bedlinen has faded to a sullen grey, the windows are opaque, and the cries of the aviary have quietened to a lesser chorus. Even his animals have noticed the change, for the zebras bray, the ostriches flap and the llamas look on with more than their habitual contempt. Briar House, once so bright and full of life and happiness, has become a gloomy place, and though Zachary never thought he would wish to go away to school, he conceives an idea that it might be for the best.

He broaches the subject with Franny.

"School, school, school," she says, "school is a poor substitute for learning. It is a muddy puddle in which one might make a toe wet, but it hardly compares to a good, clear lake in which one might swim for half a mile and be invigorated."

He knows it best to follow her metaphor for a while, waiting until it collapses under its own contradictions. "But where is that lake, Franny?"

"I am close to securing a tutor for you whose intelligence is matched by her imagination. Someone who will not bore you, Zachary, for you are like Loki, capable of great things but also terrible destruction if you are allowed to ever grow restless."

He considers countering with a different Norse god, but decides to follow the simpler course. "I am sure I would not grow bored at school."

"Are you bored here?"

It is a challenge more than a question, he thinks, and he knows he must be politic. "Samuels has taught me how to bring a rabbit out of a hat, which is diverting, and Dawkins knows more about the propagation of artichokes than any man alive, I hazard, and now I, too, have that expertise. But . . ."

"And do we not anticipate the results of Captain Cook's measurement of the transit of Venus with great excitement?"

They await the results of Captain James Cook's observations, it is true. The watching took place in Tahiti last month and will be announced to the Royal Society in as little as another year. "Yes, Aunt," he says, wearily.

"And have we not written down our estimates of the distance of our planet to the sun and sealed them with wax, and are they not ready so that we may see how our calculations match those of the Royal Society's? I have them kept in my drawer."

"You have . . . we have." He offers her a shabby smile.

Frances, overcome by agitation, speaks quickly. "I cannot, will not, absolutely must not allow it, Zachary. There could be nothing—nothing worse. Nothing. Because those schools, which I know Ratcliffe has been encouraging you in the direction of—"

"It's not Ratcliffe—" The rector has mentioned the idea of school to him, but vaguely and, having mused aloud on his own unhappy experiences, less than persuasively.

"Don't interrupt!" interrupts his great-aunt. "Harrow, Eton . . . they will place you in peril. In great peril."

"I am not afraid of being bullied, if that is what—"

"I don't care about that!" she declares. "I know how it is. I am worldly. It is not that your flesh will be battered and your spirit tested, that must happen, one way or another, sooner or later. It is that your mind will be dulled, Zachary. You will face that great peril of falling into the clutches of the establishment, and it is that which I have endeavoured to keep you from because once that happens you will find yourself devoid of imagination no less than spirit. You will wish to conform . . . *conform* . . . and there is a great conformity in the graveyard, as you will have seen. The names are various, but the stones are not, nor the lichen that grows upon them. So do not conform, my dear, dear boy. Pray do not do that. You will become like the rest of them, that complacent Eton rabble who presume to rule over all society for no better reason than that they have been told they must."

When she is in a mood like this it is pointless to attempt to reason with her. "Very well," he says, "I look forward to the arrival of the tutor."

When she is out riding the next day, he goes to her desk in the ragged library, telling himself that he intends only to check that their predictions for the distance to the sun are there, waiting. He has 92,862,000 miles. If he knows Franny, she will have put it at slightly more. But he is not really seeking out those sealed papers. She leaves her correspondence in disorder, always. During Mrs. Morley's rule the library was regimented, unsoiled and benefiting from the ruthlessness of a methodical mind, and Franny's desk a picture of symmetry, but it has since tumbled into confusion. He hesitates to look through her letters, but she has said to him so often that secrecy is a debility, a form of feebleness, and that openness is akin to bravery, that he considers it an invitation. And one thing his great-aunt truly is, is brave. He goes through her letters, the business ones, the ones from her friends, her letters from the Royal Society, though he is uncertain what he is looking for, precisely. It is that he has had a vision of his papa hiding inside a sheet, sealed with wax, and so it is his father that he seeks, though he knows he cannot have found his way into a letter. There are two pieces of correspondence from countesses in different parts of France—invitations. He glances at them, wondering whether Frances is planning a trip abroad. Another catches his eye, for it is written in the clumsy hand of his old friend Tom Spurrell. How odd. Tom's letters are usually to him, not to his great-aunt. He hesitates, wondering if he truly wishes to discover some confession that he would rather be ignorant of. Bravery is for the brave, after all.

Lady Peake-Barnes
Tring
England
5 September 1768
By the hand of a friend

Dear Lady Peake-Barnes,
We have not been regular correspondents, and for that I offer
you my humble apologies, which I trust are accepted. You will
perchance have read my pitiable letters to Zachary, which I
send him together with his new eye each year. I am no letter-
writer, madam, as what is in your hand bears perfect testa-
ment, but I rely on your indulgence to read my epistle through
to the end.

Zachary is a polite young gentleman and has always been
good enough to answer me promptly and in such manner as
to make me acquainted with your household, or of his life in
it I should say, telling me of his menagerie and his tutor and
his friend Leonora. I remember Mrs. Morley and her daughter
from Leadenhall, and those happy days when we were all
together much as like a family. I will not here deny that Zach-
ary was an unusual child, but if that was true it must also be
agreed that he was a loveable one, at least to those who knew
him best. I was always possessed of the belief that I would one
day be of great service to him, since I hold myself responsible
for the terrible accident that befell him in the workshop when he
were but six years of age, since I was distracting his father at the
time he ran on to that peacock's rod, and I have faith that God
above will permit me to make some reparation for his lost eye.

If Zachary has been good enough to shew you my letters to him you will know that I have fashioned a sort of happiness here, though it is ever under the dark cloud of Master Abel's taking. I swore I should never leave this city until I could do so with my master, or else in the certain knowledge that the good man had most unjustly perished. And so I remain and here I trade in clocks, and have a clever business partner in Mr. Ghalib, who is a black man from Nubia who was once a whirling dervish until such time as his legs were withered by the paralysis. He is a man who loves God and the stars, and who has much ingeniousness with the clockwork. I have told Zachary something of my friend, but not what I am to tell you now, for reasons you will quickly apprehend.

Mr. Ghalib's sister was taken to be a slave or odalisque to the women of the harem some six months past. Such women have duties which may be genteel or indecent, subject to the whims of the place, the place being the seraglio, as the sultan's palace is known to all. Now, we have never known with certainty whether Master Abel lives or not, having received no definite report in either direction, and it is indubitably the case that no woman held in the harem, whether as concubine or odalisque, may send missives to those of us in the city beyond. Yet Mr. Ghalib's sister has found some means, I cannot say how. She knew of Master Abel from her brother, who was employed by him for some months before he was taken.

And so, at last, I come to my intelligence: it is that Master Abel is seen! He rides within a giant wheel, driven by steam, and this he does each morning before dawn, believing himself invisible. There is a stone lattice screen that hides the women of the harem and their servants from the courtyards of the palace, and this affords them the opportunity to observe without being witnessed. Mr. Ghalib's sister was, it seems, told of the performance each day of a lunatic, and in this way came to see for herself the riding of the man inside the wheel. But I do not believe Master Abel has taken leave of his senses. I believe he is calling out to his dear boy and hoping by some miracle to be heard, for he is calling out a name, and the name is Zachary!

I thought it best to impart to you this information, since it seemed to me wrong in some way to tell Zachary of it direct, for what good does it do him to know of his poor father calling his name in such manner without obvious recourse to his liberation? But I know you are, madam, a person of great resourcefulness and acquainted with the quality, and do not doubt that you shall conceive some plan to gain Mr. Cloudesley's emancipation, and of the right manner in which to inform the dear young gentleman of his father's present circumstances.

I am your faithful and humble correspondent,
Tom Spurrell Esquire

He observes, with a detached curiosity, that his hands are shaking and uncontrollable. Sometimes he feels like this, like two people separate though entwined; one a feeling, sensitive creature, full of emotions—whether pity, rage or, lately (and with a jolt), desire; the other cool, impassive, reasoning and unmoved by whatever this bundle of humours and jangling nerves submits itself to. His cooler self wonders how long the letter has sat there and concludes that it is most likely five months or so—not much more, and conceivably somewhat less, depending on the reliability of its courier. While the self that is now crying and pacing up and down and balling its fists and muttering oaths at his absent great-aunt does what it must, his other cooler self concludes the only thing which it can reasonably conclude: that he must take matters into his own hands; that the time has come to go to Constantinople. He will set out on foot, he decides, taking a mail coach when well clear of Tring and only purchasing a horse once in France, where he knows the price of mounts to be cheaper and thus saving himself the cost and difficulty of finding one familiar with transport by ship. His own dear Gullfaxi is a pony, and already strains to go any distance under his weight.

Leaving his raging self in the library, though that fellow soon follows, he goes to the kitchen, empty and cool at this time when cook has her morning sleep. He opens the goose-fat jar where he knows forty-five guineas sits, though he has no idea why Mrs. Morley failed to take her savings with her. Now the money will constitute a rescue fund for his father, and he thinks that fitting. Next, he goes to the gun cabinet and takes a small pistol from it; it has not been locked since Mrs. Morley left, depositing the keys that always hung at her waist on the kitchen table where they have remained, untouched, ever since. His great-aunt does not believe in the locking of things. Zachary knows how to fire all manner of guns, and calculates that he will have need of defence, and possibly attack, if he is not to be robbed or worse on his journey. He notes that his trembling self trembles still.

He will say nothing to Franny when she returns from her ride, and will make an effort to be courteous and malleable, he decides. He will ask her a few questions about the tutor she is attempting to engage for him and offer to replace the wooden pole that has half rotted away on the aviary. He considers what it is that he will write in the note he will leave for her, before deciding that it will be best to leave no note at all. She will not worry about him for a day or two, thinking he is off on one of his nature rambles. And by then he will be nearly at Dover. His other self, calmer now, tells him he is happy. Yes, he says, of course we are happy, for we are going on an adventure, and at the end of it, at last, will be our papa.

CHAPTER THIRTEEN

IN PURSUIT

August 1769, Tring

Had she been more attentive she would have noticed the letter sooner, left out of place on top of her "inaction" pile whereas she felt sure she had thrust it into the midst of her "in action" pile. She allows herself to be thought disorganized—careless, even, but there is order in her chaos, method in her haphazardry.

He has taken to disappearing for a night, sometimes two, and though she is always made anxious by his absences, she reminds herself of her views on the menace of boundaries and in this way convinces herself that it is healthy for Zachary to go wandering. It is, she thinks, conceivable that there's a girl he is pursuing out there somewhere, but she sees none of the signs of exultation that she would expect on his return from such a quest. He has been changing more quickly than she can keep pace with this past year, from that startling, odd, fiercely intelligent but devoted child into an almost-man, his voice alternating from soprano to basso profundo, his complexion perturbed by red spots, his moods unpredictable, and his manner generally unreasonable.

She looks again at the letter, rereads Tom's words, and wonders how she might explain herself if, as she suspects, Zachary has already read them for himself. *I could not tell you, Zachary, without you demanding that we leave the next day, and certain preparations must be made,* she will tell him. *It is why I have been writing to certain acquaintances with whom we might stay a night or two along the way. You are excitable,* she will say, *unreasonable.* He has taken blows this past year, though they have hit her every bit as hard as they have Zachary. He cannot see that through his haze of adolescent anger.

That Mrs. Morley and dearest Leonora should have vanished just a week before Mr. Mendel expired was almost beyond the bearing. Frances had always proceeded with caution when it came to Grace Morley, sensitive to how readily that proud woman misunderstood her every motive. In truth Frances had begun to grow a little afraid of her. Leonora, on the other hand, was a delight and her great consolation, all the more so since Zachary had sprouted truculence along with his wispy whiskers.

Her striving to find mother and daughter since their sudden and mysterious flit, on which she has expended much effort and money, foundered on the simple truth that no one knew a thing about Grace Morley—not her sisters, who had not heard from her in years; not Samuels or old Reeve or Dorcas, despite taking their supper with her every day since she had come to Briar House in sixty-one. It was almost as if she had planned matters thus, believing that one day she would need to vanish into an early-autumn mist, and vanish is just what she and Leonora did, into mist and as mist, leaving not a trace behind.

It is the manner in which the letter has been put into her disordered pile in an ordered way that tells her he must most certainly have found it and read it, and that his absence these past three days is not the result of his usual wanderings but a reaction to what he read. He has, she fears, hatched some plan, rash and reckless, and acted upon it with haste.

"Samuels!"

"Ma'am?" That barely perceptible smile, that ability to appear from behind a doorway as soon as summoned, like a jinni.

"Zachary is gone!"

"Gone. Is that so?" He is imperturbable, as always.

"But not on one of his rambles, Samuels. I believe he has left for . . . well, most likely for Constantinople."

"Yes. I expect so. He has taken the best pistol, and also forty-five guineas from Mrs. Morley's goose-fat jar."

Frances, infuriated that he has said nothing to her of any of this, says, "You knew he had gone?"

"I noticed his absence, madam, as you had."

"And you said nothing?"

He waits for her to conclude her accusation.

"When did you reach the conclusion that I have only just arrived at?"

"He will have set out on foot," he says, ignoring her question, "and after taken the mail coach from a town where he is not known. He may have made Canterbury by now and will most likely cross to France tomorrow." He almost-smiles again.

"Then we must set off immediately," declares Frances, pacing the room and taking a bite out of three plums in succession, not one of them to her liking. Samuels must accompany her, she knows, for his knowledge of Constantinople as much as anything else. But how infuriating he will be.

"We may depart tomorrow morning, my lady, when con-ditions will be more favourable for us. I shall have Mary pack your valise."

It is already close to sunset. Riding through the night would be idiocy, she knows. "Very well, very well." The thought that Zachary might be lost to her forever approaches her like a wave, submerging her. "Will we ever find him, Samuels?" she cries.

"We will," he says, perfectly serene, as if he has been waiting for this moment ever since his own return from Constantinople, as if he knows every moment of what is to follow, as a clock hand knows every fraction of an inch of its face.

They reach Dover in just two days. Frances takes a room in a lodg-ing house that is not wholly unrespectable on Snargate Street, sending Samuels out to the many small inns that preponderate in and around the port, seeking information about Zachary. When he returns, he is dazed with beer and his breath foully sweet from the stuff. She has never seen him drunk and hardly cares to ask him for his report, but he gives it unbidden, forming his words like clogs on ice, slithering this way and that, the sentences tum-bling before they are quite concluded.

"Therenever . . . they never . . . they've and they haven't seen such a lad as our Zack," he slurs.

"I see. Well, very well, Samuels, I think a good night's sleep will do you good," she says, wanting him out of the tiny parlour of her lodging house and doubting she can expect any coherence from him. He is not a drinking man. If he were he might have fared better on his mission.

"Yes, but, but, Lady Beak-Parnes . . . you see, there was a man seen with a patch over his eye, and with a black beard in the Castle Inn and the New Moghul."

"Well, that is not our boy."

"His voice was . . . hmmmm"—he sways and slumps into a chair. Looking up at her his smile is for once complete, almost beatific—"thing is, I had to . . . I had to go into all the alehouses to ask, since the first dozen drew me no . . . no . . . no . . ." He sleeps.

"You drank in all of them?" She prods at him with the poker from beside the fire. It is not hot.

Samuels awakens, not knowing where he is.

"You drank in all of them, I asked."

"A man cannot go into an alehouse and ask questions and not buy a pint. It is . . ." He waves a hand, pulls a face. "Indecent."

"And you were saying something to me of this man with a patch over an eye and a black beard."

"But with the voice of a young boy, see"—he belches, turns green—"despite his disguise, and so we have him."

"He is here?"

Samuels considers this, his brow furrowed, trying hard to make sense of the question. "Here?" he looks about the room. "No, he's not here."

"I know that, Samuels. But he is here in Dover?"

"I doubt it. It was two nights ago this man was seen. He will be as far as Arras now." He hiccups. "Arras, Arras. Arras is me," he declares and promptly passes out.

Knowing that she cannot have Samuels there all night, and that if she allows him to sleep he will be a dead weight, she tugs at him and shakes him until he stirs and, having no alternative, leads him to his own lodgings a hundred yards down the road, his arm draped about her shoulder. The Snargate Street Rooming House is rowdy, even at this late hour, and she is obliged to leave him sprawled at the doorway, trusting that someone will drag him inside to his bunk. She is solicited on her way back to her own rooms by a youngish man. Since she still carries the poker she resolves to hit him over the head with it when she reconsiders, given that he is a handsome sort of fellow, and instead merely brandishes it at him in a threatening manner, sufficient to make him withdraw his indecent proposal. Back in her room she takes some small satisfaction that, at her age, she might still be thought worth propositioning.

The next day they are at sea, a light westerly blowing sufficient to fill the sails and carry them along at a good rate of knots. She fully expects Samuels to be delicate and sheepish, but he has resumed his usual demeanour, inscrutable and entirely satisfied with himself. She did not like him drunk, but she likes him no more in this, his usual condition. She wonders if she will, in the course of their long journey, see that radiant smile once more, and whether it might be induced by anything less than four quarts of ale.

◙

CHAPTER FOURTEEN

MAKING AND LOSING FORTUNES

September 1769, Republic of Genoa

◙

It rains for the first four days in France, but he presses on as he knows he must, fearing he is pursued. He uses his black eyepatch and keeps his gold-and-lapis eye in a pouch hanging from a string around his neck, together with his guineas, knowing that if seen with his distinctive eye he will be easily remembered and trailed. His false beard, which he doubted had convinced anyone as well as he'd hoped, he dropped in the Strait of Dover, watching it float along by the side of the boat, caught in its current, as if it hadn't wanted to be cast off so thoughtlessly.

At Saint-Omer he uses nine of his guineas for the purchase of a horse, a well-bred dapple grey mare, three years old and going by the name of Bouillie. As he completes the purchase, a young man who has been watching him thoughtfully steps forward, lifts his hat, bows and introduces himself as Alexander Moffatt. "I heard your French, sir," he says in English, with an odd accent, French tinged with Scots, "and surmise you are an Englishman?"

Zachary ignores the man, adjusting the saddle and stirrups and readying himself to set off.

"Where are you bound for, sir?" asks Moffatt.

Zachary, now in the saddle and feeling in a position of greater authority, says, "I am heading far from here."

"I know the road to Paris well, and where brigands lurk by the side of the road. A solitary traveler makes easy pickings for them. You will be better with a traveling companion, I assure you."

"I thank you for your advice." He encourages Bouillie to move away, but she is slow to answer. Zachary is unsure of Moffatt and though he is friendly enough, there is an undercurrent of some troubling quality about him, even though he hardly has the manner of a rogue; with his pensive, almost dreamy air, straight nose, full lips and high forehead, he has more the air of a recently appointed country curate. He wears a coat of green velvet and his own horse, presumably just purchased, is a good-looking black stallion, about three years old.

"You imagine, perhaps," continues Moffatt, not failing to observe Zachary's suspicions, "that I wait all day long at the horse market until some poor fellow comes along I can rob, but I assure you that I was here today to sell a horse on behalf of my father. Isn't that right, Delmas?" he says, seeking corroboration from the horse trader, who gives it readily enough, though without showing any great affection for Moffatt. "My father was a forty-fiver, as you have perhaps guessed, so if you have a great distaste for Jacobites, I will understand why you should you not wish for my company."

"Your father was a rebel?" asks Zachary, suddenly intrigued.

"Aye, that he was. One of Prince Charlie's colonels, all the way to Derby and all the way back to Culloden."

"Culloden!" Zachary cannot conceal his interest.

"Here, I'll ride alongside you a little way and we can converse at least. There can be no harm in that. It is a pleasure to talk again in the tongue of my native land, if you will allow it."

"Your native land?"

"I consider Scotland my own country, and always will, as does my father, though I was born here in France. We Moffatts shall ever be exiles now, I fear."

There is a natural cordiality that comes with riding alongside a man on a warm late-summer's day, and they soon fall into easy conversation. Moffatt's strange accent has a rise and fall to it, the music of the French tongue put into English with an accompanying Scottish melody, and it is almost mesmerizing. He talks of his life in Paris, his father having started a business trading in furs from Canada after his retreat from Scotland but falling on hard times after the French defeats in Canada. "My family has suffered at the hands of the English, and will suffer more, I daresay," he concludes.

Zachary wonders for a moment whether Moffatt has sought him out only to wreak some manner of revenge on an Englishman, but his amiable manner belies that suspicion, and moreover he has had the grace to resist asking what misfortune befell his eye, unlike most strangers who feel obliged to enquire about the matter before they have even made their introductions. "What brought you today to Saint-Omer?" Zachary asks.

"My brother teaches here at the English Jesuit School. It is famous, though the larger part of it has moved now to Bruges. You have heard of it?"

"I am sorry to say I have not."

"You Anglicans look neither left nor right, only straight ahead, or down at your toes," says Moffatt, repeating a line he has been taught by others, Zachary suspects.

"I am not sure I am an Anglican, not really. My great-aunt thinks all religions are the domains of scoundrels."

"What, then, is the faith she holds?"

"Reason—only that. But come to think of it"—Zachary turns to smile at Moffatt, who meets his gaze so genially he is almost taken aback by it—"she is in many ways the most unreasonable woman you could wish to meet." Even though they have hardly made each other's acquaintance, Zachary very nearly confesses her latest outrage, but thinks better of talking of his father in far-off Constantinople and of Franny's failure to tell him of the letter from Tom.

"All women of strong opinion are unreasonable."

"But a man?" questions Zachary, made alert to casual denigration of womankind by both Aunt Franny's and Mrs. Morley's teachings alike, defence of their sex being the one area of concord between them.

"A man may hold strong opinions and be considered heroic, though it makes him no less unreasonable," laughs Moffatt.

The day is fair, and they ride along a good straight road, dappled with the shadow of leaves of tall plane trees, so arched it is almost as if they were in a long green tunnel.

Realizing that they have been riding together for an hour or more and he has failed to make his own introduction, Zachary raises his hat, gives a small bow from the saddle and says, "I have been remiss, sir. My name is Zachary Cloudesley."

"Cloudesley . . . Cloudesley? The name is familiar," muses Moffatt.

"Many people know of the admiral, Mr. Moffatt; he was but a very distant relative."

"Hmm. No, it is not that I'm thinking of."

"My father is a clockmaker, and also of automata. Perhaps . . ."

"Ah yes! Remarkable creations. I have heard of them and seen illustrations in the gazettes. A silver ship, sailing on a shining sea, I recall. So intricate, so lifelike. Your father must be a man of remarkable talents."

It is as if a key has been turned deep in Zachary's soul, unlocking a swell of emotions he cannot regulate, despite the fact he cannot quite recall a silver ship, though he supposes there must have been one. "I do not know if he is alive or dead, Mr. Moffatt," he says, fighting back tears, embarrassed by the failure to smother his emotions. "He was taken by the sultan in Constantinople some seven years ago and rumoured killed. But lately I have received intelligence and have some hope that he lives."

Moffatt draws up his horse short, obliging Zachary to do likewise. "You are surely not to tell me, Zachary Cloudesley, that you are bound for that far-off place?" There is a smile of disbelief on his agreeable face.

"I am," says Zachary, not in the least ashamed to confess it. He hadn't intended to tell the man so much, but Moffatt has disarmed him with his own frankness, and most especially with the recollection of his father's silver ship.

"Well now, that is quite the thing, quite the thing," says Moffatt. "I shall be able to give you lodgings in Paris, at least, and will make arrangements with others of my father's acquaintance with whom you may stay along the way—as far as Trieste, at least."

"Thank you, Mr. Moffatt, but it will not be . . ."

Moffatt raises a hand. "I will not countenance refusal."

It is not what Zachary had wanted, to be beholden to this man, however pleasant his company, or to anyone else. He had been relishing the freedom of the road, the liberation of needing to think only of himself, yet Alexander Moffatt's presence at his side is oddly comforting. He is conscious that he is appraised by his traveling companion from time to time, and Zachary in his turn glances at him when he thinks he is not to be noticed in doing so. He is five or six years older, he supposes, twenty or twenty-one, and seems a man wholly at ease with himself, whatever resentments he harbours against the English. It is a fine day and as evening approaches he knows he would in other circumstances sleep beneath a hedge, but supposes Moffatt will recommend an inn along the way and insist they stay in it. He will probably insist on paying, too, making Zachary feel like a child. It is a surprise, then, when Moffatt suggests a good place to rest the night beside a stream where a fire may be lit. He has a supply of ham and bread he bought in Saint-Omer and, sitting beside the fire in the enveloping darkness, taking sips from his flask of fiery whisky, Zachary finds it hard to resist the candour that such companionship coaxes from any man.

Moffatt tells Zachary that he has a sister in Paris, about to marry a count, though he is worried that her fiancé is dissolute, a drinker and a gambler and a frequenter of whorehouses. He gives Zachary an odd look. "Have you ever visited a whorehouse, Cloudesley?" he asks, his manner shifting into something more determined, like a man seeking to prise open a stubborn oyster.

Zachary reddens, looks down in embarrassment. To his surprise he feels Moffatt's finger on his chin, lifting his face gently so that their eyes lock. For a moment Zachary thinks he is to be kissed. It is the strangest sensation, a delicious turmoil, yet unaccountable. He can hardly submit to it. "I will take you to a whorehouse if you wish it. I know of a place where the girls are clean and quite exquisite. It's not good for a young man to be a virgin."

"I . . . I . . ." Zachary wonders whether he should deny the truth of his virginal condition, before saying, "I thank you for your kind offer, but I do not have time for brothels, I think, given my need to reach Constantinople before the worst of the winter."

Moffatt draws back a little. "Admirably said." He frowns, cocks his head to one side. "You have spoken of your father but have not mentioned your mother."

Zachary hesitates, fearing that if he says anything at all he will say too much. But the bread and ham in his belly and the whisky on his lips loosens his tongue. "My own mother died giving birth to me. My father and I must share the guilt of that equally. It sits between us, that great calamity, and is a heartbreak for us both—for me, because I never knew the love of my own mother, though I feel I carry it with me, every day. And for my father, well, he has lost that love he had, and I suppose I will always be a poor substitute for it."

He can hardly see Moffatt's face in the light from the dying fire, which barely illuminates his gentle features, his pale grey eyes, his dusty shirt, for he has laid his coat on the ground. He sees him piece by piece, in glimpses, having the impression in one moment that he is observed with sympathy, in the next that he has spoken too freely and caused amusement. Yet as he grows drowsy he has another impression still, as if he is observed as a hawk observes its prey—patient, sure and hungry.

The morning is dewy, and he wakes to hear the sound of Moffatt close by pissing loud and long. Seeing him stir, Moffatt says, shaking himself, "You had a troubled night, Master Cloudesley."

"How so?" His mouth is parched and rank, the whisky that was sweet when drunk now leaving a foul residue on his tongue.

"You were shouting out in your sleep—terrible things. I should hope a young man such as yourself has not witnessed the terrible abominations you talk of in your nightmares."

Zachary confesses uneasily to his visions, which are so often dark and bloody, and how they come about most readily when he holds the hand of another being, most particularly when he wears his artificial eye, which seems to give him sight not of the present or of anything visible, but only of tragedies and misfortunes. He expects Moffatt to listen doubtfully, to smile and offer words of bland reassurance, but he instead comes close to him, intrigued.

"Show me your hand," he says.

"No. I . . ."

"Come now, Master Cloudesley, I wish to demonstrate something that may be to your advantage."

Reluctantly he allows Moffatt to run a finger lightly down the lines of his palm, and as he does so he receives a jolt, a vision of something perilous, forming now into the shape of a dagger, but he casts this latest vision aside, eager to hear what Moffatt has to say. "I see you will have a long life, in happy union with another." Moffatt looks more carefully. "Your heart is full of love, but you have been lonely until now. Soon you will feel an abundance of devotion and give devotion in return. That is what your heartline says. I see no children on your lifeline but other creatures. That is odd. It is what one sometimes sees with farmers. Perhaps you are to become a farmer?"

"I doubt it."

"Mmm. I see, here"—he brushes a line on Zachary's palm lightly with a fingernail; his nails are dirty, broken, not the fingers of a gentleman—"that you will face several obstacles, and a misfortune awaits you, and will come soon."

"In Constantinople?"

"Very likely."

Zachary continues to look at the palm of his hand, wondering whether those lines can really say so much.

"I read palms, you see," says Moffatt, "it amuses the ladies, and the gentlemen no less."

Zachary still gazes at his hand, as if it might have more to tell him.

"Why do I tell you this?" asks Moffatt.

Zachary awaits his explanation.

"Two reasons. The first, to show you that I do believe there is more to the world than we can see with our eyes, or touch with our skin, and so you have no need to be ashamed of those visions you told me of, though I detect your unease. Second, to assure you that you may turn your visions to your advantage. I ask for gold to cross my palm when I tell fortunes," he gives a smile, almost coy. "I make a little game of it, but it makes people more likely to believe what you tell them if they have paid. And there is a way of speaking, somewhat vague, somewhat embroidered like a dowager's pillow, that makes what one says more convincing. Sometimes I cannot read the hand at all and must invent what I say, and so you might do the same. And let me tell you, Zachary"—he cuffs his shoulder playfully—"it is a fine instrument to deploy in the art of seduction." He twinkles, all the innocence of his kind face banished and replaced with something ravenous and ugly. "Show me your eye, will you? You have not worn it."

"No, I . . ."

"Is it uncomfortable?"

"No, I have worn it nearly all my life. Or not this one precisely," he says, reaching into the pouch around his neck where he has placed it, forgetting that he had not intended to show Moffatt. He puts the eye in its place, causing Moffatt to stagger back in theatrical amazement.

"You are transformed. That eye is something powerful, and whether or not it gives you these visions, you may most certainly use it to dazzle and amaze."

Zachary is disconcerted. "I thank you for your advice, Mr. Moffatt." Embarrassed, he wants to change the subject. "Now, I must wash my face in the stream below and suggest we set off in pursuit of breakfast. How far are we from Paris?"

Moffatt ponders the question too long. "Three more nights at our current progress, I would estimate. But I have been considering the matter, and you are no doubt keen to reach Constantinople before the winter snows set in?"

"Most certainly."

"Then Paris is not your most direct route. You should head instead for Reims."

Zachary has a map in his saddlebag, and he goes over to it and opens it. Reims makes more sense. How odd that Moffatt was full of plans for Paris and has relinquished them so easily. Still, it is for the best, he sees that. "I may ride on ahead, Mr. Moffatt, since our paths must soon part."

"Oh, I would not allow such a thing. As it happens I have business to attend to in Reims and the road south of here is lawless, I assure you. It is providential that you have a friend."

Zachary cannot rid himself of the suspicion that he is being used in some way, yet Moffatt seems so considerate that he cannot admit to his doubts.

At the next village Moffatt suggests to Zachary that he buy that day's provisions, which he does gladly, though he is conscious he is watched by his friend as he finds some smaller coin in his pocket for bread and cheese and cider. He notices that Moffatt is regarded with suspicion by the shopkeeper. "Are you known here, Mr. Moffatt?" he asks.

"I have come through this place on many an occasion. I am twice a year along this road on my way to see my brother, you understand."

"You are not greeted with affection, it seems."

Moffatt bats away the suggestion. "These are country people, Master Cloudesley, suspicious of strangers. You need must grow used to the sullenness of ill-bred folk if you are to make your way as far as you intend."

That night Moffatt leads them again to a good spot, sheltered under the boughs of wide oaks, the ground dry and with plenty of kindling for a fire. There is a stream for the horses to drink from, and small trees to tether them. Zachary would think it odd that a gentleman should be so familiar with sleeping out, but he realizes, somewhat to his surprise, that he has learned nothing of Moffatt's own prospects.

Around the fire that night Moffatt asks him many questions, seeking information about the size of his great-aunt's estate and her business interests. "She must be a woman of considerable wealth," he observes.

"Not so much, I think. I have never considered it."

"You are her only relation, and stand to inherit a great fortune, or so I surmise." He puts a hand to his chin in thought before taking a swig of cider from the jar, causing him to pull a face. Zachary has tasted it, and it is sour stuff.

"Mr. Moffatt, my aunt is as likely to leave her wealth to the moon as she is to me, I assure you. No, that makes her sound stupid, and she is anything but that. But to the Royal Society for the further investigation of the landscape of the moon—that she might."

Moffatt lies on his back beside the fire, staring up at that ill-mapped moon. "Ah well," he says, seemingly disappointed in Zachary's lack of ambition for himself.

Thinking he should learn a little more about Moffatt's present circumstances, Zachary asks him whether he has marriage plans for himself. "No, no. I shall never marry again."

"You have been married already?"

He laughs. "I am twenty-four years old, Cloudesley, old enough to have had three wives, but one was enough for me."

"What happened?"

"She left me, or I her. We were not suited, let us put it that way." He grows uneasy, and Zachary thinks it best not to press the matter.

There is no moon when he wakes with a start, Moffatt's face, glossed with sweat, close to his. At first he thinks his friend unwell, and as he stirs hears himself say, "Mr. Moffatt, what ails you?" It is only then that he sees the glint of steel. The knife has a long, sharp blade, its hilt of tartan.

"Lie still, Cloudesley," says Moffatt, drawing back, "and I shall cut the string of the pouch you keep about your neck and take what I need."

Zachary makes to stand, but Moffatt brings his boot down hard upon his chest.

"I bid you do as I say, my friend, or else you will leave me little choice but to slit your throat. I am experienced in the practice, as you might expect."

Zachary looks about, wondering where he has left his pistol.

"Your weapon is in your saddlebag. It is a good one but I have not taken it, since you may have need of it further on your travels. I wish you well, you see, and think you a splendid fellow for an Englishman, but I can make better use of those guineas you keep around your neck than you can."

"Are you so sure?" gasps Zachary.

"Take my advice and use your eye and those gifts you have to make your way. You are an oddity, and people will pay good money to have their future told, especially by a Polyphemus." He steps forward, cuts the string around Zachary's neck and backs away with the prize, still pointing the dagger—ready for Zachary should he choose to fight. Without lowering his guard, he reaches into the pocket and seems pleased with what he finds there, which is thirty-four gold coins and some small silver. He casually throws a handful at Zachary's feet. "You see, I am generous." He walks backward toward his horse.

As he puts a foot in the stirrup Zachary leaps forward, but Moffatt is an experienced horseman and gallops away faster than

Zachary can get to his saddlebag. He fires a shot after him, but in the dark his aim is blind.

There is a faint grey in the sky as Zachary walks disconsolately back to his rough bed. In the promise of dawn he goes down to the stream where Bouillie is tethered, calming her, since she has been unsettled by the shot. He checks his panniers and finds nothing missing. He is tempted to weep, to despair, but his other self tells him that he has escaped lightly, reminding him he still has a few guineas and that, for all that Moffatt was a rogue, his advice was sensible enough.

He rides on, the days becoming weeks, and knows that he is changed—wary, guarded, suspicious, but the better for it. He thinks of Moffatt from time to time, wondering how much of what he said was true and how much a fancy, and of the touch of his finger beneath his chin, and upon his hand.

When he reaches Genoa he sees he is down to almost his last sou. He has kept a guinea for Bouillie's feed and new shoes for her, since hers are well worn. He uses it to put her into stables and takes a room above for himself. With half of what he has left, and remembering Moffatt's advice, he buys a mirrored tent, such as he recalls seeing all those years ago in the Vauxhall Gardens; also, a table and two stools. He makes a sign in Latin, QUID ENIM VENI UT REVELES—"Discover what is to come." The next morning, in a light drizzle, he places it in the corner of a square, not far from the vegetable market. Only two come to see him that day. The first, an old woman, probably seeking shelter from the rain, places two soldi on his palm and, her head moving like a slow lizard, looks at him defiantly. He is uncertain that his visions will come when he wants them to instead of when he does not, but as he takes her hand he sees with startling clarity the old woman beating an old man over the head again and again with a large copper pan. Abruptly, he lets her gnarled fingers drop.

"Well?" she demands.

"I see that . . ." He hesitates, remembering what Moffatt told him: the art of soothsaying relies, above all, on ambivalence and imprecision. "I see that you will vanquish all who oppose you." His Italian is poor, and he offers a clumsy approximation of the language, but seems understood.

She nods slowly, the leathery wrinkles of her neck following her chin hesitatingly. "And who is it that will oppose me?" she asks, slyly.

Disliking the woman, even considering her malign, and deciding he wants her out of his tent even if she is his only customer of the day, he says, "Your husband."

She gurgles with malevolent glee. "He is dead these past five years."

Emboldened by what he has seen and his strong sense of repugnance, Zachary declares, "And you murdered him with the copper pan!"

Her eyes widen and she leaps to her feet, her mouth falling open to reveal three broken teeth, two below and one above, and a small grey tongue, moving up and down like a parrot's, but devoid of speech. She flees.

He has, he supposes, seen something true. The past, then, not the future, but a secret all the same.

As he is about to take down his sodden tent, anticipating a night without bread or soup, since he knows that he needs to save what he has for Bouillie's oats and four new shoes, a young woman stumbles in. He hardly needs his special eye to see that she is nervous, squinting this way and that, her breaths rapid, her distress telling him not only of her unhappiness but the nature of it. She is, perhaps, seventeen, an odd blend of fragility and strength, not beautiful, her eyes set too close together, her nose long, her mouth thin, yet neither is she ugly. He can sense, this time without the touch of a hand or the use of his eye, that she is already familiar with misery, and is expecting a good deal more of it to come.

"Good afternoon," he says.

She regards him with amazement, as if she had hardly expected him to speak.

"You tell the future?"

He dips his head. He does not know the answer to that question truthfully, but he offers a reply. "I see things that may or may not be of service."

Looking about her as if she expects to be chased, she sits uneasily on the stool before his table and places three soldi in his palm.

"Just one," he says, already feeling pity for her.

As soon as he holds her hand he tastes salt, and is struck with the force of a blow, having the sense that he cannot take another breath. He hears her name called out, and the feeling of sinking into darkness.

"What is it?" says the young woman, knowing he has felt her affliction.

He cannot tell her it is a drowning. "Marietta," he says, repeating the name he heard, "there is water between you now. So much of it, too."

"Yes," she says, "and I don't know when he'll return."

I am only fifteen, Zachary tells himself. How can I know what to say to this woman, to her feelings, her hopes? You are only fifteen, the other Zachary tells himself, but you are clever, and you need to make some money in this city. Find the words that will mean whatever it is she needs to hear. He swallows. "He tells you not to wait for him. That his journey is a long one, and the oceans are as deep as they are wide, and that he wants you to be happy, that is what he asks for."

She cries, of course, because she believes in him. He knows her name, he knows that her loved one has gone to sea and she's haunted by the fear that he has drowned. She places a hand on her belly and Zachary understands all.

The next morning when he returns there is a queue of women waiting outside his tent, most wanting to know of men who have gone to sea and not returned. When he takes the hand of the first, he sees a man lying in the arms of two women in a wide bed, disheveled with lovemaking, and hears a name—Giuseppe. He tells her that Giuseppe is protected and well thought of, and the woman tells him that is just what she was afraid of, but nonetheless leaves satisfied.

He is busy all that day. Some of the women, when he sees into their thoughts, have surprising fears and worries. One seems to see nothing but squawking geese before her, and he tells her that her flock will prosper; from another it is flames, and to her he says that from the ashes new growth will rise. It is tiring work, but he becomes more and more easy with it; there is a fluency that comes with practice, as with any language. As he packs away his tent, he has almost a hundred soldi; enough to allow him to move on. A man approaches, a solemn fellow in a hat and leather jerkin. He bows, introduces himself as the city superintendent of markets and asks for Zachary's license.

"License?"

The superintendent suppresses a satisfied chuckle. "You surely have a license?"

"I am sorry to say I have not. But is there some manner of . . ."

"There is no manner of, no. There is a fine, which must be paid at the city hall. You may pay it tomorrow morning. In the meantime, you will spend a night in the gaol."

"But—"

"There is no but either, young man." He beckons Zachary to follow him, making no effort to help him with his tent, heavy with the slow rain that has fallen, or his table and stools, and Zachary struggles along behind him.

"How much is the fine, sir?" he asks.

"A hundred soldi."

After a night in the city cells shared with a drunk, a madman and an overly friendly thief, all of whom Zachary entertained with some of the tricks he had learned from Samuels, knowing that it was better to ingratiate himself for fear they might otherwise attempt to ingratiate themselves with him, he collects Bouillie from her stables, pays for her keep and his own lodgings with the last of his money, the fine paid from his earnings the day before, and rides on, bracing himself for the hunger to come and thankful it is late September, and there is no shortage of apples to steal from the trees. As he rides, he reflects on his experience as soothsayer, marveling at and unsettled by the visions he has seen in equal measure. He assures himself that all he does is tell people what they are already thinking, fearing, plotting, remembering. It is nothing, really. A trifle. Yet a man's thoughts should be his alone, the one and only thing we possess when everything else is gone. To be able to reach into a head and take them, as easily as apples hanging from a low branch, is a crime both wrong and irresistible.

Three days later, having decided to see something of Tuscany on his way, he reaches Lucca, a town so inviting he barely needs to think about what to do. Riding through one of its many magnificent gates, he stables Bouillie and sets about earning some money, checking first on the requirements for licenses. He is told by a stallholder selling live chickens that he should do what they all do and bribe the overseer with a quattrino if he comes on his rounds, this being unlikely since he was well bribed last week and is at rest.

He takes the eye from his pocket and puts it in its place. A trickle of customers come that first day, old women wanting to know if their husbands have messages for them from where they lie in their graves, young ones wishing for a husband. Zachary already has certain phrases he relies on; he has had much time to think and plan as he rides. It helps that he can usually sense a name, easily discerned in the restless conscience of whomsoever sits opposite him. "Your husband, Federico, is at peace. He wants you to know that his love is as strong as ever." Sometimes he sees children, normally ones who are a source of anxiety. "He says you are not to worry about your daughter. That she will find good sense and settle." Other times there is a troublesome neighbour. "Signora Andreotti will be trampled by a horse next week." He cannot see such a thing, only that Signora Andreotti frightens his customer with her constant harangues. The promise of a painful death for her tormentor sends her away entirely reassured.

For some reason it is always the person who comes last who is most troubling. Today it is a young man, a year or two older than Zachary, dressed in fine clothes, who wishes to know what his future holds. Zachary takes his hand, the youth's fearful, deep, dark eyes on his own. For a moment he forgets his task, so entranced is he by those eyes, by the dark curly hair, the full lips. Surprised, for it is the same sensation he felt with Moffatt, he pulls his hand away. "What do you see?" says the young man in alarm.

"Forgive me. Let me try again," says Zachary. This time he sees it: blood, broken flesh, horses, the sound of gunfire. This boy is to go to war, and is afraid that he is to be sent into battle. Zachary keeps his hand where it is, tries to feel for something more—and there it is: a canvas, brushes, paints, a model before him. He cannot sense a name, no hint of one. "Your father wants to send you to the army, but you will be a painter, and a fine one, renowned through-out Europe. You must go to a city where you are unknown, and pursue your talent," he says. He can't be sure where his words come from, but they are the right ones, the youth's face lighting with the conviction that what he has just heard matches his own intentions.

"Which city?" he asks, already standing, readying to leave.

Rome is the obvious answer, Zachary supposes, and so he says, for his own entertainment, "Naples, for the southern light."

At the end of the day he has earned a hundred and twenty quattrini. A good haul, he thinks. He will spend another day in the square, and afterward continue with his journey, it still being many weeks to Constantinople if he is lucky with the weather and Bouillie doesn't lame. He finds his fortune-telling, however tempting, exhausting, and doesn't want to have to do much more of it. There is a danger in it, he knows—of making a mistake, of being exposed. It is mind-reading of some order, that he has come to understand. How odd, then, that the boy would not reveal his name. And odder still how Zachary felt about him, feels still. He is there before him, even as he falls into sleep.

The next day he has a queue waiting for his prognostications, this time mainly young men—friends of the beautiful youth, he supposes. The city is filled with the sons of fathers who wish to send them to war. He is just about to take the hand of his first customer, a wistful-looking, frail young man, so thin he could slip through the crack in a closed door, when he hears a great commotion beyond the flapping mouth of the tent.

"Passare, passare! Stara da parta. Fammi passare!" He has no need of his golden eye to know who it is making such loud exclamations in her execrable Italian. He had expected this, perhaps even willed it. Aunt Frances bustles into his tent, casting a disparaging eye at the youth before him, and declares, "Zachary! I have you at last!"

He stands, bows, apologizes to his customer and, without further acknowledgement of his great-aunt, takes down the sign QUID ENIM VENI UT REVELES. He knows what is to come for the rest of his journey and that his solo adventure is at an end, for the present. He accepts the inevitability of it calmly, for all of a sudden he feels very, very tired.

CHAPTER FIFTEEN

A CAPTIVE CRY

September 1769, Constantinople

◙

After his discovery by the sultan those many years ago, Abel was given a choice: death by strangulation that night, or a life of service. His decision was not an easy one, Abel being more inclined in death's direction, since he expected the life that awaited him to be worse than death itself. Only the thought of Zachary, the faint possibility that he might one day see his son again, decided him in favour of survival.

Having chosen the existence of a slave, his first instructions were to construct an automaton that would fire a rifle and wield a sword. He began labouring on his task with a nervousness as great as his reluctance. To his surprise he found himself left alone for much of the time. He was given quarters—a barn-like workshop with tools and materials and, above it, a simple chamber with a bed, his meals brought to him by silent servants. Free to wander about the palace, the guards and servants shrinking from him, not meeting his eye or responding to any word he uttered, he began to learn the topography of the place, its hidden corners, its battlements, its wide courtyards, its kitchens and storerooms. If he came to a door that he was not permitted to pass it did not yield, and in this way he found the measure of his new province. It was, he thought, much like being shipwrecked on a desert island, yet he was no Robinson Crusoe, stranded and alone, but surrounded by all manner of human creatures, black, white, brown; giants and imps; men and those half-men known as eunuchs. No women, for they were hidden away from him behind doors that were always locked. There was, though, the hint of a woman from time to time, from beyond a latticed screen or high window, a gentle voice, a burst of laughter, a sigh. Yet he slowly began to believe that he could not be heard or seen by any creature—that he was invisible to all. Perhaps he had chosen death after all, and was now a ghost, though surely, he reasoned, a ghost would be able to pass through even locked doors to take what pleasure a spirit might in forbidden places.

His orders were given to him by a strange, squat, old eunuch who arrived in his workshop accompanied by several servants of dwarfish dimension, presumably chosen because they made the eunuch feel tall. His face had the quality of a wrinkled aubergine, his two bloodshot eyes peering out at a world that it was evident he owned absolutely. He bore, at all times, a smile as broad as it was unfriendly. It was only sometime later that Abel learned that his daily visitor was none other than the kizlar agha, the Chief Black Eunuch, all-powerful within the walls of the seraglio, the sultan's chief adviser, ruling over every aspect of the daily life of the palace on the sultan's behalf as his trusted deputy, reputed to have power even over the appointment and dismissal of grand viziers.

In his second month, conscious that he could not meet the orders being demanded of him, he asked the kizlar agha whether he might be given assistance. Could Tom and Naguib be sent for to help him? He might as well have been Hades asking Zeus and Poseidon to join him in the underworld. As reward for his impertinence, he was locked in a dark, damp cell for a month. When he emerged, weak and half starved, the kizlar agha explained to him, patiently and quietly, his menacing smile fixed, the impossibility of anyone from his past life ever knowing him or imagining that he was still alive. This, then, was his punishment for his attempt to spy on the sultan: to live in limbo, waiting for his entrance to hell but never quite being admitted into its furnaces. He was given no news from the world beyond, apart from being told in the early summer of the year after his capture that Lord Carteret had died that January. He had never held expectations of rescue by his old tormentor, but it was thoughtful of the kizlar agha to ensure they were dashed so conclusively.

After his punishment, Abel was once again supplied with good food and wine in his quarters and encouraged to resume his labours. One morning, early, when he was in his workshop, two eunuchs, one tall, thin and with the appearance of a Bulgarian, the other short, fat and hairless, an Egyptian, presented themselves at the door to his workshop. "We are to help you," said the Bulgarian, in Turkish. "Though we do not know what it is that we have done wrong," added the Egyptian.

Abel understood that, having been made to suffer, he might then be rewarded. "What are your names?" he asked.

"We are not to tell you our names," they replied, in unison, "since a name signifies nothing, and you are not to tell us yours."

"Then I shall call you Number One and Number Two, and since you," he said to the Bulgarian, "came through the door first, you are Number One, and you," he informed the Egyptian, "shall be Number Two." The Egyptian seeming dissatisfied with his appellation, Abel offered him reassurance. "If names signify nothing, then a number can signify nothing more—and you may call me Number Three."

Over the months that followed he came to understand that these two unfortunates had been assigned to him less because they were intelligent and willing to work under his direction than for their reliability in reporting anything he might say to the kizlar agha. Number One was most certainly not to be trusted with any confidence. But as time went on, he and Number Two seemed to reach an understanding, the hairless Egyptian being happy enough to talk of matters other than the mechanisms on which they worked together, informing him that the wizened man who governed all their lives was the kizlar agha, telling him something of his many infamies, and when Number One was out of the workshop Abel came to learn of the horrors of Number Two's own enslavement and mutilation. In his turn Abel told him something of his life in England, of Zachary and Tom and Naguib.

He felt, in those first years of his captivity, like a long clock that, its pendulum swinging, did not have the power to stop its hands from marking off the hours or the days. He even found some comfort in the making of his mechanisms—not the ones the sultan demanded, which were monstrous, but others that he made as entertainments at first for himself, but which soon caught the kizlar agha's eye and amused him enough that he was permitted to continue with their manufacture.

He thought he should keep a diary of his son's imagined life, and it gave him a measure of comfort, this memoir of nothing in particular. As he wrote he remembered that Zachary had a tutor, Mr. Mendel, and a menagerie, and a fascination for all crea-tures. He could not remember his son having a friend and so he gave him one, and a troublesome one at that, since friends were so often troublesome. He remembered that he'd had a friend, George Claxton, but he'd not been a very fine one, though he had almost forgotten his reasons for thinking so. In this invented version of Zachary's life, his son had two eyes.

In the middle of that second year of his incarceration, Abel was ready to present the soldier-automaton the sultan had demanded. The monster could stand from a sitting position, raise its weapon and fire it, but Abel and Number Two, with whom he found he could share all his doubts and dreams and trust that they would be reciprocated, had secretly introduced certain faults, ensuring that it would always misfire, aiming too high or low to kill or maim. It had occurred to Abel during its slow manufacture that he was in all probability constructing his own executioner, though that was not his only reason for making the machine harmless. He had thought long and hard about the moral purpose of an automaton that would kill a human and concluded it would be an aberration, an outrage, something that would tear at the very fabric of the universe. Guns and cannon were terrible enough, but they were fired by men, possessed of human failings. A clockwork creature had none, and so must never be permitted to do harm. He had tried to explain as much to the kizlar agha, who had lately come to share a glass of sweet wine with him in the evenings, and the old eunuch had nodded, smiling his wide and empty smile.

A small and macabre ceremony of presentation was organized by the kizlar agha for the soldier-automaton's first appearance outside the workshop. A janissary, accused of stealing from his fellow soldiers, was brought into the middle courtyard and made to stand in the flawed mechanism's line of fire. The soldier, defiant, straight-backed, proud, his demeanour more than sufficient to inform the small crowd gathered before him that he had been falsely accused, caught first Abel's eye and then the vacant glass eye of the automaton, and stared at it fixedly, as if to dare the fiendish machine to do its worst. Abel, instructed to commence the mechanism, did as he was told while praying fervently for it to fail. The creature, despite the defects Abel had built into it, caused some injury to its poor victim, grazing his cheek and drawing blood.

The sultan, from his curtained throne, declared with brief dissatisfaction, "It stands, it fires. Now it must learn to kill."

Not long after Abel began to experience strange dreams of tall crows carrying him into the sky, from which he could see Constantinople laid out below and made entirely from aspic. In the daytime, too, he began to have such dreams and visions, of dancing mushrooms and singing plates. His tools insisted on whispering to him, telling him he was the devil and must do devilish things. He slept sometimes for two or three days, and then at other times did not sleep for a week, but feverishly made all manner of automata. Number One and Number Two came less and less often and soon ceased to assist him at all. He dreamt that he made a machine that could kill, and witnessed it blowing the hearts out of man after man, the sultan cheering it on. He dreamt his automaton raised its gun and fired at his own son. All he needed to do to save him was call out his name, yet he could not remember it.

Soon after he began to experiment with different drives, ever more powerful. Clockwork was not enough, he began to understand. He needed steam. He was a clock himself, running too slow or fast, losing time or gaining it. He forgot his own name, how he'd come to be in this place, what crime he had committed. Perhaps he'd always been here, born in the seraglio, with a screwdriver in his hand and an eyeglass in his eye. Only one word kept repeating itself in his head and yet he could not hear it, though he knew it to be the name of his child.

Steam. He kept making bigger and bigger creatures, for condensing boilers were large, and needed space, and still there was none small enough to sit inside an automaton and drive it. Explosions reverberated across the seraglio and beyond the walls of the palace, out into the streets of the old city, heard by citizens familiar enough with detonations in the imperial magazine. The time came when Abel found he could not hear the blasts anymore, or anything very much at all but a high buzzing in his ears, as if a bee were caught inside his head, flying constantly from one side of its small domain to the other, yet finding no way out. He began to think of the sound as his own prisoner, his head as a prison, in turn within another prison. But still he ate, he slept, he woke, he pissed, he built his machines, though he gave up on steam and no longer strayed from the consolations of clockwork. A man came to visit him one day, a hairless, short man whom he thought familiar in some way and who presented him with an ear trumpet.

"What year is it?" asked Abel.

"It is 1179," said the man.

"Ah yes, then I must be waiting to be born, since I came into this world in the year of our Lord 1725. I understand too well that this is not life at all but some condition that precedes it. How odd, though, that I should have a birthday."

"You were born forty years ago, Number Three, or so you told me." The man's tone is gentle, almost that of a friend, though Abel cannot recall ever having had one.

"Did I so? And my name is Number Three?"

"The year in the Frankish calendar is 1765."

"Oh?" said Abel, confused by the absurdity of affixing labels to such things as stars or hours, years or people. Only the bee inside his head was real. He thought if someone were to cut open his skull, they would find it filled with honeycomb.

He remembered he had a son and wondered what life he was leading and whether he ever thought about his father with a head full of bees, or a single bee, at least. "I have a son, but I don't know his name," said Abel to this man who called himself Number Two.

"He is called Zachary," he said. Oddly, he was crying.

Since Abel has become so deaf and has the buzzing in his head all the while, the Chief Black Eunuch brings his mouth close to his ear when he comes to share a glass of wine in the evenings, so close that Abel can feel the heat and moisture of his breath, smell the decay of his molars, half concealed by cloves, as the old man grumbles on in his oddly mannered yet perfect Turkish.

Abel cannot say why the idea of his rotating wheel has taken possession of him. It was in the course of his experiments with steam combustion that he found that a wheel might be turned serviceably through the use of a boiler and condenser and piston, but the wheel was so damnably big—so big, in fact, that he could sit within it. He sets about constructing one so large it might sit upon a very majestic carriage, and a cage within it, suspended by an axle, in which he may sit. He rides the wheel in the hour before dawn around the ample circumference of the middle courtyard. The night guard is always but a few men, since that wide space sits secure right in the heart of the palace, and it is said they have only eyes to see and ears to hear, but no tongues to talk, for the comings and goings into the sultan's quarters may be observed from there, and no living being is to speak of what passes through the night.

Unremarked upon, then, if not quite unobserved, Abel Cloudesley, once clockmaker, once father, once Englishman, once living and now not quite dead, rides his steam wheel in the hour before dawn, year after year after year, hearing the bee inside his head and hollering and singing for freedom, for love, but most of all crying out for his son, for Zachary, whose name he knows now and will never again forget.

◙

CHAPTER SIXTEEN

THE UNREASONABLE

January 1770, Constantinople

◙

Oh, but it is cold.

Despite the hasty departure from Briar House, she had prepared for winter, bringing her beaver coat, hat and muff. In Venice, she bought a fur for Zachary which he obstinately refused to wear, taking deep offence that she could imagine the wearing of the pelt of any creature acceptable. She tried to reason with him, telling him that it was a matter of survival and arguing that beavers were in any case in great overabundance in North America and something like rats there. "This is not beaver," he'd said of the fine cloak she'd given him, which was in fact of wolf. "It is wolf, and should be out hunting and howling, not on my back." And he'd howled, right there by the Rialto Bridge, causing passing Venetians to regard him with abhorrence, they being a people (having both money and power) not given to great volubility. She gave the wolf cloak to Samuels, since he insisted on riding the coach up top despite her protestations that he sit with them below where it was, at least, dry. "I sit up top for two reasons, madam," he'd said, without telling her what they were until she demanded an explanation. "First, so that I may defend you, since brigands seek easy pickings, and sight of me is sufficient warning

of some inconvenience in relieving you of your diamonds. Second"—he paused, not from consideration of her feelings but for
added effect—"to be in there with the two of you is like being
at a cockfight where the roosters are featherless and bloody but
insist on pecking at each other for the entertainment of a crowd
that has long since departed in disgust." He had never been one
to express himself with delicacy or tact, but then again nor had
her tastes demanded those qualities of him. The wolf fur suited
Samuels better than Zachary, naturally enough.

Zachary had been sullen for much of the journey as far as
Bologna, and then become excited in that city, running up its
strange tall stone towers and asking the students who were gathered in the squares below questions in Latin about their studies and whether he might attend the university there, failing to
notice their bemused contempt. "Once we have rescued Papa, I
shall study here, I think, Franny," he'd said, "since I like it for its
character of learning and also because they have excellent cheese,
don't you agree?" She had and readily, relieved by his sudden and
unexpected glimpse of enthusiasm, but then a few days later had
come the argument over the wolf coat and, in Trieste, some further dispute arising from Frances's wish to stay a week with the
Countess of Friuli. He was polite in the household, courteous to
the countess, and spent much time in the library. After dinner
one evening he offered to tell everyone's fortune but the countess
mercifully took his offer in jest. Zachary's restlessness was like
a charge throughout the house, as if an agitated leviathan were
trapped in its cellars and making the whole building rumble.
On the Wednesday he went off wandering for a day, despite the
bitter weather, returning having made five thaler telling fortunes

at the port. He must have upset one of his customers though, since he had a black eye, but despite a thorough interrogation would reveal nothing of how it came about.

Two days beyond Trieste they reached the borderlands, a dismal area littered with lazarettos where travelers were required to rest in times of plague and which were peopled by all manner of odd and transitory beings: those ejected from the Ottoman Empire but not quite acceptable to Austria, and vice versa. It was at an inn there that Frances's clothes and her very being must have become infested with lice, making the next stage of the journey a torment. From Belgrade they took the Stamboulyol, the road to Constantinople, but when the snows began the journey became close to impossible. They were a week in Sofia, doubtful of the possibility of further progress, their only respite a hammam close to the rooms they had taken where, to her great relief, steam and a ferocious laundress with biceps the girth of Bayonne hams vanquished the lice.

The weather eased enough for them to press on to Constantinople at the very end of December. It was a bright, cold afternoon when they arrived on a hill above the city, looking east to the Bosphorus and beyond, just as the Salat al-Asr was being called from the wide array of minarets, barely less numerous than the spines on a porcupine. The low sun caught the golden domes of the city and the water alike, the sails of the ships sailing toward the Black Sea were full, and the whole city rippled with the call of the muezzin, causing their small party to stand beside the carriage in a reverie, casting off the trials of their journey, dispelling every memory of freezing days and itching nights, of arguments and misunderstandings. Samuels's eyes welled with tears, a sight itself barely less astonishing than the glories of Byzantium displayed below. Before Frances could make any observation, he turned away and clambered up to his usual place, behind the coachman. "Darkness comes swift at this time of year," he said. "We have another hour yet."

They are given rooms in the English Palace until they can find suitable lodgings. It is a large building, overly ostentatious—a gift, apparently, from a generous sultan of the last century; more a punishment, Frances thinks, since it is a tangle of corridors and mercilessly cold, the fire in her room succeeding in creating only enough warmth to thaw whichever part of her anatomy she places closest to it. She has no expectations of the ambassador, John Murray, other than incompetence, having been informed of his nature by her London friends, and determines to ask him little and tell him less. He is of that category of man, red-faced and spuriously jovial, by whom she has been patronized on countless occasions. Yet he gives them a good dinner that night, having the French chargé and his wife and the Portuguese ambassador also at his table. Zachary wears his eyepatch, and a jacket that she has brought for him in her valise which is a good deal too small since he insists on growing so immoderately; he also bears the faint and troubling hint of a moustache. He asks the Portuguese ambassador too many questions about the Great Earthquake of 1755, assuring the poor man that he was born at the exact moment of it, which would be true but for the fact he is out by a year and eight months. The French chargé's wife is startled to learn that Frances has read the works of Jean-Jacques Rousseau and disconcerted still further by her unconcealed admiration for Monsieur Voltaire. Each time Frances speaks she notices that the Portuguese ambassador, a small man with something of the manner of a hedgehog about him, fixes her with a stare so unshakeable she wonders if she has inadvertently enchanted him. Eventually she feels compelled to ask, "Senhor Sousa, I am flattered that you pay me such close attention, but I wonder if there is something about my countenance that fascinates you. Some blemish or peculiarity, perhaps?"

"No, madam. It is nothing, nothing at all. Forgive me. It is only that your nephew told me . . ."

"Yes?" She casts a look at Zachary, wondering what mischief he has been up to.

"It is just . . . he tells me, Lady Peake-Barnes, that you are . . ." He drops his voice so that, while it can still be heard by all at the table, it might seem as if he wishes it not to be. ". . . the daughter of a Tartar noblewoman, and I was admiring your distinguished features."

"Were you, Senhor Sousa? Well, you must forgive my nephew, who is unconscionably imaginative." She casts Zachary a withering glance and, turning back to the ambassador, offers him an apologetic smile which she nevertheless intends to hint at the possibility of her illusory Tartar heritage.

When they have done with dinner and pleasantries, and are preparing for their icy beds, Frances marches into Zachary's bedroom, where he is sitting, naked but for his pantaloons, reading a book he has found.

"Your visions are one thing, and lunatic enough, but now you have taken to lying. I do not know what else I can call it. Really I don't." She shakes herself, as if to cast off his falsehoods. "It is not acceptable."

He looks up from his book as if he hadn't noticed her entrance. "Lies?" he says. "What lies?"

"That my mother was brought to England from the Steppes."

"I made you more alluring to him. There's no harm in that, surely?"

"And you know full well you were not born on the day of the Lisbon earthquake."

"I was born at its conception, rather."

"You were not, unless your poor saintly mother was obliged to carry you for twice the . . ." She cannot say more on that matter. "I suppose I should be glad you were not telling everyone's fortune."

Suddenly he changes from that arrogant and infuriating young man into a boy again. "No, Franny. I won't do that. They frighten me. The visions." And he looks at her so defencelessly that she goes to him and places a blanket over his shoulders and sits beside him, rocking him, almost as if he were that silent infant she had loved so ardently. That is the problem with boys turned into men, she thinks: however unpleasant they become, they leave some trace of their younger selves behind, like blooms caught by the first frosts that still hold some memory of summer, and one cannot help but love them, for what they were if not for what they have become.

"Get yourself into your bed, Zachary. You'll catch a chill, sitting here with nothing on. Sleep. Tomorrow we'll see your old friend Tom. You remember . . ." She is about to say *her*, then wonders whether she should say *him*, and settles on the name: "Tom?"

"Tom is my eye, and always has been." And to her great surprise Zachary places his long, chilly arms around her neck and kisses her cheek with a yearning for that love they once had and seem to have willfully misplaced somewhere along the way.

Tom Spurrell's workshop is two miles from Galata, in Phanar, a bustling shop with six men at work around a long, low table, a profusion of clocks and springs and tiny screws and cogs upon it and in every corner. A man in a wheeled chair with a handsome face speeds over to them on their arrival, shouting greetings to Samuels in English, propelling himself from his chair into Samuels's arms and compelling the two of them into a sort of jig like long-lost lovers, Samuels spinning around and holding the poor man aloft as if he weighed no more than a child. She had never imagined seeing her servant in a condition of unabashed jubilation, but jubilant he is. Samuels introduces Frances and then Zachary to the man, who is returned, panting, to his chair. He confirms to them, as he regains his breath, that he is indeed Naguib Ghalib, Tom's business partner and, once, many years ago, assistant to the exalted Mr. Cloudesley. Seeing Zachary, who is wearing the gold-and-lapis eye Tom made for him, Ghalib's eyes moisten with emotion without embarrassment or constraint. "You are his son, then," he says, "he spoke of you ceaselessly. How he would love to see you now. What a handsome young man you are."

Frances, knowing that Zachary will only be made uneasy by unfettered emotional displays, says, "It is thanks to you, Mr. Ghalib, I believe, that we have received intelligence."

Ghalib frowns. "Mr. Spurrell will tell you what is known."

"And where are we to find Mr. Spurrell?"

"He has been called to see a client. He will be back shortly. You are to go up to his quarters. Katerina will serve you coffee."

"Katerina?"

"His wife."

Frances raises an eyebrow, no more. She and Zachary proceed upstairs, while Samuels remains below, talking animatedly to his old friend. Upstairs they enter a maze of small rooms in dark wood, cool in summer, she imagines, but now warm with stoves in each corner and rugs on the floors, and blankets on the low benches around the edge of each room. It is apparent that Tom has made for himself a prosperous business and a comfortable home. A woman, dressed in the Greek style of long skirts, tight bodice and jacket and wearing a white headdress greets them shyly and gestures to them to sit.

"You are Katerina?" Frances asks the woman in Greek.

She looks confused for a moment, but then nods, sits, and a maid brings a tray of pastries out to them.

"How long have you and Tom been married now?" asks Frances, raising her voice, thinking the woman might be deaf or stupid, and in either condition volume is, in her experience, greatly appreciated.

Tom's wife blushes and says something softly which Frances cannot understand.

"She says that she and her husband have been together for almost nine years," says Zachary.

"What language is she speaking?"

"It is Greek, Aunt. But demotic. You find it difficult to understand?"

"Demotic, demotic. What use is that to anybody?"

"To the Greeks it is useful, I think, since it is the language they speak."

"When did you learn such a thing?" she asks, resentfully.

"Mr. Mendel . . ."

"Ah yes, well." Mendel taught him too much. It was showing off.

"Tom has taught me a little English," says Katerina.

She really will not allow herself to be humiliated in this way. "We are happy to speak in Greek," Frances bristles.

"As you wish, madam," says Katerina, who proceeds again to speak in her perfectly incomprehensible tongue, though Frances hears the occasional word which reminds her a little of the Greek she learned, but only as a reflection in a pool gives some impression of the colour of the foliage hanging over it.

"She asks us," says Zachary, "how our journey was and speculates on the length of it and the difficulties of winter. She says she has never had a desire to leave the city, being wholly content with her life in it."

"Content?" says Frances, the notion of contentment not being one to which she has ever given great consideration, though she always strives to see how it might appeal, much as she has heard of people who bathe in the sea, believing it good for the joints.

Tom arrives, flushed, having hurried from wherever he has been. He bows deeply to Frances and, seeing Zachary, fights away tears before embracing him until it becomes apparent that he has no intention of letting him go without some signal that release is an unavoidable necessity.

"Zachary has grown somewhat, as you see," says Frances.

"Oh, but he has, he has!" he declares. "My dear boy. And how is the eye? A good fit?"

"I thank you, Tom, for your consideration . . ." says Zachary with surprising formality, before adding, perhaps hearing the grate of his own pomposity, "for your love. I have much to ask you about the eyes, and about their magic in particular, but perhaps now is not the time."

"It is not. Most certainly," says Frances, wanting no talk of eyes or visions or any other variety of unaccountable sorcery. Thinking it best to grasp the nettle she says, "We hope to hear further news of Zachary's father?"

Tom flushes, looks dismayed. "But that there was further news, my lady. Nothing more has been heard from Naguib's sister. It was in fact miraculous that we received the intelligence we did. The seraglio is a closed place to all but those who are invited within, and if so received one had better be certain that one may be unreceived, as it were." He pauses, presumably thinking of the capture of his master, which is the matter at the forefront of all their minds, and shakes his head slowly. "The message came from a bird, which delivered a note to Naguib's house. But the creature could not be induced to fly back into the palace, not for anything."

"What order of bird, pray?" asks Frances.

"It was, I believe, no more than a common crow."

"Naturally. A crow may be taught to do any manner of thing, having more sense than many a man, and may be a good deal more relied upon."

"Indeed, madam. I recall your great affinity for birds."

"We have zebras and llamas and ostriches, too," says Zachary, "though we rely on old Reeve to feed them while we are away, and he is forgetful."

Tom looks at Zachary fondly, seeming reassured that he is still able to speak of animals with his former enthusiasm. "You always loved nature, Zack, you did. You'd have snails in your pockets and newts in jars and I swear the sparrows would come and sit on your head when you were out in the garden."

"I still love all creatures, or those that are not human, anyway." He looks at the floor, in sudden embarrassment.

"Do you remember how you'd come and sit with me when I was busy making your father's mechanical creatures?"

Frances notices that Katerina observes Zachary a little nervously and supposes that she cannot help herself from wondering about the nature of her husband's relationship with the youth. "And your business goes well?" asks Frances, trying once more to change the subject. It is not that she does not want Tom and Zachary to be happy in each other's company. There will be time enough for that. But she supposes they must all turn their attention to the matter of Abel's incarceration and the faint possibility that he might be found alive.

"It thrives, my lady, yes. I do a good trade and have lately become clockmaker to the grand vizier's household, which is a noble house indeed. It is where I have been this morning, installing a clock. Hence my late arrival."

"Good, good," says Frances, hardly interested, until it occurs to her that some opportunity must lie in that direction. "The grand vizier must have the sultan's ear?"

Tom gives her a grin. He is not at all the man he was all those years ago at Leadenhall. Now he is confident, here in his own home, in this city, with his own business. There is almost a swagger to him. "And why, my lady, do you think I have worked so hard at raising my reputation in the city if not to that very end?"

"Aaah yes, I see. My apologies, Mr. Spurrell. I should not have underestimated you. So we have a plan?"

"Of sorts, though it is one that will require Zack's cleverness and your ingenuity."

"Tell us more."

"We have time. Let us speak of it tonight. Katerina is a very fine cook, and I trust you will do us the honour?"

"Gladly, Tom."

"Have you seen some of the sights of the city?"

"None."

"Then allow me to be your guide."

They are down by the windy shore of the Golden Horn, gazing up at the domes and minarets of Sultanahmet and the walls of the Yeni Serai, the sultan's palace, wherein lies the seraglio and, they trust to a greater or lesser degree, a beloved father. At first all is harmony.

"See the broken walls around. That is from the earthquake that was, oh, almost four years past now. The damage was very great. We had to go and live in tents outside the city walls. The minarets that you see, several toppled. Even the seraglio was moved outside the city," Tom tells them.

"You'd have thought the sultan might then have freed his hostages," says Frances.

"You'd have thought, but the denizens of the seraglio left at night, all together and with a thousand janissaries flanking them, so all was orderly. The Ottoman system is one of processions and rituals and great rigidity, or so I have observed."

"That great tall dome there, that is the Hagia Sophia?" asks Zachary. "I have seen sketches."

"It is, and a very remarkable building. The only one untouched by the quake, though it is more than twelve hundred years old, built by Justinian. It has been a Christian church and a Muslim mosque. They say it had not one but two Gods watching over it, though it is meant to be the same God, the Christian and Mahometan."

It is squat yet huge, like something dropped on to the city from the very heavens, as if God had said here is a church to set aside those little things you men construct. Yet it also looks a little clumsy, its additions detracting from its looks rather than enhancing them, like a lady finding her beauty spot admired and deciding to wear two dozen. "You have been within it?" asks Frances.

"Only once and in disguise. One must dress as a Turk to enter that part of the city, wherein the Hagia Sophia lies, but many of us do so. There is some risk to it."

"You are always in disguise, Tom, and must have become adept at it," says Frances, unthinkingly.

Tom looks at her as if reappraising her. "Disguise, madam?"

She has misspoken, she realizes, but in trying to correct her obvious error she makes matters worse. "I mean that you are always in some manner in pretence."

"Pretence of what?"

She is overcommitted and must now press on, since retreat will only bring about pursuit. "Come now, you know of what I speak." Frances observes Zachary moving a little way away, placing himself beyond hearing of their argument and busying himself petting a black cat, a creature for which she knows he feels little affection.

"I think of myself as authentic," says Tom.

"I do not doubt you are authentic, but you are a woman who must every day pretend to be a man. Every night, too, I assume. You have a wife."

Tom reddens. "Katerina and I call each other husband and wife. She is an Ottoman citizen and I am not, and so marriage is not possible for that reason."

Frances knows she should leave matters there, but she cannot help herself. "It is not the only obstacle surely?"

"What is it you are trying to say, madam? Is it that I am some sort of aberration? A curiosity? A freak? What is it that you would like me to feel or admit to?" Tom's cheeks are flushed and his eyes bright with fury.

"You are a rarity, let us say."

Tom raises his voice. "Look about you, madam, in this city, and you will see eunuchs and dwarves, you will encounter concubines who become mothers to sultans and slaves who may be made into princes and yet princes who may be enslaved. You will brush against fellows of every hue and size, with beards down to their feet and those who are quite as wide as they are tall. You will smell perfumes sweet enough to make you swoon and the vilest odours of decay. This is the centre of the world, and every variety of man and woman may be found here. And so you find me. What am I? What think you of me? Tell me!"

Frances simply cannot understand why people think her so unreasonable, when it is only reason that guides her in all things. When one attends only to reason, surely it is impossible to be anything other than reasonable. The weather has worsened over the course of their argument. "Look," she says, her face turned to the sky, "it has begun to snow. We should retreat, and I shall offer you my surrender unconditionally. Whatever your terms may be, I agree to them, Tom Spurrell."

Tom holds out a hand to catch the snow, watching the flakes come to rest on it, needing to confirm the truth of what Frances has said. "Then call me *he*, madam, and think no more about it."

"He, him, Mr. Tom Spurrell. He is quite the fellow. Yes," she says, pulling her coat of many beavers closer to her and grateful no less for its warmth than for the snow itself.

CHAPTER SEVENTEEN

CONSUMED BY FIRE

March 1770, Constantinople

◙

Tom explains the plan to Zachary, detailing what he must do and say, and Frances, at first uneasy, gains enthusiasm, adding her own unwanted ideas as to what foretellings are likely to be best received. He knows she has long regarded his visions as artifice—at best, childish delusions and lately, as nothing more than shallow attention-seeking. He's tried to tell her often enough that he has no wish to see his visions again, but she seems unable to hear anything he says anymore. Yet he will have to submit to his visions once again if he is to gain the grand vizier's confidence and, through him, find some way into the seraglio.

The next day Zachary accompanies Tom to the grand vizier's household, a mansion on the shore of the Bosphorus. Tom is calibrating an orrery, a wondrous clockwork model of the solar system he has built and installed at the grand vizier's, its Jupiter and Venus flying through the heavens on spindles so fine they can hardly be seen. The instrument's intricacies are being explained to the grand vizier and his son, Ibrahim, and they are so absorbed by its many dials and its celestial apparatus that they seem not to have noticed Zachary at all. Knowing he must seize his moment to gain attention, Zachary declares in Greek, "Mr. Spurrell also made me this eye," pointing to himself and adding, "he has been kind enough to make me an eye every year these past ten, since I lost my own in my father's workshop, upon a peacock's tail." Although the grand vizier does not condescend to look at Zachary, his son asks him, also in Greek, if the eye is made of gold and what it sees that his other cannot. He is teasing, but Zachary grasps his opportunity. "You have been told, then?"

"Told what?" says the youth, with a skeptical smile.

As he and Tom agreed before they came to the palace that day, it is Tom's turn next to speak of the eye. "It gives him visions. Why it should be or how, I cannot say, but ever since Zachary was but little he has seen into men's hearts and deeds."

The grand vizier, eyebrows raised at the impertinence of the interruption, says, with the mild impatience of one familiar with the provision of false wonders, "Tell us, then, young man, what is this magic it holds?"

"I see visions, Your Highness, visions of the future."

"And what do you see now?" he asks.

Zachary falters. What was it Franny had said to him as he left that morning with Tom? She'd wished him a light tongue and a fervid imagination. "You must give me your hand, sir," says Zachary, his mouth dry.

Grand Vizier El Gadawi obliges with a lenient smile. Zachary takes his hand, heavy with its rings, one bearing a large ruby, another burdened by a sapphire; it is, to his surprise, the hand of a man who has done arduous labour at some time in his life. If he receives no sound, no apparition, Zachary thinks he will be relieved, even though he'll be shamed before them all. The grand vizier's hand rests in his like a misdeed, and all he can hear at first is the splashing of the fountains in the courtyard. Then it comes: a shout, desperate, forlorn, for someone called Zeinab, and the crackling of fire, tearing quickly along a row of wooden houses, blown by a strong wind. Also, the shadow of wings, of an eagle or some other hawk. It lasts barely half a minute and is done before the sound of the fountains and the calm order of a fine house on a spring day is restored. "Zeinab is in your thoughts, sir," says Zachary.

The hand falls from his, the grand vizier's expression changing in an instant from forbearance to alarmed disbelief. "Zeinab? Did you say Zeinab?"

"I hear sounds, names . . ."

"And what did you see?"

"I saw fire, blown by an easterly wind, taking many houses, and a hawk, an eagle, flying over, or truer to say, the shadow of its wings upon the ground."

"And Zeinab?" he asks, urgently.

"Only the name."

He eases a little.

Zachary feels Ibrahim's eyes upon him but dares not look directly. He turns instead to Tom who, understanding his signal, draws El Gadawi and his son's attention once more to the face of the clock, and tells them how it presages the arrival of comets.

As they leave the house, with much bowing and the washing of hands in a rose-petalled bowl, Zachary senses Ibrahim watching him.

That night there is a fire in Phanar, not far from Tom's workshop. From his room in Galata, Zachary can hear the distant crackle of flames tearing greedily through the wood, and the shouts of men forming long lines up the hillside, conveying bucket after bucket from the river below. The smell is of smoke but also of hair and books, singed corn and wool, beds and rugs, shattered pots and scorched leather—the charred essence of those hundred extinguished households. A legion of rats gallops up the alleyway beneath his window, seeking a new and better street in which to dwell.

In the morning, the smell of fire still hangs, palls of smoke curling into the air over the gutted street. But the flames have not spread. The people of the city are familiar with regular blazes and expert at their containment. It has been a dry winter, a strong wind had come up from the east and, being still cold, every household's stove was burning, and these old furnaces are given to explosive misbehaviour. It was the third fire in the city that month. His prediction was barely more extraordinary than declaring a cloud will bear rain. He has, he supposes, done nothing more than interpret the vizier's own fears.

A message comes for Zachary from the grand vizier's footman at midday. *Come tomorrow, soon after you hear the muezzin call Salat al-Fajr.*

The prospect of having to account for his prediction fills him with dread and he is unable to concentrate for the rest of the day, spending it trying to persuade a sleepy tortoise to come out of its hibernation just to eat a lettuce leaf. He sleeps fitfully that night and is dressed and waiting when the first muezzin begins his plaintive cry to Allah a little before six, soon being joined by that wide chorus that stirs the half-million souls of the city into their days. At the door, Samuels waits for him, offering to walk with him to the grand vizier's, but Zachary wants none but his own company, even though Samuels is hardly one to make any unwanted demand upon a person's attention.

He breathes in the air of smoke and salt, watches the pink dawn, takes heart in the swallows returning from their African holiday, peers into alleyways where slops are being thrown from upstairs windows and trusts his reactions will be fast enough to arrive at the grand vizier's home without shit on his shoulders.

Even on that first morning of what is to be their new arrangement, El Gadawi speaks to him kindly, at first of other things, asking after Zachary's schooling, his great-aunt, his impressions of the city. Eventually, the sun casting its first rays over the tulip beds, he says, "You predicted the fire."

"I saw a fire, excellency. I saw a fire that I think you saw, too."

"You saw where it would occur."

"Did I?"

"That fire was on Eagle Lane."

Zachary has nothing he knows how to say.

"It is where Zeinab lives."

He knows he should not ask who she is.

"She is my daughter. By a woman who is not one of my wives. I tell you because I think you saw this, too, and chose not to speak it out loud, and for that I thank you. You feared the blaze, or perhaps foresaw what I feared myself, and in consequence I placed a guard there the night you came to my house, two days ago, ready to send word if fire broke out, and we were able to smother it within a few hours. Had we not . . ." He grips Zachary's wrist so hard he thinks it might break. "How do you do it? How?"

"I cannot say, sir. Really, I cannot. I do not know."

"Do it again."

"I . . . I . . ."

"Do it."

Zachary sees from the grand vizier's unwavering expression that he has no choice. Besides, isn't this what he wants? To gain some hold over the man, and through him over the sultan himself. "Your hand, Your Highness," he says, nervous. The vision comes quickly this time—a dozen heads, severed and spiked, of a baying crowd below, and again, a name, this time something like Azvourian. Zachary tells him hurriedly what he has seen.

"Yes," says El Gadawi. "I had hoped for gentler justice for these men, but it seems they will not evade the executioner's axe, after all."

"Who are they?"

"Never mind." He stands, distracted, readying himself for the day.

"Sir," says Zachary swiftly before he has lost him for the morning, perhaps forever. "I wish to ask about my father."

"Your father?"

"He is said to be held within the seraglio, a prisoner."

El Gadawi appears nonplussed, before some realization settles upon him. "Aaah," he says, "so that is why you are here, and why you have brought this sorcery with you."

"I do not know what it is. I . . ."

"Tomorrow," he says. "Come tomorrow. We will talk of your father."

When he returns Frances interrogates him. "What is he like, this grand vizier?"

"He is kind, I should say. Troubled, but surely any man with the weight of an empire on his head would be troubled?"

"You have been courteous? I know how impolite you can be, Zachary, tactless and blunt."

How is it her opinion has sunk so low, when once she thought so well of him? "I was polite. I did not poke him in the eye or spit in his face, and I chose my words with care."

"And have you yet succeeded in raising the matter of your dear father?"

"He says we will talk of him tomorrow."

She sighs, stands, then thinking of something declares, "I bought a parrot in the market. He is to come tomorrow. We shall call him Fred, I think, after my late brother."

"No spices, then?"

"Many are not so fresh as one might imagine. They are left in great heaps, spilling their perfume into the air, which makes the bazaar aromatic, but does nothing for the flavours they are intended to bear. It is as if the very point of them has been overlooked, like a fortepiano so muffled it makes no sound at all."

She comes to where he sits and, placing a hand on each cheek, says, to his great surprise, "You are courageous, Zachary, and I have always known it. You are the bravest of the brave, the bravest young man in all the world," before she turns and ascends the stairs to her chamber without looking back.

The next day, sitting once more in the grand vizier's garden at dawn, the tulips beginning to open, their serried ranks of yellow, white, red and almost-black spilling their licorice smell into the high-walled space, the grand vizier says, "You must understand, Zachary, that this happened long before I was grand vizier." He looks at him sadly with his hooded, patient eyes. He is without that pomposity or grandiosity that might be expected of one so exalted. His manner is, rather, modest and quiet, his voice kindly and patient. He sits with his back straight, his hands on his knees, and talks of his garden and of his sons and daughters and of a visit he made once to England, of the green and watery quality of the light there, as well as of the Sphinx and Nile, of the tombs and pyramids to be found in the province of Egypt, which he once governed and where he hopes he may one day return. He gives no impression that he thinks a sixteen-year-old any less worth talking to than an older man.

"I know that, Your Highness," says Zachary. "It is eight years since he was taken."

"I hear only the stories that I imagine you have heard yourself."

"What of his automata? If you saw one you would know it was his, from how like a living creature it seems."

"The chess player, the Duke of Derbyshire, I have been shown it. It sits in the armoury where it gathers dust. I have been told the tale of the Englishman who leapt from it, brandishing a pistol to kill the sultan."

"I am sure that is not true."

"I am certain none of it is true, Zachary—the monstrous machines, the riding of a great wheel belching steam, the baying at the moon. You must understand the seraglio is a place of myth and rumour, of shadows and apparitions. But of your father, your actual father, I have no reason to give you hope. I am sorry."

"I would like to search the seraglio for myself."

El Gadawi laughs, a bellow, a startling sound in the quiet of the early morning. "Would you so? And so might I. The seraglio is a closed place, Zachary. Even I am only rarely admitted beyond the gate of the third courtyard for some special audience with the sultan. Usually we viziers meet for the divan in the room set aside for it, which sits in the middle courtyard. And the sultan himself watches us there, through a golden grille set high in the wall. So you see, we are all watched, and much is hidden from us, sometimes even from the sultan himself. There is only one who sees into every part of it."

"Yes, I understand. Allah."

He laughs again. "I mean the Chief Black Eunuch, the kizlar agha. He is the one who sees all. I will ask him what he knows of your father, of what befell him, though he may not tell me."

Zachary extends his hand, ready for that morning's prognostication, but El Gadawi shakes his head. "Not this morning, I think. I have a better idea for you. Ibrahim!" From the shadows his son steps forward. "My son speaks good Greek," he says to Zachary, "but his Latin is poor and you might teach him a word or two of English, for novelty's sake, eh?"

Ibrahim comes and sits on the bench beside Zachary, and Zachary feels again that yearning that unsettles and confuses him, for he knows it is not how he is supposed to feel.

After His Highness Grand Vizier El Gadawi has left, Ibrahim declares abruptly in Greek. "We shall ride. You do ride, I suppose?"

"I'd have struggled to come this far if I did not." Zachary tells him of his journey, or the first half of it at least, boasting a little in his desire to impress, and failing to mention that he was robbed.

"Then come!" Ibrahim declares, taking him by the hand unselfconsciously, and leading him to the stables where a tall, edgy black stallion awaits him. A challenge, then. Zachary struggles to keep his steed from galloping and in the end lets it have its way, since it seems eager for the chase and to know where it is headed. After half an hour of hard riding they are in a forest north of the city.

"This is Belgrad Forest. Splendid, isn't it?" shouts Ibrahim, cantering up to Zachary, breathless from the ride.

"I should like to see it in summer, when the oak is in leaf and the birds are all at home."

"But then we would not have it to ourselves," laughs Ibrahim. Lowering his voice, as if he might be overheard by the creatures, he says, "There are bears, though shy, always, and just stirring from their sleep at this time of year."

"I love bears," said Zachary, "almost as much as porcupines and llamas and cockatoos and . . . well, I love all animals, I suppose. I cannot think of one I do not."

"No one likes a snake."

"But snakes are beautiful, with their strong bodies which move like water. In the summer I hope to keep some snakes. Look, a deer!" Zachary points to where a large red deer watches them before it turns and springs away.

"You have a good eye, though it is but one."

Zachary, pleased by the compliment, supposes it must be true. He has one eye for the present and another for the future, or not exactly the future, but for something that is not seen by light but by some other medium. He remembers when he was small that Aunt Franny had a crow with one eye, and she had explained to him that a bird uses one eye to see its present, to find a worm or spot a friend, and another to sense what is coming. He thinks it is the same for him, and that he has two eyes after all, but that they have different purposes. "Why is this Belgrad Forest? Belgrade is a long way from here," he asks.

"It's all to do with Suleiman the Magnificent, I think, and when he captured Belgrade and made thousands of Serbs come and live here. I don't know," he says, carelessly. "Well, what isn't to do with Suleiman? Anyway, you want to see a bear, there is a huge one held in a narrow cage in the seraglio. We should go and see it."

Zachary is about to say how he has no desire to see a creature in a cage when he hesitates. "In the seraglio, you say?"

"That's right."

"And you have seen it?"

"Didn't I say so?"

He knows that Ibrahim is, in his turn, boasting. "But . . ."

"Oh, there are ways to come and go. I'll show you if you like."

"Yes. Yes, I would like that."

"And when it's the season we will come to the forest hunting, and you can spot us a deer."

"I would never do that. I will never kill any creature."

"What—not even to eat?" He casts Zachary a look of disbelief.

"Animals are innocent. They cannot understand why we chase them, shoot them, trap them, taunt them, why we misunderstand them so grievously. Still less why we eat them."

Ibrahim trots his horse over to where Zachary struggles to hold his own still. "You are very strange indeed, Englishman," he says, stretching toward him and touching him lightly on the shoulder, almost a blessing. "Come!" And he sets off at a canter, Zachary following, feeling odder all the time, and very much wishing he were someone else; someone without visions, someone who could lift a gun and shoot an animal, someone whose father was not locked away or a lunatic or quite likely dead. He wishes all those things, watching Ibrahim riding ahead, his long, dark hair trailing out behind him like a mane, and wishes to be like him, or, more than that, to be him or, no, it is not that exactly either but something else, something he does not yet fully know how to put into words, even those words that he keeps enfolded and secret within his churning mind.

CHAPTER EIGHTEEN

A REFUGE

May 1770, Lundy

◙

I would not say those days were unhappy, or not always, but these past eighteen months are not better. Leonora is a worry—being as she is, though I blame only myself for that. She never talks of Briar House or Lady Pee-Bee or Zack, and I do nothing to remind her and in such manner we rub along well enough. I had no wish to go as far as Virginia, thinking the journey a long one and there being not much to America but tobacco and slaves and unfamiliar vegetables. But we had to find a place where no one would know us and no one could find us, and I thought Lundy, little more than a speck in the Bristol Channel, would do well enough, having been told by Mrs. Alsop the butcher's wife (whose brother farmed on the island) of an inn in a poor and sorry state, and of potential for good trade. The journey here was arduous, seeing as we left in a great hurry and I'd been told there was no reaching the island after the end of October when the Bideford ferry stops sailing. We arrived to find the inn broken down as promised, but also near three dozen thirsty sheep farmers and their families no less in need of ale. I had been saving those seven years in the lady's employ and sent ahead supplies I knew we would need over that winter, viz: flour, fat, sugar, malt, barley, tea, coal, paint, nails and suchlike. The island had been a place of terrible goings-on not so long before when overrun by convicts who had been meant for deportation to America but left there by a villain called Thomas Benson who was also a member of parliament. Most of those poor men were gone and Benson fled to Portugal and so all was peaceable if much depleted. The rain was soft, and the roof soon back on the inn, which we named "The Puffin" since all was puffin on the island anyway. By Christmas, with the help of two men who were happy for a day's pay through November and December, the place was cosy enough and I cooked my pies, set a fair fire and we gave credit, me keeping a book for each family (few of them being readers or writers) and in such way all knew what was owed. The lambs would fetch a good enough price at Barnstaple market in the spring and we'd be paid then and anyone who swindled us would soon find themselves with reason to regret it.

Why put myself and my girl through such hardships? Because I wouldn't have my girl at all if it weren't for the leaving of Tring. It was one thing for Lady Pee-Bee to prattle on as was her inclination about Leonora being her daughter as much as Zachary was her son (which he was not), and how they were both her own and she would bequeath her fortune to them equally and how much like brother and sister they were but for their looks and, besides, their temperaments, and I did not object for there is little purpose in objecting to that which will pass soon enough. One might as well bemoan the regular occurrence of Tuesdays. She was kind to my girl and Leonora liked her well enough. That she learned to speak French and Latin and so forth I thought would do her no good but not great harm. When I averred to the benefits of needlework and cookery for a girl's education I got my head bitten off well and proper and told there were seamstresses and cooks in the world for such things, and a young woman should have the same education as a young man, and in that way be the match of whomsoever she should marry, and be not his slave or servant, nor his cook nor seamstress but his wife. I told Lady Pee-Bee that Leonora might never take a man for her husband, and then where would she be if she had no income and must cook and sew for herself, and that it was all well and good to decry womanly skills but when a woman falls on hard times she must do those labours a woman may, not those a woman mayn't. We argued the point for many an hour, neither conceding so much as a quarter-inch, but I had not failed to notice that it was the lady who was getting her way not I, since Leonora, despite my own efforts with her, knew not how to boil an egg or stitch a sheet that needed turning, but could instead paint a pretty landscape with water paints, sing a song such as to make your heart buckle and ride a horse all haughty. She was never proud with me, since she knew she'd get a slap across her face if she was. But still, she wasn't quite the daughter I planned on having.

Lady Pee-Bee would, every few months, say how she'd adopt Leonora and how much better it would be for all, despite her knowing that each time she made such an outrageous declaration it would cause a great commotion in the household and I would be obliged to break some porcelain and lock away the tea and the Frenchy wine from them all for the rest of the week. How many times I'd told her clear and unequivocal that there'd be no adopting I do not know. She said it was not to make me any less Leonora's mother or herself anymore so, but only a matter of papers and the easing of an inheritance for my girl. I waved my finger at her and told her by no means and in no way.

Now, Lady Pee-Bee always left her papers out and in disarray, obliging me to organize them for her and in any case I had to deal with most of her affairs since, though hectic in her letter-writing as in all else, she only wrote those letters that did not need the writing, and left unanswered the ones that must without fail have an answer, as if out of fear of bringing any matter to its necessary conclusion. It was beginnings she liked, and middles a little, but endings not at all. She never kept anything hidden but that which she hid, and that which she did I'd find, and so I discovered her correspondence with her solicitor Mr. Dray of St James's Square who had sent her letters of adoption of one Leonora Catherine Morley who would become, after the addition of certain signatures, Leonora Peake-Barnes.

And we were gone the next morning before dawn, with two valises each, hats on our heads, boots on our feet and the certain knowledge that we were not, neither of us, ever likely to be made over to another by the scratch of a pen on paper.

Fourteen, fifteen, sixteen are all ages when a girl is ripe, sweet and tempting. It was another reason for my bringing her to Lundy since there had been a young man in Tring, a very typical young man with dark curls and deep eyes, an inclination toward the poetical and a great desire to give his manhood exercise in a place where it might cause a deal of trouble. He was from a good enough family, but the second born and so most likely in need of a profession. I certainly had no wish for anything so low as a lawyer for a son-in-law. As for Lundy, I had been reliably informed that all the men here were rank, their teeth loose, their hair matted and manners invisible. Their sheep had more grace, I was assured. Leonora, with her red curls and fair face, her delicate comportment, French phrases and hankering for a fortepiano would be like a butterfly set down in the ocean, though I would not let her sink but keep her safe until she was twenty-one and beyond acquisition.

What I had not reckoned on was the fact that young men, too, even in such a place as this, are sweet, ripe and tempting when sixteen and seventeen, having their hair in fair order, all their teeth, an odour about them of youth and vigour instead of sheep droppings and puffin rot, and so there presented himself one Joe Dalton, ever making himself useful about the place and mooning at Leonora and she at him, and I could not think how to put a stop to it. I says to Joe that he must desist, since she is not attainable which only makes him laugh and tell me his father has the biggest flock on the island and he shall inherit, as if he were the Duke of Beaufort, he not having the wit to see how small a thing it is to be mighty on an island three miles long and one mile wide. I nearly laughed in his face but taunting a man for being a man when being a man is all he has is not wise, and so I thought quickly and asked him if his intentions toward Leonora were of the honourable variety or no, to which he answers as you'd expect even though I daresay they weren't. Well, I says, there is a way you can win Leonora's heart and my approval, and it won't cost you a penny, which must have sounded quite the bargain to Joe Dalton or to any man. My daughter longs for a fortepiano, I tell him, which comes as no surprise, since she bemoans the lack of music unceasingly, though there is old Snape who plays the fiddle of a night in the corner by the fire, though he knows only one tune and that not a pleasant one. I tell Dalton that I have purchased a fortepiano for Leonora in Bristol but must find me some means of getting it to the island. "Leave it to me," he says, as I'd thought he would, he taking my challenge as Sir Galahad did with the Holy Grail. I wrote a note and told him it was a bill of sale, he reading it with a care equal only to his incomprehension, the only books on the island being those we had brought with us and Joe Dalton having no more means of learning to read or write than he had cause to. I trusted that a young man in pursuit of a fortepiano in Bristol would soon find better diversions than the prospect of a return to Lundy and marriage to my daughter and gave him a guinea for his troubles.

When Leonora asked where Joe had got to, I told her he had said something about being gone on business to Bristol. Then why, asked she, did he not say so? Perhaps he did not care to tell you, says I. But Leonora was not to be fooled by my ploy and, suspecting my hand in the affair has since proceeded to wage a long and bitter war against her mother, commencing with spending a fortnight in her bed and refusing to eat, then next cutting off all her hair and throwing it into the wind, after that being sullen to all and so she remains. Since none should find her desirable in her current condition my purposes are realized. Though I shall in due course have to find some means of returning her to her former character if she is to ever be capable of finding a match who is not encumbered with more sheep than sense.

It is summer now and we have fair days as well as foul. I am growing a good crop of cucumbers, beetroot, beans and so forth and shall be pickling come the autumn and quite content. I place orders for the supplies I need in the name of Ann Stevens. I have always found it easy to become something new, be it daughter, wife, mother, widow, wet nurse, hat-seller, housekeeper or publican. One day, though, I should like to be a creature of my own invention, a woman who might wake of a morning and not have to be on her guard, not have to take on the world as if it were a herd of thundering bulls. I should like to go to sleep at night and think of my daughter happy and loved by someone other than me, some man her equal. I think I should like to have deep and untroubled dreams—dreams of being loved myself. I should like to be loving and thought so. "Ah, Grace," I should like people to say when I die, "she was beloved." I do not want people to say only that I was a woman with a good head for figures and a talent for making puffin pie. What place is there in heaven for such a woman as that?

◙

CHAPTER NINETEEN

AN UNFORTUNATE FREEDOM

May 1770, Constantinople

☒

It has been two months without news of Papa and Zachary has fallen into a sort of daze, each day dreamy with hours of emptiness. There seems nothing to do but wait, as if rumours were reality and the doubting of them would prick his father's existence and make it vanish like a bubble burst by sunlight. Zachary fills his days with conversations with long, thin green whip snakes, elegant and mysterious, and with skittish lizards, weary tortoises and admirable grasshoppers the size of mice. How different the creatures are here to those at home—bigger, bolder, more abundant. He studies them and asks them what they think of him, dressed in shirt and stockings, breeches and waistcoat. He is hardly dressed for heat. Once he is out of the city and into the forest he sometimes discards his clothes, hiding them beneath a log and wandering free and unencumbered; careless.

He presents himself each morning to the grand vizier, who continues to require his predictions, though he regards them lately more skeptically, as if Zachary were an outcast priest encouraging him to sin. Rituals have their place, and he supposes the grand vizier has need of them more than most, his thoughts being troubled and dark, overshadowed by great assemblies of the dead and dying, by torment and misery. He has seen into them after all, though Zachary can offer him neither forgiveness nor consolation, only unformed dreams. Turkey is at war with Russia, and second sight is not needed to know that it goes badly. It is a war that Grand Vizier El Gadawi has counseled against, but its disastrous course is no vindication, merely a stay of execution. Zachary dreads the day when he sees the grand vizier's head upon a pike.

Three or four days each week he spends with Ibrahim, and Zachary has never known such comfort in another's presence, or not since he and Leonora were small and used to play their childish games. He teaches his friend Latin, as he has been asked to do by the grand vizier, and Ibrahim in return teaches him a little Turkish. But they are more interested in other languages—most particularly that of swallows, since the birds converse with each other with such obvious purpose. Ibrahim and Zachary hope soon to be able to explain to all mankind what it is the busy creatures speak of all day long, though it may be nothing more than where good swarms of flying insects are to be found.

Zachary has worn the Turkish disguise Ibrahim gave him, taken his hand and been led across to the old city, tumbling up the steps of the Hagia Sophia, wide and shallow enough so that the Emperor Justinian's horse could canter up them. He has leaned with his friend over the high balconies to feel the old stone carvings and gazed in wonder at saintly frescoes in ancient Christian churches. He has followed him into the salty dark of the Roman cistern, and by the light of a flaming torch gazed upon the upturned Medusa who lives down there. He was not turned to stone, not even when he and Ibrahim embraced as lovers do, seen only by that angry goddess whose snakes had petrified so long ago.

Ibrahim has two older brothers, both away at war, and two sisters, one older and one younger. Though Zachary is a regular visitor to the household, since he is neither brother to them nor husband, and being, moreover, a Frank, he sees them only in their shadows; the rustle of a gown, a laugh from their chambers, sometimes a whisper close at hand, as if he were being watched. His sense of the two young women is unclear. There is an air of clemency about them, as if he were already forgiven for some sin he would one day commit.

Ibrahim has promised to take him swimming that afternoon in the reservoir in Belgrad Forest. By the time they have ridden there they are both sweating, stripping off their dusty clothes and jumping into the cold water. Ibrahim shouts and laughs and Zachary swims, listening to him and happy. After, they find a spot in dappled sunshine to dry off, and Zachary glances when he is unobserved at his friend's muscular body, covered with short, dark hairs, the bush between his legs and those beneath his arms forbidding and enticing in equal measure. He tries not to think at all of his friend's touch, his voice, tries not to think about what the feeling in the pit of his stomach might denote if it is not love.

"See, there!" says Ibrahim, quietly, but urgently.

Zachary follows the line of his pointing finger and sees a falcon in a tree, a peregrine.

"It's watching us, working out whether we are too big for its dinner," says Ibrahim.

Zachary has heard a rustle in the leaves. "There is a snake behind you, and it is that which it plans for its dinner, not you."

Ibrahim sits up, alarmed, looking about. "A snake? It will bite me!"

Zachary senses the snake retreating and in that moment the falcon swoops, just after soaring skyward with a viper hanging, broken-backed, in its hooked beak. Ibrahim watches, mouth open, eyes wide, and stands, as if to get a better view of the disappearing bird. Looking down at Zachary he says, "How did you know the snake was there just behind us?"

"I sensed it, heard it." He feels suddenly and unaccountably disturbed by the terror of nature, the swiftness of death. The falcon did only what it must, after all, as the viper must catch its prey, as even a flea must bite. But he wonders if God could not have ordered the universe in some gentler manner. He thinks too much of death, he knows; seems to see nothing else with his gold-and-lapis eye. Sometimes he is drawn down into a place that might be the underworld and does not think he can raise himself up from it.

Ibrahim squats down beside him. "What's wrong, Zaki?"

"It knew it was about to die, that snake. Knew it had been seen. Have we been seen, do you suppose? Are we being watched? Will we end badly?"

Ibrahim considers this, drawing circles in the dust at their feet before he laughs. "Who says we will end badly, you and I? We will change the world, Zaki!"

Zachary turns away. How it presses all about him, like a dark, heavy cloth that wants to stop him from ever seeing the light again. His love for Ibrahim is something else inside the darkness; a secret, yet another thing to fear.

"Why so sad?" Ibrahim asks, kissing him lightly on the forehead.

Zachary places his lips tentatively against his friend's, unsure of response. When they had stood there before the stone Medusa it had been Ibrahim who had embraced him, kissed him, and it had been a delicious jest, or so it seemed. Yet now he can feel Ibrahim's answer, can taste the wonder of him as their tongues, their breath, their souls seem to find their unexpected harmony, as if they are viola and cello rehearsing a sweet prelude. For the first time in his life Zachary cannot feel himself at all, but only another, and it is the man he knows he loves. "I love you," he says, before he knows quite what words escape him. He looks up, almost in apology, and then his friend's hands are on his shoulders, pushing him down to the ground and he's on top of him, and the weight of him is the lightest thing Zachary has ever felt. It is enough to make the darkness lift.

Franny wonders aloud how he can be so happy when they still have no firm news. "It is the first time I can ever remember you having a friend, Zachary," she says, her voice laden with accusation.

He supposes it is true, unless he counts Samuels and Dawkins. Unless he counts Leonora. He flushes with unease.

"It is all to the good that you have a friend," she continues, "and certainly that you've won the trust of the grand vizier and so forth. And I am making modest progress in my meetings with the ladies of quality here in the city, who tell me what they know of life in the harem, which is a good deal less shocking than one might have expected. But—"

"But tomorrow, Franny," he interrupts, "we are at last going into the palace, into the seraglio."

"You are?"

"To see a bear."

"A bear?"

"Ibrahim has arranged it, or his father has, knowing how much I like the creatures, though it took a deal of negotiation. It is the sultan's own, caged. It will be miserable of course, but I reasoned if I can see a bear, well, why not . . . why not Papa?"

"If your father is . . ."

"Is what? Is there to be found?"

"Is, is . . ." She stands, does a turn around the room like a stalled ship drifting slowly in the hope of catching a breeze. "Is alive at all." She hesitates, then rushes on, "I'm sorry to say what I must, Zachary, but it is as if we have been sent to see a mountain and find instead an endless expanse of swamp and are told that we must march on and on until we see a high summit, but there is no summit, and we are at risk of sinking."

"But tomorrow . . ."

"I shall await your report of the bear with great interest." She fans herself. "But if we are to learn that your father has perished, Zachary, then it is best that we learn it soon, for then we can leave this fetid city and start out for England. We cannot conjure your father from the seraglio unless he lives, and the longer we are here the less, it seems to me, that we learn. It is something like being dissolved."

He cannot raise a protest. Even Tom Spurrell has begun to doubt Naguib's sister's note. Ibrahim's father has been good as his word, finding out what he can about the man who sprang from the chess-playing automaton. He has learned that the sultan did not have him killed, and that he lived long enough to make a further machine, capable of firing a gun, but that he fell ill and is said to have died of an apoplexy. Zachary does not believe it, for he hears the sound of his father's calling each night, and it has grown loud, so loud he is amazed it cannot be heard by all.

The day of the bear is a Friday, the day the sultan leads the procession to prayer from the Yeni Serai to the Süleymaniye Mosque, flanked by a hundred janissaries dressed in red and gold, all the viziers and other high officials walking at a trot behind him in order to keep up with his stately horse, white and tall, upon which sits the sultan himself, the shadow of Allah upon the earth, also white and tall by virtue of the towering hat he wears, adorned with diamonds and sapphires. The ritual means the seraglio will be, if not empty, then emptier than at any other time, though the harem will be busy with its own prayers, the eunuchs bustling about their work, and the kitchens noisy with the clanging of copper pans and the shouts of furious cooks admonishing those who have the misfortune to toil beneath them.

Why the kizlar agha consented to the grand vizier's request that his son and his friend be permitted to visit the bear is a mystery, but when Zachary asked the grand vizier whether the kizlar agha knew that he was the son of Abel Cloudesley, El Gadawi said, "I have told him all about you, and about your prophecies, too, and I daresay it is for that very reason he has permitted it, so be careful what you say. Be subtle, be wary, be sensibly afraid."

They enter the Yeni Serai a little after eight, through the Imperial Gate into the first courtyard, an area so large that Zachary can barely see across it. There is a mosque in one corner, also an ancient church. Soldiers parade, gardeners tend to flower beds, and gazelles graze on a field. At the next gate, the Gate of Salutation, there are formalities, but they are to be expected, and Ibrahim is known anyway, since his father has been grand vizier for five years. The middle courtyard is only a little smaller than the first, lined with buildings, some rebuilt since the earthquake, others still being repaired and covered in wooden scaffolding. There is a parade ground, in its centre a rose garden and fountain, and peacocks displaying. Along one wall is a low stone lattice, and Zachary wonders if it was from there that the ladies of the harem watched his father howling at the moon. In one corner, near the high Gate of Felicity to the inner courtyard and the sultan's own chambers, is the meeting house for the viziers, the divan. Zachary looks up to see what he thinks at first to be a statue of an owl atop it, but it moves its head, blinks once and continues its afternoon doze. The janissaries who are guarding the tall, studded wooden doors of the Gate of Felicity swing them open to reveal beyond a garden laid out with beds and terraces, pergolas and fountains, dotted with pavilions and kiosks with a view down to the Golden Horn, the Bosphorus and all the city below, set out much as earth must look from heaven. He glances at Ibrahim in wonder, who in turn grins with pride as if he had built the place himself. To one side are the sultan's private quarters, guarded by a single janissary. The day is warm, and all is peaceful.

"Come," says Ibrahim, who is his only guide.

As they walk down a flight of steps Zachary sees that they are watched by other janissaries, up on the walls, each holding a long rifle. There is a cage, tall and narrow, something like that which might belong to a giant bird, and within it a huge, dejected brown bear. At their approach the creature lets out a low rumble which grows louder and louder until the ground seems to shake. She stands, the bear, towering over them both. She must be eight feet tall. Her breath smells of old meat and seawater.

"Oh, poor bear," says Zachary. "You poor old girl. Has she a name?"

"She is called Catherine the Great, of course."

"You should be out in the forest," says Zachary to the bear, "hunting berries and squirrels. Not in here, however well tended your view." He places a hand on one of the bars, and the bear brings a paw to it, so it is almost as if they are touching, her long claws seeming profligate. She is chained, and though the chain is long enough to allow the miserable creature to pace the circumference of her cage, she is cruelly constrained.

"Why keep this creature so?" asks Zachary.

A shrill voice, high and piercing, says in Greek from behind them, "His Majesty the Sultan comes to see the bear each morning and feeds her and they console one another."

Ibrahim bows low before the stump of a man who has appeared stealthily behind them. He is dressed in robes that trail around him and is rumpled and wrinkled and black as a raisin. "Your Highness," says Ibrahim.

Zachary follows suit, peering up at him. He puts him in mind of a cairn of dark, flat stones, topped by a cap of blue silk and gold, beneath which peer a pair of small, blinking eyes.

"Our emperor talks to him, and the bear talks back. Here." He approaches the cage, takes a long, rusty key from his belt and opens the door, at which the bear leaps forward straining on her chain and growling.

Zachary had wanted to talk to the bear, calm her, but this creature is in such a torment it makes him recoil.

"Don't you like the royal bear?" taunts the squat man, whom Zachary realizes is the kizlar agha himself, the Chief Black Eunuch, and the man responsible for his admission to the seraglio.

"She seems to me a tortured creature, highness. She would be happier in the forest."

The kizlar agha contorts his face into what Zachary supposes must be a smile. "She would have been happier free, yes, at one time, but now she is used to her cage and wouldn't know what to do with freedom, any more than an octopus would know how to ride in a coach. Look." His smile fades and he approaches the bear once more, this time unlocking a padlock that fixes the chain to its thick, studded collar. The creature shakes her powerful, hunched shoulders, dust and a brume of flies rising up from her shaggy coat. She stands on her feet and roars again, causing Ibrahim and Zachary to jump back in alarm, yet the curious, crumpled kizlar agha barely flinches. In that moment the ground shakes, followed by the searing noise of an explosion, loud enough to rend the air, causing all to put their hands to their ears to block out the sound, so that the janissaries' rifles all clatter to the ground. The bear, alarmed, lurches toward Ibrahim and, as casually as if she were swatting a wasp, knocks him to the ground, gashing his face and shoulder with her long claws. Zachary shrieks and rushes over to his friend, heedless of the bear, which is sniffing at Ibrahim's unmoving body as if surprised at her own strength. The kizlar agha mutters something under his breath in Turkish and shouts for a janissary to come and assist him in encouraging the bear back into her cage. Another shout and another guard appears. They struggle with the bear, trying to push and shove her, but now, with the smell of Ibrahim's blood on her claws, she bounds away. The kizlar agha's expression contorts as he issues an order. The janissaries pick their rifles from where they have dropped them and begin to shoot at the creature, but this only slows her, and she is shot again and again, now from many angles as dozens of guards appear on the walls, firing. The bear felled at last, the kizlar agha says in Greek to Zachary, who is holding his beloved friend in his lap, "That was not at all expected. I fear I know all too well the cause of that explosion. His Majesty will be most displeased."

"My friend . . ." croaks Zachary.

"Ah yes, and His Highness the Grand Vizier will be no more pleased to have his youngest son attacked, I suppose. What a business." Astonishingly he laughs, a high, tinkling sound blending with the echoes of the ricochet of the volley of rifles that still reverberates around the walls of the court-yard. The kizlar agha claps his hands twice, and a eunuch comes running from near the inner gate. "Call the imperial surgeon," he orders, impatiently.

Two janissaries carry Ibrahim's limp body into a pavilion nearby, and Zachary follows, hardly believing that what is hap-pening can be real. He sits beside Ibrahim, who is laid out on a cushioned bench, onto which his blood flows, and places a hand on his clammy brow. There are two gashes on his face and a deeper one on his shoulder. He listens to his rapid breaths. A few moments later a sombre man enters, bows, places his ear to Ibrahim's chest, cuts away his robe and pours some liquid, yel-low and with a sharp smell, on to his wounds. Frowning, he takes from his pocket a vial and holds it under Ibrahim's nose, making him gasp and open his eyes in shock. Seeing Zachary, he smiles and falls back onto the cushion in a faint.

"Hmmm," declares the doctor. "You speak what, Greek, I suppose?" he says to Zachary.

"Yes, sir."

"Wait outside. I am going to have to clean and stitch his wounds. I do not like to be watched."

Zachary does as he is told and, looking up at the entrance to the courtyard, sees a figure dressed all in white appear in the gateway. As he begins to walk, all those he passes prostrate themselves. It takes Zachary a moment to realize he is coming toward him, the kizlar agha now at the figure in white's side, murmuring to him. Zachary does as he sees others have done and throws himself to the ground.

"This is the boy who is responsible. He freed Catherine and taunted her and the poor creature, disturbed by yet another accident with steam, went berserk, majesty, I am sorry to say." He says all this in Greek, for Zachary's benefit, he assumes.

The sultan asks, "Is this true?"

Zachary can see only a pair of white slippers. He has heard that no one may look directly into the sultan's eyes. Hearing a gasp of pain from the pavilion behind him, he turns. If he tells the sultan that it was the kizlar agha who freed the bear then he will bring fury down on that strange man without, he suspects, gaining any better opinion of himself. Yet if he agrees, what fate awaits him? Before he can answer, another yelp of agony comes from the pavilion. "What is this?" asks the sultan, striding toward the place where his surgeon is at work. Some discussion takes place behind him, and Zachary gets to his feet to see the kizlar agha's collapsed features facing him, a finger on his lips.

"Keep quiet, young man," he whispers, "and you will see what it is you have been waiting for. That was always my intention, but I had not reckoned on yet another explosion. The bear was not meant to run amok, I assure you."

The sultan emerges, scowling. "That is El Gadawi's son in there. How did these two, the Frank and the grand vizier's boy, come to be here?" he demands.

"I have no idea, majesty," replies the kizlar agha, almost nonchalantly, as if teenage boys entered the inner sanctum of the seraglio every day, freeing bears to run rampage and be shot dead.

"You, boy," says the sultan to Zachary, who throws himself again to the ground. "No, no," he says, placing a slipper beneath his chin and raising his foot so that Zachary is obliged to look into his face, which he sees is dragged down with weariness. His nose is long and straight, his mouth small and beard full and, to Zachary's surprise, fair. "Who are you?"

He does not feel courageous, but remembering Franny's words he thinks, yes, I am brave, or can be if I choose to be. "I am Zachary Cloudesley, majesty, son of Abel Cloudesley, clockmaker and, I believe, your prisoner."

The sultan's mournful face shows no surprise. "Now I have the son, when before I had only the father. Well, someone must give his life for that of my bear. That is only reasonable. Who is it to be, I wonder?" He leans down to the ear of the kizlar agha and whispers something to him. The wizened old eunuch nods, and bustles away, but soon returns, in his wake a man hunched and grey and confused, bearing the sooty marks of undue proximity to the recent explosion.

He looks about, muttering in English, "It is not yet twelve o'clock, and there should be some peace. . . . I am in ill sorts today, what with the size of screws. . . . I will not tolerate poor wine, when I know there is better to be had. . . . Mercury is visible in Taurus tonight. . . . Did I tell you that we are making a rat, since it seems only right to honour the creatures. They are better than us rats, oh yes . . ." His eyes come to rest on Zachary and he says, "A Frank! What is he doing here? What am I doing here?"

All his life Zachary has carried a clear memory of his papa, strong and tall, his blond hair tied with a blue satin ribbon, his eyes light blue and laughing, a man who drew every eye to him, yet who always seemed withheld in some way, only part there. He remembers the feel of his father's hand enclosed about his own; the reassurance of it, how he held him close in those weeks after he lost his eye. Even when his father seemed so unsettled and nervous with him, even after he was sent away to Franny, he still came to visit him before he left for Constantinople, and that visit had been like a gift, not for the things that he brought with him—creatures of clockwork and living ones, too: a frog, a marmoset that Zachary cared for tenderly though he died not long after Papa left on his voyage—but for the love he showed in hints and glimpses, before he stole away, body and soul.

But this is not the memory that stands before him now, this husk of a man. He feels cheated, betrayed. "Papa?" says Zachary, tentative, uncertain. "Father?" he takes a step toward him, but the stooped, grey-haired man retreats as far.

"What's that?" he puts a hand to his ear. "I had a son once, yes," he laughs. "A son with a gold-and-lapis eye, just like yours. But he was small, oh"—he puts a hand down to the level of his waist—"this high, I should say."

"That was over nine years ago, Papa. I have grown."

"I cannot hear you. Whoever you are, you shouldn't be here."

The sultan speaks. Zachary had not seen him sitting beneath a pergola, watching. "You see how sometimes it is best to leave a thing in its cage, once it is used to it. It is cruel to set it free, when it might be confused by the unfamiliar world. It is as likely to be terrified as to run wild and attack those it should not."

"Papa?"

"He cannot hear you," says the sultan, without emotion. "He is quite deaf, the result of his experiments, the most recent of which you have just heard. He has a workshop and makes things for me from time to time, objects to entertain. Or terrify."

Zachary faces him, unafraid, but his voice cracking with emotion. "It is cruel. You have made him into something he was not. He must have served whatever punishment you saw fit to give him." Remembering his place, he bows his head. "Majesty."

A bee buzzes between them, and the sultan swats it away. "Perhaps he has. But now there is a new punishment to be paid for the death of Catherine, and I do not know whose life to take for it. Yours or his. Or perhaps the son of the grand vizier. Which shall it be?"

Zachary doesn't hesitate. "Take mine," he says, puffing out his chest. "Take mine, majesty, for this was all my doing. All of it. To come and see the bear. To come to the palace, in the hope of finding my father. To come to this city at all."

The sultan beckons to the janissary who stands closest and says something barely audible before Zachary is held. "Admirably brave, boy. Your request is granted."

"But free my father in return for my life."

"What? You think yourself in a position to lay down conditions? To lay them down to me?" Bemusement more than anger marks his expression.

Abel has been watching the exchange all the while, not hearing the words but perhaps understanding the nature of it. He says to the kizlar agha, in Greek, "Does this boy say he is my son, highness?"

"Yes, Cloudesley," says the kizlar agha, nodding his rumpled head, the pendulous folds of his chin wobbling.

Abel steps forward, examining Zachary's features more closely. He reaches out to touch him. "You are real, then. Whoever you are."

"I am, Papa."

His father pats him on the head, sorrowfully, as if pitying his delusion. "I have called out many times for my son, but you have come in his place. That is a shame, a very great shame."

The janissary who holds Zachary loosens his grip, and he twists himself free to see that the sultan and kizlar agha have withdrawn to the pavilion in which Ibrahim lies, and are in conference. A moment later the kizlar agha comes to where he stands and says, "Your proposal is accepted. Your father will be freed."

"Let him be well cared for, sir. And, may I ask, what is to become of my friend?" he asks.

"We have sent a message to El Gadawi, who will be here soon to take his son home and care for him."

"May I talk to him?"

He gives a brief nod.

Ibrahim is woozy but smiles as Zachary enters. "Ah, my friend, my sweet friend."

"Your father is coming."

"I heard. I heard everything they said, Zachary, the sultan and the kizlar agha. They thought me unconscious, but I was not."

"And . . . ?"

"The kizlar agha told the sultan you are a better prize than your father, since he is out of his wits."

Zachary groans.

"He has persuaded him to permit you to give him a prophecy, and if he is convinced by it, he will let you live."

Zachary clutches Ibrahim, making him wince with pain so that he releases him quickly.

"I will find you," says Ibrahim. "That is my prophecy for you. That we will one day be together again."

Zachary has a sinking, sickening feeling in the pit of his stomach. All the lightness that he had felt since first meeting Ibrahim seems to have left him; he can hardly move.

"Go to your father," mumbles Ibrahim. "Haven't you come halfway across the world to find him?"

◙

CHAPTER TWENTY

ZACHARY CONFINED

June 1770, Constantinople

On his first morning as prisoner, he is taken to the sultan's audience chamber by the kizlar agha, who tells him to be sure to mention tumbling walls and fires and shouts of victory, since a battle is under way against the Russians in Moldavia, and it will be best to be vague about who the victors might be. Zachary, though nervous, thinks he will have no need to dissemble—his visions usually come whether sought or not. He bows low as he enters His Majesty's presence, aware of dozens of pairs of eyes upon him, the walls of the surprisingly small room lined by janissaries. The Grand Seignor the Sultan sits on a squat throne that rests on many cushions in one corner of the room, over him a canopy. No other officials are in attendance but the kizlar agha, who appears to be the sultan's intermediary to all in the palace and everyone beyond. The sultan permits Zachary to take his hand, which is soft and cold and pale as a bejeweled slab of dough. Zachary waits until the noise in his head stills sufficiently to reveal that deeper voice, and for his sight to occlude into a glimmer of something dreamlike, that glimpse into the consciousness of whoever it is whose hand he holds. He waits and waits and feels . . . nothing. Nothing but anxiety, not for himself but for Ibrahim, seeing in his mind's eye not some strange, shimmering apparition or presentiment or prophecy but only a bear's claws tearing at his beloved's flesh, at Ibrahim's terror, his body prostrate on the ground. What he feels is not that empty, hollow, falling sensation that usually accompanies his visions but a fullness that is love. Yet love does not serve him, for he must speak—his life depends on it. Sensing the sultan's impatience, he says in a weak, stuttering voice, "I see the walls of a city ablaze, the shadow of a two-headed eagle in retreat, the shouts of men, shouts of victory. A name, *Mehmet, Mehmet*. A table of gold coins overturned in a street." He falls silent, his brief attempt at sophistry spent, and fears it cannot possibly be enough.

The sultan gives a grunt, though whether of approval he cannot judge. "Very well. More tomorrow," he says.

Zachary stands, bows low and withdraws, walking backward, his eyes on the sultan's slippered feet, as the kizlar agha has told him he must. As they return together across the middle courtyard to what, until the day before, had been his father's workshop and, above it, sleeping quarters, the kizlar agha says, "I enjoyed your embellishments. You have imagination, even when afraid, like a true daemon. Overturned gold coins . . . very good, very good," he chuckles approvingly. "He wishes to see you tomorrow."

"And if he had not?"

"Your head would now lie at an inconvenient distance from your body, your lips moving with surprise, yet having no breath to utter another word in this life." He turns, smiles at Zachary, as if he had been speaking of nothing more troubling than an imminent change in the weather. "It would have been a swift, painless death. Almost a comfort."

Zachary wonders whether to confess that he saw nothing, had no vision, that he might as well have been headless.

"You are far from the first called upon to be soothsayer to His Majesty nor will you be the last. I bring them to him, watch them stutter and fail, get the blood mopped up after they do. It is daunting, after all, and even those who are only partly counterfeit cannot perform their usual tricks and magic." He places a fat hand around Zachary's shoulder and brings his face close, so that the smell of cloves and rot is overpowering, making him swoon. "I grew to have a great affection for your father, you understand. We became friends, and I am sorry for the lunacy that overcame him. I shall protect you with my advice, my dear, but in return you must promise me something."

"What?" gasps Zachary.

"You must always deliver my words, not your own." He tightens his hold on his shoulder, and though he is shorter than Zachary, portly and with every appearance of being in morbid health, his strength is such that Zachary almost buckles with the pain of his grip.

They have reached the other side of the wide courtyard and enter his father's workshop, a jumbled bestiary of bizarre, nightmarish automata. The smell is of old wood, metal, oil, dust and heat. It is cluttered, oppressive. Zachary sits heavily on a low wooden bench, his head in his hands, involuntarily checking it is still firmly on his neck, ruing his fleeting courage of the day before. He should have pleaded for mercy, not offered his own life like a woefully overconfident hero.

He'd sat yesterday on this very bench beside his father, since they'd been permitted an hour together, though Papa hadn't known him and it was worse than not finding him at all, to meet a man so collapsed into himself that if recognition was there at all it would have to be hacked out of the tangle of his lost senses. There were moments, perhaps: his papa stumbling over to a drawer and taking from it two handfuls of sunflower seeds. "He counted these," he said, eyes bright with recollection, "counted them in an instant, and I have kept them ever since as a remembrance of his intelligence. Could you do that, count this number in a second?" he asked, wanting to confirm his belief that Zachary, by committing the sin of growing, must be an imposter. Zachary had shaken his head slowly in defeat, obliged to accept that he was indeed a different person from that boy the sorry figure before him had once loved. Now he would think of some method to count such a great number of seeds, and in thinking lose the ability to do it so readily. But that child of six is still in him, as a sapling is in the trunk of a grown tree.

All through the long years of their parting he'd envisaged a joyous reunion, played it over and over as if it were already a memory. But this bitter betrayal of his longings—an hour of shouting into an ear trumpet in a room surrounded by the crazed emanations of a disordered mind—it was worse than death.

He looks up now to see the clockwork apparitions clamouring for attention, and the eyes of the corpulent old eunuch on him like those of a cat, waiting to pounce. He can hardly be the man to trust, yet what other friend has he in this place? He hopes the grand vizier might come to see him, give him some news of Ibrahim, but waits in vain. The prospect of his next audience with the sultan fills him with dread, the one that must follow with even greater foreboding until, soon enough, he knows that his counterfeit predictions will be found wanting and that he will be followed from the audience chamber by a janissary, who will take from the loose folds of his robe a scimitar, and there will be a glance of cold air, a keenness of steel upon flesh and then . . . nothing. Death has never seemed very far away, but now the breath of it is on the back of his neck, and it is too intimate. He begins to weep.

The kizlar agha places a plump, moist hand on the exact spot where Zachary had imagined the sharp blade slicing into him, making him jolt. "I will give you each day an excellent prophecy, do not worry. You will soon have His Majesty amazed by your preternatural powers."

"How can you?"

"Never mind how I can. Worry only that I will. When next summoned you must tell His Majesty that there will be a fight between two janissaries, Selim Masjid and Tuleman Fateh— repeat these names."

"Selim Masjid and Teleman Fateh."

"Tuleman, Tuleman!"

"Tuleman, yes. But will the sultan care about two janissaries?"

"Tuleman is his favourite. He looks after His Majesty's person most intimately, and he will be killed in this fight, and naturally Selim must be punished for it."

"How do you know all this?"

"Because I shall arrange it," he grins a toothless grin and giggles wheezily.

Zachary has no wish to be responsible for the death of anyone, not even a janissary. "I don't want to be the cause of that."

"You will not be. You will simply predict it."

"But it has not happened."

"Surely, my dear little Cloudesley, that is the very point of a prediction?"

"So I give the sultan their names, and say what?"

"No! No, tomorrow you will simply say that you see a fight close to His Majesty, and blood and so on and so forth . . . a janissary, greedy and covetous. Murderous. You must be vague. And say something else, something about an emerald that is stolen. He will be intrigued by that. That you know of the stolen emerald."

"There is a stolen emerald?"

He taps the side of his nose.

"And the names?" asks Zachary.

"You may declare the name of the murdered and the murderer at your meeting the following day, and in such manner you will have won the sultan's confidence entirely. I shall have Tuleman killed tomorrow night, and then, when you have identified Selim Masjid the morning after, he may be executed that afternoon, without the need for protracted enquiries." He slaps his hands together in glee, which immediately causes a servant to appear at his side, as if conjured from vapour. The kizlar agha dismisses him with an irritated flick of his fingers.

"But . . . but . . ." Zachary is horrified to be drawn into this lethal intrigue.

"I assure you both are most unpleasant men. I shall introduce you to them if you wish, so that you might satisfy yourself on that count?"

"No! No, thank you."

"Tuleman has been whispering things in His Majesty's ear to make him doubt me. Can you imagine? So it is time he was stopped."

"With death?"

"I cannot think of a more reliable way."

"And Selim Masjid?"

"I just don't like him." He wheezes again, squeezes Zachary's knee, lets his hand drift up his thigh and squeezes again before he stands and waddles away, giggling to himself merrily.

Zachary spends that night examining his father's quarters inch by inch. He is brought a supper, birds stuffed with rice and sultanas, salads of strange fruits, breads encrusted with seeds. He says a small prayer for the birds and eats the fruits and breads, before continuing his systematic examination of the strange assembly of automatic creatures that stand about, some half built, others complete. It is like something ancient—an Athenian stonemason's where the statues are hewn from mother marble, but here they come to life with the turn of a key, the swing of a pendulum. There is a metal ostrich that blinks its long lashes, takes two strides before its long neck swoops sorrowfully to the ground; a snuffling wild boar that raises its silver tusks into the air and grunts; an armadillo, each scale of its armoured back exquisite, with a long tongue on which a row of silver ants march into its throat and that rolls itself into a ball until its key is turned again. There are creatures in human form, too: a steel skeleton, accurate in every particular, which dances and nods its skull in affirmation of an unspoken question; a dwarf, in long beard, dressed in silks, who holds an axe and raises it, ready to strike. They are a grotesque medley of companions, hardly conducive to sleep. He searches in vain for the great wheel which he read about so long ago, though he doubts it was ever real.

He is about to climb the ladder to the loft where his bed awaits him when he sees a leather-bound book bearing on its cover his own name. Turning the title page, he sees that it is written in his papa's hand, and begins to read:

Zachary Cloudesley is a remarkable boy, who talks without words, and makes birds flutter down from the trees to sit on his shoulders. He runs as fast as a horse and it should be no surprise if one day he learns to gallop. But will he ever make a friend? I shall give him in these pages a companion, whose name shall be Nathaniel. Nathaniel plays pranks on the ladies of the village, such as putting salt in their sugar bowls, and pepper in their horses' nose bags. He picks all their roses at night and puts cochineal in their duck ponds so that they seem to bubble with blood, but he blames Zachary for all his misdeeds, and soon Zachary is in great trouble, because he does not want to get his friend whipped. What to do? . . .

There is page after page of Zachary's adventures, though after sixty pages his father's hand becomes erratic and after a hundred much of what is written makes no sense at all, viz:

When the giraffe told him he was an omelette he declined to boil, and said instead that he would prick a cheese with his snout. Far from this, said the dandelion, you will moult. A thousand timpani rattled the clouds, but still the hour was obstinate.

Was there sense in it? A hidden code? He lies on the bed, falling into the dip made by his father's body, and wonders if he, too, will be made mad if he slumbers too long in this strange crib.

In the morning he is given a good breakfast of fruit and curds and is summoned for his audience with the sultan. He does exactly as the kizlar agha told him, and his warning of murder amongst the janissaries is received with mild disbelief, but he is permitted once again to withdraw from the exalted presence without having his head removed. Wandering across the courtyard, he hopes to find a lizard for companionship, or a grasshopper, at least, but the palace seems shunned by such innocent creatures. Even the birds are reluctant to settle on the branches of the trees. He sees again the owl he noticed the first time he entered the palace; unmoving, resolute, patient for its night prey. The peacocks parade, but joylessly. Finding a centipede, he lifts it gently but it gives him a sharp bite and obliges him to drop it, his palm burning.

He squats in the dust of the yard, of no more interest to the guards who stand about its perimeter than the centipedes and ants, and wonders why his visions have deserted him. All his life they have been his affliction, yet now when he truly needs them they have cursed him again by evaporating. Is it only that he cannot stop his mind from racing to that moment of Ibrahim's mauling, or is there, rather, a spell at work in the seraglio, or more properly a curse that brings time itself to a juddering halt along with thought and vision? He rubs at the bite on his hand, which is turning red and swelling. What is the point in a centipede's bite? Yet what, then, was the point in his visons? To bring him to his father but having done so their sting is spent. Now he must trust to Franny and Tom to find some way of rescuing him. He hopes their approach is more adroit than his: a dead bear, a wounded lover; captivity. Could matters have taken a worse course? He has won his father's freedom, but to what end if his father is so used to his cage that, like a bird that has forgotten how to fly, he can only sit and peck at his own feathers? He stands, kicks at the dust in despair and wanders back to the workshop.

There, waiting for him in amongst his father's odd and gloomy automata, is a visitor—a gnomish man who stands and greets him as he enters. "Aah. You are Zachary," he says in Greek. He places a hand on Zachary's jacket, smooths it down, then caresses his hair, his cheek. His eyes bulge from his skull, as if they are being pushed out of it.

Zachary recoils. "Who are you?"

"My name is Mofeed Moussa, but your father always called me Number Two."

There is something oddly beguiling about the little man despite his unsettling looks. He has an innocence, a wish to please. "Why did he call you that?"

"Because I walked through the door after Number One!" he smiles.

"I fear my father was not in his wits."

"He was sensible enough in those days, I assure you. We had been instructed not to give him our names, and though in time your father came to be trusted, he never asked and I never told him." He winks—a tic rather than an invitation to conspiracy.

Zachary gestures to the man, Moussa, to sit. "Will you tell me something about my father?"

"It is why I came, Zachary Cloudesley," he says, extending his hands as if the truth were something to be caught, a substance light enough to float down through the dusty air of the room.

For the next hour Mofeed Moussa tells Zachary about the work he and his father did together, how often Zachary was talked of, and of the endless efforts to get some word out into the world to reach him. He describes how his father won the confidence and even the friendship of the kizlar agha, a man who terrifies all others.

"But my father did not seem at all like the man you describe when I saw him the day before yesterday."

"Ah no, most unfortunate."

"What happened?"

"You must understand that your father refused absolutely to invent a creature, a machine, capable of taking a man's life. But the sultan insisted. And so we introduced small faults and failings into the automata so they could not perform that function. Secretly, of course."

"Of course."

"I am sorry to say that your father was given certain potions, powders to make him more compliant, concoctions that caused him to see phantasms, to suffer deliriums. The kizlar agha put a stop to that in time, he being one who much prefers old-fashioned means of slaying a man—a strangling, a beheading." He rocks on his stool, looking down at his belly with a sly smile, knowing he has said something disloyal but amusing. "Then came our experiments with steam, but the condensing boilers kept exploding, and this resulted in his deafness, and though he regained his senses somewhat after the potions ceased, he suffered not to hear the birds in the morning, or his own voice, which cried out for you in the night and could be heard even in the eunuchs' quarters." ·

Zachary feels stricken with pity for his papa and for all that he has suffered. He has so many things he would like to ask Moussa and begins by pointing to the collection of strange metal creatures that surrounds them. "You and he made all of these?"

"We had no other duties."

"All for the sultan?"

"His Majesty lost all interest in your father and his machines many years ago. No, these we made for the amusement of the ladies of the harem."

"Then why are they here?"

"There are others there in the harem. We change them from time to time for novelty's sake. There is a giant silver cricket with wings made of sheer glass and that jumps, and also a lobster with claws that pinch mercilessly." Moussa turns and begins to walk away, which is when Zachary notices that his feet are bare, his toes pink and unsettling.

"Wait," says Zachary.

Moussa turns, expectant.

"Why was my father not freed long ago?"

"The kizlar agha wished you to come. You are the bird, you see. Your father was the worm. But you are the bird, yes." He smiles as if he has only just thought of the allusion, before he pads away on his small, blameless feet.

CHAPTER TWENTY-ONE

A QUESTIONABLE PLAN

July 1770, Constantinople

◉

Abel has come more to his senses this past month, little by little, though Frances cannot think he will ever be quite the man she first met twenty years ago, nor even that figure broken by Alice's death, or the one still more demolished after Zachary lost his eye. He seems to have crumbled away in stages like a Suffolk cliff falling piece by piece into the sea, bringing down its fields and houses and churches with it, so that the only trace of what went before are lanes ending in air and signposts to villages that lie beneath waves.

Each morning, Frances brings Abel to Tom's workshop, and they talk to him as best they can, encouraging him to speak of times past and in such manner bring him more to himself.

It is on the fourth morning that Tom makes an announcement. "It was an automaton that got us into this quandary and I do believe it will be an automaton to get us out of it."

"How so?" asks Frances.

"The master may not be fully in his own mind," says Tom, quietly, "but he sits with us and makes things all the while. Have you seen? See." He holds up a clockwork soldier, minuscule, exquisite, dressed as a janissary, and winds the key in its back to make it march up and down the table. "This he made in just two days, while you were out visiting. Katerina made his uniform. Isn't it beautiful?"

"Yes," says Frances, not quite understanding.

"We shall manufacture here a perfect resemblance of Zachary, but as the child he remembers, not as he is now. It will help the master recover his senses. I know it will, and we may then use it to free Zack."

"But how long will it take? Zachary is in peril. I know his prophecies to be haphazard and often delusional. They are unlikely to convince for long. What if the sultan tires of him, but instead of freeing him commits some further unspeakable cruelty?"

"That is just the point. We can work quickly, my lady, Naguib and the master and I, and when the automatic boy is ready we shall find some way to present him to the sultan, and have him write prophecies, and it will be a wonder that will soften even that cruel man. The work of constructing the automaton of his own dear boy will be a manner of healing for the master, but when complete it will be our means of winning Zachary's release. Clockwork in trade for flesh, and flesh in trade for clockwork. There is a symmetry in it, do you see?" He is excited, and Frances cannot deny there is a certain elegance in his proposal. Even if it is a course of action which carries only the slightest chance of success, it is a better prospect than waiting for the grinding cogs of diplomacy to achieve any progress. She watches Abel, busy making some new gewgaw, absorbed completely in his work, next Naguib, his serene face, his eyes upon her own, quietly trying to convince her with his gaze, and finally Tom, his hair trimmed short and carelessly, his jerkin smeared with grease, and his gruff manner that does not quite make her forget what he was when she first met him. "Since we have no other schemes . . ." she says at last, without conviction.

She pleads with Ibrahim's father, the grand vizier, to win Zachary's freedom, but he tells her the best to be hoped for is that the sultan keeps him alive. His own star is fading, he confesses, and he is certain to be dismissed from his exalted office in the coming days. The moment of greatest peril will come when the sultan tires of Zachary's prophecies. He is worried to distraction about his own son, naturally enough, since the poor boy shows little sign of recovery, lying in his bed in a delirium.

Frances maintains an outward calm, pretending to her usual confidence and irascibility; if all think her obdurate, so be it. In truth she is in quiet despair at the many calamities that have befallen them all since their arrival in Constantinople and is exhausted. For once in her life she wishes she did not have a fight on her hands.

Work on the automaton proceeds quickly. She walks each morning with Abel to the workshop, his gait easier day by day, and his talk lately is more of breakfast, the weather and the new buildings being constructed along their route rather than of eunuchs and shadows, of locks and chains. Each day the machine they are working on takes shape, its half-human frame filling with springs and levers and misshapen cams. All work in the shop has turned to the construction of the automatic boy, and she finds herself sharing in the absurd hope they all feel in the deliverance of clockwork. It is as if they were constructing a winged carriage that will fly them free, escaping this land of troubles. But she is too experienced in life's tribulations to believe in the thing quite as she should. She feels as she does whenever she is obliged to attend church, wanting to submit to the idea of God; envious, in truth, of that touching faith others seem to have, but however hard she prays she finds no answering voice, hears nothing but her own doubts and misgivings. And deep within those misgivings is the certain knowledge that she has been the cause of all of their misfortunes, for as sure as a key once turned sets a mechanism in motion, it was she who set the mainspring moving and the wheels spinning when she wrote a letter all those years ago that she can never confess to, for the truth of it will be enough to make all those who think well of her now see her for what she knows herself to be.

◙

CHAPTER TWENTY-TWO

PLAGUE

August 1770, Constantinople

◙

Zachary chalks them on the wall. It is his seventieth day in captivity, and he has had enough of obedience, of deference. He knows he must do something to change the pattern of his days if he is not to be caught in them for all eternity. Last month he was told the court would move to a palace in Belgrad Forest to escape the worst of the summer heat, and he felt certain he would then make his escape, even imagined Ibrahim rescuing him on horseback. But the war against the Russians goes badly, and the court has been kept at work in the swelter of the city, for empires that take a holiday when they are crumbling are thought unseemly.

He starts to wonder if he has been forgotten by all. Was this how it was for his father—caught like a bubble in glass, unnoticed? He is kept here only to make his false prophecies, much as a canary is caged for its chirping, cheerful to the unwitting ear, wretched to those who are sensitive to the many agonies of its song. Yet each day he forges the kizlar agha's false futures from foul deeds.

"Tomorrow," says the kizlar agha, spitting out a plum stone and throwing it over his shoulder, "you will tell His Majesty of a fire in Fundukli, in the street of the fishmongers."

"A fire in Fundukli tomorrow?"

"The fire will in fact be in Tophani, in the alley of the gold merchants. I shall have my men set it at midnight, and ensure it burns until morning."

"You are asking me to mislead, to give the wrong place?"

"I ask you nothing. You will tell His Majesty what I tell you to tell. The sultan is a great one for the putting out of fires. But I wish the alley of the gold merchants to be razed."

Zachary is barely interested anymore in the kizlar agha's motives. At first he was surprised to be given explanations so easily until he came to understand that the old eunuch is so bereft of moral feeling that he thinks there is nothing wrong in murder or arson or other human suffering in pursuit of his ends, being one of those men who believes his purposes are transcendent by simple virtue of being his own. And who, anyway, would Zachary tell? Those who might believe him already know, and those who do not know will not believe.

"I have hired an architect to build it anew. It is a slum. It shames the city."

Zachary knows it is hardly worth speaking, but he cannot help himself. "If the fire is not put out, people will die."

"Little Cloudesley, a good smoking clears the corruption of the air that brings the plague. So do not trouble yourself. We stagger from fire to plague and from plague to fire. Such is the pitiable condition of Stamboul."

"I will be blamed for telling of a fire in the wrong place."

"Be vague. Say there will be a fire near the sign of the fish, in a place by the water. Make it sound enough like Fundukli so it might be thought Fundukli. Spundukli, Yundukli. You know what to do." He hands him a plum, purple, with a bloom on it like mould.

The fire in Tophani, fanned by high winds and wood parched by the long sun of summer, kills two hundred souls. Every one of the sultan's fire engines was deployed miles away in Fundukli. Yet the kizlar agha seems pleased the next morning that so many old houses were cleared. "The flames even melted the gold—a blessing, since the work of the smiths there was fussy, overdone. I detest filigree. Don't you?"

"You have no conscience," says Zachary, as a fool kicks a wall knowing his foot cannot hurt the brick, but the brick is sure to hurt the foot.

"Conscience? You might as well say the autumn has no conscience when it makes the trees lose their leaves, or the churn when it turns milk to butter. It is change, that is all."

"And death."

"That too. Death has no conscience. Only life has that misfortune." He smiles, but it is not quite his usual thoughtless grin.

"The sultan will be in a rage," says Zachary.

"He will not see you today. When he got word of where the fire had struck he went to fight the flames himself and is exhausted."

"Then he is a man with some love for his subjects."

The kizlar agha seems caught by the word. "Love?" he says, as if the sentiment is unfamiliar to him. "It is possible. Do gods love, or do they only play with us, as we might choose to step on an ants' nest or step over it? To be a king is a strange disorder, half god, half man—both everything and nothing. I would not wish it on any being." He smiles, taps the side of his nose and marches away. Over his shoulder he says, "Plague is come to the city from Trebizond," with as little concern as if he had announced the arrival of a sack of walnuts.

Zachary is lying on his bed reading Horace when a servant calls out for him. His father had a good library, and it is a slight comfort to him to lose himself in hexameters during the long, airless days. Hearing his name called out again he climbs down the ladder and into the workshop, where the servant bows, turns and bids him follow. He is led to the sultan's audience chamber and thinks at first he is to be required to provide an unrehearsed prophecy, obliging his heart to quicken and mouth to parch. The kizlar agha is waiting for him outside the chamber. Zachary enters the dark room, its ceiling decked in heavy red and gold cloth. It is the first time he has been there when the sultan has not been upon his throne, and he takes the opportunity to look about. The windows are small and set high on the walls. Usually it is lit with a chandelier hanging on a long brass chain and heavy with candles which make the room bright and stately; but now, in the afternoon heat, it is sepulchral and surprisingly cool.

He feels a breath on his neck and spins around, startled, fearful. The kizlar agha says, "Don't you see who sits before the throne?"

His eyes take a moment to adjust to the gloom before he spies, sitting at a desk, a boy, dressed in Frankish clothes, his shoulders rising and falling almost imperceptibly with each breath. "Hullo?" he calls out, but the child does not turn. Approaching him he sees that he is writing something. The boy looks up, seeming to see Zachary and giving him a nod of recognition. Zachary sinks to the ground before him, just as he would before the sultan, yet he is on his knees not from terror but from astonishment. What confronts him is no stranger but he himself—a living, breathing simulacrum of that child he once was, though one with two eyes, blue and blinking and looking directly at him. This is an automaton, he tells himself, though his other self demands belief, wanting the magic of the moment to continue, for some miracle to occur. He reaches out a hand to touch his own face, half expecting to feel warmth, the pliability of flesh. But it is plaster and paint, an illusion, as it only ever could be.

When the kizlar agha speaks, his voice comes as a blow, reminding Zachary of his prison and his predicament. "What is it you are writing?" he asks.

"I?"

"You see yourself, do you not?"

"I . . . I . . ." he stands at the writing boy's shoulder to see that he is producing a prophecy, one that bears all the marks of one of the kizlar agha's familiar schemes.

A baker called Vissarian shall put poison in his bread, because he is mad, and will by such means kill seventy of his customers on the twenty-ninth. He will flee the city heading for Bulgaria but be pursued by his neighbours and hanged from a tree.

"You have given this automaton your cruel predictions?" accuses Zachary.

A voice, soft and familiar, speaks out. "It was I," says Tom, stepping forward from the shadows. "With some assistance, I confess."

"Tom!" declares Zachary, embracing him without restraint as if Tom were life itself, and the resurrection to boot, before he draws back, puzzled. "How are you here? This is a prison. Oh, do not be here! You are captured?"

Tom nods in the direction of the kizlar agha. "Your father and I and Naguib, we made the creature before you as our means of setting you free."

Zachary feels lightness rising up in him with strength enough to lift him clean through the roof and into the sky. He puts a hand over his mouth, as if to prevent the feeling from escaping him, before he turns, stricken with doubt, and asks the kizlar agha, "Will I be free?"

"The court will move tonight to the hills, to escape the plague. It would have passed, but a southerly wind has blown up and brought the fetid, poisoned air into every neighbourhood. The Spurrell will know of it already, I am sure."

Tom nods. "Seen it, smelt it."

"It is a great undertaking, moving all out of the palace," continues the kizlar agha, "we will begin at midnight and I shall pretend to His Majesty that you are ailing, and that your father made this automatic boy in secret, and that I have brought it in your place and left you dying here in the seraglio. I knew, naturally, of its manufacture. I have had your aunt, your father, the Spurrell watched all this time—your aunt most particularly, since she has taken to stirring agitation against order and tradition with the women of the city."

Zachary bows deep to him in mock gratitude. "Thank you for your efforts to familiarize yourself with my family and no less for allowing me to die alone." He is filled with a sudden urge to show Tom all the remarkable creatures his papa made during his long imprisonment, knowing he will be astonished by them. "Before we leave I'll show Tom some of the wonders my father made," he says. "Here—" Zachary reaches for Tom's hand, ready to lead him to his father's quarters and its collection of strange machines, but suddenly the kizlar agha claps his hands and two janissaries appear, one seizing Zachary, the other Tom. "To the Canoglu dungeon," he orders.

They are dragged protesting to a door in the back of the audience chamber. Zachary is hardly surprised by this latest betrayal, but he feels desperately for Tom, duped into creating the remarkable automaton, only for it to be used to bring him to this calamity. They are pushed, the two of them, down steep steps, hauled along a corridor lit by torches, its walls leaking ferrous water, then down again, the slippery steps now rank and salty. Farther and farther they go along narrow passageways. Tom is silent, bearing his treatment bravely, and Zachary wonders whether to shout out to him, but he cannot think of a single word of comfort or reassurance. They begin to climb from the damp passage, up steps that are at first rough-hewn but, as they ascend, of carved marble. A door appears before them and they are all of a sudden in a bright and orderly chamber, set out with desks and chairs. Windows look out on to the street beyond. The kizlar agha appears from the outside doorway like a jinni, a wide, satisfied smile on his face. "Welcome to the Canoglu dungeon, where, it is said, victims are sent and from which they never return." He laughs gleefully. "Never speak of your egress. In fact, never speak of what you have seen of the seraglio at all," he says quietly. "You will only be disbelieved."

"I am free?" asks Zachary.

"What is freedom, little Cloudesley? Am *I* free?" he directs a pudgy finger at his own heart. "Is your friend free? There is no such thing as freedom, never believe that. But you may leave this place, once and for all, and, if you are wise, you will never think of it again. Quit the city forthwith, before word reaches His

Majesty that you live. Know that it will be promulgated that you and all by the name of Cloudesley are in all perpetuity banished from the empire." He extends the stubby fingers of both hands as if to make the two of them vanish, yet it is he who disappears, shuffling behind a curtain like a maladroit magician.

Zachary and Tom stare at each other wide-eyed, as if expecting some further trap or test, but they are alone in the strange room and after a few moments in which they look at each other and at themselves, examining their feet, their hands as if doubting the reality of their own flesh, they step out into the street, giddy with expectation. The cobbled road is usually crowded with traders, officials, others on their way up the hill to the Sublime Porte or on their way down from it; it leads to the Fish Market Gate by the water, but today is almost empty. "People are in their houses, Zachary," says Tom.

"Why?"

"The plague has hit us hard. Hundreds are dead or dying already."

"Then we must leave the city straight away."

"I cannot leave, Zachary. Katerina will not go. She will stay home. We have lived through other pestilences and survived them."

They reach the water of the Golden Horn and pay a ferryman, whose face is covered in a cloth so he cannot breathe in the contagion, which it is known is carried on corrupt air, and most particularly near foul water. On the Galata side Zachary sees carts carrying bodies, and a plague doctor wearing his Thoth-like mask and a long black robe. Zachary grows fearful that those he loves might have succumbed. "How is Papa?" he asks, already sensing devastating news and shaking in expectation of it. He wonders whether release from the sera-glio has restored his preternatural powers, though he would wish them gone forever.

"He is more himself, if not quite as he was in the olden days, but perhaps he never will be after his long confinement." He reaches out, puts his hands on Zachary's arms, to keep him still. "He will know you, Zack, and be overjoyed to see you, but he cannot be seen beyond the confines of the house, since he is ban-ished, as are you now, so leaving as soon as you may is wise. But all who can are leaving now, and you might not find a horse easy to come by. The ships are not sailing for fear of being quarantined wherever they seek port."

"We have legs, Tom, and can walk."

"There is something else."

"Oh?" He fears something has befallen Ibrahim and almost blurts out his dread.

"It is . . . well, it is a great worry for us all, Zack."

Zachary urges his friend to speak what news he must, but he can see that Tom is struggling to find words. "Your great-aunt ails, I am sorry to tell," he says at last. "She was going about the city to her acquaintances who were fevering, bringing them water and figs and dates and raisins and light white wine—all that is known to alleviate the malaise. She said, in her usual manner, that she could not suffer it since she had had the measles as a girl and was immune to all diseases but melancholy."

Zachary cannot think of Franny as anything but invincible. "Is she very ill?" he asks, doubtfully.

"She is, Zack, yes." Tom is on the edge of tears.

"Then we will have to wait for her to recover."

In all the streets in Galata and high on the hill in Pera the doors and gateposts of the prosperous Frankish households bear daubs of yellow paint, for they have been caught by the disease's rude and swift intrusion into their quarter, which failed to give its customary nod and bow, its announcement of its intention to pay its morbid visit. This time, many were deprived of the chance to flee the corrupted air and make for the cool glades of the forests to the north, where the wealthy keep their plague houses.

Zachary enters the house to find it dark, the air filled with the scent of burning thyme and rosemary. Papa is at the table, head down, working away at some device, and does not hear Zachary call out to him. Tom waits in the doorway, though whether for fear of breathing in the contagion or from a reluctance to intrude on their reunion Zachary cannot tell.

"He will know you now, Zack," he says, "but his hearing is only a little improved."

Zachary approaches his father and watches over his shoulder as he works intently on a watch of a small and simple design. His papa looks up and, seeing him, says, "I am making this for Katerina, Zack. It is in keeping, I think, with her character, which is kind and plain, do you not agree?"

Zachary, conscious that Tom is at the door and hearing all, puts an arm around his father's shoulder, brings his mouth close to his ear and asks, "How are you, Papa?"

"Sit with me a while, Zack," says his father quietly, without turning away from his work on the watch. "Let's be together and grow familiar in an easy way, with no tears or uproar. You have seen a little, I understand, of what I have endured, and no doubt suffered in similar manner, and it is a hard thing to get out of one's thoughts, is it not? I am sorry you have been subjected to all of that on top of all else in your short life. I have been the worst father in all the world, and even now am no better since I am too frightened to know how to play the part. Old King Lear made such a mess of things, didn't he? But he had the excuse of three daughters and a divided kingdom. For my part I only had you, and though you have always been more precious to me than any other thing, I have failed you."

"No, Papa, no," says Zachary, embracing him. Despite his papa's injunction against tears their faces are both wet. He sits with him, asking him questions about the device he is making for Katerina, and about Tom (who he sees is no longer waiting in the doorway), and also about his sleep and diet, since he does not wish to raise memories of the seraglio by speaking of the strange automata in his papa's old quarters, or of the kizlar agha. Zachary knows he must be gentle, yet he asks as he must about Franny.

"Franny?" says his papa, almost as if he had forgotten about her. "She is upstairs I believe. She is not well, Zachary. She has an ague."

Zachary wonders whether Abel has quite understood that it is the plague that is once more in the city.

Franny's chamber is dark, her rasping breath audible from ten feet away. He enters, holding a sprig of fragrant herbs before his nose as Samuels, who is in there with her, instructs him to before he retreats, giving him that half-smile that could mean anything.

"No more bleeding," she says, faintly. "If I must die let me at least die with a little blood in my veins."

"Franny, it is I, Zachary."

"Oh, Zachary, Zachary, Zachary. My beloved little boy." She turns to face him, her eyes tiny, her skin tight upon her bones. He sees buboes upon her neck, seeping clear liquid, slightly yellow and foul-smelling. Her tongue is black and swollen, so that he has to strain to understand what it is she is saying. "Didn't we have happy days together, for a while at least?"

"They were always happy days, Franny."

"We should never have left Briar House," she murmurs, "and how will we get all the birds to fly? Will the horses be fed and watered? Who will be giving Mr. Jepherson his dinners? Where is Leonora? I must ask Mrs. Morley for the keys. She keeps them on her belt, you know." Her face oozes sweat.

"You are in a delirium, Franny. A good sleep will help."

She coughs, her body racking with spasms, and blood dribbles out on to the pillow. He steps forward. "Do not come close!" she gasps. "I was mopping at the sweat and blood of my dear friends this past week, and in such manner fell victim to the contagion. I will not permit you to die, my dear, for otherwise all has been in vain." She laughs, faintly. "All is in vain in any case, since we are all of us nothing more than . . ." But the thought fades and she falls silent.

"I will sit here, in the corner, and keep you company from a distance, and shall keep these herbs before me."

"Herbs," she croaks, "whoever heard of a life saved by oregano?"

"Can I bring you water?"

"I have beside the bed rosewater to treat me, but it is not efficacious. Samuels has been attentive, but he is not made of flesh, is he? Sometimes I think your father must have made him, though he is not built of steel, but of some stony matter. Flint, perhaps. He is made all of flint and impervious to infection." She lies back on the pillow, exhausted, and seems to sleep.

After an hour Zachary gets up from his chair and begins to creep out of the room, but like a lioness that always has one eye open, she sees him. "Zachary," she says, her voice a little stronger, "I must tell you something, and you need hear me out."

He steps closer.

"You know I have not always been as attentive of my affairs as I ought."

"I . . . I . . ."

"Do not dissemble, my dear. I have liked to sow confusion, for there is nowhere to hide in order, or so was my reasoning."

"Do not speak of it now."

"It is my will. I fear it is likely to bring you all difficulties, for being . . . for being . . ."

"Another time, Franny. We can talk of it when you are well."

"But I must!" she hisses. "I must, because you will be bound by it. I long intended to write a new one, but then you left in such a hurry and I followed, and . . ." She lies back, sapped.

"Do not worry about such things now."

She stirs once more. "You see, I was so keen to ensure one deserving of a fortune should have it, whatever their status, and so . . ."

"I do not care if I am disinherited. Truly."

"You haven't been . . . do not think . . . and I do not care at all about your proclivities. Why you should prefer men I cannot imagine. Women are far more interesting, being subtle where men are, on the whole, vulgar and unwholesome." Her speech is rambling, and Zachary stands, making to leave. "And the male sex is an odd thing, like a riddle, hard one moment, soft another. I had a few in my time."

"Franny!"

She looks at him as if she does not know him. "What was I saying?"

"Nothing. Nothing that made any sense."

"Go, then. Go," she says, raising a hand feebly in dismissal.

He creeps out of the room. Samuels is out on the corridor and, without a word or look, takes his place.

Downstairs his father is still absorbed in his work. Seeing Zachary, he says, "The doctor will come at seven in his strange costume. But your great-aunt won't let him near. She always was an obstinate woman, of course." He inserts a spring with minuscule tweezers. "I have secured us places on a coach bound for Salonica," he adds.

"When?"

"What?"

"*I* have secured it," says Samuels, from the stairs. "For when her ladyship is recovered or . . . when she is not."

Zachary goes to his own chamber and, finding clean clothes, decides he must seek out Ibrahim. No one has spoken of him and he has not dared ask, as if to speak of him at all would break a spell and bring a hideous truth into existence. As he tiptoes along the landing, he hears Franny calling out his name, and steps back into her noisome chamber.

"Is it you, Zachary?" she says. "I cannot see. I am blind. It is near the end, I know."

"Do not say so."

"I must speak to you on some matter . . ."

"I have said, you are not to worry yourself about the will or some such. Use your strength to grow well."

"It is, it is . . ." She struggles for breath. "Bring the candle near, will you?"

He does as she bids and stands before her, as close as he dares. "No, I am blind, it is true. I should have liked to see your face one last time, for I have loved it so."

"Franny," says Zachary, choking back tears.

"I must tell you something of the greatest importance, and you must listen. I may then meet my maker, whether she be up above or down below or nowhere at all, more likely, having told at last a truth I should have told you long, long ago."

Zachary squats by her bed, dutiful but uncertain whether it is Franny or her delirium that speaks to him.

"I always wanted you to myself, Zachary, greedily, selfishly for myself, because I had lost your dear mother and I hated . . . yes, I hated your father for it."

"Franny?"

"And when you lost your eye, you poor boy"—she casts her sightless stare in his direction, as if she might see again his glinting gold eye—"and your father put you into my care at last I was overjoyed. But you must know, Zachary, that he regretted his decision almost straight away, and soon after wrote to say he wished to take you back into his care. And it was then I did something wicked, so that I might keep you in my custody . . ." She gasps, cries out, struggles for breath, causing Zachary to lift her head from the pillow to ease her breathing. Recovering a little, she whispers, "I wrote to his old schoolfriend, a man called Claxton . . . a man Alice once told me would be your father's nemesis." She takes a breath, shallow and insufficient. "I had read in the *Gazette* that Claxton had recently been put into a position of power and I wrote to him and told him to seek out your father and put the idea into his head that he should flatter Abel into taking a position in Constantinople."

"Papa could have said no," says Zachary, calmly, wishing her needless confession at an end.

She sits upright, almost as if recovered, her eyes ablaze. "But that is just it, child. He could not!" she declares. "For when Claxton doubted the venture, or at least his ability to persuade Abel of the logic of it, I told him that his master should make some threat against your welfare, and that it would be sufficient to gain absolute cooperation." She sobs, falls back on to the bed. "There. That is my great shame."

"Why tell me all this?" says Zachary, feeling his anger rise, more at the needlessness of Franny's confession than at Franny herself. "It is past, and I would have you well and then we can speak of it more if we must."

"I shall not recover. You thought your father unloving all those years, yet it was I who stood between his love and yours . . . it was I," she weeps, muttering words that are incomprehensible.

She sleeps at last, and after sitting with her a while longer Zachary steals from the room and out the house, casting an eye at his papa as he goes, seeing him still hunched over his workbench and oblivious to his departure. Franny's revelation is sensational, and yet Zachary has always understood the landscape of her sentiments. He asks himself what has changed and thinks not so much. She loved him enough to fight for him, and that is not so shameful, even if it led his father into peril. He resolves to tell her just this when he returns, but first he must seek out Ibrahim, for he knows he will not sleep that night if he does not find him, or at least some news of him, and he must sleep, for he is exhausted.

He walks the empty streets, which are being cleaned with buckets and brushes, it being well known that the miasma that carries the plague settles on cobbles, on clothing, on market stalls and all else, and so must be rinsed away.

The grand vizier's palace is cloaked in a strange silence. Not even a guard is on the door. He walks through the gardens, the fountains splashing innocently, unobserved. "Hello," he calls out in Greek. "Who is at home?"

He expects a servant, a cook, someone to emerge. He walks on through the house, into the main room, where no lamp is lit, the low cushions bearing no sign of recent use, the tables empty. Here and there a brass pot, a lamp, is overturned, suggesting a hasty departure. He goes up the stairs to Ibrahim's chamber, a feeling of creeping dread upon him. It is growing dark and he knows he should have waited until tomorrow, should have stayed with Franny. "Hello?" he calls out again, more tentatively. Ibrahim's chamber is empty, the sheets on his bed still rumpled. He runs the palm of his hand across them to feel for warmth, but they are long cold. He sees spots of dried blood on them, and there is the lingering odour of sickness in the room. He goes to the wardrobe where Ibrahim's robes hang, pushing his face into them, wanting to be reminded of the scent of his friend, breathing in a faint memory of summer, of laughter and friendship. Of love.

"*Efendim?*"

He is startled out of his reverie by a servant, ancient and hunched, who holds up a lamp to peer into Zachary's face.

"Where is Ibrahim, sahib?" he asks in his rudimentary Turkish.

"Gone."

"Gone?"

The old man shrugs, turns.

Zachary grabs his shoulder. "Gone where?"

"They are all gone," says the servant, waving a hand toward the south. "The master is banished to Egypt."

"And Ibrahim?" Zachary is certain he is to be told he is dead.

The old man shrugs again, juts out his lip, which could mean anything. "The plague is here. Why are you?" he says.

"To find Ibrahim. He is my friend."

"I remember you, with your predictions," he says, or so Zachary surmises, since he cannot understand precisely what it is the old man is saying. The servant beckons him to follow, the light of the lamp needed to pick their way down the stairs. At the bottom the old retainer bids him wait, returning a moment later with a leather-bound book and handing it to him. Zachary is led out of the house, through the dark, jasmine-scented garden and onto the street, the heavy wooden doors cluttering shut behind him. In the light from a doorway Zachary sees that the book is Virgil's *Eclogues*, with passages speaking of love and reunion underlined. In the front, in an unsteady hand, an inscription in Greek.

ζ

Aς μην θρηνούμε για αυτό που έχουμε χάσει, εσύ και εγώ, για αυτό που είχαμε ήταν καλύτερο από ό, τι πολλοί εραστές γνώριζαν ποτέ.

I

Z

Let us not grieve for what we have lost, you and I, for what we had was better than many a lover ever knew.

I

Zachary hurries back to Franny and Papa. The city now seems to him a vision of Hades, carts in every alley, the bodies of the dead being lifted out and piled high upon them, the call of the plague doctors muffled by the long-beaked masks which poke from their hoods and gowns, making them look like tall birds greedy for human carrion. Abel knows what it is they call out in their muted Turkish, and he knows, too, that in some households there is no one to lift the lifeless bodies and bring them out into the street. It will only be several days after the contagion is past that the smell of putrefaction will bring some neighbour to batter down a door and lift out the raddled, rotting flesh to be found within. Sometimes a child is found, unmarked by the disease but starved to death, their last terror frozen there on their innocent face.

Bring out your dead.

It is the call of all time, of every place.

When he arrives home, his papa's face tells him. Franny is dead.

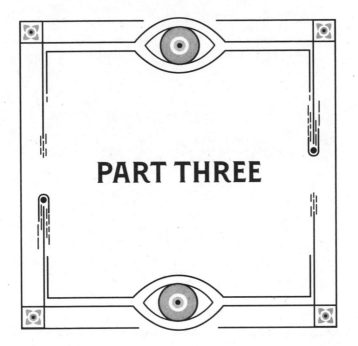

PART THREE

CHAPTER TWENTY-THREE

A SLOW FORGIVENESS

November 1770, En Voyage

◙

Franny was buried with what few dignities could be mustered. At least she was consigned her own grave and headstone in the English churchyard, and not thrown into a common plague pit. They left that night, stealing out of the city in the coach that Samuels had mysteriously procured and were on the road for nearly two weeks before they reached the gates of Salonica, where they were examined by a plague doctor and, after the payment of certain bribes, permitted to enter the city. Papa wished to return to England as quickly as possible and calculated that if they sailed from Salonica to Venice, avoiding the plague gripping Belgrade and Ragusa, and then took the road from Venice to Calais, they would be in London before Christmas.

It is on the voyage out from Salonica that they begin to talk at last. Finding themselves on deck together, looking out at the wooded hills of Skopelos, Zachary ventures, his mouth close to his papa's ear, "Your automata, sir, that I spent seventy days with, they were part heaven and part hell, were they not?"

His father seems, at first, startled, and then confused. "Were they?" he says, uncertainly.

"There was a creature with a long neck, an ostrich, yes, and a dancing skeleton, an armoured pig that rolled into a ball, a dwarf, a . . ."

"Do not make me think of them!" groans Papa. "Help me forget, won't you?"

"Yes, Papa. I'm sorry."

His father stumbles away in an agitation. He has barely asked Zachary a single question on the entire journey—not about his life in Tring with Franny, or even about his efforts to win his freedom. Is he not interested in what books his son has read, what creatures he has studied?

The next night, as they eat in the ship's mess, Zachary says, "I have llamas at Briar House—or had. They are from Peru and—"

"I know what they are," Papa snaps. "And you have no need to shout."

"I—"

"You want me to know you, Zachary. I understand, but I am . . ." Papa looks at him while Zachary awaits his explanation, but then takes to gazing into his soup as if the keys to their future lurk somewhere in the bottom of the bowl.

The awkwardness eases a little as they pass Corfu. Out on deck, looking up at the billowing sails, Zachary finds that he has his papa's attention and so tells him about Mrs. Morley coming to live at Briar House, and of how poised and ladylike Leonora became, though still given to occasional fits of temper. He tells him of Franny's great affection for the girl, and how the house was splintered by her sudden, unexplained disappearance along with her mother.

"Why did they leave, do you think?" asks Papa.

"It was Franny, I think. She was always so careless with her correspondence, as I have told you. My suspicion is that Mrs. Morley saw something that upset her beyond measure, and though she was broad-minded, once resolved upon a course of action there was no persuading her otherwise."

"That I do recall."

Zachary is close to telling him of Franny's confession, but decides against and tells him instead about Mr. Mendel, his universal knowledge, his remarkable skill as teacher, also of his melancholic nature. "Can a man die of melancholy, do you suppose?" he asks.

"Oh yes," says Papa with conviction.

Zachary wants to ask about the great steam-driven wheel, but he knows he cannot without risking causing his papa distress. There is, though, another thing Zachary wishes to know, and it is the most important thing of all: he wishes to learn about his mother. Franny had told him stories of her beauty, her willfulness, her talent at the fortepiano, her tendency to the whimsical. Once, when he had been troubled by one of his visions, Franny had told him that his mother had visions, too, but they had passed, just as his would. He hadn't believed her.

"I should like you to tell me about my mother, please," he asks Papa as they sail from Ancona, where they had made port for the night. They are sitting in their cabin, his father on his bunk.

"What's that?" Papa asks, turning to face him, since he struggles to catch words without sight of the lips that utter them.

"Tell me about Mama," he repeats.

Papa leans his head back on the pillow and stares at the cabin roof in silence. Zachary sits at the small desk, writing an account of his incarceration in the seraglio, which he intends to send to the *London Magazine*. Thinking his father will not respond, he picks up his pen, dips it in the inkwell, and resumes his writing.

When his father begins to talk, his voice sounds disembodied, almost trance-like. "She was a wonder. I never could believe she was mine, though she never was, not really, no more than a bird that sits in your favourite tree and sings to you is yours. She was always given to odd sayings, strange memories that she claimed to be her own, but could not have been."

"Such as?" asks Zachary, but he is not heard. He thinks it best, in any case, to let his father speak on.

"She had other suitors, many I suspect, being Frances's heir and, besides, being both beautiful and clever. Why I was chosen from them all I cannot say. I am not sure it was your mother who chose me, or not exactly. Your great-aunt Frances thought me suitable because she saw something in me out of place, like a crack on a plate, or a pulled thread in silk. That was what she was look-ing for, someone who had a flaw, a blemish I should say, to match Alice's own. We were both apart, a little, you see, from the bustle of the everyday, a little caught up inside our own worlds, and so we made another world of our own together, and we made three girls in quick succession but none . . ." His voice catches and he lets out a great shaking sob, taking Zachary by surprise. ". . . not one lived. The smallpox came next and took away my mother and sisters and left us alone but for the men in the workshop and the servants, and we were close with them all. What else? We were equals, I should say, for your mother was not a woman for meekness, any more than I was ever a man for dominion." He turns his head to one side, looking at Zachary to see if he is listening, and then, turning back to face the low wooden ceiling, continues. "With my mother and sisters dead, Frances came to stay often, telling us how we should run the household, and how I might increase the business of the workshop by manufacturing telescopes and other astronomical instruments. She was ever impractical, your great-aunt. We should have given up on our hopes of a child, losing three in quick succession and Alice a little weaker after each. But it was Aunt Frances who had the notion of a new manner of midwifery, with more books, more instruments, more advice on diet and rest and suchlike, and so . . . and so"—he takes a breath, a sigh—"so we came to your mother's confinement with you."

"It were better I had never been born."

If he hears he makes no sign of it. "There were signs, early on, that all was not as it should be. Alice had dizzy spells, ate unusual quantities of eels, felt cold when she should have felt hot, and hot when she should have been cold. Pike, the midwifeman that Frances had engaged, came nearly every day to listen at her belly and cast his opinions about. But how we wanted you—you, Zachary," he says, turning once more to him, "and thought we could conjure you into the world from nothing more than the threads of our desire. We should not have wanted you so much."

His father's soliloquy only serves to confirm Zachary's worst fears. He can never be forgiven for being the cause of his mother's death. He looks down at the page he has been writing to see it blotted with tears. As if deafness were a contagion passed from one to another with the ease of a cold, he finds he cannot hear whatever else it is his father is saying. Soon after that his voice falls quiet, and Zachary blows out the candle, crawls into his bunk and sleeps.

After that Zachary asks him nothing, and it is Papa, rather, who begins to ask questions, about his friends in Tring (none), his animals (he lists them, without further detail), his preferred reading (the Roman poets).

"You made a friend of the grand vizier's son, I was told?"

Zachary's breath stumbles, and he has to force himself to gasp for his next. "Yes. Ibrahim."

"There was that accident with the bear, the same day I was freed and you were taken. Did you see him after?"

"Never, no." He doesn't wish to say anymore.

"Oh?"

Reluctantly, he adds, "His father was banished, and he must have gone with him. I fear he carried a great wound from the bear attack."

"You were close?"

He hesitates. "Very."

His papa nods. "I had such a friend at your age. We were educated together by a tutor as remarkable as your Mr. Mendel, a man of wildly liberal opinion called Catchpenny. George Claxton was my friend's name. Still is, I suppose, unless he has been ennobled for services to villainy and taken the name of some poor village as his own. We were like brothers, George and I—more than brothers. We were something powerful when together, something like a battalion, and felt the world could be turned whichever way we chose at our bidding. Was it like that for you and Ibrahim?"

Zachary feels that deep ache, a hunger that can't ever be satisfied. "Something like it, sir. Yes."

"But it was George that got me into the terrible business with the spying machine, and had it not been for that . . ." He seems lost in his thoughts, before adding, "Well, your friends are ever likely to let you down, Zachary. Mark my words."

Zachary begins to say something about Claxton, about Franny's involvement with him, wondering how he can do so without betraying his own memories of Franny and his papa's alike, yet as he speaks, he sees he has lost his father's attention, and he thinks he will leave the matter for another time, if that time will ever come.

When they arrive in Venice, Papa is eager that they visit Murano, having heard of a glass blower making perfect replicas of eyes. He takes Zachary for a fitting and the next day Zachary is once again a young man with the appearance of having one more eye than is strictly necessary.

"It looks well on you, Zachary," says his father over dinner that night, leaning back to admire the glass eye with pride.

Feeling an urge not exactly to ingratitude, but certainly to independence, Zachary says, "I am used to having but one, and still have but one. It is a deceit, to pretend to two." He resolves to wear it a while to please his father, but to revert to his golden eye as soon as he may.

His father smiles nervously. He has been anxious all that day, Zachary notices. At first he thinks it because of the fitting of the eye, yet it becomes apparent that it is because he wishes to make some announcement. "I have given you the impression, I think . . ." He dabs gravy from his lips, coughs to clear his throat, preparing Zachary for the import of what is to follow. "I am guilty," he begins again, "very guilty, I fear, of giving you the impression that you were not wanted by your mother and me. But you were wanted, and above all things. We talked of you, and though we did not dare give you a name, since we had given your sisters each names and none lived to use it on their lips nor we on ours, we thought of you, and of what you might become, and she knew you were a boy."

Zachary, unprepared, allows his emotions to spill out on to the red check cloth that sits between them. "You have never forgiven me," he declares.

"Forgiven you?" says his father, confused. "For what?"

"For killing Mama."

"No, Zachary. No, that's not true." He leans toward him, puts a hand on his cheek, but Zachary recoils.

"You sent me away!" declares Zachary, all the hurt he has been storing up, not just on the journey, not even that of the past months, but all of it, all his pain and confusion, everything he'd felt all his life coming tumbling out, as unstoppable as oil from a tipped jar, and even as the words spill, and even though he knows his father's actions were, at least in part, the result of Franny's plot, even as he tries to stop himself, he finds he cannot. "You sent me away, first putting me with Mrs. Morley, and when I tried to make you see me, notice me, when I ran into the peacock's tail, you sent me away again. You sent me to Franny. And then you went away, and I knew you lived even when all told me you were dead and even then, when I found you, even then"—he hears his voice, loud and cracking with sorrow—"even now you cannot love me!"

Papa, already stooped from his years of incarceration, and no less from all his hours hunched over a workbench, seems to rupture before his eyes. "No," he rasps. "No, that is not how it is at all."

But Zachary has already stood from the table, crumpling his napkin and throwing it onto the cloth without being able to bring himself to look again at his papa before stalking out of the place alone, watched by the other diners, whose eyes have been drawn by their argument as flies to sugar.

It is not until almost a month later, in Paris, that they speak again of anything other than the road or their supper. They are lodging on the Île de la Cité, close to Notre-Dame, flecks of snow falling from high clouds. He feels his papa's hand on his shoulder, and then he is being pulled close to him, warming him in the chill. "You must hear me out, Zachary, here beneath the gaze of these grotesques, since we know their evil look is not to do evil but to keep evil away, and it seems to me we have used words too often these past weeks like grotesques, not to give meaning but, somehow, to keep meaning away."

"Best it were kept away, then," says Zachary, "if it were to do evil."

He is not heard in the wind, which is enough to howl out his papa's already poor ear.

"I wanted to tell you the truth of it the day we got your new eye, but you walked away and we were both upset and I did not know quite how to say what I wanted to say—needed to say."

A chestnut seller pushes his cart close to them, shouting out, *Chauds, les marrons, chauds.* His papa waves him away and continues with his speech, seemingly well prepared. "I had no choice but to have you nursed by a stranger, and that we found Mrs. Morley that day you came into the world, and that she became so much more to us than a stranger, that seemed to me the first good sign after you were born. Your great-aunt was always full of ideas for your upbringing and came to stay, but she and Mrs. Morley argued so bitterly I thought it best to keep Mrs. Morley and let

Frances go, since the other way around would not have served, and Frances, besides, had her estate to run and businesses. You were fiercely clever, Zachary, always, even as a tiny infant, and like your mother in so many ways. And it was as if you had an extra eye, not just two, and a tongue that could speak to us without words.

"You were always special, Zachary. More ingenious than any other child, and you were interested in the work of the shop, in the mechanisms we made there. And Tom, well, you and Tom were close always, he was like an uncle to you. I did not like to keep you out of the place, though I should have done. I was always afraid I'd do you some damage, because, you see"—he takes a breath, stumbles—"because I knew I could not make another you, not from clockwork, not from brass and china clay and glass, however great my skills."

Zachary turns at last to face his papa. "But you did. You made an automatic me."

"That was not you. It was a shabby trick. You are warm and full of hope and life." He puts his hands upon Zachary's cheeks. "You are unusual, and think your own thoughts, thoughts that no man could put in your heart. I know this. It was always true, Zachary. You are unique. But when you lost your eye . . ."

Zachary remembers even now the running, the sharp point, his father not seeing him, his crazed desire to win his father's attention. "You went away, and even though I know now that it was not what you wanted, not truly, it hurt me," he confesses.

"That is what I wanted to tell you about most particularly, but . . ." Abel looks about at the falling snow and says, "Let us find somewhere warm."

They go into a small wine shop, each taking a glass of red wine and sitting in front of a fierce fire. "I was made to go to

Constantinople against my wishes, and to make that infernal chess-playing machine. I did not want to go."

Zachary knows he must wait for the explanation that will surely follow.

"You were threatened, Zachary. I was told you would not be safe if I did not do as the minister wanted."

"What minister?"

"Lord Carteret, long dead now. I don't know if he would have carried out his threat, perhaps not, but I could never take another risk with you, do you understand? I had damaged you enough."

Zachary, understanding now that he can never reveal the truth behind that threat for the injury it will cause to his father, says, "I wrote to every prime minister about you, sir, and to the king."

His father gives him a look of bafflement. "If you were so convinced that I did not love you, then why you were so determined on my behalf?"

Zachary knows the words he will use, since they are the ones he has carried in his heart all his life. "Because I do love you. And all I wished for above all else was to be loved by you in return."

His papa leans forward, tipping over his glass of wine but paying it no attention, and kisses his son on the forehead. "So there we were, the two of us, like Jupiter's moons, orbiting and thinking each other icy, simply because we could not touch."

One of the drinkers in the wine shop turns to observe the father and son embrace, the father kissing the son's head again and again, as if in absolution.

CHAPTER TWENTY-FOUR

A STRANGE BEQUEST

March 1771, London

He hears his papa shout up to him from down the stairs. "Zachary, are you awake?" Although today is his seventeenth birthday, today they must visit the offices of Mr. Dray at St. James's Square for the reading of Franny's will. Reverend Ratcliffe is executor and is due by noon.

"Aye, Papa!" he shouts. His father's hearing is much improved, but not so good as he thinks it to be.

"I'll send Samuels in to dress you."

"I shall dress myself."

"What's that?"

"Never mind."

Samuels dressed him yesterday and the day before, but that surreptitious smile of his made Zachary feel as if he were carrying some defect much greater than the lack of an eye, besmirching him for the rest of the day.

His father's voice is at the door, whispering through the wood. "Zachary?"

"Yes, Papa," he says loudly.

"Smart now. Your best. You will most likely be a young man of means by this afternoon."

"Very well." He doesn't know what Franny told Papa about her will and he has resolved firmly never to tell him about her confession. He has no wish to draw out the past, and even less any desire for a fortune. All he longs for is Ibrahim, or if he cannot have him, that his longing for him might lessen into a duller ache. Soon, he thinks, he will be back on the road. He was happy those weeks riding Bouillie, free to make himself whatever he wanted to be. Even the swindling Moffatt seems, in retrospect, an encounter more intriguing than upsetting. Besides, he and his father have only recently begun to speak to each other without those stubborn silences and misunderstandings, and he hardly wants to argue about an inheritance he has no wish for. Let the will say what it must—it cannot change him.

Correspondence from Tom Spurrell awaited them on their homecoming, in which that good man reported on the return of sweet air to Constantinople, and of several new commissions for the seraglio. In still-happier news he wrote of Naguib's marriage to a woman who had once seen him dance at the Mevlevihanesi. It was only in closing that he revealed his great surprise—that he and Katerina had become father and mother to a little girl, having found the infant laid in a basket at their door one morning. On learning that the little one had been orphaned in the terrible plague that fell upon the city they made her their own, naming her Hephzibah, after Tom's late mother.

Zachary is sitting at his desk writing a reply to Tom when there is a sound through the window of singing, off-key yet resonant, the voice as familiar as a pair of old boots: *All people that on earth do dwell / sing to the Lord with cheerful voice . . . dum-de . . . dum . . . dum. . . . We are the flock he surely feeds / the sheep who by his hand were made.* A knock on the door, cheerful; desperate. Soon after, Papa is calling Zachary down.

"Aah. Ah. Yes indeed," says Ratcliffe, once through the door and standing in the hallway, as always racked with some embarrassment that only he perceives. Dogless as he is, he can only carry his own mortification. He pulls off his hat and holds it before him, looking Zachary up and down. His wig is in need of powder. "Zachary. You have had quite the adventure, I hear."

"I have, sir. Many excitements."

"Oh, but Lady Peake-Barnes. Oh, oh . . ." He bites his lip and looks from Zachary to Papa. "I do not know what to say," says Ratcliffe with a tear in his eye. "Ah! Prayer," he declares, as if remembering with relief its utility. "Let us pray for her dear departed soul."

They stand, the three of them, and are soon joined by Samuels, who attempts to take Ratcliffe's coat from his shoulders while the reverend resists, engaged as he is in the process of praying, head bowed, hands clasped. "Dear Frances, our wise companion, aunt, great-aunt, mistress of Briar House, irregular congregant, fine horsewoman, astronomer and ornithologist, may the Good Lord accept you into His loving arms and, and . . ."

"Not argue with you," mutters Samuels, wrestling the coat into his arms and retreating.

"Give you rest. Amen," says Ratcliffe, quickly.

"Amen," say Zachary and Papa together. After a silence to permit some consideration of Franny's soul, Zachary, remembering that Ratcliffe has a wife—a frail and permanently perplexed woman, asks, "How is Mrs. Ratcliffe?"

Ratcliffe cocks his head to one side, as if he had not thought of his wife for a good long while. "Elisabeth is well, very well, thank you, Zachary." He frowns, puzzled. "She still has ambition on my behalf, I am sorry to say. I have long told her it is a hopeless cause, notwithstanding her facility at writing my sermons. She proposes that I have them published. Can you imagine?" He laughs, forlornly.

They take tea and discuss the meeting that is to come. "It seemed to me best that we should hear the will together, since Mr. Dray could hardly send you a copy of it what with you being on the road in far-off places and . . . and . . ." He coughs, turns first red then puce, prompting Zachary to hammer on his back, imagining a macaroon had become lodged in his throat. "Thank you, thank you, dear boy," says Ratcliffe, turning to him, "I am choking merely on a predicament."

Papa leans forward and offers Ratcliffe an encouraging smile.

"I should declare my surprise, first of all, that your aunt should have made me executor of her will, given that we were in such profound disagreement on almost every matter."

"Then it is surprising," says Papa.

"On the other hand—and I have thought about this a good deal, as you might imagine, ever since word reached us of that good lady's demise and I received a letter not a day after from Mr. Dray to inform me of the contents of the will—as to why she might have thought me in any way a suitable person."

"You are a man of God," says Papa.

Ratcliffe regards him with bafflement. "I hardly think that a qualification. Were it not for Elisabeth our affairs should be in great disarray. It is a miracle that she runs the rectory on three hundred a year."

"Well, if there's a miracle to be had, best it comes to a rectory," says Papa.

"We are not papists, Cloudesley," declares Ratcliffe in mild alarm. "They are the ones for holy visions and bloody tears. Our Lord performed miracles and they are there in the gospels and let that be the place for them. Faith is its own miracle."

"Indeed."

"I have concluded—with respect to my own role in this matter of the will—that it is because I was so fully acquainted with both the principal beneficiaries." He colours again, and breaks out into a perspiration. "Oh dear, it is all so very difficult."

"Proceed," Papa urges, gently.

"I would prefer not to, if you do not object, Mr. Cloudesley. The stipulations of the will are complicated and I came to the view that it would be a great assistance to me in my duties as executor that we three hear the terms of the, of the . . . equally, and you may help me understand how best I should proceed."

The poor man looks stricken. "How are your dogs?" asks Zachary, trying to ease his discomfort.

"I am glad to say they are not beneficiaries of your great-aunt's will, Zachary. They almost alone are not." He exhales and, having shared a little of his wretchedness about the room, leans back in his chair and looks about as if only now permitting himself to see it. "Was that your father, Cloudesley?" he asks, pointing at a portrait.

"It was. Joseph Cloudesley."

"What sort of man was he?"

"A crab. Closed in his shell one day and all pincers the next."

"Oh? Oh dear. Yet you are not in the least crabbed."

"That I attribute to my mother," says Papa, but Zachary wonders whether a little of the crab persists in his father's nature, all the same.

Dray's offices are, as solicitor's offices are in every place, endowed with a fine address and nothing to justify it, like a noble title without so much as an acre. They walk up narrow stairs, along narrower passages, squeeze around corners barely wide enough for a man, up further stairs and eventually reach a door, tap upon it and are admitted to a garret, piled high with papers and two desks, a clerk at one, harried, and at the other Mr. Dray, beneficent in his empire.

"Please sit," he commands graciously, his voice a drawl, sounding as if he is chewing a recalcitrant toffee and cannot quite get it out of his teeth.

"Now then, this will, of which Reverend Ratcliffe has the misfortune to be executor, is, appropriately enough, given your recent excursions"—he looks up at them, his face round, his eyes round, everything about him round: his spectacles, his nose, his mouth— "byzantine." Pleased with himself, Dray waves his fingers in the air as if releasing a flutter of butterflies. "I knew Lady Peake-Barnes better than many of my clients, given the regularity of her correspondence." He catches the eye of Stubbs, and some silent pain is exchanged between them. "And there were disputes of great variety to resolve, you understand"—he sniffs, pulls out a snuff-stained handkerchief and blows—"particularly relating to her many efforts to adopt one child or another, which never came to aught since she never could find one who had the good fortune of a mother or father willing to forsake it." He peers over his spectacles first at Papa and then at Zachary with great meaning. "I should have thought there no shortage of orphans in this world but there we are, Lady Peake-Barnes never had one come sufficiently to her attention." He releases another flutter of butterflies and smiles.

It strikes Zachary that the solicitor is not being very respectful to Franny's memory. In fact, he is not being respectful at all. For all Franny's eccentricities, she was everything to him. "The will, sir?"

"Ah yes, the young man wishes to know his fortune, naturally enough," says Dray.

"It is not that at all."

"No? Ah well. Perhaps that is for the best. And so . . ." He waves his small fingers in the air and drops them, as a cat pounces on a vole, onto a batch of papers enclosed with a pale blue ribbon, which he flicks from it dexterously and begins to read. "*In the Name of God Amen I Frances Harriet Peake-Barnes of Tring in the County of Hertfordshire being of sound Mind and Memory . . .*" Dray glances up mischievously from his reading, hoping, presumably, for a moment of hilarity, but none forthcoming he continues, only a little dismayed, "*. . . do make and ordain this my last Will and Testament in the manner and form following. Item: I give and bequeath unto Leonora Catherine Morley of Briar House, in the County aforesaid, Briar House, its lands, stables, its fixtures, fittings and all within its curtilage and, for the maintenance of said property and whatever other uses she may see fit, eight hundred pounds a year, payable at four quarterly payments payable within three months of my decease or the aforementioned Leonora Catherine Morley taking ownership of Briar House, whichever may come sooner.*" Dray pauses again and looks up, his eyes teary with the triumph of what he has just read out and the consternation it must have provoked. But Zachary feels only relief and offers a quiet smile. His father seems equally unmoved.

It falls to Ratcliffe to speak. "She is a lovely girl. Delightful. But . . ."

"We have the damnable difficulty of finding her, do we not?" says Dray. "Shall I proceed?"

"Pray do," says Papa.

"*I further bequeath to William Reeve and to Dorcas Tull the sum of fifty pounds a year to be paid for the rest of their Natural lives in four quarterly payments and to John Dawkins the sum of twenty pounds a year for the rest of his Natural life. Furthermore, the aforementioned William Reeve and Dorcas Tull shall have the right to reside in Briar House for the rest of their Natural lives. I give and bequeath to my great-nephew Zachary Cloudesley of Briar House . . .*" Dray pauses. "Would anyone like tea?" His offer being declined he continues: "*. . . all my remaining Goods, Chattels, Stocks, Ready Money, Bills, Bonds, Stock in Trade, and Writings whatsoever and wheresoever on condition that he . . .* a glass of water, perhaps?"

"No, thank you."

"*On condition that he open a . . .*" Dray pauses again, and it is apparent that he has been relishing this moment for some weeks. He struggles to keep the mirth from his voice as he reads the next words: "*. . . menagerie for the education and edification of the general public, ensuring that the creatures are not*"—he takes a breath, the air seeming to curdle in his throat—"*tethered or caged, but permitted to roam as freely as they may within necessary enclosures and to exhibit their natures and manners. They shall be encouraged to be as if they were in their wild locale, and information shall be given to those who come to visit about their diet, breeding, etc.*" Dray skims the rest of the document but, finding nothing so amusing in it as he has just read, concludes hastily with, "There is then a bequest to Mr. Mendel, but he being dead he may not enjoy it, and so what he would have had goes to you, Zachary. And the usual provisions for the executor, which you may read for yourselves, and the witnessing, which is all in order. And the date, for this was signed on the seventh day of June in the year of our Lord 1766, when matters were somewhat differently arranged in all of your lives, I hazard. I urged her, the good lady, that is, to make a new one, I assure you, but as you know, for a woman of such great energy in matters of opinion and taste, she had little to spare in matters of organization."

"Indeed," says Papa, rising from his seat.

"But," says Dray, "there is the matter of the absent principal beneficiary."

"Zachary is the principal, though as it happens, despite the injunction against tethers, somewhat tethered," says Papa, glancing at Zachary, who wonders how he will go about making a menagerie, or what on earth Franny was thinking of, apart from knowing full well his love of all creatures. He supposes he must have talked about the idea of a grand menagerie and Franny, failing to notice that he was twelve years old, conceived the notion that she would put such a thing in her will.

"Also that both of the principals are, in fact, minor beneficiaries, being under twenty-one," adds Dray.

"There are no directions as to trustees?"

"Ah yes, yes. How silly of me to have omitted to mention who is trustee."

"Reverend Ratcliffe, I assume?" says Papa.

Ratcliffe gives an uneasy laugh. "It is Mrs. Grace Mary Morley. Leonora's mother, as was and, I trust, as is."

"For Leonora?"

"For both, Mr. Cloudesley," says Dray. "At the time of the writing of the will, you were thought deceased," he adds, as if resurrection were simply another tedious legal detail for which he would be obliged to make a small charge.

Ratcliffe rises from his seat with the look of Sisyphus at the moment when he has pushed the boulder to the crest. It is only as he stands, letting his burden free, that he watches in despair as it tumbles back down into the valley of his duty. "You understand, now, Mr. Cloudesley, the difficulty of my position. I am simply unable to discharge my obligations as executor without some communication, at least, with Mrs. Morley and her daughter."

"Indeed. You have tried?"

"There is no trace. But . . ."

"But what?" asks Zachary.

"I have in the past week come across a piece of intelligence that may lead us to them, and I trust you may take on that part of my task, since Easter is almost upon us, and I shall be obliged to conduct services which celebrate the resurrection while at the same time satisfying my parishioners' great desire for flowers and eggs and chicks and, well, every single pagan symbol of fertility that might be imagined. It is a stressful time, Easter, I do declare." He commences to sound a note, a middle C, but no words come, just a hum.

"Share your intelligence over a cup of wine, Reverend," says Papa, his hand upon the Rector of Tring's shoulder, "and Zachary and I will do all we can to find Mrs. Morley and Leonora, won't we?"

CHAPTER TWENTY-FIVE

A FORTEPIANO

April 1771, Lundy

◙

The journey to Bideford is a hard one at the dog-end of winter, with the roads muddy and the trees bare. Daffodils along the way cheer, and the first blackthorn leaf starting to show gives promise of greenery to come. His first English spring in ten years and, despite the chill and rain, Abel is exultant. His son sits opposite, gazing out the window of the coach and taking no less joy than he in the countryside, pointing out badger setts and hedgehog runs and, overhead, the circling swallows, early this year, or so he tells him. They are easy now in each other's company and, Abel believes, not so different from one another, though for Zachary it is and always has been nature itself that fascinates, not those ticking simulacra of living creatures that Abel once made. He has discussed Zachary's strange inheritance with him along the way, reassuring his son that he will assist him in constructing the menagerie, telling him that all is possible. He might use his clock-work skills, he thinks, to explain to the public how a giraffe's neck extends to the highest branches, or a python slithers through the undergrowth. For Zachary's part, he says he foresees frequent journeys to Africa to acquire exotics and bring them safely back to Hertfordshire.

Abel is sanguine about Mrs. Morley's sudden dominion over their lives. He knows her well enough to believe her forthright, honest and sensible. That she should have quit Frances's employ without leaving so much as a crumb to follow is no great surprise—he remembers her determination to live independently, to make her own way. He found her trail thanks to intelligence that Ratcliffe had gained: a parishioner with a brother on the isle of Lundy, a Mrs. Alsop, had told the rector that her brother would not come this year to Tring for his holiday because there was now an excellent inn on the island, run by a woman called Ann Stevens, stern yet kind, and with a daughter having oddly refined manners yet given to outbursts of terrible temper. Ratcliffe had the presence of mind to ask his parishioner, the butcher's wife, whether Mrs. Morley had perhaps been a customer in times past and, it being confirmed that she had and that they often spoke of Mrs. Alsop's brother, drew his reasonable surmise.

The Bideford ferry only sails when there is a westerly, enabling it to tack its way to the island over most of the day and to sail back to port safely of an evening. Yet the winds are from the north when Abel and Zachary arrive in town, and they must take rooms in a hotel by the port for three days, awaiting the first sailing of the season. Bideford is a rowdy kind of place, like most other ports, for all that its sailings are few, with much carousing through the night, the streets littered at dawn with broken cider jars and puddles of puke.

Zachary goes out alone into the hills each morning, returning with pockets full of snails and grasshoppers, yesterday bringing back to their room a hessian sack holding a grass snake, glossy with scales that, despite their look, were dry to the touch, its startled eye observing all.

When at last word comes that the ferry is preparing to sail, they go down to the quay to see it being loaded with supplies much needed after the long winter of isolation: potatoes, grain, cheeses and barrels of sack. It is a surprise, therefore, when Abel observes a wooden case the shape of a fortepiano being winched aboard. "What is in the case?" he asks the young man who is watching it with fixed attention.

"It is a fortepiano," says the man, not adjusting his gaze to see who is asking him.

"That is unusual freight. Is there an orchestra on the island?" asks Abel.

"No, sir, and never has been," says the man, looking up. "It is for my fiancée," he adds.

"Well, well. A fortepiano. She plays it well?"

"I never heard her, since there is none on the island, like I said, but she used to play, she told me, when she lived in a great house, and she is the most beautiful creature in all the world, and I am bringing her what she desires and deserves."

Zachary lights up with mischief, and a moment later a question tumbles from his lips. "Does she have red hair?"

"Then you have heard of her!" exclaims the man. "Leonora Stevens . . . Dalton, as will be."

Abel introduces himself and Zachary to Dalton, who is a broad-shouldered, unguarded, friendly-faced fellow. As their voyage commences, he proceeds to tell them how he came by the piano and, believing he held a bill of sale for it, was informed that he had been duped. "I shall carry this piece of paper with me for the rest of my life, to remind myself how no man should allow himself to be taken for a fool through his ignorance or pride." He presents the scrap, on it the words, *This fool thinks he has a bill of sale for a fortepiano, whereas, instead of being in the sum of nineteen guineas and five shillings, it is a warning to him that he should learn to read and write and exercise some good judgment if he is to ask for the hand of my daughter in marriage.* "Well, what think you of that?" asks Joe Dalton with a wide smile.

Abel imagines he must have been humiliated by it. "Were you not made angry, once you knew what it said?"

"No . . . or, well, a little, yes, but then I reasons Mrs. Stevens is doing me a favour, since she is telling me what I surely need to know, and if I'm honest I been too lazy to learn to read and know I must be a better kind of man than that if I am to deserve Leonora's hand."

Abel wonders whether they should admit to knowing both Leonora and her mother since the truth of it must be revealed soon enough. He glances at Zachary, who must have been having the same thought, but before they can confess, Joe, speaking with the urgency of a man in need of confession himself, says, "I was determined, see, to do as I promised and bring my sweetheart a fortepiano, and went to Bristol as Mrs. Stevens had told me I must, and asked about for a shop where a fortepiano might be bought and was directed to the premises of Mr. Valentine, and when I presented him with the paper he looked at me long and careful and then interrogated me in several particulars, such as where I was born and whose son I was, and for whom the fortepiano was being purchased and so forth, which I thought were questions reasonable enough to establish that I had right to hold the bill, see?"

"Indeed," agrees Abel.

"But then Mr. Valentine says to me, 'And what is your ambition in life, young man?' Which is not the sort of question I'd have thought of, but since he asked, I told him, because I am a believer in answering a man unless there is reason not to."

"And what was it you said to him?" asks Zachary, eagerly.

Abel suspects that Zachary has taken a liking to Joe Dalton just as he has himself, much as one might adopt a stray on the street, however disinclined one might be in the direction of the acquisition of puppies, simply from the innocence of its wagging tail and warm eyes.

"I told him I should like only to be a good man, a loving husband, a proud father and to find some farmland in Devon, since Lundy is only good for sheep and then not much good for them. I like cows and pigs, and there is nothing better to see than a field of corn in July, golden and rippling in the sun—though I never yet seen such a thing for myself."

"And what did this Mr. Valentine do next?"

"He told me that the fortepiano under order was being built and it was, anyway, his understanding that there would be no sailings to Lundy until March or April." He stops, looks about the boat and raises his arms wide, declaring with his broad smile. "I do believe this very sailing!"

"And so you were stuck there?"

"Oh no, not a bit of it. Don't you believe that. "Cos Mr. Valentine says I might work for him over the winter if I am handy with my hands, and I says I am, which I am, since, he says, he is having a house built in Clifton, one of them grand places with colonnades and doors wide and tall enough for a giant to walk beneath and not ruffle his hair, and I says I will do so gladly. And he makes one condition, which is that I must learn to read and write with him, four times a week I am to have lessons. And so I do and spend a happy winter laying bricks and plastering ceilings and learning to read in the evenings."

"Mr. Valentine must be a very good kind soul," says Abel, wondering at how Joe Dalton stumbled upon such kindness, but perhaps angels are ordained to meet other angels, all arranged as if by chance.

Joe agrees with teary vehemence. "Oh, he is, he is so good to me. He kept the bill of sale and told me it was good for the purchase of this fortepiano that is now sliding about so alarmingly on deck." He gestures in its direction, and then realizing that it is indeed skating across the boards, leaps up to try to secure it, Abel and Zachary assisting him. Breathlessly, each of them now holding a corner of the crate, Joe concludes his tale. "So it was only last week, me taking my farewell supper with Mr. Valentine and his mother, who is a very old, deaf lady and also a little blind and who kept mistaking me for a son of hers also called Joe but long dead, that Mr. Valentine hands me the paper what you have seen. And he says, 'Well, Joe, now you and I have read *Gulliver's Travels* together and you have a good collection of books to take back to your island, and we both know which end of a boiled egg to slice off'—and I laugh, I do—'and we know that a man may be a giant but have a Lilliputian within him or may be very small yet but may still become a giant'—and his eyes were misty, I swear, and no less misty were my own—'it is time you read what was on that bill of sale you gave me.' And so I read it and I laugh and laugh, and I says to Mr. Valentine, 'Well, she is a sage and shrewd lady, that Mrs. Stevens, and who can say but that she were right. But Mr. Valentine, says I, how shall I pay you for the fortepiano?' 'You have worked for me all winter, Joe,' says he. 'But my labours are nowhere near the price of such an instrument, Mr. Valentine.' 'Then you may pay me when you have your first hundred head of cattle,' says he."

The island rises before them, a long, rocky strip of land which looks like the back of a great beast, most of it submerged in the grey waters.

"Ain't that a thing?" says Joe, though whether of the island or the kindness of Mr. Valentine, Abel is uncertain.

"He has been like a father to you," says Abel.

"Yes, and more. Though my own father is a loving soul and always cheerful, even when giving me a beating. Especially so, I should say. Not that I haven't deserved it."

The boat ties up at the rickety wooden jetty and, though the disembarkation of the dozen souls who have business on the island is quick, the unloading of the freight is slow and awkward, for fear of it tumbling off the jetty onto the spume-covered rocks below.

Abel signals to Zachary that they should speak in private. "He will be planning, I imagine, to present the instrument to Leonora as soon as it can be dragged up the hill to the inn." He looks up the steep slope that leads from the jetty and can see the roof of the inn half a mile away, a sign before it, hardly necessary, swaying in the breeze. He is gripped by unexpected nerves, even though the news they have come to bring is surely welcome. It is, he supposes, always possible that Mrs. Morley will be obstinate in some way—she is more than capable of it.

"He won't be the man for delay, I am certain," says Zachary.

"We should get to see Mrs. Morley and Leonora before the commotion is upon us all. She will be surprised enough to see us, and to hear of Leonora's transformation into the mistress of Tring without the appearance of a fortepiano being pushed up the hill and into her life by Joe Dalton."

Zachary, thoughtful, says slowly, "On the other hand, it may be best that we appear after the fortepiano and good Mr. Dalton have made their own appearance, and in such manner we might then be seen as the solution to what will otherwise seem to Mrs. Morley a great predicament."

"Ingenious! Yes. I agree. Let us help Mr. Dalton up the hill, stay back a little as he calls at the inn, which would only be polite, and then make ourselves known."

They return to Dalton's side, and together with one of the deckhands, help him to manhandle the fortepiano onto a cart and assist him in pushing it up the track to the top of the hill. "This is right good of you two gentlemen. I suppose you must be headed to the Puffin yourselves, since there is no other place to lodge on the island, unless you count the old gaol, and I wouldn't recommend a night there, since it is jostling with ghosts."

Dalton, Abel observes, is preternaturally strong, pushing the cart, laden as it is, with just one hand, and it is apparent that his own assistance is quite superfluous. As they near the inn he and Zachary fall back, allowing Dalton to present himself. A young woman of striking beauty runs from the door and throws her arms around him. A shriek emits from within. "Do not tell me you have returned with that damned fortepiano, Joe Dalton." It is, unmistakably, the voice of Grace Morley.

"I have done as I promised to Leonora and, moreover have done as you bid me do in your bill of sale," says Dalton, "since I have learned to read and write, and so now"—he drops to one knee—"will you, Leonora Catherine Stevens, do me the great honour of becoming my wife?"

Leonora bites her lip, as if doubting for a moment that she will say yes, causing Dalton to look stricken before she admits to her tease and says, joyfully, "I will, Joe Dalton, I will!"

Abel steps forward, Zachary a little behind.

"Bloody hellfire," declares Mrs. Morley, "you have conjured up not only a piano but a man from the dead and a babe I thought lost to me forever." She holds herself steady, a hand on the door frame of the inn, and though the wind has dropped to a gentle breeze, she rocks backward and forward as if being battered by a gale, until that imagined squall blows her clear off her feet.

Abel rushes over. "Mrs. Morley, I appreciate this must be a great surprise to you."

"Surprise?" she bawls from her prone position. "Oh good grief, oh good lord. Surprise. I should say so. What, what . . . ?" Suspicion settles upon her features. "Oh, I know, I understand everything now," she says, bitter, standing and brushing herself down. "You have purchased this fortepiano and conspired with Dalton—"

"No, no, I assure you—" says Abel.

"Do not you interrupt me! You have conspired with Dalton to take my girl away from me. Well, she will need my consent and I will not give it."

Leonora, entwined with her beloved and, until then, watching the unfolding argument with detachment, much as a person on foot watches two coaches collide as they try to pass each other on a too-narrow street, reddens with fury. "Mother! You gave Joe your word."

"What word did I give? I said he might win your heart with a fortepiano, that is all. But your heart has already been given to him, I see, and a measure too freely, I should say."

It falls to Zachary to try to calm the tumult. "Mrs. Morley," he says quietly, "I assure you that my father and I met Mr. Dalton for the first time at the quayside at Bideford this morning. We had no idea who he was until we spoke on the voyage. That he should have brought this fortepiano for Leonora is all his doing, I assure you."

"Well," harrumphs Mrs. Morley, a little steam released from her fury. "So be it, then."

Leonora beams at Zachary, leaving Joe's side to give him a fond kiss on the cheek. "Oh, Zack, I have missed you so."

Joe, confused, looks first to Abel, then to Zachary and then to his beloved, it gradually dawning on him that the two persons he met on the voyage are known to Leonora Stevens and her mother and, indeed, that Stevens might not even be their real name. "So, I'm thinking you lot all know each other pretty well," he says.

"These two," says Mrs. Morley, pointing to Leonora and then to Zachary, "I looked after each as my own," she puts a hand to her bosom, "though one were my daughter, ungrateful though she be, and the other this here gentleman's son"—she nods in Abel's direction—"a gentleman I first met the very day Zachary was born, and who is much changed, though given he was dead and is now alive we can hardly be surprised at that. What brings them here I cannot say. In fact, what brings any of you here I cannot say. This being the first day the boat has come

I have pies in the oven and rooms to prepare and guests already in them, so I have no time to dally." And with that she is gone.

Abel calls out after her, "Do you have a room for Zachary and me, by any chance, Mrs. Morley?"

A shriek can be heard from somewhere beyond the door. It is Leonora who replies to Abel's question. "The rooms are all taken, I'm afraid, Mr. Cloudesley." She takes Zachary's hand in hers and gives his fingers an affectionate stroke. "We cannot have you stay at the gaol though"—she looks around at Joe— "can we, Joe?"

"No. I already told them about the old gaol, about it being haunted 'n' all."

"Your father will put them up, won't he?"

Joe beams. "'Course he will. He did ever like a man of quality, my old man. And I can hear your stories over a jar or two tonight, gentlemen, since I never did ask you about yourselves."

"I should like to hear it, too," says Leonora, "since I have a notion their adventures have been extraordinary. It is so good of you to seek us out here, Mr. Cloudesley"—she gives him a demure smile—"and clever, too, since my mother hid our trail thoroughly, I think. But tell me, how is Franny?"

Abel and Zachary's expression tell her all she needs to know.

"Oh? Oh dear. Oh, oh." Leonora takes a small, embroidered handkerchief from her sleeve and dabs at her eyes. "Oh, I am so sorry. I always said to mother that we should at least write to let her know our reasons for leaving and to reassure her that we bore her no ill will. That lady was so good to me and I shall never forget it."

"She may have been kinder to you than you suspect," says Abel.

Leonora gives him a puzzled look, but before he can say anything more Zachary says, "I hoped for some word from you, Leonora."

She again goes to Zachary and kisses him, this time embracing him and telling him how sorry she is about it all, but that her mother, once possessed of a notion, is not to be dispossessed of it, however wrong. "She was most certain, that morning we left in the mist of dawn, that we should never, ever see Briar House again. She bid me not to look back, for fear I would turn to salt."

"But you did look back, didn't you?" says Zachary.

"Of course I did, Zack. I was never so happy anywhere as I was there, with you."

Joe steps forward, unconcealed concern written on his candid face.

"Oh, Joe," says Leonora, understanding, "Zack and I are brother and sister, almost, but even better than brother and sister, since we are different, and it is the curse of brothers and sisters to see that they are alike and to find all those things they most dislike about themselves in their sibling. Isn't that right, Zack?"

"Very likely," he says with a smile. "I have not made a study of it."

Abel watches how easy they are with each other and is reminded that, thanks to Frances, they did indeed grow up together as near to brother and sister as in many a true family. Perhaps there was method in her madness, after all. "It is as well you looked back, Leonora," says Abel, "for you are to see Briar House again."

"I should like that," she says, "perhaps I will be able to visit you and Zachary there, if that is where you are now to live?"

Abel considers whether to tell her that it is, rather, they who will be visiting her there, but knows he must speak first to Mrs. Morley. He enters the inn, which is freshly painted, comfortable and orderly, as he would expect, the smell of pastry and something vaguely fishy filling the air. He finds Mrs. Morley in an upstairs bedchamber, plumping pillows with great ferocity.

"Mrs. Morley, a word if I may?"

"Grace, it is Grace. And I shall call you Abel, since you are no longer my employer nor in any way am I beholden to you."

He bows.

"Well, spit it out. And no, you may not stay, since all my rooms are full. And no, I am not pleased that Leonora is smitten with that oafish shepherd, but he has a good heart, and that is something, I suppose."

"I can attest to that, Grace."

"Yes, well, I have no great need for your attestation. You came here to give us some news, I take it?"

"We did. Aunt Frances fell ill to the plague in Constantinople, I am sorry to say, and is buried there."

She stops her work, looks at him quiet for a moment. "Dead, then?"

"She was not buried alive."

"Well, there's a blessing in that, at least," she says quickly. "I am sorry to hear of her passing. Truly. I liked her and she was generous to me and Leonora both."

More generous than you can imagine, thinks Abel.

"But she had designs . . . designs upon my daughter, to make her in some way her own, and I could not countenance it." She attacks a pillow with such force that feathers explode from it, and she sits heavily on the bed, goose feathers descending about her like a heavy but gentle snow. "I could not countenance it," she repeats, wretchedly.

"I understand, Grace. I do. Dear Frances was, I always thought, a little like the Romans, straightening the roads, bringing laws and armies and wine and oil, but paying little attention to whatever went before her, thinking us all somewhat too primitive for our own good. It was a desire to improve that made her such as she was, rather than any wish to subjugate." From her position on the bed, the feathers having now descended, Mrs. Morley regards him with doubt. She has barely aged and is a handsomer woman now than when he first met her seventeen years ago, as if she has been filled out with her own convictions and with the confidence that her choices had been the right ones, however unwelcome the making of them may have been at the time. She is ampler in the face, the body, but not to the point of corpulence, and that anger that has always simmered beneath the surface of her is like steam in a well-constructed compressor, powerful but controlled.

"You were taken prisoner by the Turks, then?" she says.

"Aye."

"Well, you are not the first."

"Not the first, no."

"You did not want to go, I know that. I remember, you see," she says, "I remember there was something you tried to tell me that day we met for tea before you sailed. You did not want to be separated from your Zachary. And you must know, that was why I agreed to go work for your crazed aunt, that above all, to try to be a goodly influence on the boy and stop him from turning wild under her influence. He is a fine boy that one, Abel. Full of love for all of nature. A queer one, right enough, and full of the unexpected. But *good*." She bangs her chest, her heart. "*Good*," she says again.

"He is, Grace. That I have seen for myself. I might be in that cage in the seraglio still were it not for him. I owe him my life, very probably."

"Very probably you do," she says, rising. "Well, I have work to be getting along with, and so if you will forgive me. It is good of you to come and deliver this sad news of Lady Pee-Bee and to present yourselves as living no less, but . . ."

"Grace," he says, with urgency, "there is something else I must tell you."

She turns in the doorway, and there is some foreshadowing in her expression of the importance of what she is to be told. "Go on, then," she says, reentering the room.

"Grace. Leonora is now mistress of Briar House. And you are trustee of all her estate, and of Zachary's inheritance, too."

She sits again on the bed, heavily. "Oh," she says. "Oh." She looks neither surprised nor unsurprised, but in that place where she has always been, a place where the unexpected must be faced with fortitude.

From below comes the sound of the fortepiano, Bach's Concerto in D Minor, but the instrument is in need of tuning and the notes fail to linger as they should, the air being too damp for their enduring.

◎

CHAPTER TWENTY-SIX

LOVE'S NOT TIME'S FOOL

August 1771, Briar House, Tring

◎

Sneezing. I never was such a sneezer till after Lundy, where the air was clear and salty and any pollen was blown clean away before it had a chance to do any mischief. But all that fresh air must have lowered my tolerance for flowering things, like when you put your feet up on a footstool for a few minutes of an afternoon and only make yourself more exhausted than you were before. Now I find myself at the mercy of a lily. I don't know whose idea it was to fill the church with quite so many blooms. The smell is enough to make an elephant giddy, and my eyes are streaming so bad I can hardly see my girl walk up the aisle. I'm blowing on my nose every two minutes and all those in the congregation, which is large, must think I am weeping either with joy or with despair. Not that her condition shows. The dress is well cut and the veil long and she is, my girl, a beauty. There is Zachary at her side. They make such a fine couple and always did. My sisters are here and their husbands and there is a gaggle of their children and their grandchildren, too, and so I have a family at last. They were surprised to get the invitation, me having been disinclined to maintain any correspondence with them this many a year. It was not that I did not like or love or care for them, but their business was theirs and mine was mine and I have liked to keep my affairs private, but that must all change now. There is no longer any hope of a secluded life. I have not yet told them that the house where they will go to eat peacock pie and gumballs and cheese wiggs this afternoon and drink French wine and dance until they can dance no more is Leonora's own. It will come out in the course of the afternoon, I daresay, and there will be several degrees of amazement, and then there will be as many or more expectations of charity. I shall deal with those requests in such manner that they will not be repeated. It is not that I am uncharitable—I shall give to those in need and have resolved to establish a foundation for the benefit of wet nurses so that their own little ones shall always be well cared for and never be left to starve. I shall name it for Lady Pee-Bee, since it is her money after all that is making all possible: it shall be the *Frances Peake-Barnes Foundation for the Welfare and Relief of Those Who Suckle Infants.*

They can see Abel sitting here behind me, my relations, and must think it kind of him to have consented to attend his old wet nurse's daughter's wedding. And there is Mr. Jepherson, not that you'd guess him a gentleman until he opens his mouth, and old Reeve and Dorcas, she not having a great notion of what it is she is at or why, and Mr. Dawkins and his wife, but they are all of them servants and won't count for much in the eyes of my sisters, not that they are of any higher rank themselves. Samuels is in the very backmost pew, as if he must be ever ready to leave in a rush to resolve some quarrel or skirmish. Mr. and Mrs. Alsop are here, and Mrs. Ratcliffe, naturally enough since she must keep an eye on the lilies. Other townspeople are standing about in the graveyard out of curiosity. It's a funny thing in its way, marrying and baptizing next to all those skeletons, but it is only right that we are reminded to make the most of that life we are given.

Over on the groom's side sits that rabble of Dalton's, laughing and talking so loud as to make noise enough to fill the church five times over. They are such a family as might settle a colony without need of supplement, the men being strong and the women fecund by the look of the squirmage of infants now crawling over the pews. They are testimony to the advantages of deportation, though 'tis a shame they got no further than Lundy. In amongst them sits a kindly fellow called Valentine, he that took a liking to Joe and taught him to read and thus to my present misfortune of being about to acquire him as son-in-law. Joe comes bouncing along the aisle now, smiling to all and shaking hands, his brother at his side, who is as Joe will become in short order, having acquired a sagging belly and grey hairs in the decade of his advantage. Zachary, who walked my girl down the aisle in the absence of her father, places now her sweet hand in Joe's rough paw, and Ratcliffe coughs and, oh dear God above, starts to sing without assistance of the organ and so we all must stand and try to do our best, Zachary coming to stand beside me.

When 'tis done and we sit and the ceremony begins with *If any person present knows of any lawful impediment*, I take Zachary's hand in mine and squeeze it hard. "Common sense and reason," I says to him quietly, "that should be the impediment," and he leans his mouth close to mine and whispers, "He is as full of love and goodness as any man she could find on the face of this earth, Mrs. Morley. Let us be glad for my sister." And the lilies get to me then right and proper, what with Ratcliffe saying *Do you take this woman* . . . and Zachary calling Leonora sister, and me having that family I hadn't seen in so long all around me.

I trust Zachary will not go scuttling off to Africa too soon. There are the plans for the menagerie to be decided upon first, though the walks and fences can go up all around the estate while' he is busy catching rhinoceroses. A letter came for him two days ago. I should not have opened it, but it bore a strange script upon it, which some good person must have been able to read, for they had scribbled upon it *Briar House, Tring, Hertfordshire, Royaume d'Angleterre*, but the rest of the address was a scribble, and inside more of it and it cost me three shillings in the receiving! I show it in passing to Samuels, asking him what form of gibberish it be. He looks at it as if he is about to stroke an old cat of his acquaintance, very nearly purring himself. "It is Greek," he says. I ask him if he can read it and he does not answer but gives that smirk, like as not to mean that there is no tongue on earth he cannot comprehend. When I ask him what is in the letter, he says do I want the gist or the specifics? I tell him the gist being as I don't have time for specifics, and he says it is a letter to Zachary from an old friend he made when in Constantinople. Oh? Then perhaps some of the specifics would be best to know, says I. And he reads, ". . . the old sultan being dead, my father is forgiven and is made governor of Alexandria, and so that is where I now reside." Oh, says I, not caring greatly. And he reads on and says how the correspondent has now but one arm, his fox—no, he corrects himself, his other—having been consumed by a bear, and I concede that is more interesting. He concludes, sly as ever, by saying that the young man wishes Zachary to know how fervently he would like to taste again his sweet lips and how he should like to lick the salt off his belly. Goodness, what manner of friend is this, I ask. His name is Ibrahim, and I do not doubt he would lay down his life for our Zachary, he avers.

I keep a hold of the letter, thinking I will give it to Zachary the day after the wedding, and then ask him about his friend, but that evening I hear Samuels telling Zachary that he has decided he will accompany him on his trip to Africa and he proposes that they commence their journey straight after the nuptials. He hopes they might sail first to Alexandria, he says, where an old friend awaits them.

Samuels, I think, you scheming old bastard. Still, if any man is to help Zachary bring gentle giraffes and irritable hippopotamuses to Briar House it is him, and we are all of us obliged to carry out the terms of Lady Pee-Bee's will and to pursue for evermore her many lunacies. I shall give the letter to Zachary as soon as we are out of the church, and trust to God and Samuels that he will be happy. Oh, I shall miss Zachary, though. He was ever mine and we have become close again these past months as I have set about bringing the late Lady's estate into order.

Abel is on his feet. He is to make a reading. He stands not in the pulpit but at the lectern, which is a golden eagle, very highly polished. *Let me not to the marriage of true minds*, he begins, at first looking at Leonora and Joe, but then only at Zachary,

> *Admit impediments. Love is not love*
> *Which alters when it alteration finds,*
> *Or bends with the remover to remove.*
> *O no! it is an ever-fixed mark*
> *That looks on tempests and is never shaken;*

It is the star to every wand'ring bark,
Whose worth's unknown, although his height be taken.
Love's not Time's fool, though rosy lips and cheeks
Within his bending sickle's compass come;
Love alters not with his brief hours and weeks,
But bears it out even to the edge of doom.
If this be error and upon me prov'd,
I never writ, nor no man ever lov'd.

They are in tears, father and son, and it seems it was a reading for the two of them, not for Leonora and Joe at all. Still, bride and groom seem happy enough. It must have been taken from one of those Old Testament books, since it is not a verse I recognize from the gospels. "Is it from the Book of Ruth?" I ask Zachary, since he is conversant most especially with the Old Testament. "No," he whispers, wiping away his tears, "it is one of Mr. Shakespeare's sonnets." Well, that fits, since Abel and Ratcliffe are ever talking nonsense together, and will have cooked it up between them.

That loud music by Jeremiah Clarke plays now, ever popular for the recessional, Samuels playing the trumpet, which would be a surprise but that Samuels might turn into a tiger before our eyes and we would only think it another of his strange faculties. The bride and groom start their slow procession out and into the sunshine that, for this afternoon, at least, bathes their new life together. Zachary stands and walks behind with Joe's brother beside. Next goes Abel, extending an arm for Mother Dalton to take. I stand and find Father Dalton putting out his arm for me to take, and it is like putting a hand about the belly of a fat hog, firm and broad and hairy.

I look at the back of Abel's head. He wears a peruke today, his shoulders are rounded and his back bent, and I think to myself that I only ever saw him suffer, from that day we first met when he watched me take his child away from him all the way to this. He has sold Leadenhall and put his workshop into the old pigeon loft, where he has begun again to make his strange clockwork creatures, little singing silver birds and croaking frogs and such-like. He gave me a ladybird for my birthday, with silver legs and red enameled wings with black spots on them, and it is as like a living creature as you could wish for and though I have never desired such a thing as that, I keep it in my chamber. Each morning when I wake, I turn its key and watch it scuttle. I do believe it is trying to fly. I do believe that one day it will.

◙

EPILOGUE

March 1772, Alexandria, Egypt

◎

A strong northerly blows the *Syren* along at sixteen knots or more, and Zachary has been on deck all morning admiring the lush green fields scattered with slender date palms, the bare rocky hills rising in the far distance, with their promise of mirages to come. The ship is close enough to shore that he can see the *fellahin* working the land, their patient mules pulling wooden ploughs. The sea is shallow, hardly enough for the draught of the vessel; he can smell the toppled gods and desiccated papyrus of Egypt now, and the waters of the Nile carrying silt a thousand miles or more from Nubia. Samuels is busy down below, unmoved by the prospect of adventure, building cages for all the crocodiles and lions they are to capture, but Zachary thinks he will have no need of coops and crates, for he has other plans.

By afternoon, Alexander's city can be seen on the low horizon, though its once mighty Pharos and Cleopatra's palace have lain long beneath the waves, and the great harbour is a disappointment, backed by squat brown buildings, the only sense of that grandeur it once held resting in the domes and minarets of the city's mosques. It is not Constantinople, and for a moment Zachary's buoyant mood falters until, in amongst a gaggle of porters dressed in *jalabiyas* of grey and brown, he sees a figure sitting tall on a white horse, his black hair tumbling down his back, his gaze fixed firmly on the deck on which Zachary stands.

Samuels is beside him, a hand on his shoulder as if he has read his thoughts and knows Zachary must be obliged to desist from diving into the harbour and swimming into his beloved's arms. Zachary raises a hand and sees his answer in Ibrahim's wide, carefree smile.

At the moment the ship makes dock, he rushes down the rickety gangway, jumping onto dry land and sprinting to where Ibrahim is saddled. He reaches down for Zachary with his strong, good arm and hoists him up on to the saddle behind him. Samuels appears at their side and shouts up to them to ride on ahead, assuring them that he will oversee all at the port.

As they canter away, Zachary sees that men walk hand in hand here as brothers, as friends—perhaps as lovers, too. Let them suppose us brothers, then, he thinks, his chest pressed hard to Ibrahim's back, his breath already finding a new rhythm. "Let us be all three!" he shouts to the wind, causing Ibrahim to slow the horse and turn, permitting Zachary to take in the wonder of his face, to see the glint of his golden eye captured in Ibrahim's own steady gaze.

"Shall we always be together?" Zachary asks.

"Zaki . . . Zaki. Why always so full of questions? Is this moment not your answer?"

Zachary pulls Ibrahim to him, and finds that reassurance he was about to seek by peering into that other, darker future that he has always until this moment carried within him.

No, he thinks. He has no more need of prophecies, of futures foretold or withheld, of visions and charms. He is set free.

◙

HISTORICAL AND OTHER NOTES

I was inspired to write this novel after coming across an Ottoman clock in a small, almost hidden shop in Istanbul's covered bazaar. The clock was made by George Clarke of Leadenhall, around 1750. Wondering why the Turks were so keen on importing clocks from England, I set off on several years' research into clockmaking, the Levant Company, Anglo-Ottoman relations during the Seven Years' War, and a host of other eighteenth-century diversions. For my efforts, I was rewarded with a truly terrible first draft, wildly overburdened with research about wet nurses, the Julian calendar and grand viziers. The novel in its present form shows, I hope, only a hint of hours spent in the British Library reading the delightful diaries of British ambassador James Porter and of days wandering the Topkapi Palace in Istanbul, known in the eighteenth century as the Yeni Serai, or, more commonly, the seraglio.

Astonishing automata really were built in the second half of the eighteenth century, particularly in England, France and Switzerland, most notably by James Cox and Pierre Jaquet-Droz. One of these, built by Hungarian inventor Wolfgang von Kempelen to impress Austrian Empress Maria Theresa, was the famous chess-playing Turk, which, like the Duke of Derbyshire, was a fraud concealing an operator. Unlike the Duke, the Turk was not, it seems, ever used for spying, though it did on one occasion play a game against Napoleon. Lord Carteret was an accomplished diplomat, linguist and Lord President of the Privy Council, but whether he was ever the sinister spymaster described in this novel, I doubt.

Grand viziers came and went with great speed during the 1700s, often lasting only a matter of months before being dismissed by the sultan if their policy advice displeased. Turkey remained neutral throughout the Seven Years' War (1756–63), but was soon after embroiled in one of its frequent wars with Russia which, in 1774, ended in a decisive victory for Empress Catherine's Russia. Sultan Mustafa Khan III's rule (1757–74) was troubled by economic difficulties and military setbacks. The Chief Black Eunuch, or kizlar agha, was an all-powerful figure in the Ottoman administration in these years. In this novel, I have based his character to some extent on what is known of Morali Beshir, originally from Borneo, who held the office from 1746 until his execution in 1752, and who was notoriously unprincipled and corrupt. But Abel and Zachary, Aunt Frances and Mrs. Morley, Tom Spurrell and Ibrahim El Gadawi, Joe Dalton and Mr. Valentine are inventions, sprung from an Ottoman clock built in 1750 on Leadenhall Street.

◙

FURTHER READING

FitzRoy, Charles. *The Sultan's Istanbul on 5 Kurush a Day*. London: Thames and Hudson, 2013.

Mansel, Philip. *Constantinople: City of the World's Desire, 1453–1924*. London: John Murray, 1995.

Porter, Sir James. *Turkey: Its History and Progress—From the Journals and Correspondence of Sir James Porter; Continued to the Present Time, With a Memoir of Sir James Porter by His Grandson, Sir George Larpent*. Farnborough, UK: Gregg International, 1854.

Webb, Nigel, and Caroline Webb. *The Earl and His Butler in Constantinople: The Secret Diary of an English Servant Among the Ottomans*. London: I.B. Tauris, 2009.

White, Ian. *English Clocks for Eastern Markets*. London: Antiquarian Horological Society, 2012.

Wortley Montagu, Lady Mary. *The Turkish Embassy Letters*. London: Virago, 1994.

◙

ACKNOWLEDGMENTS

It's a long old journey, from that first wish to become a writer at the age of, let us say, ten, to the first novel being published; a journey of many years or, in my case, of rather more than half a lifetime. On such a long journey you make many friends, and receive much advice, and it is journeys and friendships and advice that make a life, after all. Permit me to thank some of these friends here: the miraculous David Headley, the agent I always dreamed of, the one who loves your books and fights for them, and his colleagues Helen Edwards and Emily Glenister for making sure nothing (and none of us!) fell through the cracks. In the UK, the Transworld team of Larry Finlay, Eloisa Clegg, Charlotte Trumble, Kirsty Dunseath, and Bella Bosworth, who worked so skillfully to bring Zachary heart and soul into the world; Jett Nyx for a sensitive sensitivity read; Izzie Ghaffari Parker and Sara Roberts for publicity and marketing wizardry, and the genius who is Marianne Issa El-Khoury with that oh-so-beautiful cover design and James Weston Lewis for executing it so beautifully. And in the US, my (patient!) executive editor Barbara Berger at Union Square & Co.; the design team of Igor Satanovsky and Gavin Motnyk; and production editor Michael Cea, together with the amazing folks in sales and marketing.

I want to thank Liz Jensen, mentor extraordinaire as well as a very fine writer, who kicked me into plotting properly and giving my characters beating hearts and Bill Ryan for spotting the spark. Michael and Maria Start at the House of Automata for giving clockwork advice and for performing the magic of bringing automata back to life.

ACKNOWLEDGMENTS

I want to thank my dear friends from the Curtis Brown Creative course back in 2015 and the amazing Barmoor crowd, who have been with me every step of the way: the late and great poet Ann Atkinson, Rosie Ford, Jo Bell, Robbie Burton, Matt Black, Chris Eagles, Rosie Garland, Sarah Jasmon, Lesley Richardson, Tania Hershman and Nell Farrell. Tania read an early draft of this novel and gave me the confidence to finish it. Nell gave me so many brilliant editing notes that this book should probably bear her name on the cover as well as my own. To Clem Cairns and Lorraine Bacchus, who used to run the amazing West Cork Literary Festival with a swashbuckling panache. Peter James, who taught me much in a remarkable evening class he ran in Burgess Hill, and Deborah Painting, who always wrote better than me. Kate Wilson and the team at the Bridport Prize, who in choosing one of my short stories as runner-up gave me the confidence to continue, and the same to the team at the Manchester Fiction Prize, who were kind enough to go one better. To Rupert Dastur and his TSS publishing. To countless Arvon Foundation tutors, and the wondrous Ty-Newydd in North Wales. To my brother Andy, who gave me the original idea for this novel and has believed in it from the first; to brother Paul who read and encouraged; to niece Beth who has always believed; and to Miriam, too. To Molly, who has been the only person on the planet to have looked regularly at my website. To my amazing children Jess and Ben, who fill me with pride and joy every single day, and to Rory, Poppy, and Josh and Mia, who magnify it and a new arrival, Zachary (born February 2023)! And to Sally, who has put up with an awful lot, and who, in cutting the first line of this book, made all the difference. She makes all the difference, every day.